Praise for Elizabeth Everett

"Beautiful and important."

—*New York Times* bestselling author Julia Quinn on *The Love Remedy*

"Smart is the new sexy, and Elizabeth Everett does both better than anyone else!"

—#1 *New York Times* bestselling author Ali Hazelwood

"Fizzy, engrossing romance . . . a wholehearted celebration of women who choose to live gleefully outside the bounds of [the] patriarchy's limitations."

—*Entertainment Weekly* on *A Lady's Formula for Love*

"Dazzling. *A Love by Design* is full of heart, brains, and white-hot sizzle."

—*New York Times* bestselling author Lynn Painter

"Explosive chemistry, a heroine who loves her science, and lines that made me laugh out loud—this witty debut delivered, and I'd like the next installment now, please."

—*USA Today* bestselling author Evie Dunmore on *A Lady's Formula for Love*

"A witty, dazzling debut with a science-minded heroine and her broody bodyguard. Fiercely feminist and intensely romantic, *A Lady's Formula for Love* is a fresh take on historical romance that's guaranteed to delight readers."

—*USA Today* bestselling author Joanna Shupe

"Sparkling, smart, moving, original—just delightful from start to finish."

—*USA Today* bestselling author Julie Anne Long on *A Perfect Equation*

"A phenomenally courageous romance with a wonderfully tenacious heroine that also manages to deliver on one of *the* swooniest and most complex heroes I've read in a long time. *The Love Remedy* is a perfect mix of delicious banter, crackling chemistry, and phenomenally cozy moments with Lucy, her siblings, and the deliciously grumpy Mr. Thorpe. A gem of a romance, and a brave one."

—*USA Today* bestselling author Adriana Herrera

"A delightful romp."

—PopSugar on *A Lady's Formula for Love*

"A brilliant scientist and her brooding bodyguard discover that love can find you when you least expect it. *A Lady's Formula for Love* is full of wit, charm, and intrigue."

—Harper St. George, author of *Eliza and the Duke*

"Elizabeth Everett's writing absolutely dazzles. Fiercely feminist, deliciously sexy, and bursting with intoxicating enemies-to-lovers goodness, *A Perfect Equation* is an instant historical romance classic and Everett an auto-buy author."

—*USA Today* bestselling author Mazey Eddings

"Poignantly feminist and perfectly feisty! Letty and Grey's romance is a delicious journey from sharp-tongued disdain to smoldering desire."

—Chloe Liese, author of the Bergman Brothers series, on *A Perfect Equation*

"I've always loved Everett's Secret Scientists of London series—historical romances that revolve around the early women of STEM and the men who are either bowled over by their smarts or self-preserving enough to get out of their goddamn way and let them do their thing."

—Paste

"*The Love Remedy* firmly establishes Everett as a trailblazer and truth teller whose daring historical fiction lights the way forward."

—Joanna Lowell, author of *A Rare Find*

"A brilliant balance of comedy, sensuous romance, and smashing the patriarchy, the second installment of the Secret Scientists of London is a triumph!"

—Libby Hubscher, author of *Heart Marks Spot,* on *A Perfect Equation*

Also by Elizabeth Everett

THE SECRET SCIENTISTS OF LONDON

A Lady's Formula for Love

A Perfect Equation

A Love by Design

THE DAMSELS OF DISCOVERY

The Love Remedy

The Lady Sparks a Flame

Magic and Mischief at the Wayside Hotel

Elizabeth Everett

Ace
New York

ACE
Published by Berkley
An imprint of Penguin Random House LLC
1745 Broadway, New York, NY 10019
penguinrandomhouse.com

Book design by Alison Cnockaert

Library of Congress Cataloging-in-Publication Data

Names: Everett, Elizabeth author
Title: Magic and mischief at the Wayside Hotel / Elizabeth Everett.
Description: First edition. | New York : Ace, 2026.
Identifiers: LCCN 2025023358 (print) | LCCN 2025023359 (ebook) |
ISBN 9780593955741 trade paperback | ISBN 9780593955758 ebook
Subjects: LCGFT: Fiction | Fantasy fiction | Novels
Classification: LCC PS3605.V435 M34 2026 (print) |
LCC PS3605.V435 (ebook) | DDC 813/.6—dc23/eng/20250604
LC record available at https://lccn.loc.gov/2025023358
LC ebook record available at https://lccn.loc.gov/2025023359

First Edition: March 2026

Printed in the United States of America
1st Printing

The authorized representative in the EU for product safety and compliance is Penguin Random House Ireland, Morrison Chambers, 32 Nassau Street, Dublin D02 YH68, Ireland, https://eu-contact.penguin.ie.

Dedicated to my husband, a real-life romantic hero.

Magic
and
Mischief
at the
Wayside
Hotel

Chapter One

"I propose we move ITEM NUMBER ONE: DISCUSSION OF IMPENDING DOOM down on the agenda, Maddy."

The speaker, a tiny man swathed in a frothy white beard, stood on a folding chair in the hotel ballroom. His tall, red, cone-shaped hat was too big and kept sliding down his forehead when he gesticulated.

Which he did. A lot.

"I got a plugged-up crapper that needs to be addressed first."

"If you varied your diet, Denis, you wouldn't have so many issues," Maddy scolded. She pushed her black cat's-eye reading glasses farther up her nose, her hair writhing beneath a strawberry-pink headscarf.

Denis huffed and rolled his eyes. "*I'm* not plugged up. My *toilet* is plugged up."

Pax Nomen would rather eat dragon shit than run a meeting, but he did have a sense for danger and this crowd was already bubbling with tension and magic. The werewolves were eyeing the faeries a little too hungrily, the ghosts kept corporealizing in compromising positions, the dragon from the third floor had broken four folding chairs, the Fate siblings were quarreling, and the centaur refused to put on pants. Throw in the constipated gnome and an irritated medusa, things could get ugly quick.

He stepped forward from the shadows and put a hand on Maddy's shoulder. She was an incredibly efficient assistant manager, emphasis on *manage*, and sometimes got carried away.

Although, it wouldn't kill Denis to eat a piece of fruit occasionally.

"The agenda doesn't change," Pax said in the voice he used to discipline his troops. "Doom first. Toilets are for number two."

Denis turned red and the faery princesses broke into laughter, sending a spray of faery dust from the rafters where they perched.

It might have been actual dust—the room having seen better days. The curtains were yellowed with age, the beige Berber rug showed burn marks, and cobwebs swung gently in the corners of the ceilings.

A month ago, sheer curtains had been tied back with silk ribbons and blinding sunlight had blanketed the parquet floor. Thousands of crystals hanging from the grand chandelier had tossed confetti of tiny rainbows onto the walls and everything had smelled of roses and dancing.

The chandelier disappeared last week. In its place now hung three banks of fluorescent lights, one out of every four burnt out.

"Let's get back to the agenda," Maddy said. "Are we ready?"

Per the check-in agreement, meetings at the Number Five Wayside Hotel and World Travel Hub began with a recitation of the Wayside Oath.

We shall not kill within the walls of the Wayside.

We will show respect for the customs of all creatures.

No loud noises after ten in the evening.

The hotel manager will be informed of
any and all damages.

To break this oath is to suffer eternal torment
and a fifty-dollar service fee.

After a century of leading soldiers into the worst of battles, of hunting the kinds of monsters that nightmares were made from, of sacrificing his soul and sanity in the protection of innocents, Pax had assumed being a hotel manager would be easy.

Only took one week managing Number Five Wayside for him to accept how very, *very* wrong he'd been.

Number Five Wayside was the fifth and smallest of six World Travel Hubs that managed the ebb and flow of magic throughout the universe through a schedule of tides. Anyone wishing to visit another world checked into a Wayside until they traveled far enough down the flow to reach their destination.

Although the general length of time between worlds was common knowledge, there were no guarantees on this journey—Waysides had a mind of their own.

Literally.

They were living organisms: six hearts pumping rivers of magic through the universe. Beacons of hope and light to worlds under constant threat from the forces of Darkness, the Waysides were the only truly safe places in the universe.

And they were dying.

Pax had been dying as well. Lying in the mud, trapped beneath his injured horse, bleeding from a hole in his gut when lightning had flashed across the sky. He'd been promised a glorious ending as a reward for his service as a paladin in the Army of Light—a knight sworn to protect the roads between the worlds from the forces of Darkness.

Instead, a building had appeared. Manny Quintas, Number Five's previous hotel manager, had ambled out and crouched at Pax's side, oblivious to the screams of dying men and the stench of rotting bodies around them.

"I'm retiring to a time-share by the beach," Manny had explained. "Used to be the Waysides were a place to gather and get to know one another. Grand bargains agreed to, symphonies written, and legendary love stories played out in its halls. Now, it's in and out and no-kill be damned. I don't want to live like that anymore. So, you got about five minutes to decide. Burn up in a blaze of glory with a hole in your stomach or be a hotel manager as your universal reward."

If Pax had known what was in store for him, he might have chosen the gruesome death from a gut wound.

Unclogging Denis's toilet had certainly taken a few years off his life.

"Are we talking impending doom for the universe or just us?" Denis asked.

"When are we going to talk about the laundry room rules?" someone else called out. "Some people may have forgotten it is not okay to take out someone's wet clothes and leave them out—don't give me that face, Denis."

"Number Six Wayside disappeared last month," Pax said.

The room quieted at the reminder.

"Number Three Wayside is flickering in and out of existence," he continued. "Numbers One, Four, and Five are the only functioning Waysides left."

It began with a stuck door.

One of the gargoyles, Ernie, had taken the elevator up from

the games room. Instead of the quiet *ding* that usually accompanied the opening or closing of the elevator door, there had been a low rumble, like a burp, and the shuddering doors had refused to open.

Pax had never heard of an elevator malfunction, and it had given him a bad feeling. He had dutifully consulted his handbook while Ernie complained about his fear of small places and a need for the bathroom and other guests complained about taking the stairs.

The problem was a case of *cantankeropenup.* After an incantation of soothing words and a wave of cherry-scented incense, the elevator doors opened.

As soon as the elevator doors came unstuck, the exit stairway lights went out. The second Pax changed the light bulbs, the decorative wrought iron railing where the iron birds lived came loose.

The golden needle on a small gauge labeled "±Þ˜š¬¥‡" affixed to the main boiler dropped from 100 percent to 75 percent. The ±Þ˜š¬¥‡, or *hypsidoodle,* was the measure of fuel left in Number Five's "tank."

No one had ever heard of a Wayside running out of fuel.

Ever.

A trickle of small nuisances turned into a river of damage. Doors disappeared. Frantic pigeons had been sent between Number Five and the other Waysides with the shocking news that all the Waysides were stricken by the same strange malady.

The *hypsidoodle*'s golden needle dropped again to 35 percent.

Five days ago, a series of low silvery chimes rang out through the building: a signal of a new world approaching. When Number Five stopped, however, it was in a world no one recognized.

No one left and no one checked in.

Days passed before the truth became clear.

They were stuck.

Stuck on a world with only the slightest trace of magic, like a ship thrown up on a beach after a storm.

The *hypsidoodle* was empty.

Number Five was out of gas.

Without the Waysides, travel between worlds would end. Trade would cease, families would be torn apart, and, worse, the flow of magic keeping them alive would be blocked and would stagnate, and eventually magic would disappear altogether. The battles Pax had waged for the Light to protect magic would have been for nothing and the forces of Darkness would win.

Nothing like this had ever happened before. No one knew what would come next.

"Doom" was putting it mildly.

"Impending doom for the entire universe unless we figure out what is happening with the Waysides," Pax clarified.

"What did the Wayside Operating Manual say to do when Number Five runs empty?" asked Denis.

"The manual says, 'In case of dire emergency, reboot,'" Pax said.

"Reboot? What the heck does that mean?" Denis asked.

"Well," Pax said, rubbing the soft stubble on his chin, "I have an idea."

Josephine LaChiusa took comfort in the fact universally acknowledged that a lunchtime walk with two women in their mid-fifties will include discussion of what their twentysomething children are doing wrong (everything), what their husbands have gotten right (nothing), and the daily indignities of aging.

All she had to do was nod every so often and her officemates, Barbara DeVane and Jenna Brown, would tow her in the wake of their conversation, leading her across slush-covered streets and down haphazardly shoveled sidewalks, braving the stinging wind on the stone pedestrian bridges crossing the river bordering the university campus where they worked.

Josie would give anything to live in one of the old mansions renovated into lovely condos sandwiched between campus and the riverbed. Picturing mornings with a steaming cup of coffee on an unstained couch and sunlight drenching the Persian-carpeted floor, Josie decorated her apartment in her head, adding an eat-in kitchen, a clothes closet of her own, and a reading nook where she and Amos could curl up for bedtime stories.

The whiplash of reality when her daydreams faded gave her a headache. A widowed mom with no savings and no family support, Josie spent every waking moment keeping her head above water. There were no such things as leisurely mornings with coffee and certainly no such thing as a beautiful home.

Her landlord had raised the rent again, and this time, Josie wouldn't be able to swing it.

They turned the corner, Jenna and Barbara holding on to each other as they traversed craters of ice formed on unshoveled sidewalks. The enormous oaks and skeletal sugar maples on the riverside were cramped, their roots pushing through the sidewalks, adding to the treacherous footing. The larger homes were interspersed with small apartment buildings and a Donuts Delite hunkered down at the end of the street, its cheerful white-and-blue facade loud against the fading charm of the older structures.

Nodding along as Barbara complained that the drier her insides, the wetter her outsides, Josie drew in a deep breath. She exhaled a wish, one of many unheard pleas to the universe that she could find a safe place and the world would be gentle with her child.

Gradually, Barbara and Jenna ran out of complaints so only the shushing sound of tires over wet snow accompanied them. Waiting back on Josie's desk were three more hours' worth of work, a slew of emails from her insurance company about her son's latest checkup, and her boss's infernal premeeting packets. Just another day in the fascinating world of student financial aid at a private university. None of that was going anywhere, so she slowed her pace, even though her toes were turning numb.

Until her phone pinged in her purse.

She couldn't ignore the pings. Not with Amos's finicky heart. That wasn't his official diagnosis but try saying "tetralogy of Fallot" to a four-year-old and all you get is a blank stare. Josie pulled the phone from her purse and paused. She'd set up notifications for an apartment search when she found out the rent on her place was going up.

There had been nothing for three weeks and Josie was pretending not to panic. This notification said . . .

"Guys?" Josie looked up. Her walking companions were half a block ahead of her.

Jenna and Barbara turned around. The cowlick in the back of Jenna's white hair stuck up over her knitted ear warmers, and with her monochromatic white snow pants and parka, she looked like a stork. Next to her, Barbara's long gray locs were wrapped in a multicolored crocheted turban, and her green wool coat and red moon boots contrasted violently with both Jenna's ensemble and the gray-on-white snow covering everything.

"I got a notification of an apartment matching my requirements," Josie told them.

"Probably something wrong with it," said Jenna.

"Did you hear about that landlord hiding a secret camera in his tenants' bathrooms?" Barbara asked.

Josie nodded. "So, it turns out it's on this block. Can you believe the luck?"

"You'll be two minutes away from work. Don't think the boss won't take advantage of that," said Jenna.

"That's suspicious you got a notification of an apartment on this block while you were walking by. How do you know it's not a cyberkidnapping?" asked Barbara.

Again, Josie nodded. The best part about Jenna's and Barbara's intense absorption with the worst case was Josie didn't have to argue with them about the likelihood of either of those things happening.

"I'll only take ten minutes," Josie said, walking backward and waving at them as she squinted at address numbers on the buildings. "No one will miss me."

"Okay, no problem," said Jenna.

"Don't die," Barbara called, and the two of them turned their backs to Josie and started walking again.

That was Barbara's standard goodbye.

Even at Christmas.

Josie counted the building numbers as she walked down the sidewalk. "Here's 4473 . . . 4481 . . . 5555. Oh, would you look at that?"

That was the six-story wine-colored brick building sitting far back from the sidewalk. A blanket of untouched spring snow covered the front lawn, and the walkway had been neatly shoveled.

The notification had said apartment tours were available today, beginning every half hour in the front lobby. Josie sent Barbara a text as she walked up to the building, telling her she would let her know as soon as she finished.

Better to head Barbara off at the pass. Josie didn't want to come back to work only to find search parties assembling.

Hedges of waist-high holly bushes flanked her at the entrance. The outside doors were made of a heavy, dark wood, and two brass knockers in the shape of opened eyes hung on each door.

Josie's skin tightened over her bones and her stomach flipped like it did at the slow climb of a roller coaster.

Something was very right about this place, on this day.

Pushing inward on the dulled brass door handles revealed a high-ceilinged lobby with black-and-white-tiled floors. A bank of stairs at her left had wrought iron banisters twisted in the shape of birds, roses, and fleurs-de-lis. The stairs stopped at a landing, where a tall, thin table held a vase of dried flowers before it continued out of sight.

A wall of mailboxes stood to the right and the elevator was directly in front of her, flanked on either side by two niches holding truly hideous gargoyles.

"How . . . whimsical," she said aloud; her voice bounced briskly off the walls and ceiling in a satisfying echo.

The lobby had an air of faded grandeur. Beneath her feet, the tiled mosaics were dulled by blackened grout and the walls needed a good scrubbing.

The floor lights above the elevator lit and Josie checked her watch. The heirloom had been a gift to her great-grandfather during the war from a family he'd rescued from a camp. Josie had never seen it anywhere other than her grandfather's wrist until the day he died. That day, he'd taken the watch off and handed it over to her, unable to speak, but making his wishes known by gently curling her fingers over the watch and wrapping her fist in his hand one last time.

God.

Where had that memory come from?

Before Josie could decide if it was a good or a bad sign, the elevator doors opened with a melancholy shushing sound.

". . . don't care what you say. I heard what I heard. You can't tell me the noise was anything other than—" A pasty, nervous-looking man stepped off the elevator and tripped, nearly landing facedown in front of Josie.

"This place is a deathtrap," he complained as he straightened. When he noticed Josie he paused, a greasy leer spreading across his face like an oil spill.

"Do *you* live here?" he asked.

Before Josie could answer, the elevator doors closed, and a shadow fell over them both.

"You are here for the tour?" the shadow caster asked.

Josie looked up to meet the eyes of a tall man who'd exited the elevator after Pasty-Face.

Impossible to say exactly how dark a brown they were in the low light of the lobby, but his eyes were bracketed by starbursts of tiny wrinkles in his deeply tanned skin. His eyelashes were long, as long as a child's, and the dip beneath his cheekbones slightly shadowed.

A sense of safety so strong her bones hummed with it washed over her in that moment—could have been two moments, ten minutes, an hour, Josie had no idea.

However long it was, it was too long. The tall man cleared his throat, one thick eyebrow rising into a triangular question mark.

"The tour?" he asked again.

Those eyes were set in a ruggedly handsome face. He looked like a hero from an old black-and-white movie, broad-shouldered with a strong, squared chin. Two scars ran parallel to his right eyebrow, ending at the streak of white hair at his temple.

"I'll take your tour again," said Pasty-Face. He sent Josie a tight, hungry smile.

Before Josie could speak, a high tinkling sound echoed through the lobby.

Pasty-Face spun around.

"Did you hear that?" he hollered. "This place is haunted. Haunted, I tell you!"

The tall man ran his fingers through thick black hair long enough to reach his chin and grimaced at Pasty-Face's voice. His brows rose and he looked at Josie as if asking for help. She shrugged and the tall man's head dropped to his chest for a moment in exaggerated defeat.

"I hear them laughing at me." Pasty-Face pointed at the staircase. "Girls. Teenage girls. I can't see them, but I know it's me they're laughing at." His voice thinned to a whimper. "Haunted by *teenagers*."

Again, the tall man glanced at her, tilting his head to the right as if asking for a favor. Josie wanted to smile but this unspoken conversation made her nervous.

Was he flirting?

No. Why would he?

"Yes," Josie said, the word barely making it past her thick tongue and dry lips. She pulled her scarf to her chest and cleared her throat. "Yes, I am here for the tour."

The tall man nodded, his eyes crinkling. "This is the lobby. Over there are everyone's mailboxes, and packages are left on that ledge."

Josie took a step toward him, but Pasty-Face set himself between her and the man, and gripped her upper arm tightly.

"Don't go with—I can take you, I mean, can I take you for

coffee?" the man asked. "You wouldn't want to rent an apartment here anyway; it's creepy and you can't get cell phone reception in the lobby."

Josie's mouth opened in astonishment, but nothing came out. Twenty-eight years old and *still* conditioned to react quietly and politely no matter what the circumstances.

What she wanted to do was tell Pasty-Face where to put his hand and what to do with it but her inbred instinct to avoid unpleasantness kicked in. Josie smiled instead.

"Thank you for your invitation, but I'll take the tour," she said, stepping back so it wouldn't be obvious she was pulling her arm away.

Why? Why couldn't she be more like Barbara and call the guy on his rudeness?

With a meaty *thud*, the tall man's hand landed on Pasty-Face's shoulder. "Your tour is over."

There was no hint of menace in the tall man's voice, but still, his dismissal was final. Pasty-Face turned a sickly gray color and sidled out of the front doors without another word, leaving Josie alone with this man. A stranger. A tall stranger with kind eyes.

"Who are you?" she blurted out.

The giant cocked his head and Josie blushed.

"I meant, um, do you work for the management agency or for the building? Not that you don't appear trustworthy, but . . ."

But she'd listened to Barbara's and Jenna's horror stories for too many years to trust her instincts.

Monsters come in all shapes and sizes.

"My name is Pax," the man said. "I am the building superintendent."

Josie waited a beat, but he said nothing else.

"Just Pax?" she asked.

He gestured at the gargoyle to the left. On the wall, next to the gargoyle's head, were two frames, below which were small brass tags. The first tag was engraved PRESIDENT, TENANTS' ASSOCIATION, and above it was a picture of a beautiful Black woman in a white-and-gold headwrap. Above the brass tag reading BUILDING SUPERINTENDENT was a picture of the man standing next to Josie, his sympathetic eyes seemingly fixed on the woman in the picture next to him.

"If you feel comfortable following me, we will take the stairs," he said quietly.

Outside, the clouds lifted, and the tepid sunlight warmed the lobby's dingy walls to the color of a candle flame. A sound like the shushing of wings came from somewhere and it smelled like violet gum.

As Josie followed the man up the stairs, a scraping noise came from behind her and she whipped her head around.

Huh.

She would have sworn one of the gargoyles had moved.

Chapter Two

The tips of Pax's fingers had tingled with the urge to pull out his sword and pin the pasty-faced man to the wall of the elevator.

What stopped him wasn't fear of retribution for breaking the no-kill oath. It was a disinclination to clean something like that up since, after two hundred years' service, the hotel's housekeeping staff had quit the day after Denis checked in.

Pax knew the Waysides never did anything by accident. Number Five stranded itself on *this* particular world for a reason. Rebooting meant starting fresh. What could that mean other than allowing a human inside Number Five's walls?

A new resident. A fresh start.

At least, that's what they hoped.

Maddy had put out an advertisement. They were looking for a single, quiet tenant with impeccable references and the ability to pay three months' rent up front.

The kind of tenant who wouldn't be home often or ask too many questions.

What would happen to the tenant once Number Five recovered

and was on its way through the universe was a question for another day.

Pasty-Face had been the fifth human to come look at the apartment and Pax had decided he would be the last.

There was a reason this world was unvisited.

These people were assholes.

As soon as Pax thought this, the elevator doors had opened, and she was standing there.

The new tenant.

It wasn't her face that decided him, although she was lovely in a quiet way. Short—the top of her head barely reaching his chin—with straight brown hair parted in the middle, smooth white skin, high cheekbones, and serious gray eyes.

With her presence came a silence Pax hadn't experienced since becoming a soldier. The roar in his head of angry men and dying beasts had been such a constant he didn't notice it until it stopped.

She smelled like the rikkonberry pancakes the children in the orphanage got as a special treat on high holy days. Pax was taken aback by this and couldn't form a proper sentence at first.

"Who are you?" she'd asked.

Sweet-smelling or no, she was a woman alone with a large man in a foreign place. His instincts as a paladin told him to step away from the space around her, keep his movements slow and his voice even.

Pax couldn't risk scaring her.

The faery princesses had already done enough damage teasing Pasty-Face.

There was so little magic on this world, the tenants had agreed they would not reveal their identities or purposes. The most human-looking among them volunteered to interact with the outside world until Number Five started up again.

Unfortunately, the faery princesses' idea of "interaction" was a lot different from what Pax or Maddy had envisioned.

While Pasty-Face was wrong about the building being haunted, he was correct to fear teenagers.

Adolescents were universal terrors.

Not that it mattered, because the new tenant was right here. Pax gestured for her to follow him and led her up the staircase.

She reached out and trailed a finger along the banister. "When was this built? I can't identify the ironwork. It's certainly prewar, but other than that, all I know is it's beautiful."

Pax stopped on the landing and looked beyond her. Where she'd rested her hand, the decorative vines had gone from black to green.

"What is your name, if I may ask?" he said.

"You may," she said, a dimple appearing right next to her mouth. When Pax said nothing, the dimple smoothed out and a faint blush traveled up her neck to her cheek. Had she said something funny? Pax was a lost cause when it came to jokes.

"I mean, sorry. My name is Josephine. Josie."

"Josie," he repeated. No bells rang and the dust on the side table didn't disappear, but the vine on the banister stayed green.

Was that enough?

A hundred years of responsibility for thousands of soldiers' lives had shaped Pax. Even if no ogre hordes waited to descend upon them, the fate of every living being in Number Five Wayside was in Pax's hands. This kept him up at night wondering if the job had truly been meant as a reward, or if he'd failed somehow along the way.

If failure was to be his fate.

Turning away, Pax trudged up the second flight of stairs, turned left, and kept going until he stopped at the door of apartment 3C.

"This is it," he said as he slid the key into the lock and opened the door. "I hope you will like it."

Holy hell in a handbag, this apartment was perfect.

Josie should have turned around and left as soon as Just-Pax opened the door. She could see from the hallway the place was huge and bright. For a woman trying to make sensible decisions, Josie sure liked to test herself.

So she followed him into the apartment, not really caring if he was a serial killer. On second thought, now was a good time to text Barbara.

Just in case.

Josie once had a vivid dream where she and Amos had been sitting at the kitchen table when the waters of the river outside began to rise. The two of them lived on that table from then on, floating past the dangers around them while playing patty-cake and eating fried bologna sandwiches.

She'd figured out the dream was a metaphor for how she felt when her partner, Dan, died of an aneurism while she was pregnant with Amos. Alone but not alone. Endangered but safe enough as long as she kept moving.

The kitchen of this apartment came furnished with a round wooden table like the one from her dream. Josie stopped in her tracks and stared, forgetting she didn't have enough money for a place like this, forgetting medical bills for her son were slowly bankrupting her, forgetting her lonely nights.

Atop the kitchen table sat a jelly jar filled with cabbage roses that looked as though they'd just been picked. A few peach-colored petals had fallen to the table and Josie focused on those while she got herself together.

"You do not like the table?" Pax asked.

"Oh, no," she said, tearing her gaze from the roses. "I do. It's lovely. All this is lovely."

"Lovely" was an understatement. The ceilings were high and the corners where they met the wall were free of any webs or dust. The floors were linoleum tile in the kitchen and hardwood in the rest of the space. The windows were large and had wrought iron flower holders, and the living and dining areas were joined by an archway.

Not until they reached the first bedroom did Josie want to cry.

This room was made for Amos: full of light from the southern-facing windows fronted by a cushioned window seat, beneath which sat two bookshelves and a row of cubbies. The walls were a soothing moss green, and the curtains were the yellow of sunflowers.

"Hmmm." Pax walked past her into the room and examined the bookshelves, running his hand over the back of his neck while tilting his head. "I have not seen these before." He glanced at her. "This is a child's room."

Was that a question?

Her toes already at the edge of a gravelly slope down to the canyon of depression, Josie had to leave before she saw any more.

"I have to go now," Josie said, horrified she'd had to force the words through her constricted throat.

She would not cry. She would *not*.

Instead, she would squeeze her feelings into a tiny ball and swallow them alongside every other strong emotion she'd had in the past four years.

"You have children?" he asked.

"A boy."

"Ah. This is his room." Pax pulled the pair of curtains apart to let in more light.

"I can't afford this apartment," Josie said. "Or any apartment in this building. I'm sorry for wasting your time."

He frowned at the floor for a moment as if listening for something.

"I haven't told you the monthly rent yet," he said when his gaze returned to hers. "How can you know?"

They faced each other, Pax's hand on the curtains while she leaned against the doorframe, hesitant to fully enter the space. He didn't move other than the steady rise and fall of his chest. No fidgeting, no jokes to break the silence. The gaze resting on her was light, unencumbered by anything other than patience.

What a gift.

She told him her rent—before her dick landlord jacked it up—and waited for Pax to usher her out. Instead, he shrugged.

"That's more than I would ask. We have no cleaning staff," he said, looking up at the lighting fixture of colored bulbs hanging from the ceiling. "The railings are wobbly, the exit lights don't always work, and a bag of wet cats is more amiable than our tenants' association meetings."

Josie clasped a hand to her heart.

"The elevator is . . . temperamental and there is a man named Denis on the fourth floor with a foul mouth and IBS who has no respect for personal boundaries. The laundry room has only two washers and a recalcitrant dryer. Our residents have gotten on each other's nerves ever since . . . er, the pandemic, and the most socializing anyone does is the Thursday afternoon Scrabble competition in the games room. Even that is over with since someone stole the *e*'s."

Josie stared. "Nothing you said makes this place any less appealing."

"Hmph." Pax moved past her out into the hallway. "You are the first person who has said this." He turned on his heel. "The internets are weak here. If your existence is predicated on 5G, like the man before you, you will not be happy."

That feeling in her stomach, the one Josie had when she stood on the stoop, was the same swooping sensation she'd had when she'd met Dan. When she'd found out she was pregnant. When, twelve years ago, she'd gotten on a Greyhound and never looked back.

"Is heat included?"

Chapter Three

"If you shove me again, I will reach down your throat and rip out your intestines."

"Joke's on you. Zombies don't have intestines."

"Shut up, everyone, they're coming."

A crowd of guests had gathered in the common area this morning in anticipation of Josie LaChiusa's arrival. There was no way all of them could see out the windows in the double doors leading to the lobby, but that hadn't stopped anyone.

"I count eighty-five corporeal and sixteen noncorporeal beings in this room," Maddy announced. "The room capacity limit, according to the handbook, is two hundred corporeal. We should be fine."

The faeries rolled their eyes, not bothering to smother their giggles.

"Thank you, Maddy," Pax said loudly, "for your vigilance."

Maddy nodded, then wandered over to the billiards table to inspect the efficacy of the chalk cubes.

Another negative effect of Number Five's illness. The guests were becoming too familiar with him and Maddy. Normally, a journey on a Wayside took less than a month, a short enough period to keep him and Maddy both distant and intimidating.

Once the staff of a Wayside lost the respect and fear of the guests, havoc would ensue.

Havoc was Pax's least favorite ensuence. Right up there with pandemonium.

"They're here," whispered a faery.

Pax put a hand on the double doors and gave everyone his best stern gaze. "Remember. They can't know the truth about Number Five or about who any of you are until we are certain they are the cure. You are tenants, not guests, and I am the building superintendent."

"This is a mistake." Prince Raphael Darksson's smoky voice drifted from behind a set of drapes in a shadowy corner.

The heir to the Vampire Throne pushed aside the material, revealing his face and form, setting the faeries to swooning. He pretended to ignore this though he turned his head so they could better ogle his profile.

Raphe had not been the only guest vehemently against the decision to let in outsiders.

For the past three weeks the entire building had been readying themselves in preparation for the LaChiusa family's arrival. Computers and cell phones irritated Number Five and often died, so a handful of residents had ventured out to a nearby oracle, the Public Library, where they found the annals of *People* magazine and could view the YouTube.

Thanks to the library, the faeries now worshiped a demigoddess known as Taylor Swift, the zombie family had been indoctrinated into a cult known as veganism, and Denis and his fellow gnomes had almost rioted after having watched the Disney

Channel. It took Maddy days to calm them with a promise not to turn them into garden decorations before they would even listen to Pax's plan.

As for Pax, over the years he'd learned that the less magical a world, the less pleasant the people. Nothing he'd seen in the library had convinced him to change his opinion.

Among the revelations at the Public Library was the seemingly infinite slander of the vampire species.

Raphe, however, insisted his opposition to the plan had nothing to do with the ridiculous rumors about turning into a bat or sparkling skin.

"Once again, I believe you have mistranslated that damn handbook," Raphe said.

Pax felt for his sword, forgetting he now left it off, and Raphe bared his fangs. Yet another reason they needed Number Five to get better. Two legendary warriors in one confined space would inevitably lead to bloodshed, and those fifty-dollar service fees could add up.

Maddy walked over and set herself carefully between the two soldiers, one hand to her headscarf as a warning to both.

"Pax isn't the only one who can read," Maddy said to Raphe. "I looked at the handbook as well. In the universal language, 'reboot' is the closest word there is to 'rz∂"iϖL.'"

"The best translation is 're*blood*.'" Raphe's emphasis left no doubt about how literally he took the meaning. "We don't need a human from this world coming to live here. That makes no sense. These creatures have no magic. If Number Five's *hypsidoodle* is empty, fill it with their blood."

Denis nodded. "The vampire has a point. A lot less bother to sacrifice the humans than to keep up pretenses around them."

"No. Number Five is clear. No bloodshed," Pax said.

"What, then?" Raphe demanded. "If it isn't blood she needs to refill her *hypsidoodle*, what *does* she need?"

As it had during the last meeting, the subject cleaved the guests in two, neither side in the mood to compromise. Understandable, perhaps. Some of them, like Raphe, faced a matter of life or death once Number Five reached his destination.

However, the guests had made no effort to come together to solve the problem. Instead, they split into factions, each regarding the other side with suspicion. This meant a handful of the loudest and angriest made decisions—not the ideal climate in which to defuse a crisis.

Pax lacked the patience to negotiate. This was why he became a soldier instead of a diplomat. Easier to stick someone you don't like with a sword than spend time arguing.

"This squabbling is redundant. We had a vote, and the majority agreed to let the humans live within our walls for a trial period," Maddy reminded him. "You aren't the only one who has a pressing rebellion waiting for them, Prince."

Raphe's lips thinned and his exposed fangs elongated, the clean line of his beautiful features thickening, turning his spectacularly handsome face harsh and brutal. One of the faeries did swoon now.

Pax rolled his eyes.

Drama king.

"I want the trial period defined," Raphe said. "Two weeks. If nothing changes, we sacrifice the humans on the altar in the basement."

"Tcha." Princess Naliti, the firstborn of the faery princesses, sucked her tongue against her teeth, signaling disdain. "Sacrifices are *so* last century," she drawled. Her sisters murmured their agreement.

"I propose we table the subject until the next meeting. That altar needs to be brought up to code before any of us discuss sacrifices," Maddy said. "Besides, we don't have a cleaning staff, remember?"

Pax had never let emotions steer his choices on the battlefield and he wasn't about to start now, but no one would be touching a hair on the new tenant's head.

Not that he had any emotions about the new tenant.

Or the hair on her head.

"The matter has been settled. The LaChiusas are under the protection of Number Five. Remember. *No* magic around them." He pointed up at the faeries swinging from the fluorescent ceiling lamps. "I mean it. None. Everyone just act normal. I mean, normal for human beings."

With that, Pax left the room.

He opened the outside entrance door as Josie set her back against it, her arms occupied with a large cardboard box, and caught her before she fell backward.

She smelled like winter and peppermint chewing gum.

"Good morning," he said. "If you will allow me to help—"

"You like 'Pider-Man?" asked a high voice.

A child had followed Josie into the foyer and was staring up at Pax with round blue eyes. They wore a puffy yellow coat, a hat in the shape of a duck with two long legs hanging over their ears, and padded blue boots.

"Who is Pider-Man?" Pax asked.

"'Pider-Man is the best," the child said, eyes narrowing as if waiting for Pax to admit he'd been joking.

Pax had planned on taking the box from Josie but instead stood frozen, completely flummoxed.

"The best what?" Pax asked.

"Knock knock," the child said.

What the hell was happening here?

"Sorry. I haven't introduced you. This is my son, Amos," Josie said, nodding her chin at the child.

"Knock knock," Amos repeated.

"He's got a new knock-knock joke," said Josie. The wavering smile on her face told Pax she expected him to know what she was talking about.

A joke?

Shit.

His soldiers would tell jokes, especially before battle when their nerves were strung tight. Pax had never understood what they found funny. At first, he'd asked, but explaining a joke turned out to kill the magic of it all and he learned to pretend amusement.

The little boy was bending backward with his whole body in order to gaze up at Pax and it looked uncomfortable. Pax could barely remember his own childhood and, as a soldier, had no experience with children, but he assumed they had the same feelings as adults, only smaller. Pax never liked it when larger soldiers used their size to intimidate smaller troops.

He knelt to one knee so the child could stand straight when they spoke.

"You're 'posed to say, 'Who's der?'" Amos explained.

"Who is there?" Pax asked.

"Orange!" the child shouted.

"Orange?" Pax repeated. He looked at Josie for guidance but couldn't understand the words she mouthed to him.

Shit. Shit.

"Orange who?" Amos squealed, his tiny face split with a huge smile, as though his entire body readied itself to laugh.

Utterly lost, Pax echoed the boy, "Orange who?"

"Orange you glad I'm not a banana?"

Josie didn't laugh, but she did lie to the little fellow, telling him he'd made a funny joke. Pax nodded as though in agreement, stood, then took the box from her arms. She tried to object but he led them up to their apartment.

What did oranges have to do with bananas?

He would have to consult the YouTube.

Although he was only one child, once he removed his boots, Amos made more noise than a herd of goats, running from room to room and shouting to his mother whenever he saw something interesting.

Everything was interesting, thus there was a lot of shouting.

Pax didn't mind. It had been ages since he heard anyone shout in excitement and there was a sweet, porcelainlike echo to the child's voice.

"These curtains are perfect. They weren't here before, were they?" Josie asked when she joined Pax in the kitchen.

A set of plain white curtains with scalloped edges and a spray of forget-me-nots now adorned the kitchen windows.

"Ma. Ma! I have a 'Pider-Man room," Amos hollered.

"Wait for Mommy, Amos. Don't touch anything," Josie said as she left the kitchen and made her way down the hall to the bedrooms.

Who the hell was Pider-Man? What was he the best at? Did it have anything to do with oranges?

A clicking noise caught Pax's attention. Where the old gas stove had sat two seconds before was a new electric stove, dozens of push buttons and lights replacing black plastic knobs.

A thud of his heart, like a punch from the inside out, nearly sent Pax to the floor. He would have to tell Raphe.

One new stove did not mean they were out of the woods.

Still, it was a beginning.

Josie gripped the door handle and tried to appear calm even though she was freaking out.

She'd toured this apartment three weeks ago and this bedroom had not been furnished, the walls had been green, and yellow curtains had hung in the window above the cushioned reading nook.

Amos ran around the room, pointing out the blue curtains above the red window seat cushion, the blue metal-framed bed covered with a plush Spider-Man blanket, and a shelf full of books about trucks and nature—and Spider-Man.

"I will open the back entrance and unload your possessions into the elevator."

Pax had come up behind her and she'd jumped a little, then spun around. It pissed her off to have to look up to speak to him. His height might not be his fault, but Josie decided she could take it personally if she wanted.

A headache pounded directly behind her eyes, adding to the pain in her neck and the exhaustion from lying awake last night wondering if this had been the right move. Like every other major decision she'd made since Dan died, Josie had second thoughts.

Third thoughts.

Abject terror, really, that everything she'd done up until now was a mistake.

If Dan were alive, Josie could have shifted some of the burden. He'd taken in stride his family's disappointment with Josie as a partner and been achingly sensible. For him, the world was a place that made sense; he had been blessedly free of anxiety or self-doubt.

"Never cry over spilt whiskey," was his motto. It was the second thing he said when Josie told him she was—thank you, antibiotics—pregnant with Amos.

The first thing he said was "Holy shit."

Once Dan made a decision, he never questioned himself. That was his most compelling attribute, as far as she was concerned.

Josie had never managed that, and Dan's parents knew it.

The last time Amos was hospitalized, Dan's mother had asked in a saccharine-sweet voice whether it wouldn't be *safer* for Amos to live with her instead.

Josie had pulled herself together enough to decline politely, but the look in her mother-in-law's eyes was the stare of a raptor who'd found a nest full of eggs.

". . . their father?"

Mr. Pax had asked her a question. Josie's headache morphed into a pair of wings, battering the inside of her skull.

"What did you ask?" she said.

Rocking back on his heels, Pax lifted his chin in Amos's direction. "I asked whether Mr. Amos's father or another family member would be joining you at some point, and should I issue him a key?"

Josie shuddered at the thought of Dan's mother, Gloria, having access to Amos at any time of day.

"No," said Josie with emphasis. "*No one* else gets a key."

"Is there conflict with the boy's father?" Pax's jaw clenched and his hand went to his side in a gesture straight out of a cowboy film. "Tell me what he looks like."

Confused, and a little bit turned on by his protective reaction,

Josie pressed her fingers to her temples and tried to focus. "No conflict. It's just us. Me and Amos."

The right corner of Pax's mouth twisted.

Ugh. That sounded pathetic when she said it out loud.

"Mom, Mom, can I go to sleep right now in my 'Pider-Man bed?" Amos asked.

"The fact I'm a single mom isn't the point. The point is, who did this?" Josie asked. "Who decorated Amos's room? How did they know his favorite superhero? I can't afford to pay anyone back for this. Who was in here?"

The questions spilled out like dominoes even as she winced at how thin and high her voice sounded.

She could stand to learn a thing or two from this guy's poker face. For years, Josie had done a beautiful job denying her fear, but with the arrival of Amos, her fear had grown thorns and poked holes in her pretentions.

Pax rubbed his chin over the shadowy promise of stubble to come.

"There is no cost to these furnishings," he said, no hint of what he thought anywhere on his face. "This was organized by the building."

"The building?" She cocked her head, signaling her dissatisfaction with his answer.

"Yes?" He raised his eyebrows, voice pitched up at the end as if asking for permission to be obtuse.

"Maaaaaaaaaaaaaaaa. I has to poop!"

Dammit.

"But someone came in here and left these things. Who was that?" Josie asked, rummaging through her handbag, looking for wipes in case there was no toilet paper in the bathroom.

Unless the mysterious decorator had already supplied that, in which case, cool. Still creepy, but cool.

Pax's eyes darted back and forth between Amos's and Josie's faces.

"Maddy," he said, nodding as though he'd figured out the answer to a quiz. "Maddy is the . . . president of the tenants' association and . . . and she loves children."

Hmmmm. The sharp scent of cinnamon wafted from the hallway. Shit. A bottle of room spray must have cracked open during the move.

Pax continued. "She loves children so much she knew exactly what a six-year-old boy—"

"He's just turned four," Josie said.

"—what a just-turned-four-year-old boy would enjoy in his bedroom."

"My son is the most important person in my life, Mr. Pax," Josie said sternly. Fear tugged at her stomach and settled in her guts. "My sole priority is keeping him safe. Please don't let anyone into this apartment again without me present, no matter how maternal their urges."

Pax made a small bow. "Amos will be perfectly safe in this building," he said. "I swear to it."

Chapter Four

With Number Five sick, the air inside the building grew stale by afternoon. Pax opened a back door and propped it with a sleeping gargoyle.

"Ernie won't like it does he wake to find you've used him for a doorstop," opined Bert, the other gargoyle, who lay sunning himself in a small dry patch.

The absence of the small birch forest that used to lie here stung Pax like the spiked kiss of a whip. Instead, Number Five's courtyard was now paved with pockmarked cement, entirely bare except for one lone bench, the wood tinged with green and listing to the left. Stepping outside, Pax tilted his head up, closed his eyes, and let the puny sun's rays sink into his skin as a garbage truck roared past.

So much noise in this world.

The humans here went from stationary noisy boxes to mobile noisy boxes and back again. What could the appeal be in driving these autos? How did they commune with a case of aluminum and plastic?

The hardest part of becoming the hotel manager had been saying goodbye to his horse, Butthead.

Pax hadn't named the horse. Like most horses, it had named itself without consideration for what the name might sound like in other languages. Pax had hated shouting, "Charge, Butthead!" but Butthead had been a good horse.

Pax held out his hand, palm down, into a shaft of light. The invisible heat sank deep into his bones—only once he was warm could he appreciate how cold he'd been these last few weeks.

A high-pitched scream followed by a torrent of giggles drifted from the open windows on the top floor, signaling the faery princesses were awake.

To entice a faery, all one had to do was pull out a fiddle or a ¢¤î§çç•wll and play a tune. Before Number Five got sick, there had often been music ringing and rolling through the building. One by one, the guest's instruments had fallen apart, rusted shut, or simply vanished. No faery circles could be held while Number Five sickened. The princesses' moods had been dark indeed.

Unfortunately for the furniture, they'd decided on competitive cheer as a substitute.

"Oh, hello, Mr. Pax."

Josie and Amos stood in the doorway behind him. Pax pretended to be startled, but he'd heard their footsteps as soon as they'd left their apartment. A "perk" of being a hotel manager was the ability to hear guests whenever they moved around the building. When Number Five was fully booked, it sounded like a small army was in residence.

"It's waundry time," Amos announced. "We been trying to find waundry machines for two hours and all we finds is stairs."

The boy wore a magenta sweatshirt, a purple hairband, and yellow plastic shoes with holes in them. Two of the holes were plugged with what looked like tiny blue gnomes with white puffy hats.

Denis would have a fit.

"Two hours is an exaggeration, but I have gotten us turned around a few times," Josie said, her mouth lifted to one side in a sheepish smile. "You will have to draw me a map."

Number Five sent you where it wanted you to go. Disconcerting if you didn't know what was happening, but not something Pax could tell her about.

"This is an old building," he said instead. "Everyone gets lost sometimes, even me."

During a long siege, soldiers had an aura about them. Not resignation exactly, but a state of acceptance that the barricades might fall, and a final battle loomed around the corner; a fragility revealing itself in the shadows under their eyes or how they drew out their goodbyes.

This same aura surrounded Josie. Pax could tell she would never break, but the signs of exhaustion after a siege were there—she couldn't stretch her smile to fit her face and the furrows between her eyes were deep enough he wondered how often she laughed.

Amos walked past Josie into the courtyard, adept at avoiding the piles of dirty snow. The child raised his face to the sun and smiled, then went to stand over Ernie.

"He likes to be petted?" the boy asked. Obviously, the question had been rhetorical, because Amos began to pat Ernie's stone head without waiting for an answer.

"This courtyard is . . . well, there is a basketball hoop. That's promising." Josie followed Amos out into the sunlight, carrying a plastic basket piled with clothes.

The net of the basketball hoop was dirty and ripped on one side.

It hadn't been there when Pax had stopped to speak with Bert.

"Do you like basketbawl?" Amos asked. He'd squatted next to Ernie and looked up from examining the gargoyle's ears to meet Pax's gaze.

"I don't know much about basketball," Pax admitted. "These teams of men who call themselves warriors, do they not have a cause to fight for? What sort of battle calls for a man to be revered for throwing a ball into a hoop rather than for his courage or foresight?"

Amos's mouth opened and his little head tilted to the side. Obviously, Pax had given the wrong answer.

"Yes. I like basketball."

This turned out to be the correct answer, and Amos promptly stuck his fingers up Ernie's nose.

Josie examined the courtyard, frowning at the broken bench. Here, March was the end of winter. In Pax's world, it meant the beginning of spring when the air smelled like wet leaves and crushed mint.

Josie's delicate lips were the same color pink as the earliest flowers on Pax's world. They were called "tentatives," those flowers, because they came after the first thaw and were gone by the next frost. Their fleeting purpose solely to give folks hope that spring would come soon.

"This looks a little worse for wear. Is it nicer in the summer?" she asked.

She must think he was slow to understand, because every time Josie asked him a question, Pax paused, searching for an answer that wouldn't give away any magical secrets.

There were no outward signs of impatience, no fiddling with her clothes or tapping her foot. She waited, unmoving, her serious gray eyes fixed on him without judgment. They were pretty, her eyes. He looked away and stared at the rotting bench. What he wanted to do was compliment Josie. Tell her something nice about her eyes or how she smelled like cherries and powdered sugar.

What a bad idea. She might take offense and leave the building. Where would they be then?

Pax did wonder if she knew.

If Josie knew how lovely her eyes were.

"Yes, I find it nicer later in the year." He watched Amos's little hands pat Ernie's back. "I will see to a new basketball net and . . ."

What did just-turned-four-year-old boys play on?

"What else might Mr. Amos enjoy?" he asked. "A horse? Not a real horse, of course."

Oh.

The way Josie's face lightened, the worry lifting from the bed of wrinkles across her forehead, the way those soft, pink lips drifted into the prettiest of smiles; he'd done this with only a kind gesture?

If she'd been his soldier, Pax would have clasped her on the shoulder and headbutted her lightly, armored helm clinking against armored helm.

This did not seem to be a common form of encouragement on this world, however.

"He doesn't need a horse, but that is a kind offer."

Kind.

Josie thought he was kind. On some worlds they called him The Butcher. On others, his name meant "drowned in blood."

They watched Amos singing softly to himself, comfortable in the silence.

"It's too bad there isn't any green space back here. The one drawback of living in the city is not having a piece of earth to work. It would be a nice spot . . ." She looked around. "Oh, I didn't notice that tree until now. Is it a pear tree?" Josie asked.

Pax spun on his heel and confronted the sight of a pear tree newly sprung up in a corner.

"I believe it is," he said.

Josie set the plastic basket on her hip and shifted her weight. She smelled better than cherries and powdered sugar. She smelled like something you make with cherries and sugar. Like a pie.

"Funny how I missed something that big," she said.

"Most people don't see what's in front of them until it becomes important."

He winced at how officious he sounded.

"Let me guess. Were you in the army?" Josie asked.

"Yes," he answered, letting his gaze brush the side of her face. "All my life."

"My grandfather was, too," she said quietly. "You remind me of him."

Ouch.

Grandfather, eh?

Good thing he had no interest in this woman aside from a building superintendent's concern for a tenant. Her comparison might have stung. Might have made him wonder how old he looked or remember how Number Five stayed in one place for only a short while before always moving on.

Sometimes Josie visualized her brain as a villain. A thin, unhappy woman who chain-smoked Pall Malls, leaving only a ring of CoverGirl's Candy Red lipstick bleeding into the wrinkles around her mouth.

In other words, her gramma.

Most times, Josie could stay in control, but sometimes Josie's brain had its own agenda. When she was supposed to be listening to her boss, her brain would focus on the slight stain inside the collar of his button-down oxford. Once she latched on to the stain, her brain went on a lightning-fast journey, from questions about the sustainability of mass-produced clothing, the relative toxicity of laundry soaps, whether her boss would ever remarry, did she remember to pack Amos's lunchtime pill for daycare, to why was she still in this job, treading water, the rent is why, would her mother-in-law surprise her with a visit that afternoon, and was the apartment clean enough to pass muster.

All those thoughts would cascade through her brain in a matter of seconds, distracting her so she missed half of what her boss had said.

Then, when she asked him to repeat that last part, her brain would scold her with a familiar litany, like a recording looping over and over.

Josie's brain shouted at her right now. *Why do you say the things you say? Why can't you keep your thoughts to yourself? Why are you so* stupid*?*

Always, so stupid.

"Not that you're old," Josie said quickly. Pax had flinched when she compared him to her grandfather. That flinch would settle into her brain like a pea beneath a mattress, only to pop out at random times.

Clouds covered the sun. Josie wanted Pax to look at her. The weight of his stare did something to quiet her brain.

"You're not as old as he was. At least I don't, um . . ."

Ugh, that was embarrassing. Josie slapped her palm over her eyes.

"Are you covering your eyes so you don't see the wounded look on my face?" Pax asked.

The tenor of his voice remained soft and even, giving nothing away.

Either he was teasing her, or he was supersensitive about his age.

She spread her fingers and peeked with one eye.

He wasn't smiling.

Then he winked.

Oh. That wink did something weird to her stomach, leaving her a little lightheaded as though she'd been pushed and wasn't expecting it. A swoop almost.

A swoop was close to a swoon.

Josie needed to get out of here before she said something else to keep her up at three o'clock in the morning.

"I—oh, hey, Amos." Josie set down her laundry and scooped up her son. "I doubt Mr. Pax wants you to ride his gargoyle."

Amos's sweatshirt rode up when she grabbed him. Josie took advantage and made a loud raspberry on his belly below his surgical scar. As always, his giggle evoked a tiny thrill. She looked up at Pax, but he proved impossible to read. With a palm covering his mouth as though stifling a yawn, he cleared his throat while staring at the gargoyle.

"I'm sure Ernie enjoyed the attention," he said.

"He wikes me," Amos insisted, giggles trailing off like tiny golden burps. "He said so. He laughed at my jokes."

Pax scowled and his face closed in anger.

Josie's joy shriveled, and the clouds above turned the color of a bruise. His classic features turned from marble-like to granite when he lifted his chin. The broad shoulders and muscled thighs she'd admired now intimidated her with their implied strength.

Josie didn't know this man. Not really.

Instincts honed by a childhood spent at the mercy of powerful men kicked in. Josie picked up the laundry basket and directed Amos toward the propped door with her knee.

"Well, see you later," she said.

"You are leaving?" Pax asked, sounding perplexed. As though his expression hadn't turned as dark as the clouds.

"There isn't much to keep a little boy occupied out here," she said apologetically, her impulse to smooth things over kicking in. "I'll take him to the park later. The sun has been out and maybe melted some of the snow. I'm sorry he climbed on the statue," Josie said. "He won't touch anything again; I'll make sure of it."

Pax opened his mouth, to say what, she didn't know, because it snapped shut and he glowered at the statue once more.

"I'm sorry," Josie whispered, then hurried after Amos, her brain berating her the whole time.

Chapter Five

"We need a planning meeting for the premeeting meeting. Can you schedule that?"

Josie rolled her lips inward and bit gently to keep from saying a single word.

"I picked six random accounts to audit this weekend. I'm going to need office supplies, and I noticed our supply checklist is missing. I can't take office supplies home without recording it on a supply checklist. Should we have a quick meeting about this?"

For once, Josie and her brain were in accord. Her boss, Ben Jorgenson, was a well-intentioned *menace.*

"Ben. No one can fit another meeting into their schedules this week."

Josie spoke calmly and without rolling her eyes or flicking her fingers against his forehead. Her gold medal in patience awaited her. What she wanted to do was ask him why he'd spend the weekend auditing when he should be spending it getting laid, but that would bump her down to bronze.

Ben glanced up at her, confused, and for the thousandth time she wished Nordic blue-eyed blond hotties were her type. Her boss smelled good, liked to cook, and never talked down to her—catnip for most women.

Instead, all day Josie had mulled over Pax's expression when Amos had been playing with the gargoyle, trying to come up with an interpretation putting him in a better light. Maybe he was worried Amos might fall and hurt himself? Maybe he had a sudden bout of gas? Maybe . . .

"What if we held it to fifteen minutes? Fifteen minutes is reasonable," Ben said.

Josie was finished, though. "No. No meeting. I'll print out a new checklist."

A wrinkle of disappointment arced between Ben's eyebrows, but Josie had no sympathy. Since menopause had descended on the office, she was the only one who had the patience to deal with the director of financial aid. Yesterday, Jenna had threatened to set fire to his premeeting packets and Barbara had begun researching assassins on the dark web.

"Gotta run." Josie backed out of the office, smiling apologetically. "Time to pick up Amos from daycare."

Luckily, Ben was a single parent as well. He waved her off without saying anything, even though she could tell by the way he tightened his mouth he felt a few more meetings were in order.

The best part about working for the university was on-site daycare. Within a half an hour of leaving work, Josie and Amos were walking home in the slowly gathering darkness. Once past the university they turned onto East Avenue. This street was home to a few of the city's largest homes as well as a science museum and planetarium. Josie sent another quick thanks to the universe for providing a place for her to live that didn't require a bus everywhere, since she couldn't afford a car.

Amos told her a story about his best friend, Jalyn, while

groups of students ran past, kicking up dirty wet snow. As cars sped by, Josie grabbed Amos's hand at the stoplight, her brain deciding to treat her to a scenario where she lost her grip on his mitten, and he went flying into the road.

The apartment building shone like a beacon in the late-winter dusk, lights blazing through the Palladian windows in the lobby and the holly bush's glossy leaves sparkling in the borrowed light.

Amos sang the wrong lyrics to pop songs while Josie stopped in the lobby to check the mailbox. They had been here a week and Josie hadn't gotten any mail. This was in direct contrast to the family living on the top floor. Every day enough cardboard boxes to fill Josie's apartment two times over sat on the ledge.

Josie glanced around the deserted lobby. A thin layer of dust had settled on the metal lip overhanging the mailboxes and a large crack in the shape of a finger on the plaster wall pointed east. Pax had said something about not having a cleaner when she first toured the apartment, and it showed. Even one of the gargoyles was missing.

"Where's that guy?" Amos asked, pointing at the empty niche.

"I don't know," Josie answered. Intrigued, she leaned over to read the labels on the boxes. Nosy, yes, but what if the recipients were movie stars or Mafia or hidden royalty?

Smith. The last name on the packages was Smith. There wasn't an apartment number, just Seventh Floor. Did they have the entire top floor of the building?

In the pile were three BoxyCharm, one Illumicrate, and two Adore Me subscription boxes, all made out to Miss Smith. Hidden royalty started to sound plausible.

Oh my God. That huge box was from Bergdorf Goodman.

The only time Josie had been in Bergdorf's was by accident

and it had left her shaken for days, discovering there were enough people in the world wealthy enough to keep a store selling $6,000 handbags in business.

When Josie had confided this to Dan, his mother, Gloria, had overheard.

Ever since, Gloria would make a point of mentioning which pieces of clothing she'd bought at Bergdorf's, tilt her head, fake-smile, and say, "I know you're thinking I'm part of the one percent, but being well dressed doesn't make me a bad person, does it?" in a high voice, like a little girl.

The lights in the lobby flickered and dimmed.

Josie let Amos lead her away from the piles of packages to climb the stairs. Amos sang a song to the birds entwined in the decorative balusters and Josie forced her brain to focus on what to make for supper instead of worrying about Gloria and any new ways she might have come up with to torture Josie.

"This is unacceptable!"

Amos and Josie froze in their tracks as the scent of burnt sugar filled the air. Slowly they turned and stared down at the lobby.

A woman so beautiful she didn't look human stood there, hands on hips. She wore a formfitting blue silk dress with a star-pleated neckline showing off her flawless black skin. Her hands were hidden by wrist-length gloves and covering her hair was a shiny black turban with a gold starburst pin sitting in the center—like a '50s model come to life.

The woman looked up and snared Josie with a pair of remarkable amber-colored eyes. She held a clipboard in one gloved hand and wielded a sharpened pencil in the other.

"Are any of these yours, Mrs. LaChiusa?" the woman asked, pencil pointing at the stack of cardboard boxes.

"Ah, no. And it's Ms., umm, *Ms.* La—"

"The apartment rules and regulations are posted prominently," the woman said. "Packages are to be retrieved in a timely manner. These have been sitting here all day. This is a fire hazard."

Josie simply nodded, her words having dried up from intimidation.

The elevator doors opened and out tumbled what appeared to be an entire cheer squad. The noise of so many young women talking at once and the jaw-dropping bedazzlement of their cheer uniforms pushed Josie's question about how the elevator fit that many people out of her head.

Twelve teens bounced around the lobby, each in a different color and style of cheer uniform. Most of them resembled professional football cheerleaders, thousands of crystals adorning every centimeter of their satin hot pants, belly-baring tops, and enormous hair bows. Some were short with wide faces and round calves, others were tall and almost skeletal, their skin varying in shade from the darkest black to a creamy peach and the hair colors ranging from a hennaed red to bright blue.

"Misses Smiths," the older woman snapped. "I am warning you . . . and you and you . . ."

"M-A-D-D-Y! Maddy's in charge, we don't ask why!" The spontaneous cheer rang out while the teens fell into a loose formation, stomping their feet and clapping their hands in time with the rhyme.

The two smallest cheerleaders hopped onto the shoulders of the larger ones and another cheer rang out.

"We've come to get our pack-a-ges and take them home, then win, win, win!"

The two tiny cheerleaders flipped off their supports and stuck their landings while the rest of the group jumped up and down, cheering like mad.

A cheerleader walked over to Maddy, whom Josie now recognized as the tenants' association president from her photo on the wall. This cheerleader might have been a coach or a chaperone. She was in a vintage cheer costume and the only bedazzlement to be seen were the sequins sewn on the letter *H* adorning her sweater. Of average height with dusky olive skin and ebony hair pulled back in a ponytail with a discreet little white bow, she looked to be in her early twenties.

"Sorry, Maddy," the quiet cheerleader said. "We had a little delay—"

"Cindy had a meltdown," someone interjected. "She lost a bet to Mindy and had to eat ten of those silicon pouches labeled 'Don't eat this silicon pouch.'"

"You'd have a meltdown, too. You don't know constipation until you eat a handful of those," a green-and-silver-bedazzled cheerleader, Cindy most likely, announced, hands on hips.

"—but we'll clear this away, right this minute."

The others cheered again and grabbed boxes.

"What's conthipashon?" Amos asked. Josie took hold of his hand, meaning to lead him back to the apartment, when a cheerleader squealed.

"That's them. The new gu—ow, the new tenants!"

The entire sparkling horde advanced on them and Amos pressed himself against Josie's leg.

"Oh. My. God. That child is cute!" one squealed.

"Do you like Taylor Swift?"

"How many times have you streamed the Eras Tour?"

"How old are you?"

Josie and Amos walked up the stairs backward, one step at a time, unable to answer any of the rapid-fire questions.

"Did you get your boots at a thrift store? Thrifting is the new buying, you know."

"Have you ever been to an outlet mall? Is it truly a paradise?"

"Noticed anything different about this building since you moved in?"

"Stop!"

The cheerleaders paused, one having already reached the staircase, a greedy look on her thin face.

"Misses *Smiths*," Maddy spit the words. "As president of the tenants' association I am obliged to remind you this is a *normal* apartment building with *quiet* tenants and rule number 436 of the Wayside Rules and Regulations state no cheerleading allowed in the lobby between the hours of six p.m. and ten a.m. It is now"—Maddy looked at her watch—"six-oh-one. We are officially spared from your high-spiritedness. Hurry up and get your packages or I will have to call *Mister* Smith."

A flash of something feral twisted the face of the cheerleader nearest them and Amos let out a tiny gasp. In the blink of an eye, the squad surrounded Maddy, menace in their expressions.

The scent of ozone permeated the air, and the light bulb in the sconce to the left of the mailboxes made a popping sound and died.

Visions of a cheerleader-led *Lord of the Flies* flitted through Josie's head as the squad tightened their circle.

Maddy, however, was obviously badass. As though she had all day, she removed her blue cat's-eye-frame glasses, hung them from the bodice of her dress, and put a hand to the pin in her turban.

"Yes, ladies?" she asked, one perfectly plucked eyebrow lifting into a sharp point.

The threat of violence hovered, but none of the cheerleaders moved, as though Maddy setting a hand to her head created an impasse. The quiet cheerleader whispered in the tallest girl's ear and got her to step back, defusing the threat.

A deep voice cut through the tension.

"No need to call anyone."

Josie jumped. Pax stood behind her on the landing. She hadn't heard his tread on the stairs but now he was here, a scent reminiscent of the early-morning air high in the mountains settling around her like a blanket.

He nodded hello to Josie and Amos while passing them on his way down the stairs toward the angry cheerleaders. The teenagers shrank in his presence, their limbs turning more sticklike, their faces narrowing and eyes widening.

The phenomena must have been due to Josie's perspective from above. Pax's height was so great everyone else looked smaller in comparison. He parted the sparkling sea and faced Maddy, his shoulders rising and falling with a silent sigh.

"I don't understand this hostility. Number 436 of Wayside Rules clearly states . . ." Maddy began.

"I'll bet she's memorized all seven hundred rules," a cheerleader said, not bothering to lower her voice.

"You wish you could remember seven hundred of anything," snapped Cindy. "You can't even memorize the lyrics to a Taylor Swift song."

"I know the words to Tawor Swift songs," Amos said quietly.

The acoustics in the lobby must have carried his voice, because the cheerleaders' heads swiveled in unison to examine Amos with thoughtful expressions.

"She means the real words, Amos," Josie clarified. "Not the words you put in yourself."

"Rules are important." Pax looked around at the cheerleaders. "They keep us safe, especially when we find ourselves in *unknown territory*," he said, putting a strange emphasis on the last two words.

Maddy's perfectly made-up mouth tightened in satisfaction, and something squirmed in Josie's stomach. From where she stood, it looked like Maddy wore the same shade of candy-red lipstick as Josie's grandmother.

"However. When there is no immediate danger, sometimes rules can be loosely interpreted." He nodded at the teens. "Especially when the prohibited action is a joyful one."

Like flipping a switch, the cheerleaders went back to their bouncy, sparkly selves, all traces of animosity and otherness gone from their faces.

"Pax, Pax, he's our man. If he can't do it, no one can!"

Backflips and cartwheels ensued. Pax nodded tentatively, backing slowly away from the chaos.

The quiet cheerleader gave Pax a grateful nod, then hustled the squad back into the elevator. Josie forgot to watch to see how they fit because while she'd been staring at Pax, he'd turned around and caught her watching him.

A prickle of heat itched at her cheeks and the realization she was blushing made Josie blush even more.

"What is the point of writing down rules if no one bothers to follow them?" Maddy asked. "The only way this whole thing will work is . . ." Maddy paused and looked over at Josie, then at Pax.

When she frowned the faint odor of cabbage filled the lobby and Amos tightened his grip on Josie's hand.

Maddy directed her attention at Pax. "The only way this tenants' association will work is if *everyone* takes the *rules* seriously." She made her way to the far end of the lobby, where a small plastic tag reading BUILDING STAFF ONLY hung above a door, paused, put her hand on the doorknob, and spoke. "Rule number 312 is no children allowed unsupervised anywhere in the building." She stared directly at a spot behind Josie's head. "That rule is nonnegotiable."

Maddy shot one more glance at Pax, then exited.

"I better get myself a copy of those rules, huh?" Josie asked.

Pax nodded, then shook his head no.

"Maddy is dedicated to her position," he said in an apologetic tone. "She takes the association presidency seriously."

"I can tell," Josie said. The weirdness of the entire scene left her off balance. "Those cheerleaders . . ."

She let her words trail off, but Pax gave no sign he was interested in small talk. Probably worried Amos was going to touch stuff again.

"C'mon, buddy. There's leftover potpie or I can make a tofu scramble. You decide," Josie said as she turned away from Pax.

"I decide cake," Amos said, seriously.

"I decide no cake," she replied.

"What Maddy said." Pax's voice stopped Josie as abruptly as if he'd put a hand on her shoulder. "About children left unattended."

She twisted her neck to look back at him.

"For everyone's safety, rule 312 is nonnegotiable."

A wriggling worm of anxiety woke in her belly.

"He's only four," she said, her throat dry from disappointment and fear. "I will try my best but sometimes . . ." Exhaustion sucked at her legs and Josie let out a long sigh, along with a piece of truth. "I don't know how to do this."

Pax tilted his head. "I don't understand." He climbed up the stairs and halted one step below her.

Amos decided now was a good time to lie down. He lowered his body to the stairs, reached his chubby fingers out, and hooked them among the wrought iron leaves of the balustrade, singing quietly to himself about birds.

"It's an impossible task, parenting," Josie said, the words rushing out of her like water bursting through a crack in a dam. "No matter what you do, you're confronted by books and websites and magazines and a whole horde of people ready to tell you you've done it wrong."

Pax startled her as he folded his body with a liquid grace and sat on the steps, tilted his head, and stared up at her without saying a word.

Listening.

Shrugging, Josie sat on the stairs as well. The calming scent of violet gum wafted on a draft, and Amos tapped his toes against the marble stairs as he sang nonsense words.

"Those same people spend a lot of money and time scaring you into hyperawareness of how many ways you can screw up or how close you are to ruining everything," she said.

Pax frowned and rubbed his chin, silent but still listening.

Dear God, how attractive.

Men should put it on their Tinder bio. Silent listener.

"He's four," she said. "He's a child. At any other time in human history, the expectation would be if I keep him fed and clothed and educated, I've done my job. That if he runs around in circles or gets dirty or lost or scared or bored or sits on a stone gargoyle that's normal."

She hadn't forgotten Pax's face when they last met in the courtyard. This wasn't an apology, because Amos hadn't done anything wrong. More of a reminder that Amos was a kid.

"Children learn a lot by touching things," she said.

"Boys like to hit things, too," Pax added. "And push things over, I remember that."

"Right," Josie agreed. "They're fleshy, stinky little tornadoes and that used to be okay. Not today, though. Today, they're . . ."

What were children expected to be these days? Perfect? No, if you demanded perfection from a child, you were a bad parent. Perfectly imperfect? Imperfect in ways that could be solved by a column in a parenting magazine or a vlog post?

"It's not the rule itself," Josie explained. "Of course, you don't want four-year-olds running around an apartment building without anyone knowing where they are or what they're doing. Trust me, I can imagine a hundred different scenarios where it ends up in tragedy."

Amos stuck a finger in his ear and wiggled it around.

"A hundred?" Pax asked.

A thousand if she put her mind to it, but Josie didn't say that. She continued. "The weight of my expectation something terrible is bound to happen, the way I raise my voice when he takes one step out of my sight, how I'm constantly telling him 'No, you can't touch this' or 'Go there' or 'Do this'—I don't know how to keep him safe without making his childhood smaller than it should be."

"Do you come up against many rules like 312?" Pax asked.

Josie nodded. "Dozens and dozens. All day, everywhere."

"You are a biwd named Unique and you have frwee brothers

named Bird, too," Amos sang, quietly serenading a wrought iron sparrow. "Tomorrow you will eat some cake because cake is the best dinner in the world, and I love it so much."

Pax cleared his throat and stood, frowning at the floor.

"Caaaake is so good and has flowers on the top and I love it soooooooo," Amos crooned.

Josie hid her smile with her hand. She loved Amos to the moon and back, but Frank Sinatra he was not.

"For some reason, I am thinking of getting cake for dinner," Pax said.

Amos was into his song now and didn't hear him, but Josie raised an eyebrow at Pax and waited.

"What if I cannot finish my dinner, though?" he said. "I don't like to think of sugar going to waste."

If it were only possible to see inside Pax's head. Did he pity her? Did he pity Amos for being saddled with an anxiety-ridden mother who insisted on tofu scrambles? Was he truly craving cake?

"You can saves it for breakfast if you don't finish it." Amos had stopped singing and started to pay attention to them at some point.

"I could. Or, if you are not too full of your tofu scramble, perhaps I could share the rest with you and your mother?" Pax asked.

"I will never be full from tofu," Amos said seriously. He wrenched his fingers free of the wrought iron ivy and sat, gazing up at Pax with wide eyes. "I always has room for other food when it's tofu scramble for dinner."

Pax looked to Josie, and she nodded.

Amos certainly did not need to believe his freestyling about cake would work every time but the way Pax grinned when she nodded yes was the most genuine expression of joy she'd seen in a long time.

Fuck it. She was going to make a mistake at some point today anyway, right? Might as well make one that came with frosting on top.

Chapter Six

Pax leaned back in the squeaky swivel chair behind the metal desk in his office and sighed. Before Number Five stopped working, this office had been elegantly furnished except for the beer hat and dartboard Manny had left behind.

It hadn't suited Pax—luxury. In fact, he'd found it distasteful. Even now, his former troops—those who survived that last battle—were living in barracks or out in the field, eating what they could catch, some of them having to deal with menstruation during weeks-long campaigns while sleeping on the ground in oilcloth tents. Pax, meanwhile, had left them behind.

What if Number Five was reacting to his guilt?

Was *he* responsible for Number Five's illness?

Leaving the office, Pax crossed the lobby and wished for an enemy he could see, a place to put his frustration. Bert was asleep in his niche.

Ernie, however, was missing.

This was Pax's fault as well. He'd delivered too fierce a scolding after Amos and Josie had left the courtyard. Ernie's defense—Amos had tickled him until he had to beg the boy to stop—had fallen on deaf ears.

Pax considered the notion of apologizing when he heard the door to 3C open. The soft shush was too quiet to register in a human's ears in the silent lobby, but not Pax's. He took the stairs so fast he almost knocked Josie over in the hallway right outside her apartment.

"You must be a mind reader," Josie said. "I was going to see if you were in your office. You know, I don't have a number for you."

She'd wound her hair into the shape of a cinnamon bun and stuck it on top of her head. Most women he knew were soldiers and kept their hair cut close to their skull. In his world, the only women who created shapes with their hair were noblewomen who had maids and time to spare.

Josie did not have a maid nor time to spare. Should he compliment her cinnamon bun because it took work to create, or should he hold his tongue because it looked ridiculous?

"What number?" he asked, deciding to skip the subject altogether.

"Your cell phone," Josie said, raising her eyebrows and tilting her head.

"I don't have a cell phone."

Cell phones were abominable creations unique to this world. They had an unhealthy hold on people's attention. Even worse, they had the disconcerting effect of draining magic from whoever held them. Since every human he'd seen had one in their hands at some point, it might account for the dearth of magic here. This might also account for why they refused to work for most of the residents except for Maddy.

"No phone?"

Pax shrugged. "I am almost always here. You are welcome to come and knock on the door to my office at any time."

"Can I knock, knock?" she said, her voice rising and falling in that way folks used when they told a joke. Her shy half smile when she bit the side of her mouth right after confirmed Pax's guess. She had stepped outside her apartment but still held tight to the door handle and had to look up to meet his eyes.

"You are referencing Mr. Amos's joke from before. When he knocked into being a banana again."

When she laughed, Josie covered her mouth and stepped away from him, leaning back into the door, and Pax tensed. Had he mistakenly made a ribald joke? Said something embarrassing?

"You were nice to humor him."

Pax shrugged. "Being kind is the simplest of pleasures. It takes no effort and the rewards are infinite."

"That's a lovely sentiment," she told him, a dimple appearing to the left of her mouth.

A wave of warm pride washed through him, and he fought the satisfied smile buoying up from his chest.

Imagine, a woman thought The Butcher nice and lovely.

Was it pride keeping him from smiling or years of training himself to appear tough and emotionless kicking in? Pax was no longer at war. Perhaps it was time to lose his wartime habits.

Something heavy fell to the floor in her apartment and interrupted them. Josie's shoulders bent inward as if the sound had snapped whatever willpower was holding her upright.

"I would like to help." Pax meant help with whatever had gone awry inside the apartment, but the words came out thick with intimacy. He hadn't meant to use that voice.

Strange things happened when Pax was with Josie. She might even have a drop or two of magic in her blood and it did something to his brain.

Josie nodded once, then looked up at him with a worried gaze. "Thank you."

The words fell into a soft shape between them. He reached out to catch them but turned the gesture into a pat on her elbow at the last second.

Whatever lay between her and Pax included recognition of a kindred spirit and the gift of appreciating a fellow soldier in whatever war they may be fighting. An intimacy not necessarily tied to attraction but certainly paving the way for friendship.

If he wanted to be Josie's friend.

Except . . .

Number Five would somehow refuel and resume its travels. Soon the birds would fly again, and he would leave this world and this friendship behind.

"No thanks are necessary," he said overbrightly, tapping again at her elbow as though there were a button there. "This is my job."

One of the ceiling lights in the hallway burned out with a loud *slap.*

"Right," she said. "Of course."

The bitter black licorice taste of disappointment coated his tongue as Pax followed her into the apartment. He admired the newly painted entry hallway and peered closely at the photos hung along the wall: vibrant pictures of produce in a farmers' market, magnified shots of multicolored spirals at the center of a petunia, a riotous bed of jewel-toned nasturtium.

Josie stopped when they got to the kitchen and crossed her arms over her body.

"I did this," she said. "Didn't take me long, but once again, I managed to ruin a good thing."

* * *

My God, Josie could be a dramatic bitch when PMS collided with stress. Her brain thrilled to the moment, its raspy voice berating her so violently she could smell Pall Malls.

"I meant . . . I don't know what I did, but I can't fix this."

This was the hole in the wall, the multiple half-inch nails fallen on the top of the oven, and a battery-operated clock from the hardware store that had fallen from its perch—again.

"I hung this clock yesterday using a picture-hanging kit, and everything seemed fine. Tonight, the clock falls off the wall. When I put it back up, it falls again. Like the wall turned soft. Whenever I hung it back up, the hole from the previous nail grew larger. The whole mess got bigger and bigger the more I tried to fix it."

Josie didn't need a clock over the oven. She was looking for comfort. Craving assurance. There were only so many mantras Josie could repeat or tasks to perform before the lady with the Pall Malls sounded less and less like her grandmother and more like her mother-in-law, Gloria.

Pax moved the oven to the side—holy moly, how did he do that so effortlessly?—and ran his hand along the wall near the hole as though he were stroking a wounded animal.

"I'm sorry," she said softly. "After the third time I had to stop because I felt . . ."

Josie bit her bottom lip and her stomach flipped. The sensation she'd felt each time the hole got bigger had freaked her out.

"What? What did you feel?" Pax asked, still examining the wall, not looking at Josie like she was a nutcase.

"Like I was hurting her. It. Something."

"It's mostly cosmetic," he said. "You didn't do any lasting damage."

The sleeves to his gray henley were pushed up past his elbows rather than rolled neatly. Small scars stood out on the knuckles of his large hands and a swath of fine dark hair beginning at the knobby bone in his wrist covered his forearm. She imagined there would be calluses on the fingertips examining the wound.

Wall. Examining the wall.

The light over the sink was dimmer than usual and the sensation of standing in the only safe place intensified with the encroaching dark in the rest of the apartment. Josie forced her gaze down to the blue flowered pattern on the linoleum floor until his toes appeared at the edge of her sight. What did she care what her building super thought of her? So what if she got a reputation as the crazy tenant?

He was only here to do his job.

"You have a watch," he said. "Does it keep time?"

"He's late," she said.

If Josie's brain had hands, she would have smacked herself in the forehead. She'd delivered a soliloquy on how hard it is to parent to the poor man the other night and he'd brought her kid cake. Was she going to subject him to another cascade of her boring anxieties? He had things to do and places to be large and reassuring.

"Mr. Amos is late," he said.

On Saturdays, Dan's parents took Amos out for pizza and arcade night. Because he had Sunday school the next morning, they always promised to bring him home by nine p.m. While Josie bit her tongue when they showed up early to get him, in the past few weeks they'd also brought him home late.

At first it had been five minutes. Then ten. Last Saturday, they didn't bring him home until nine forty-five. Amos's bedtime was nine thirty, and when Josie remarked she'd been worried when they were late without calling first, Gloria had smiled as though she'd told them a joke, then patted Josie on the shoulder, the stench of Givenchy and gin wafting from her neck scarf.

"He was with his grandparents, Josephine. This is safer than him being with strangers all day at his nursery school."

Amos's nursery school buddies didn't smell like cocktails and bitterness.

"Is he in trouble?" Pax asked, his gaze sweeping her body. Not in a creepy way, more like he was taking stock of her messy bun and ratty sweats and lips chapped where she chewed when she was nervous. As if he was assessing her readiness to handle whatever came next.

"Not trouble, exactly. He's with my in-laws. They run on their own time." She set her hands on her hips, as if by looking like a grown-up, she could act like one and cast a glance toward the front door. If he hadn't been here, Josie would have checked her watch. Again.

Pax said nothing, loudly.

"Amos's father's parents," she said, when she caught sight of his expression, one eyebrow raised. When his eyebrow remained raised, Josie told him the rest.

"His father died. Dan."

Not like this was a secret. Still, whenever she said it out loud, Josie always felt as though she was defending herself.

"Ah," he said. "They lost their son, so they hold on tightly to their grandson. Grief can make you selfish."

What a kind way to think about it.

If only she believed Gloria held tight to Amos because she loved him, not because she thought he belonged to her.

Josie debated whether to tell Pax about Gloria and confide in him her fear she was skirting close to the edge of losing Amos to his grandmother but the sudden scent of roses distracted her.

Josie looked around, and her blood ran cold.

There, on the kitchen table, a small vase held three cabbage roses. With the shushing sound of a sigh, one large petal the color of a ripened peach fell to the table.

Those roses hadn't been there ten minutes ago and there was no way Pax could have brought them in without her seeing them.

"Can you fix this tomorrow?" Wiping her now sweaty palms down the sides of her pants, Josie forced a smile and stepped out of the warm light, breaking the circle. "Sorry, I . . . he will be home any minute, I'm sure, and he needs to go to bed."

"Of course," Pax said, putting the oven back into place, chin down and eyes averted. "Tomorrow."

The muscles holding her smile in place trembled until he left. Josie turned the lock and put her ear to the door until she couldn't hear Pax's footsteps anymore, threw the flowers away, and turned on every light in the apartment until Amos came home.

Chapter Seven

Regular Goldfish or pizza Goldfish?"

Huh. That was a stumper.

Josie and Amos crunched the edges of frozen waves of slush covering the sidewalk, two white pastry boxes with greasy stains on the outside tucked under Josie's arm. They'd stopped at Donuts Delite and their discussion with the girl at the counter about jelly versus cream-filled donuts had grown into a debate over which flavors in general were the best flavors. A debate that continued even after they left.

Obviously, watermelon anything was the best.

"I like the taste of regular Goldfish," Josie said, "but pizza Goldfish feel better in my mouth."

"My dad liked grape pie best. We can make grape pie?"

Josie's stomach plummeted, but she didn't stumble.

The shock of Amos speaking about Dan's likes and dislikes had slowly worn away. Gloria, of course, was the source of such information. "Your father liked to fish. Your father loved golf." That last part was bullshit. Dan liked to drive around in a golf cart drinking spiked Arnold Palmers.

Who didn't?

When Josie grew frustrated with her mother-in-law, she would look at Amos and try taking a mental step back. She understood a parent's love for their child. How big and dangerous and cold the world is and how small you are in comparison with all the terrible things out there. How aware you become of your shortcomings. How crazy it makes you to think of them gone.

Amos's aim when he asked questions like *Did my dad hate broccoli, too?* or *Dad's favorite superhero was 'Pider-Man, right?* was to have a relationship with Dan, even though they would never meet.

It hurt, but pain didn't always mean you'd been wounded. Sometimes, it just meant you were human.

"Sure, buddy," Josie told Amos, keeping her voice level. "Pie is a great idea."

"Jalyn's dad likes gummi worms," he said, oblivious to her reaction to the mention of Dan.

"Gummi worms are a waste of sugar," Josie mumbled, her attention caught by the lights on the seventh floor where the cheerleaders lived. Unlike the homey golden glow spilling out of the other apartment windows, the Smith residence emitted multicolored flashes, and someone was growing pot in a windowsill, the purple heating lamp turning the snow on the ledge a sickly indigo hue. Mafia family on the DL? Secret reality show filming the hijinks of a blended family?

What was going on up there?

More important, had she bought enough donuts?

A flyer had been taped to the mailboxes advertising the tenants' association meeting tonight. Someone had slipped a highlighted copy under her door the day before.

1. Discussion of Laundry Room Etiquette
2. Reminder of Elevator Use Etiquette
3. Welcoming of New Tenants
4. Reintroduction of Package Pickup Rules and Regulations
5. Mingling and Snacks

**NB The collection jar for snack money will be outside of the building's office from Monday to Wednesday 12 p.m. Your choice of snacks depends on your generosity of donations.*

Josie's first instinct had been to ignore it. What would they think of her, these other tenants? How would they judge her? Should she bring Amos with her? Did any of them have something to do with the roses?

Josie couldn't hide, though. When Gloria dropped Amos off Saturday night, she'd come inside the lobby and flipped out over the dingy floor, dim lights, and strange smell in the lobby.

"What sort of neighbors live here?" Gloria had asked, mouth thinned in displeasure. "You can't let Amos leave the apartment on his own. A building like this could attract the worst sorts."

"It's an amazing location and a gorgeous apartment, considering how reasonable the rent is," Josie had countered.

Gloria's derisive sniff had set Josie's teeth on edge. "If the cost of rent is an issue, Josephine, you can always tell me. We can work something out."

As if Josie would ever let Gloria know the state of her finances.

Before the conversation with Gloria, she hadn't doubted the safety of the building but now Josie thought it prudent to check out the other residents.

She'd dithered and forgotten to put money in the snack jar, so twenty minutes before the meeting was supposed to start, she and Amos ran to Donuts Delite, ate bear claws for dinner, and brought a ridiculous amount of half-price, day-old pastries home with them.

When she pushed open the lobby door with her back, arms around the precious donuts, Amos slipped past her.

"Don't run in wet boots," Josie called as she got the door open completely and nearly wiped out when the noise from the lobby hit her.

"Rule number 212—"

"Shut up, Maddy!"

"Donuts!"

"D-O-N-U-T-S! DONUTS! Dunkin', Tim's, or Krispy Kreme, anytime they're good to eat!"

"Whoa!" Amos shouted, turning around in the center of the lobby like a Spider-Man-booted ballerina. "Is here a party?"

If it were a party, the guest list was *eclectic*. The cheerleaders were back, in matching outfits this time, pink-and-green hot pants and crop tops plastered with rhinestones everywhere, even places rhinestones shouldn't be plastered. Maddy was there, wearing a white pantsuit, white turban, and clear-framed cat's-eye glasses, arguing with a short man who must not realize how much he looked like a garden gnome with his white beard and red dunce cap.

To the left of the elevator, double doors Josie had never noticed before stood open. Beyond them was what looked like the waiting room of a 1970s dentist office. Inside, rows of rusted folding chairs were set in front of a plywood lectern with a projector screen open behind it.

Josie did a double take and, helpless, a third take at a dark-haired man with the face of a European model and the body of Batman who leaned against the double doors. The man's hair grazed his shoulders and his eyes smoldered—finally Josie understood the metaphor—with what she decided was pent-up desire.

Whew. Was it hot in here?

Behind him stood three elderly people dressed in pastel-colored velour track suits, one pink, one blue, and one purple, their silver hair cut into perfectly angled bobs. All wore dark sunglasses and held the type of canes used by folks with visual impairments.

One of the gargoyles was still missing; someone had dressed the other in a Kansas City Chiefs jersey.

Josie immediately took offense.

This was Bills country.

"I'm glad you came. We were about to begin, and everyone has wanted to meet you." The quiet cheerleader from the other day held out her hands toward the donuts, and Josie let her take the top box. The teen wore pink and green and rhinestones as well, but instead of hot pants she sported a short, pleated skirt, and her long hair was down.

"Hi," Josie said. "This is quite a turnout. I'm Josie, by the way."

Like her . . . sisters? . . . cousins? . . . the cheerleader had slightly feline features: tilted eyes, broad cheekbones, and a narrow chin. If asked, Josie wouldn't be able to name a single characteristic that stood out, but the combination up close gave the girl an otherworldly look.

"It is a tremendous pleasure to meet you, Josie Bytheway. I am Pri—" the cheerleader stuttered. "I am Naliti," she finished.

"Hi, Naliti. Actually, it's LaChiusa." Josie's explanation went unheard as another cheer went up from the crowd.

Holy God.

In the blink of an eye, Amos had somehow ingratiated himself with the teenagers and now stood on a cheerleader's shoulders. Thankfully, his boots were off, but the cheerleader was tall, and Amos still had a tenuous grasp on gravity.

"A-M-O-S! Like 'Pider-Man he is the best! He's so cute and very small, but we sure hope he'll save us all!"

The dark-haired Model Guy pushed away from the door and stalked toward the cheerleaders at the same time Maddy advanced on them, her finger jabbing the air in their direction.

With a twisted grin the cheerleader holding Amos's ankles hoisted him from her shoulders and held him over her head.

The lobby floor was wet from melted snow. Josie wasn't wearing boots and her sneakers slid, slowing her down as she ran toward the cheerleader.

He wasn't far off the floor. The cheerleader was six feet or so, and after lifting Amos above her head, she'd only added two feet at most. Still, the sight of Amos's tiny knees buckling, the fug of too many bodies in the overcrowded lobby, and the anxiety simmering in Josie's gut combined to unbalance her. Josie's feet splayed in opposite directions, and she slid toward an unattractive windmill-like collision with the floor.

Except it didn't happen.

"Steady."

Pax grabbed the falling donut box in one hand, took hold of Josie's elbow with the other, and pulled an honest-to-God save the day. Before Josie could open her mouth to ask where he'd even come from, he'd handed the donuts off to the man in the cap, kept her upright, and caught a toppling Amos literally in the *palm* of his hand.

More like assisted Amos in a paper plane–like landing. Pax was an island of calm in the chaos of the lobby.

Ninety-nine percent of Josie's brain gave him a standing ovation and even the one percent had to shrug and nod through a cloud of smoke.

Competence is a universal turn-on.

"It's six fifty-eight," Maddy announced to the crowd as her three-inch stilettos clacked across the floor. A look passed from her to Pax to the quiet cheerleader to the ridiculously handsome Model Guy. "Meeting commences at seven."

"Get inside, now." Model Guy didn't raise his voice—didn't even look around—he just made the announcement, and by the time Amos was on his feet and running toward her, the entire crowd had funneled through the double doors into the meeting area.

"Sheep," Model Guy muttered, closing the double doors behind him without looking back.

Amos in one hand, a slightly squished box of donuts in her other, Josie had to wait for her breathing to return to normal in the now empty lobby.

Empty except for Pax.

"They are especially active," Pax said. "The tenants' association."

"Active," Josie repeated weakly.

Model Guy poked his head out through the doors. "Is that raspberry or strawberry preserves in the pastries?" he asked in what sounded like an Eastern European accent, brows furrowed, voice resonant and obscenely sexy.

"They're tawberry jelly," Amos told him.

Model Guy rolled his eyes and frowned in an expression of disgust.

"There are Bavarian creams in this one," Josie said, holding up the box in her hand.

Model Guy sniffed. "*Bavarians.*" He pulled his head back into the room and the doors swung closed behind him.

Silence again.

"This has something to do with the rent being low, doesn't it?" Josie asked.

Halfway to his head, Pax's hand stilled, then fell to his side. "They have all had sufficient"—he looked up and to the right—"background checks. Our tenants. You are in no danger from them."

Pax mentioning danger unprompted didn't make Josie feel better. Neither did the sinking feeling there weren't any members of Gloria's country club in there.

"Please come," he said, the tiniest lift of his brows and widening of his eyes taking years off his face. How many years? "They are excited to meet you. The zombie . . . Zombino family have even composed a welcome song. Joey, the youngest, was inspired by a television program called *The Partridge Family.*"

Pax trailed off, something in her expression having clued him in that none of the words he'd said made any sense. At all.

Eyebrows lowering, the years crept back into the planes of Pax's face, and the prickly sting of loss itched Josie's skin.

Once, a long time ago, Josie had believed in a man. A boy really. He'd been tall and strong and quiet, too. He'd lied to her and left her, and Dan had left, too.

Her brain sucked hard on a damp, lipstick-ringed filter and reminded Josie she was a shit judge of character and shouldn't try to make friends.

There was too much at stake.

"It's getting late," Josie said, grabbing on to a truth so she wouldn't stutter or blush. "I've gotta give Amos his dinner and bath. Why don't you take the donuts? The Bavarian creams are on the bottom for"—she gestured toward the door—"the guy with the . . ." She gestured at her face. "The guy."

"Raphe," Pax said.

Of course Model Guy's name was Raphe. Probably Raphe Midnight or Darkmoor or something equally black-velvet-and-red-rose-ish.

"Mom," Amos whispered, and tugged at her hand. His Spider-Man tuque had fallen off and a hank of sweaty hair stood up in the center of his head like Big Bird's feathers. "We can go in. I won't let go your hand the whole time."

Damn.

If Amos could be courageous enough to stand on top of a cheerleader's shoulders, Josie should at least have the guts to go to a stupid tenants' meeting.

"I will—" Pax stopped himself. "Um, that is to say, if you find crowds difficult, I can . . . we can stand in the back and be the first to leave. If that is of any comfort?"

The concern in Pax's eyes couldn't have been faked and the warm pressure in the center of her chest from knowing someone was looking out for her gave Josie the strength to take a risk.

"Okay, buddy," she whispered to Amos, then glanced up at Pax. "Okay, Mr. Pax. Let's go eat some donuts and make some friends."

* * *

"The laundry room rules are written in large font, Ms. Fate."

Maddy stood at the lectern and spoke into the superfluous microphone, her voice venturing into nails-on-chalkboard territory. "I am happy to have a committee meet to agree on standard font size in all building communiques if that's why you continually violate rule 44 and use a full-load setting on what is obviously a small-to-medium load. However—"

A chorus of voices drowned her out.

"They came!"

"They're here!"

"More donuts?"

"Should we make up another cheer?"

Pax had hoped to slip Josie and Amos into the back of the room without a lot of fuss. Tiny wrinkles in the shape of question marks had bracketed Josie's mouth after he'd helped Amos down from Cindy's shoulders.

He couldn't assure Josie that the hint of nutmeg in the air meant Cindy was using a faery freeze-fall spell.

The way Josie watched her son while at the same time reacting to everyone else around her—this was the look of a soldier on point, ready for danger, expecting the worst. As evidenced by Number Five's reaction to Josie's clock, having the new tenant be a bundle of nerves wasn't helping the situation get better.

Somehow, Pax and the rest of the guests had to convince the young mother of Amos's safety without using magic.

Raphe flicked his eyes at Josie, then at Pax, his opinion easy to read. The king-in-waiting was restless and wanting blood.

Time moved according to the tides of magic, which meant one day on this world might equal ten on another. Without fuel,

Number Five's universal clock was frozen and none of them knew how much time had passed since they came here.

Raphe had checked in expecting a journey of two weeks. Three at the most. A month could have gone by on his world, and he'd never know it.

Few had expected Raphe's father, the vampire king, would perish in a coup while his son was on an extended diplomatic visit to the Gnoman Empire. When Raphe got word of the king's death he'd rushed to the closest Wayside stop, frantic with both panic and rage. Rumors swirled around Number Five about who had been responsible for the coup, but Raphe said little on the subject, only that he was returning home to claim his rightful throne.

Raphe's initial panic had since subsided, but his rage kept building the longer he was forced to wait for retribution.

Not every guest had stakes as high as Raphe's, but that didn't mean they enjoyed sitting around and waiting.

Not to mention, the guests on the sixth floor wouldn't stay asleep forever.

"As I was saying . . ." Maddy's voice flattened and slapped at the air like a pancake spatula, indicating she was losing patience. Mindful, the crowd's exclamations dampened and most of them turned back to face her. Like *normal* humans.

Speaking of which, Pax would have to tell the owl shifter in 4B to stop turning his head all the way around.

"Item number two on our agenda is an etiquette reminder. I have received more than a few complaints about some of you leaving strong spells—"

"Derp!" Joey, the youngest Zombino, shot up out of his chair, eyes bugging out of his face. Hopefully, they wouldn't fall out while the humans were here. "Strong *smells*, you say?"

"Ahem." Maddy caught herself. "Leaving strong *smells* behind in the elevator. Kindly think of others who must endure the vestiges of those . . . smells . . . in a small, confined space. Now, on to item number three—"

"That's an ableist take, Maddy." Denis stood on the seat of his folding chair, arms across his chest, beard quivering—the model of an outraged gnome. Not that they were usually anything else.

Pax's head dropped.

He should reconsider the blood sacrifice and put Denis's name up for consideration.

"I challenge you to find any evidence of the tenants' association discriminating in any way, shape, or form," Maddy snapped. "Our guidelines are both *inclusive* and *holistic*, Denis."

"Those of us who suffer chronic conditions cannot control their symptoms on cue. If I am in the elevator after a meal and happen to—"

"She means smells," Joey said. "You know. *Smells*. Smeeeeelllss??" His pale, spindly fingers wiggled like spiders in Denis's direction.

Denis did not get the hint. Denis was impervious to hints unless they were in the shape of an anvil and fell on his head.

"What I wanna know is who stole the *e*'s from the Scrabble letter bags," demanded Future Fate, the youngest of the Fate siblings. They crossed their arms over the front of their purple velvet tracksuit jacket. "Bunch of sore losers. Just because *xinczrthyn* isn't spelled with a *c* where you come from, doesn't mean it's not a word."

"It's not a word," muttered Denis.

"I have to get Amos his supper," Josie whispered to Pax, her eyebrows so furrowed they looked like a confused caterpillar marching across her forehead. "We should go."

"When are we gonna talk about the pile of dirt out there?" the owl shifter piped up, his glasses slipping down his nose when he thrust a pointer finger at the window facing the courtyard. "The new tenant needs to tell us what it's for."

Every single head not already on backward now turned toward Josie. The air around her chilled.

"Right." Maddy grabbed for control of the meeting. "Item number three. Our new *neighbors* in our *apartment building* here on this delightful *Earth*. Everyone welcome Josephine LaChiusa and Amos LaChiusa."

"Hi!" Amos, unmoved by the same anxiety that had turned his mother to ice, waved happily at the dozens of folks who examined him intently.

Some more intently than others.

"Well?" the owl shifter asked, arms still crossed. "What's the deal with the dirt?"

"The deal with the . . . ?" Josie twisted around and looked at Pax. Looked at him to save her. That's what knights were supposed to do for ladies in distress.

How, though? He could cut someone's head off, but Pax couldn't work out how that would help her. It would probably do the opposite. Plus, he'd have to clean it up.

Amos pulled his hand from Josie's and clonked over to the window, then mashed his face against the glass.

That couldn't be hygienic.

"Mom, the backyard got ruined," he cried.

Pax, praying to the gods he wasn't fucking everything up, squeezed Josie's shoulder once. He joined Amos at the window and the rest of the tenants followed at a small distance, still observing the newcomers.

"What happened there?" Josie asked him, her eyes wide with surprise.

The courtyard was no more. The cracked cement and rotting benches were gone, replaced with a towering pile of rich, black soil.

"That's what I want to know," said Denis. "If I have to sit through these meetings to get one little thing fixed, so do you. You can't go wishing for dirt piles without asking the tenants' association first."

Josie gaped, her astonishment and discomfort so strong the air vibrated with it. Pax stepped forward, putting himself between Josie and the tenants.

"*Number Five* decided on the dirt," Pax said, gesturing to the courtyard.

Amos frowned, and Pax quickly followed up. "I mean to say, the dirt is for a *building* project. *Our building* needed dirt, so I bought some."

"You bought dirt?" Josie asked.

Shit. How else did one acquire dirt?

"Is it a unique blend of soil that cannot be found anywhere else, perhaps?" Raphe inquired, his eyes wide and brows lifted to his forehead, overenunciating as though speaking to a child.

Dick.

"Yes," Pax snapped. "Yes. I ordered special soil to . . ." What had Josie said the other day in the courtyard? ". . . to create some green space."

"A garden?" Josie asked.

Was there a note of hope in her voice?

"A *garden*," Denis hissed in horror. "With *statues*?"

"Will we be burying anyone, er, anything in there?" Raphe asked, true interest shining in his eyes.

"This is exciting," Princess Naliti piped up. "We can grow flowers."

"Oooohh." The princesses made a collective sound of appreciation. After loud music and shiny things, faery princesses loved flowers most of all.

Before they could break into a cheer, Maddy strode to the window. She glared at the enormous pile of dirt, glared at Denis, then at Pax, at the cheerleaders, and finally at Josie, who turned a little green.

"If *Number Five* is to have a garden, there needs to be a garden committee," she announced. "The committee will meet once a week and report back at the biweekly tenants' association meeting."

"There will be night-blooming flowers," Raphe demanded.

"And hellebore," Joey added.

"Peppermint," Denis offered.

"When do we start?" Naliti asked while her sisters did a few cartwheels with typical faery excitement.

Josie, however, had turned from green to gray when everyone in the room stared at her in expectation. Except for the owl shifter, who had turned his head around to leer at Maddy's legs.

Pax was going to kick that guy's ass.

"We?" Josie echoed, sounding nauseous.

"Mom," Amos said, bouncing on his toes. "Mom, you always say you wished you could put your hands in dirt. You said so, Mom."

Put her hands in the dirt? Pax waited for Josie to deny it, but she opened her mouth, then closed it, a stricken look in her eyes.

"We can help dig, right, Mom?" Amos asked.

One of the fluorescent light bulbs sizzled then dimmed, and the smell of burnt popcorn mingled with the fumes of the ugly brown carpet beneath their feet.

"Mom?" Amos asked quietly.

Josie lifted her head and examined the tenants with her steady gaze, a hint she knew this moment was important, even if she didn't know why.

"A garden committee." She looked at Pax quickly, then at the pile of dirt out back. "What a wonderful way to get to know our new neighbors. I would love to join."

Maddy rolled her eyes and clapped her hands over her ears as the faeries cheered and backflipped the length of the room. Denis designated himself vice president in charge of decorative objects, Joey Z. whistled, and Raphe left the room with the box of Bavarian creams under his arm.

Josie didn't see any of this. Her attention was on Amos, who twirled around in his snow boots and laughed as though he could hear someone whispering something silly in his ear.

Chapter Eight

Your gargoyle is hiding in the basement."

Pax shrugged.

"He's been *whining*."

Pax flinched.

Raphe sniffed in triumph. "Get him back upstairs or I'll chisel off an organ."

"Wheeeew," Denis said with admiration. "Creative. Evil but creative."

The tenants' association meeting over, the common area was empty except for the two stragglers. Pax had told Maddy to go to bed and he would finish putting away the folding chairs. She'd taken one last look at the dangling fluorescent lights, nodded, and left.

She missed the chandelier.

They all did.

Even Denis.

"I thought you didn't like strawberry jam," Denis said.

As he stood next to a folding table near the window, Raphe's hand hovered over the bakery box, but his expression remained blank.

"I was checking to see how many were left," the vampire lied.

Cinnamon scented the air and Raphe glared at the ceiling.

Number Five was allergic to lies.

"I didn't know you liked sweets," Pax said, not bothering to hide his amusement.

Pulling his lips back to expose the sharp points of his fangs, Raphe retracted his hand and brushed an invisible speck of dust from his lapel.

"I don't like sweets," Raphe said, sniffing as the cinnamon scent intensified.

Pax hadn't needed the hint. The vampire had left the meeting twenty minutes early with an entire box of Bavarian cream donuts under his arm and returned with a sly grin.

"I am a deadly warrior," the vampire said curtly. "Deadly warriors don't *like sweets.* We steal them from children and rejoice in the sound of their subsequent tears."

"Okay. Whatever you say." Pax picked up his chair, folded it, then set it on a cart.

"*You* like them."

Pax ignored the vampire's comment while he folded and stacked more chairs. He knew Raphe wasn't talking about donuts.

"It was a mistake, letting a pair of humans through the doors," Denis remarked. He'd been eyeing the donuts as well and had stayed after the meeting to see if any would be left over. "Now you'll have a guilty conscience no matter what. You'll feel bad if we kick them out and even worse when we slit their throats."

Pax kept his expression blank despite the acid burn of rage at Denis's words. They were only words. Denis was all talk. "No one is slitting anyone's throat."

"Pussy." The vampire who did not like sweets lifted the lid of the white cardboard box with one finger and examined the contents as he spoke. "Ironic that The Butcher has a resistance to slitting throats. I'd thought after all your kills you might have figured out how to do it without worrying about the mess."

From a bucket beneath the snack table, Pax took a spray bottle and a microfiber cloth. Not as soothing as grooming his horse but he felt the same urge to instill order he often had after battles.

The meeting had been a battle of sorts.

Josie had fought to remain calm while the merits of the garden committee were "discussed." Her smile hadn't reached her eyes, and her gaze had volleyed between Amos, the pile of dirt outside, and Denis, who glared at her in return. The tenants who sided with Pax and were amenable to having the humans among them now took the position a communal garden was an excellent idea.

Others had come up with alternate ideas. The werewolf from the fourth floor wanted an orchard, the naiad on the first floor whose windows faced the courtyard wanted a water park, and a ghost in corporeal form suggested a dog run. Maddy had done her best to remind everyone to be well-behaved *humans*, but the atmosphere had been tense. Three more lights had burned out and the carpet had turned the greenish-yellow shade of bile.

Hopefully, Josie hadn't noticed.

"This has nothing to do with liking or not liking them," Pax said. "This won't work if we make her uncomfortable. Number Five is changing—"

"A single vine turned green?" Denis scoffed.

Pax held up his spray bottle as though it were a sword. "A new stove," he pointed out, "redecorated itself for the boy."

"He is a liar, that boy," Raphe remarked, sniffing the last of the powdered jelly donuts. "This isn't strawberry."

"Focus," the gnome snapped. "We don't know how time

passes on this world. The pigeons stopped coming and we don't know what's happening in our home worlds, either. We need to get out of here and back to reality. Remember, some of us have shit to do." Denis frowned as Raphe bit into the donut. "Or asses we need to get kicked."

Raphe ignored the barb, but the vampire coup had repercussions on dozens of worlds. Similar to the controversy over Josie and Amos, one faction of guests supported Raphe, and another, who benefited from the demise of the Vampire Kingdom, opposed him.

A handful from each group could be found in Number Five, but no fights had broken out, although a good deal of wagering took place out of Raphe's earshot.

The vampire pretended to be too intrigued by the donuts to be baited. "This tastes like the fruit of a *hoornegghi* plant. They're carnivorous, you know." He licked his lips. "Delicious."

Whatever impatience the guests felt, Pax felt it ten times over. He was responsible for not only their fate but for Number Five itself. Now added to this weight was the fate of Josie and Amos.

It would be Pax's fault if someone like Denis drove them away. He'd have to find them another place to live at the very least.

At the very worst . . .

Pax put his head down and set to cleaning the tables.

There wouldn't be a worst. He'd promised Josie that Amos would be safe within the walls of Number Five and nothing on this world or any other would cause him to break that promise.

Unlike the administration of the university where Josie worked, when Number Five's tenants' association undertook a project, things happened immediately. Sadly, much like the university, subsequent action was accompanied by paperwork.

The day after the TA meeting, Josie stood next to Pax amid a small group of tenants in the back courtyard, having been summoned by memos slipped under their doors, in their mailboxes, and pinned in the lobby informing TENANTS WHO WISH TO HAVE A SAY IN THE OUTCOME OF THE GIANT DIRT PILE were to report to said dirt pile at five thirty p.m. sharp. The wind was bitter cold, and the hill of dirt now sported a snowcap.

"She's like a steamroller with a clipboard," Josie said, slightly awed and sincerely terrified as Maddy finished handing out the premeeting meeting agenda and argued about the order of items on it with the person in the purple tracksuit from last night who had made a fuss about the *e*'s.

Josie stared down at the premeeting agenda in her hand. She would have to make sure her boss and Maddy never met.

"She's inexhaustible," Pax confirmed. He had to lean down to speak quietly, and the puff of his breath tickled the edge of Josie's ear while prickles of awareness pebbled the skin of her arms when his shoulder brushed against her. Warmth from his big body seeped from the top of his woolen peacoat.

If the world was a fair and kinder place, Josie would figure out a way to sneak her hands beneath his coat and put them flat against his chest.

For warmth, *obviously*.

Not like she would gratuitously feel him up.

Her hands were cold. That simple.

"Every time I'm tempted to tell her to cool it, she does something miraculous. Like save us money on recycling or tamperproofing the fire alarms."

Josie turned her face toward Pax's, letting his breath stroke her cheek.

"Do a lot of tenants mess with the fire alarms?" she asked.

He frowned, looking as though he was trying to find the simplest explanation.

How hard could yes or no be?

"You would be surprised what some of the tenants mess with," Pax said finally.

". . . all I'm saying is fungi grow faster when they are part of a decomposition process. I didn't mean anyone *here* should be decomposing." Joey Z. held his hands up in a warding gesture. Poor kid, he had terrible psoriasis. "You don't have to take everything literally, Denis."

Denis.

"Now, Denis, I doubt anything he messed with would surprise me," Josie said.

Pax's silent laugh curled beneath Josie's ear following the curve of her neck in a quick caress and she flushed. As if she could hear the pair of them from where she stood, Maddy looked over at Josie and frowned.

"C-A-K-E. I like cake and cake wikes me!" Amos squealed.

Pax chuckled at Josie's reaction to the chant the cheerleaders were teaching Amos, complete with jumps, stamps, and an impressive number of backflips on the far side of the dirt hill.

He'd claimed not to know how the teens had found out about Amos's love of cake, but she didn't buy it.

The cheerleaders had caved to the cold and sported thick, fuzzy jackets and wide-hemmed sweatpants in a bizarre pink-and-yellow color scheme. Amos's head in his duck hat bobbed up and down amid a sea of giant bows sparkling in the fading sun as they taught him the steps.

Maddy looked over at the noisy teens and frowned, then directed her disapproving stare over to Josie.

"I get the sense Maddy doesn't like me," Josie said quietly to Pax once Maddy's attention shifted.

"Maddy likes you," he assured her. "She has resting stone face. Deep down, she's got a huge heart. Simply because she makes the tenants cry, she gets a bad rap."

"Who did she make cry?" Josie asked, picturing Maddy tearing into the cheerleaders.

"Denis."

Whatever Maddy was saying now to Joey Z. didn't look warm and fluffy, either. The poor kid's head hung so low it looked like it would fall off.

Wait.

"Didn't you tell me *Maddy* was the person who decorated Amos's room?"

Josie hadn't meant to question him and might have been as surprised as Pax that she'd blurted this out now.

"It was her idea," he said, turning his head to watch Amos so she couldn't see his expression. "Not Pider-Man, specifically, but that we should find a novel way to welcome you."

Josie considered his answer.

She wanted to trust Pax.

No matter how hard her chain-smoking gramma tried to kill it, no matter how many times it led to the shittiest moments in her life, Josie was a romantic. She wanted to believe people had good in them and someday she would get her own happy ending.

Except . . .

For all his presence woke a familiar tingle in her bones, Josie knew better than anyone that attraction could happen between two people who should *never* sleep together—let alone be in the same *state* together.

A spicy shot of cinnamon suddenly filled her nose and Pax sneezed, then looked at her as though she'd sprouted horns.

"It's not a lie," he blurted.

Josie stared.

In no scenario would she have spoken her thoughts out loud. That sort of nonsense belonged in bad rom-coms. How then . . . ?

"*All* of Number Five wanted you to feel welcome," he said.

They were brown. His eyes. She knew they were brown but not until today had she known they were a dark brown, like the bark of an oak tree, with a few ribbonlike twists of coffee-with-cream spiraling out through the irises.

The pleading expression on his face drew wrinkles at the corners of his eyes and tiny butterflies woke in her belly.

"Did it work?" Pax asked. "Do you feel welcome?"

Words sat like pebbles on the back of Josie's tongue, too heavy to shape.

"I . . ." What did that even mean, *feel welcome*?

As a child she had been an unwanted burden—to her mother, to the state, and then to her gramma, passed around from shelter to shelter with her mom, group home to group home by the state, coming to rest for a bit with her grandparents, but leaving shortly after Grampa died and Gramma had given up. When Josie took off for New York City on a Greyhound, she'd bounced from YWCAs to rented rooms until, finally, when she'd met Dan, they'd moved into a place of their own.

Even that apartment hadn't been welcoming. Gloria had it painted without telling them and Dan had insisted it was a kind gesture. By the time she'd had Amos, Josie had stopped wishing for a home or searching for welcome and was happy to be warm, fed, and not on the streets.

"Welcome" meant safety, and safety was forever beyond her reach.

"You can change that," Pax said.

The smell of wet paint overtook the last hint of cinnamon. "Change what?" Josie asked. Change the direction of her hope, or her certainty the worst outcome awaited her?

"Amos's bedroom. Any room. Say what you want and . . . and we'll change it." Deep and hoarse, as though he'd spent years calling out orders like a drill sergeant, when Pax lowered his voice, it sounded like wool might feel. As if Josie could take his words and wrap them around her.

"It took me a long time to settle in after the . . . after I left the army," Pax said. He rubbed his chin and looked up at the sky, took a deep breath, then looked Josie right in the eyes. The impact of his stare made her insides jump.

"After so many years of living with other soldiers, I had no picture in my mind of what 'home' meant." A breeze riffled through his hair. Pax pushed the hair out of his face and continued. "It came in spurts. The way my shoulders dropped when I came home and hung up my jacket. How I have a certain spot on my couch where I like to have my tea in the morning. A section of my entry wall is bare because I'm waiting to find exactly the right picture to hang."

This should have felt uncomfortable, the intensity with which they gazed at each other, the way he spoke, as if securing a promise between the two of them. It wasn't, though. It was like he was answering a question she'd forgotten she'd asked.

"Of course, it took time. I changed what I didn't like and brought in things—things like flowers and art—I would have dismissed as too nice for me before. It took intent. I had to force myself not to expect a bunch of soldiers to come tromping through at any minute. Mostly, I had to believe I deserved a safe, warm space to myself."

Josie had thought it impossible that Pax, or anyone, could understand the allure of what he offered. Feeling welcomed, able to place her worries aside and take her contentment for granted, but he'd somehow seen into her heart and voiced what she needed more than anything.

"Maybe you can begin with the courtyard. None of us know what we're doing when it comes to creating a garden," he said, gesturing with his chin at the knot of people milling around the dirt like colorful ants. "You can make the outside a safe place for you and Amos, and I'll wager the rest of the tenants will benefit, too."

A lock of her hair twisted in the wind like a tentacle, and Josie held her breath when Pax reached over and gently pushed it back over her ear.

He stood so close the lapels of his coat brushed against her.

"If there is something missing in your apartment I can get for you, please ask me." His gaze locked on hers and the noise of the crowd around them lowered to a gentle murmur.

What was the apartment missing that would make Josie trust she and Amos were safe?

Something suggesting permanence and normality.

"If Mr. Amos enjoys music, you might consider a piano," he said softly.

A piano.

Talk about permanence and normality.

Unnerving, this man's ability to see her thoughts.

Too easy to get her hopes up. Too easy to watch them fall again.

"Thanks for the offer, Mr. Pax," Josie said, using the title deliberately. Distance. She needed distance from this man, any man who might tempt her to lower her guard. Josie's life wasn't the only one that could go off the tracks in a fiery wreck.

She stepped away from his warmth, and the wind took the opportunity to rake its talons down the front of her body.

"I don't need to change a thing, so don't give us a second thought. Amos and I are fine," she told him. Josie shivered when Pax mirrored her actions and took a step back as well, but she forced a smile anyway. "Everything is fine," she said, "just the way it is."

Chapter Nine

"I was trying to make things easier for you, Josie." Gloria sighed and everyone but her winced.

Gloria's sighs scraped away at Josie's confidence like a dull blade peeling the skin of a fruit. Every so often they pulled up a chunk of tender flesh and the wounds would weep for hours, sometimes days afterward.

Josie tried floating away from her body as she spoke, looking down at the group of figures huddled in the Beech Room at Amos's daycare. Amos in his puffy yellow jacket and purple hat looked like a mushroom surrounded by a flock of adults in drab-colored coats.

"I'm sorry you were inconvenienced, Gloria, but it helps me," Josie said, "and all of us at the center, when we are consistent with the pickup and drop-off protocol."

When Mr. Tim and Miss Alysha nodded in approval, Josie knew she'd pulled it off and had come across as calm and reasonable. None of the adults in Amos's life could know Josie was sometimes seconds away from screaming in a fear-fueled rage.

Gloria had her suspicions, though. That's why she pulled shit like waltzing into Amos's daycare class without calling ahead and trying to bully the staff into letting her take Amos without permission. Yes, they had switched nights so Amos could go to a hockey game with his grandparents, but the pickup was supposed to happen at home, not at daycare. Miss Alysha had not been happy when she called Josie at work to explain why Amos couldn't be whisked away unexpectedly.

"It's silly. It's not as though I am a stranger. I am his grandmother. I take Amos all the time," Gloria complained.

Mr. Tim's jaw clenched at the artificial sweetness stretching Gloria's voice into a tinny sort of whine.

"The rules are the same for everyone, Mrs. Donovan," Miss Alysha said. "No child leaves without a parent's permission and three hours' advance notice. This is how we keep our children safe."

Miss Alysha had no time for women like Gloria.

Josie wished she had a piece of whatever it was—disdain? disinterest?—buffering Miss Alysha and keeping her from apologizing when she'd done nothing wrong.

"Well, I don't know what's more upsetting for Amos. Watching you treat his grandmother like a criminal or keeping him imprisoned until his mommy comes to free him."

Judging from Miss Alysha's clenched fist, it was lucky for Gloria one of the kids spilled a jar of paint and defused the tension. Josie apologized again to Mr. Tim and planted a series of loud raspberry kisses on Amos's cheeks as she collected his belongings from his cubby and walked him to Gloria's car. Dan's dad, Al, sat in the front seat of the leased Buick listening to a call-in sports show. He nodded at Josie and gave Amos a thumbs-up but said nothing.

Gloria spoke for them both.

Josie stood for a while in the parking lot after watching the squinting red eyes of the Buick's taillights as the car drove away. She vacillated between an after-work stop at the wine store or Donuts Delite. Neither method of settling her nerves after a Gloria encounter was on any list of healthy ways to self-soothe, but Josie hadn't even learned what those words meant until she was twenty-one years old.

Sugar and alcohol had been the go-to pacifiers for generations of LaChiusas, and Josie was all about keeping tradition alive.

The wintery smell of dirty snow and wet pavement did nothing to improve her mood. By the time Josie reached her building, brown bag and white box in hand, she'd given up on mantras and positive self-talk. She'd made a quick stop at the campus bookstore earlier and scored a package guaranteed to take her mind off everything—at least until the wine and sugar did its thing.

Nothing hit like a new Ali Hazelwood novel.

"Where is the boy?"

Josie jumped and almost peed her pants. When she'd entered the building, she would have sworn the lobby was empty.

"Um, hello?" Josie said, craning her head and still not seeing anyone. "Did you mean my son?"

"What other boy could there be?"

A stack of Amazon packages next to the mailbox shuddered, then fell, revealing Denis. The Menace.

"Hello, Denis," she said, knowing her smile looked weird but unable to summon a genuine grin. "How are you?"

Denis's nose twitched, sending the white hairs in his nostrils aflutter. "I am alive."

Among the conditions the man suffered, one gave his skin the oddest gray coloring. Almost like a river rock: smooth and weirdly nonporous. Denis stomped around the fallen boxes without bothering to pick them up.

"Where is the boy?" he asked again. "Why isn't he with you?"

For a kid with a crappy upbringing, Josie's manners had always been a curiosity to folks, but her politeness and avoidance of conflict were a survival strategy. A way to deflect any unwelcome attention and keep her out of the crosshairs of the sadistic men and women who were drawn to children's services.

Not all of them, but a lot of social workers, juvenile court officers, and "counselors" got off on the power they possessed. Far more power than the average adult has over a child. Unwanted and lost, kids in the American child services system had less agency than a stray dog in some states.

So, while Josie wanted to tell Denis the way he looked at her and the way he called Amos "the boy" were creepy, she deflected. Gesturing to the lobby doors, she backed up to the stairs, hoping Denis would look away from her.

"He's with his grandparents," she said. "Off to a hockey game at the arena."

Denis's squinty gaze remained fixed on Josie. "You sent the child away to a game that glorifies violence? With elderly folk to guard him?"

"I didn't send him away." Josie's nerves snapped and crackled beneath her skin, frayed into a buzzing tangle by Gloria's stunt and the anxiousness creeping into her belly at the thought of a long night alone. Her words came out too fast and too sharp. "His grandparents are taking him to a hockey game. That is perfectly normal. Normal families do it all the time."

Denis raised one eyebrow at her tone and Josie closed her fist against the urge to flip him off.

"Denis."

The ice in Maddy's voice slid beneath Josie's ribs like a blade and Denis sucked in a breath and turned around quickly. Not before Josie caught an expression of real fear on his face.

Josie hadn't noticed the door to the employees-only room opening, but in the doorway now stood Maddy. Directly behind her was Pax, his arm casually placed on the wall next to her head.

Not a single thread of Maddy's outfit was out of place. There was no reason for the rash of jealousy breaking out on the back of Josie's neck at the sight of the two together.

Except . . .

What did the two of them do in that office? Why was the door always closed?

One of the radiators hissed and a network of pipes below clanged as though someone were smacking them with a hammer.

Maddy's eyes narrowed as she looked at Josie, and for some reason, Pax's ears went bright red.

"What do you want?" Denis asked Maddy. Surly as a teenage boy being told not to throw rocks at cats, he set his hands on his hips.

Josie had seen his fear, though. His bravado was flimsy at best.

"I'd like to discuss the unauthorized changes you've made to your apartment," said Maddy.

Josie hoped for some tears, but Denis was made of sterner stuff. His feet slid slowly across the floor as if he were compelled but he managed to keep his gaze on Maddy's face until he walked past her into the office.

Pax set his hand on Maddy's shoulder for a second, perhaps as a gesture of solidarity before he came out into the lobby and picked up some of the fallen boxes, checking the addresses and dividing them into stacks.

The metallic *smack* of the office door behind Maddy and Denis echoed against the walls and Josie groped for her bearings.

Something was not normal in this building.

Pax glanced over at her, frowning. Again, again Josie hoped he couldn't hear her thoughts.

"Did Denis say anything inappropriate?" he asked.

What was she supposed to say?

"Why? Is there a building fine for being creepy?" Josie tried for flippant but knew she'd failed when Pax let the box in his hands drop to the floor without flinching.

"What did he say?" The question rolled from his throat like a growl and god*damn* if it wasn't the sexiest sound she'd ever heard.

"He . . ." Josie cleared her throat. Good God, why was she blushing? "He was asking about Amos. It's a little strange."

Pax did not seem appeased. He picked up the box he'd dropped and stared at it for a beat.

"This is yours," Pax said. "I will carry it for you."

He held a pink box in his hand and Josie's blush heated even more. That was her romance book club box. The logo was emblazoned across the top in bright gold font.

Would he think she was pathetic? Horny? Pathetically horny?

Before Josie could blink, he was at her side, the box tucked under one arm. He held out his other hand toward her as if asking her to dance and she stared at his palm, frozen with indecision until he reached out and took the box of donuts from her clawed hand.

Oh. So. Not dancing. Cool, cool.

His jaw set, Pax walked up the stairs and Josie followed. Without saying a word, Pax stopped at her front door. He planned to come inside, that was obvious from the iron grip he had on her box.

One might describe his manner as commanding. Especially if one read the kinds of books included in Josie's book box.

Pax followed Josie inside, placed her book box on the tiny end table next to the door, walked down the hallway a few feet, and turned into the kitchen. She waited a beat before following him, her heart pounding for no good reason. Even though she knew they were red, she set her palms to her cheeks.

Whatever was happening with her body must be messing with her eyes, because the hallway sconces threw off a softer golden light than her long-lasting light bulbs should have done.

Josie had thought long and hard about why she'd sent Pax away abruptly the last time he'd been in here. The appearance of the roses had been an excuse, not a reason. The reason was cowardice.

In that circle of the stove light, Pax had seen her. Certainly seen past the politeness and the deflection. If he'd found the next layer in, the uncertainty and apprehension that came with being a single parent with zero experience in healthy relationships, it wouldn't have scared her off.

Anyone who navigated this world and didn't second-guess themselves on occasion was a sociopath, enviable as that might be.

This man, though, could see past the uncertainty if she let him look long enough. Whatever lay beneath, the unhealed wounds, the damage done by the lipstick lady in her brain, the reason she skittered away from memories as if they were a hot burner on the stove—not only didn't she want Pax rummaging through there, but Josie would prefer not to have to look too deep herself.

The sound of metal sliding over linoleum sent Josie into the kitchen. There, Pax stood next to the oven and inspected the clock, checking behind its face to see if the nail holding it up had created any lasting damage.

"Are donuts your usual choice of supper when Amos is not with you?" he asked.

She set the brown bag down on the kitchen table, the paper wet and wrinkled where she had been clutching it. Denis's interest in Amos had unsettled her. The pipes beneath the kitchen sink gurgled. Pax looked up quickly at her and frowned.

"He doesn't have a good sense of boundaries, does he?" she asked. "Denis."

Pax walked past her to the kitchen sink, where he washed his hands. Josie peeked but the only object on her kitchen table was the potted shamrock plant she'd bought at Wegmans yesterday.

Despite this, the scent of roses persisted, overpowering the fake lavender smell of her hand soap.

"I will speak to him," Pax said as he dried his hands carefully on her Buzz Lightyear dish towel, holding it up to examine the characters. "Buzz Lightyear. He is a flawed hero."

Was that a question or a declaration?

Pax folded the towel and put it back on its hook, then turned to face her, leaning back against the sink. A foot of space sat between them, but he was such a large man, the warmth of his body was palpable even from a distance.

"I suppose so," she said, just to say something. His presence threw her off-kilter. You'd think Josie had never been alone with an adult male.

"Just like Spider-Man," he continued.

Josie opened her mouth, then closed it. Maybe this was leading to something. Hopefully something interesting, not something weird.

Pax must have sensed her confusion. "Mr. Amos is enamored of Spider-Man, so I went to the library and did some research."

She'd flipped the switch to the kitchen overhead light when she walked in, but the room remained dim, and the smudged hollows of Pax's cheeks turned his skin the same shade as the dark oak cabinets behind him.

"You researched Spider-Man?"

He nodded. "I researched a few superheroes."

"Because of Amos?" Her question came out as a whisper.

"It seemed important to him," Pax said, his voice catching on the last few words. "I . . . am fond of Mr. Amos." He glanced at the floor. "Fond of you both."

Fond of you *both*.

He cleared his throat and looked up at her, all traces of softness now vanished from his face.

"Having become familiar with the classic canon of the two major producers of superhero lore, I agree with Amos's choice of favorites."

"You prefer Spider-Man to Superman?" Josie asked. Personally, she liked Black Panther and Scarlet Witch, but mostly because they would be superhot as a couple.

Pax raised his chin as if in defiance. "Peter Parker is a compelling hero. On the one hand, he has been granted superhuman powers of both strength and perception, but these powers were foisted upon him accidentally."

"True," Josie agreed.

Pax waited with one brow raised.

"No, really," she assured him. "I want to hear your reasoning."

"Well," Pax said, slowly at first, "he was not tempered, as most heroes are, by fulfilling a series of quests to gain this reward."

When animated, Pax's face looked younger, despite the shadows darkening the lines at the corners of his eyes. "Once in possession of the gift, he cannot reap the rewards of fame and gratitude for his actions. He must keep them hidden, even though this means he lives with embarrassment and rejection."

Raindrops clacked on the windowpanes like the keys on a keyboard. Josie considered making a joke and breaking the mood. The earnestness in Pax's voice disarmed her.

It made her soft. *Soft* meant stupid.

"Most men would never willingly show the world the weaker version of themselves," he kept going, enthusiastic now, "but Peter Parker has a hero's heart and sacrifices his ego for the greater good."

If he'd delivered this like a spiel, arms crossed, self-satisfied smile, and twinkling eyes, Josie could have handled it. Most men had a bit they did like this, a tongue-in-cheek deconstruction of something so geeky yet so iconic it was cool.

Pax, however, showed no hint of irony. He'd truly considered the character of Peter Parker. He'd done it to better understand Amos.

He was fond of them *both*.

"That's a generous interpretation," Josie blurted to cover her nervousness. "I don't know if it's why Amos likes him best, but the way you see him . . . it certainly endears him to me."

The tiniest curve of Pax's lips was another man's blinding smile, and it sent zings of awareness through her veins. A cloud of giddiness rose in her chest.

"I've always rooted for the villains," Josie confessed. "I stan the Joker and Harley Quinn, for sure. Those two are sexy."

Not what Pax had expected to hear, obviously. He tilted his head and narrowed his eyes as if he could see inside her heart. Or was he staring at her chest?

"You find evil attractive?" he asked.

Well, if he was trying to see inside Josie's heart, he was out of luck. She hid that part of her anatomy from everyone but Amos.

"I find it attractive when men and women who are considered misfits or mutants, who live with their worst self painted on their faces, have the balls to go out in the world and demand something from it instead of hiding from the judgment of others," she asserted.

The declaration surprised Pax. His eyebrows furrowed as he mulled over her answer, standing with his fists on his hips in a superhero-ish posture.

"You sympathize with them?" he asked. "Even though they do terrible things to people? To children?" His voice held a note of . . . was it concern?

Josie met his gaze easily but weighed her words carefully. She had the sense her answers carried an outsize importance, as if he'd asked her a different question than the one she heard.

"I don't believe in heroes and villains," she said at last. "These are archetypes we use to teach children simple lessons. We're all a mishmash of good and bad, kind and uncaring—all the shades of gray. When you hurt other people, it's usually because you've been hurt yourself."

Pax's gaze changed from assessing to something else. Something more intense.

"Would you forgive a villain if they believed their crime was essential to righting a terrible wrong?" he asked. The lights in the kitchen flickered on and off, only stopping when Pax set his hand on the kitchen counter next to him. "Could you forgive them for hurting someone you love if it were in pursuit of the greater good?"

A heavy sense of expectation weighted the air around them and Josie hesitated.

"We aren't talking about superheroes anymore, are we?" she whispered.

What was Pax asking her? Had he committed some wrong in his past Josie would have to forgive in order to be with him?

Was he asking her to be with him?

"I suppose the questions facing superheroes can come up in the lives of regular folk," he said. "You never know when you might be called upon to make a heroic sacrifice."

"Well," Josie said hesitantly. "What kind of sacrifice?"

When she crossed her arms, her elbows brushed his chest. They had inched closer while talking and the accidental touch sent a spark of electricity shooting up her arm. In response, Pax's pupils dilated, darkening his eyes to a velvet black.

Oh dear.

This wasn't a good idea. Alarms should be sounding—any second a robot would come in waving its arms shouting, *Danger, Will Robinson!*

The distance between them could be measured in inches. It felt like a mile. It felt like nothing. She ought to say something sensible, something to defuse the moment and send this man on his way, but her mouth was dry so she had to lick her bottom lip—a signal Josie had forgotten she could send.

Or not forgotten, because she didn't step back or put out a hand to stop Pax from closing the distance between them to put his thumb on her damp bottom lip and pause. He was waiting for Josie to be sensible and send him away. Instead she gasped with surprise at how fucking amazing it felt to be touched by a desirable man. By this man.

The gasp was a sign of permission for Pax to sweep his thumb up over her cheekbone and cradle Josie's face between his two large hands, his attention solely on her mouth while she trembled like a stupid girl.

Stupid, warned the angry old woman in her head. *Thinking with what's between your legs instead of what's between your ears.* The familiar warning drowned beneath the buzz of blood rushing through Josie's veins when she grasped Pax's shoulders, stood on her tiptoes, and brushed her mouth against his so lightly it was an exchange of breath more than it was a kiss.

They stared at each other and Josie could have sworn she heard the whooshing sound gas makes when a spark sets it aflame.

He held her like a piece of crystal in stark contrast to the force of his kiss. Teeth knocked, lips bruised, Josie wrapped her arm around his neck and kissed him back, just as starved.

His tongue twined with hers in an undulating rhythm with the slapping of the rain on the window and the low buzzing of the doorbell as counterpart.

Shit.

They broke their kiss, but Pax kept her face in his hands a second or two longer, unable to look away until the doorbell rang again.

Josie raced to the intercom. "Hel-hello?"

"I frowed up, Mom." The words squeaked through the speaker and Josie pressed her forehead against the wall next to it, trying to remember how to fucking breathe.

"I will be right down, buddy," she said, not moving when Pax walked by her, set his hand on her shoulder, then let himself out of the apartment.

Another second passed until Gloria's voice burned away the last vestiges of lust. "Josephine, your son is covered in vomit. I don't know what they fed him at daycare . . ."

Josie was out the door before Gloria could finish her tirade, not knowing whether she should be disappointed or grateful.

One thing she did know.

Her body had woken after a five-year lull, and it was going to be hard to get it back to sleep again.

Chapter Ten

Were you fixing the pipes or getting your pipe fixed in the little human's apartment tonight?" Raphe asked.

Instead of walking down the front stairs, where he might encounter Amos and his grandparents, Pax had left Josie's floor via the emergency staircase at the back of the building. There, the surly vampire had ambushed him, jumping out from the shadow of the stairwell and tossing insinuations around like confetti.

Walking past Raphe, Pax opened the door to the basement, pretending to ignore him, but the vampire followed in his wake like a shadow. A shadow with a snarky attitude.

A shadow who knew too much.

"I thought paladins were eunuchs," Raphe said.

"We remain *celibate* during our service," Pax replied. "Celibacy is different from castration."

"I don't see how," Raphe said.

"One is temporary."

Instead of turning down the corridor to the left, which led to his lair, Raphe followed Pax through the door marked BOILER ROOM. Inside the gray cement walls stood what looked like an eighteenth-century stove with pipes sprouting from all over it, some as thick as branches, others thin as adders. The pipes attached themselves to the ceiling and the floor, throbbing in time with the low pulsing beat emanating from the belly of the stove.

"She doesn't sound like she's out of gas," Raphe said.

"I don't know if anyone other than Maddy and I can hear it," Pax said quietly, "but she sounds . . . sad."

"Sad?" Raphe echoed the word as he drew closer to the stove.

Waysides were comparable to complex structured cells. This stove was like a mitochondrion, the powerhouse to the whole. Ever since the elevator stopped working, something in this mitochondrion—or perhaps heart would be more accurate—had been diminished.

The golden needle on the *hypsidoodle* still rested on its side, pointing to zero.

For hours Pax had sat down here listening to the rhythm, trying to hear a hitch in the pulse, a drag, a whine—some hint of what ailed this magnificent creature. He would do anything for her.

Number Five had surrounded him with comfort and warmth, asking little in return. Polishing the railings when they were tarnished, sweeping dust from her corners, and keeping her windows clean so light could blanket walls and floors—these were small favors in return for the first true home he'd ever known.

Paladins were chosen from orphanages. Girls and boys with no family, and sometimes without even a name, were recruited to the Army of Light. It still struck Pax as a small miracle he now had a room of his own, a door to close when the world outside grew too loud, and a clean pillow and soft bedding cradling him when the nightmares came.

"Have you tried?" Raphe asked.

Rubbing his face, Pax regarded the other man warily. Not

good to let his attention wander when in the company of a predator. Were they still speaking about Number Five?

What was Josie doing right now? Why had Amos thrown up?

Had the kiss affected her as much as it had affected him?

"Tried what?" he asked, shoving those questions out of his brain.

Raphe smiled, the low light of the stove's flames reflecting off his pointed teeth. "Blood."

That again.

"She doesn't want blood. I would know if she did, and I'd give mine without question." Pax sighed. "You're wrong, Raphe. She might be looking for a sacrifice, but not the kind you're thinking."

"'Reboot.' What does that even mean?" Raphe muttered. "'Reblood' makes more sense."

"'Reboot.' 'Renew.' 'Restart.' It doesn't matter what lexicon we reference," Pax said, cutting him off. "We've been doing things wrong. Somehow, we've drained her of what she needs to keep moving."

Raphe scowled at the stove. "Yes, but what? What have we done wrong? How are we supposed to rectify this mistake if we don't know what it is in the first place?"

When Manny had come to save Pax on the battlefield, he'd said something about the Waysides having changed.

No.

Travelers had changed in the way they treated the Waysides.

"Manny said Waysides used to be a gathering place," Pax said.

Raphe squatted down and peered through an opening in the stove belly, gently tapping the glass over the golden needle as if he could wake it.

"Waysides are still the only places we can coexist without violence," the vampire said. "'Safe as a guest in a Wayside.' Quite certain it's a saying on every world in existence."

"Except for this one," Pax pointed out.

The men shared a glance.

"Do you think that's why Number Five stopped on this world?" Raphe asked. "It has something to do with how little magic is here?"

"Maybe?" Pax shook his head. "She doesn't speak to me directly."

The vampire stood and stepped toward Pax; fists clenched. "How do you know she is against a blood sacrifice if she doesn't speak to you?"

For vampires, blood meant life. To them there was no such thing as needless bloodshed. All blood was needed, all blood sacred.

"I am the hotel manager," Pax insisted. "I *know*."

"Pfft," Raphe dismissed Pax's protest with a wave of his fingers. "You also *know* the sixth-floor guests can't sleep indefinitely. At some point you'll have a floor full of the most powerful—and the most dangerous—beings in the universe up and around and hungry. You *know* the Fate siblings will tire of staying in one place without meddling in folk's affairs. The Zombinos will give up on that vegan nonsense, and the shifters will lose control of their forms. This building is full of creatures existing only in myths for this world. At some point, we will be found out. What do you *know* about our fate when that happens?"

Nothing.

Pax knew nothing about what the future held except that he was responsible for the outcome.

* * *

"Out with it."

Josie looked up from her computer screen.

Shit. She did not have time for this today.

Jenna dragged a chair from the waiting room in front of Josie's desk and sat herself down while Barb put the CLOSED FOR LUNCH sign on the door out there, then joined her. Ben's office door was closed but the occasional buzz phrase could be heard from the weekly administrative Zoom meeting the provost scheduled during lunchtime.

"Is it cancer?" Barb asked.

"Barb," Jenna admonished, rolling her eyes. "Always with the worst case." She leaned over the desk and pushed Josie's monitor to the side. "Are you safe in your home, honey? You can blink the answer if you think someone's listening."

Barb turned in her seat and stared at Jenna. "If she's being recorded, they heard you tell her to blink her eyes."

"Well, okay, smarty-pants. What should I have done?" Jenna snapped.

"You should have held this up." Barb held up a sheet of paper with the words *Are you safe in your home?* written in orange Sharpie.

"I'm not in danger," Josie said.

"That's brilliant," Jenna said admiringly to Barb. "I'm going to make a smaller sign and laminate it to carry in my purse."

"I don't have cancer," Josie added.

"Ooooh, lamination. Genius," Barb replied.

"I do have the summary of three different financial aid audits to finish before I can leave," Josie said. "So, now we're clear . . ."

She pulled the monitor back in front of her face, only for Barb to pull it away again.

"We're not clear," Barb said. "Something is going on."

Josie stared at the women. They stared back. The provost's tinny voice came from the other side of Ben's door, droning on about "synergy" and "team-building" and "platforming."

"How do you know something is going on?" Josie asked, forfeiting the staring contest, knowing she would never win. Barb might give up, but Jenna was part lizard.

"You've had three students in a row come in and complain about their aid packages or work-study jobs," said Jenna. "When the first student complained ten was too early in the morning for them to be expected to show up for work, you told them their entitled lifestyle ended the minute they couldn't pay for it."

Josie shrugged. "It's true."

"Of course, it's true," Barb said. "The point is you said that. To one of them. Out loud. Without backtracking or apologizing or giving them all the cash from your wallet."

What the . . . ?

"I don't give students cash from my wallet," Josie protested.

"No, you Venmo them," Jenna said shortly. "When the second student sat there and said how the university should be paying them to be here instead of the other way around, you played a tiny violin for them, then told them to get back to class."

"That was wrong of me," Josie said.

"No, girl," Barb held up a hand, palm out. "No, that was the *right* answer. The answer you should have been giving all this time."

"We knew for sure something was going on when you told that boy who left that his parents weren't emotionally blackmailing him when they emphasized how difficult college was to afford, what he felt was guilt and guilt was good for him."

The boy had been outraged his parents had asked him to apply for financial aid now that he was twenty-three and still an undecided sophomore after six years of college.

"I shouldn't have made him cry," Josie said.

Jenna slapped her forehead with a palm. "Josephine, he was crying when he walked in here because he had to show his ID to come behind the front desk and felt violated by having to be perceived. You didn't make him cry. His default is crying. You told him the truth."

"Exactly," Barb chimed in. "I've never seen you be so honest before. It's as if Mary Poppins channeled Cruella de Vil."

"Point is," said Jenna, "you are not yourself. Who are you and what have you done with Polly Pleasant?"

Josie slapped her hands on the desk. "Is that what you guys call me behind my back? Polly Pleasant?"

Without even trying to look embarrassed, Barb and Jenna nodded.

"You two are the ones always telling me to be assertive!" Josie exclaimed. "Now you're complaining?"

Someone knocked at the office door. It was one o'clock. They should be opening back up for afternoon hours. Barb and Jenna didn't even blink.

"We aren't complaining," Barb said, "we're worried."

"You're not being assertive, you're losing patience," said Jenna.

"What could cause *you* to lose patience?" Barb asked.

"You're so patient you make my teeth ache," Jenna put in.

"The only explanation we could come up with was cancer—"

Jenna shook her head. "Cancer was Barb's explanation. It's always that or cyberkidnapping."

Barb whipped her head around and glared at Jenna with a look of betrayal. "You're the one who said cyberkidnapping."

"I said trauma from sex trafficking, not cyberkidnapping."

The knocking on the office door continued.

"We should open the door. I have a one thirty—" Josie stopped talking. They weren't listening.

"And I told you if Josie was getting sex, she wouldn't be so tightly wound," Barb argued.

Tightly wound?

"I hope you aren't equating forced sex with—"

"Of all people, you should know I would never—"

Did she come off as tightly wound?

". . . because some people's menopausal symptoms don't interfere with their sex lives . . ."

". . . taking my words out of context . . ."

One kiss wasn't enough to unwind a woman who had gone without sex for almost five years. One very long, very hot, very unforgettable kiss.

". . . everything about sex . . ."

". . . everything about sex . . ."

Josie daydreamed for the one hundredth time about what would fully unwind her and in how many positions it might occur.

"Excuse me?"

Barb and Jenna, who were pointing at each other's faces, now twisted in their chairs to point at Ben, who'd emerged from his Zoom meeting with the dazed expression most people wore after an hour of the provost's corporatespeak.

"Was there a meeting I didn't know about?" he continued, the dazed expression morphing into one of panic.

"We were staging an intervention with Josephine," said Barb. "Trying to get to the root of her abrupt change in personality."

This was getting ridiculous.

Ben tilted his head. "I thought you'd settled on some sort of traumatic brain injury?"

"What?" Josie stood, furious. "I don't have brain trauma, I don't have any trauma, and I haven't been kidnapped, and I'm certainly not a sex slave," she snapped.

"Well, we know *that*, don't we?" Barb said out of the side of her mouth to Jenna.

Goddammit.

"I'll tell you what I am, though," Josie said, yanking open the bottom drawer of her desk and pulling out her purse. "I'm taking a mental health day. My mental health is suffering from the trauma of inappropriate workplace psychoanalysis."

Ben scratched his head. "I don't remember that being an approved condition for . . . ah . . ." He spluttered to a stop at the look Josie gave him. "Well. Okay, then. You . . . go do what you must to get better."

"Go shopping," said Jenna.

"Take yourself out for a milkshake," said Barb.

"Don't worry about the audits," Ben called as Josie yanked open the office door and three students came spilling in. "Not to worry. No worries at all. Just, don't worry they aren't finished—"

Josie slammed the door behind her and stalked out of the Admin Building.

Cyberkidnapping.

Sex slave.

Traumatic brain injury.

Gahhhhh.

Josie wished she knew what her face looked like so she could re-create it the next time she wanted someone to get out of her way. Like a woman who has been cyberkidnapped and suffered a traumatic brain injury, no doubt. Students scattered the instant they caught her eye and even the hypersocial Sam the Hot Dog Guy ducked behind the umbrella of his cart.

Rage took Josie as far as the doors to the pre-K room, but she stopped there. It would be hypocritical to give Gloria a hard time for disrupting Amos's routine and then do the same thing. Instead, she walked off campus toward the surrounding neighborhood.

Three blocks in and Josie came to an avenue lined with cafés, small stores, a few hairdressers, and an ice cream shop she and Amos visited often in the summer months.

Maybe a new haircut? Treat herself to a fancy latte? The choices overwhelmed her as she peered in the window of a vintage clothing shop. Their mannequins were elegantly styled, complete with seamed stockings and shiny patent leather pumps in contrast to Josie's faded Old Navy pencil skirt and tired-looking Reeboks.

One of the lush red dresses glowed in the afternoon light. Slightly boxy in the shoulders, it narrowed to a point at the hem, with rhinestones adorning the belt buckle. The kind of dress the Scarlet Witch would wear when off duty.

"Red is not your color."

Josie's head reared back when Maddy's reflection appeared in the window behind her shoulder.

"That dress isn't your size, either," Maddy continued.

Josie had been thinking the same thing. Obviously, women hadn't had hips in the 1940s.

"Hello, Maddy," Josie said warily.

There was the tiniest smudge in Maddy's lipstick, and the reminder the tenants' association president wasn't perfect made Josie happy.

"Is this where you shop?" Josie asked, gesturing to the red dress in the window.

"Sometimes," Maddy replied. She stood next to Josie and peered at her reflection in the window, fixing the tiny smudge of lipstick with her pinkie. "I appreciate the structure of the fashion from the postwar period."

Nodding—because of course Maddy liked structure—Josie looked around. Most of the people on the sidewalks and in the shops were college students.

"Do you work around here?" Josie asked.

"Work," Maddy repeated. "Employment, you mean." Today she wore a large-brimmed black hat beneath which her hair was covered with a black scarf. If indeed there was hair under the scarf. Baldness could explain why Maddy covered her head. Maybe she was self-conscious about the condition and that's what made her frosty.

"I mean, it seems as though a lot of the tenants work from home," Josie said. "I wasn't sure what you did."

"Yes," Maddy said slowly, staring at Josie as though she'd asked about her personal finances or something. "I work from home."

Josie smiled but Maddy kept giving her the hairy eyeball, saying nothing else.

Walk away, Josie's brain hissed. Go home and do something productive like clean your windows or scrub your baseboards.

Normally, Josie would let her brain browbeat her into leaving, but her kiss with Pax had sparked something more than a little bit of sass in her step. Once upon a time she'd had confidence in herself. Not only the confidence to catch a cute boy's eye but confidence enough to take charge of her life, to turn around when she'd reached a dead end and start over somewhere else.

Fuck you, brain.

"The weather looks good this weekend," Josie said. "Maybe the garden committee could meet again and finalize plans?"

Maddy's frown was a master class in muscle control. Not a single wrinkle pulled at the corners of her mouth or between her perfectly symmetrical eyebrows. "Oh, yes. The garden committee. Now, that's an experience I cannot wait to repeat," she said.

Last week's meeting had gone from chaotic to downright acrimonious despite Maddy's premeeting planning. No one could agree on what to plant, or where to plant things, or even if they needed plants. Raphe kept insisting on a night garden and Joey Z. was worried about strange smells, which made no sense. Any chance there might have been for agreement was derailed by the animus between the cheerleaders and Denis, who kept calling Josie "the new guy."

"Is it the garden interesting you, or the amount of time you spend with Pax keeping you involved?"

Whoa.

Maddy's voice remained even and there was no sign on her face she'd asked the question for any reason other than curiosity.

"Ummm." Josie's brain short-circuited, whether because of what happened with Pax last night or with awe at Maddy's bluntness, Josie didn't know.

"It's not . . ."

Maddy's smirk sliced through Josie's spine like a blade. She had a way of tilting her head that made her look like a falcon eyeing a mouse from far up in the sky.

Focused.

Predatory.

A terrible thought occurred to Josie.

"Are the two of you together?" she asked Maddy. "Because if you are, you need to know . . ." Josie paused.

What was she going to say?

Need to know . . . you are pretty fucking lucky?

Need to know . . . in any fight over something Josie didn't think she deserved, she would back down in an instant?

There was only so much fight a person had in them, and most of Josie's fight went toward figuring out this parenting thing and not cracking under the pressure of getting by in a world that didn't seem to give a shit one way or the other if folks made it through the day.

"I don't need to know anything." Maddy waved a gloved hand as if to disperse Josie's words into the air. "You are correct. We should have the garden committee meet again. I will draw up a schedule for planting that aligns with forecasted weather patterns so we take advantage of optimal growth conditions."

Of course Maddy would figure out the best timetable by which to plant.

"Perhaps you will stay with us long enough to see the fruits of this labor," Maddy continued. She set a gloved finger to her lips and smiled. "Ha," she said in a tone bordering on cheerful yet remaining icy and intimidating, ". . . fruits of your labor. Clever, no?"

Josie nodded but Maddy had already turned on her heel and walked away without a word of goodbye or an explanation as to why she thought Josie and Amos might not still be in the building a few months from now.

Chapter Eleven

I want to go home.”

“I know it can be overwhelming, but I promise we won’t lose you,” Pax said.

“There are miles of corridors here and everyone looks miserable and confused, it’s loud and cold and . . . oh, look. I didn’t know there were so many kinds of duct tape.”

Delighted, Joey Z. ran over to a display of duct tape right inside the entrance of Home Depot, his initial panic subsiding thanks to the marvels of plastics and the promise of candy at the end of the trip. Pax only hoped Joey could keep his body parts intact for the length of the visit.

“There are no homes,” Denis was saying to Maddy, oblivious to the stares he attracted, mostly from children, due to his size—or to his headwear.

Miss Nekesa, Head Librarian at the Oracle of the Public Library, and Guardian of both the Bathroom Key and Computer Time, was attending a conference this week. Without her vigilance, Denis had circumvented the computer time limit and overdosed on the YouTube. He’d come back to Number Five yesterday babbling about conspiracies and lasers, trading in his standard gnomic red cap for a similar cap made of tinfoil.

"Why is it named a depository of homes if there are no homes?" Denis asked. "Doesn't that sound like something the Freemasons might have a hand in?"

Maddy failed to answer him, having caught sight of a vast wall of drawers housing screws, nails, bolts, and other small fasteners.

"Someone put 2d finishing nails into the same box as 4d box nails!" she exclaimed, one hand over her heart in an expression of horror. "Who would do—oh, Hera, they've mis-shelved a box of drywall nails next to the framing nails. I cannot let this stand." Maddy left the group for the hundreds of small boxes containing what seemed to be every conceivable nail one might need in this world and a few Pax suspected no one would ever need, but they would be bought just in case.

This emporium obviously catered to the *male* of the species.

"Why don't we keep going?" Pax asked Josie. "They'll catch up, I'm sure."

Josie watched Joey duct-tape two of his fingers together as Denis disappeared somewhere in the bathroom fixtures department.

"I honestly thought this would be a good idea, but now I'm having second thoughts," she said. "It's odd. They act like they've never been in a Home Depot."

Josie was exactly right. The residents of Number Five had agreed only a select few of them would be allowed outside of the building. Those who most resembled humans had ventured as far as the library, Wegmans, and of course, Donuts Delite. None had ever been in anything like the Home Depot.

There were emporiums on other worlds, of course: labyrinthian markets made up of individual stalls, entire sections of cities given over to commerce.

Near Pax's last encampment, wares were sold in an ocean of brightly colored tents covering the savanna. Women with skin wrinkled by an ambivalent sun would sit cross-legged on straw mats and sing out obscene taunts if folks passed by without stopping. By afternoon the sun had sapped the men and animals of energy, but the women never ceased in their loud speculations of whether a soldier might have testicles large enough to handle their fermented goat's milk or pungent cheese.

Other than a whiff of something almost like fermented cheese, this place was nothing like the stinking, loud, and enormously entertaining markets where Pax felt most comfortable.

So many things in one place. At first, the bright shiny labels and attractive pictures fooled him into reaching out, but Pax shook off the spells easily enough. He could read this world's script, and no amount of packaging could disguise the sheer superfluousness of the products for sale. An entire shelf full of gardening gloves? What did it matter if the rubber hands were blue or gold, or how much longer would one pair last than another if they were all manufactured in the same country—identical except for the logo? And why would one need a package of twenty gloves? Of twenty anything?

None of the other humans in the store seemed concerned with these questions. They lurched about like ghouls, blind to everything but the tiny devices in their hands leading them to this *sale* or that *bargain*.

Amos sat in the front of a wheeled cart and swung his legs back and forth, mouth open as he gazed up at the expansive roof, laughing whenever he saw a bird make its way from orange-colored beam to orange-colored beam far overhead.

"Be happy at us, Mr. Pax," Amos said.

Pax looked to Josie for a translation.

"He means, don't be mad at us," Josie said and pointed to Pax's face. "You're looking a little, uh, grim. I take it you don't like shopping."

"I don't," Pax said.

He, Josie, and the six others were the pre-garden planting subcommittee, a position none of them had asked for but Maddy had assigned them anyway. They had already lost one committee member, Princess Naliti, who had walked past the Depot without even turning her head and sailed into a store called Marshalls. Maddy's resulting scowl had given Pax goose bumps, but a faery's urge to shop rivaled the pull of the moon for a werewolf.

When they reached the garden portion of the Depot, Josie pulled Amos from the cart and let him loose among the towers of plastic bags filled with soil. He'd recently learned to count—sort of—and occupied himself with counting how many bags there were on each shelf.

"One hundredy-two, one hundredy-five . . ."

This was the first moment Pax had alone—alone-ish—with Josie since their kiss last weekend and he was at a loss. Should he bring it up? Josie hadn't mentioned it. Had she forgotten?

Should he kiss her again?

Pax had considered asking Raphe for advice. The vampire was the object of amorous attention from all manner of species and genders, and must have a wealth of experience, but Raphe still wasn't convinced Josie and Amos were the cure to Number Five's illness. What if he gave bad information, scaring Josie off?

Perhaps Pax should try kissing her again?

"What was the square footage of the space we're setting aside for the patio?" Josie asked.

Pax told her and she bent over her phone again, then looked up suddenly.

"That's per square foot, not square meter, right?" she asked.

"Per square foot," he assured her. "I've seen the meemees. The metric system is a tool of the devil."

Josie's mouth fell open.

Maybe she wanted him to kiss her again?

"Was that . . . did you make a *Simpsons* joke?" she asked.

"No," Pax said quickly.

Wait. Had he made a joke?

Her blue knit cap was slightly too large and fell to her eyebrows, which were raised in surprise. A fluttering sensation filled his belly and he forgot for the moment the universe was in existential danger and lives depended on him and instead lost himself in the spiral of her animated gray eyes.

"Yes?" he said, stupid from the dizziness of desire. "I am not good at them. Jokes."

At his admission, the promise of a smile hovering at the corner of her lips turned to something else Pax couldn't interpret. A grimace?

Dammit. He should have just kissed her.

"Don't they tell lots of jokes in the army?" she asked.

The faint scent of blood and smoke made his eyes water, and for the first time in decades, Pax wondered who he would be if he'd been born into a family, like Amos. If his life hadn't been an unending march toward violence.

"They did tell jokes," Pax admitted. "I grew up in an orphanage, and there wasn't any . . ." He searched for an analogy that would make sense to Josie. "... any television or computers at the orphanage."

Josie's eyes went wide, and her mouth shaped a pretty, round O.

"You're kidding me," she said, clearly horrified.

Although Pax had discovered the charm of black-and-white movie musicals and *Sesame Street*, his childhood wouldn't have been bettered by something like television. If anything, it would have made his deprivation more difficult.

He could not covet what he didn't know existed.

"Because my upbringing was different, most of my soldiers' jokes made little sense." He spread his hands out before him, as though presenting himself to her. Nothing shiny or special here. Just a man who knows how to fight and yet craves a life of peace. A man without charm who wishes desperately he could make her laugh.

"You have a sense of humor, even if you aren't especially good at telling jokes, though," Josie said.

Pax scanned the garden department, but aside from Amos now counting the rocks in a cardboard box labeled River Stones, he and Josie were alone. He stepped close enough to see that the freckle next to the corner of her mouth was in the shape of a heart.

"I've never been accused of having a sense of humor," Pax said happily.

The corners of Josie's mouth twisted like the tails of a *linger-fisk* as though she fought her smile. "I don't know if you remember, but the first day I met you, you were giving a tour to a pale gentleman—"

"Ugh," Pax shivered. "Pasty-Faced Man."

Her smile jerked and shimmied, not fully loosed yet.

"Your reaction to Pasty-Faced Man is how I knew you had a sense of humor."

"There was nothing humorous about that man," Pax insisted. "His company was torturous."

Josie put her hand over her mouth to hide the smile.

"However, I am grateful if my suffering was what convinced you to trust me," he said.

Her hand dropped and revealed the absence of a smile.

Dammit.

He shouldn't have tried to be humorous.

Jokes were a stupid way to hold a woman's attention.

He should have stuck something on a sword.

Or punched something. Common wisdom held that women were impressed by men who punched things.

"I trusted you because you asked me if I felt comfortable following you," Josie said seriously. "It meant you cared about how I felt, even though we didn't know each other."

Oh.

This was a *good* reaction.

Did this mean he should kiss her again?

"I don't know how to dance, either," Pax blurted.

Wait.

Did he say that? Why did he say that? Who cares if he couldn't dance?

What he meant to say was he *did* care about how Josie felt.

Instead, a completely different set of words left his mouth.

Something about the lack of magic in this world turned Pax into an *idiot*.

Josie chuckled. "I'm sure your dancing skills are as good as your joke-telling skills, you just need to practice them."

Yessss. She'd laughed.

It hadn't been a full-throated laugh, but he'd take it. She thought he was funny. This was going well. He was turning into quite the charmer.

A strange buoyancy pressed against his breastbone, and he smiled back at her.

"Oh, I've never seen you smile like that," Josie said. She swallowed and shook her head sharply. "Sorry. I'm . . . I'm not saying you're humorless, it's . . . you have a nice smile."

The buoyancy spread through Pax's limbs, leaving him weightless.

A blush crept over her cheeks like a sunrise. Pax rubbed his chest where a pleasant ache made itself known.

"The other night," he said, forcing the words out over a bubble of fear right next to the pleasant ache, "I kissed you without asking for consent."

This had been in the back of his mind all week. In the front of his mind had been the nicer parts, how soft her lips had felt beneath his, how the burdens he felt so keenly had melted beneath the tentative brush of her fingers across the nape of his neck.

How hard he'd been when the pressure of the kiss increased, and he knew she wanted him as much as he'd wanted her.

He hadn't asked her, though.

"Can I kiss you?" Pax felt his own face heat and he shook his head as though that might clear whatever confusion Josie ignited in him alongside the lust. "I mean, not now, but before."

"Not now?" she asked, her elusive smile reappearing, flickering up and down until she pinned it with her top teeth to her bottom lip.

"Yes? No. I mean, it's not that I expect to kiss you again, I wanted to retroactively, uh . . ."

Shit. Who was this nitwit inhabiting Pax's body? What was he even saying?

Josie blushed harder and looked down at her feet, one toe sketching a half circle in the space between their bodies. When she looked up, he took the opportunity to move closer and inhaled the scent of cherries, saying a silent greeting to her heart-shaped freckle.

He cleared his throat. "I didn't want to presume."

That sounded reasonable, right?

Josie's smile reached to the corners of her eyelids and Pax lost his mind a little.

"You were welcome to kiss me," she whispered. "Are welcome."

Pax caught her coat sleeve between his fingers and began to pull her closer. Josie's serious gray eyes stared up at him as she lifted her head the tiniest bit. Desire pooled at the base of his spine, and he dipped his head to meet hers.

"Moooom."

Shit.

"Mooooooooooom!"

Amos ran over and grabbed Josie's hand. "I hafta go potty."

For a moment, Josie remained motionless, her gaze locked on his. Snippets of poetry, talk overheard at the alehouse, certain paintings Pax had never understood were suddenly translated in the language of prickling beneath the skin and warmed cheeks and breathlessness despite the fact they both stood perfectly still.

"Right," Josie said to Amos, still staring at Pax. The boy pulled on her arm, and she turned her head, breaking the connection with a snap. She turned back and shrugged, then followed the boy inside the store.

Pax had no idea how long he might have stood there while the world rearranged itself, but Maddy came stomping across the garden center toward him muttering about nonlinearity and fractal patterns.

In other words . . .

"Chaos." Maddy spit the word out like a foul taste, folded her arms, and tapped the toe of her shiny red shoe. "This world is a mess."

The heel of the shoe looked impossibly high. He almost asked her if the unnatural bend in her foot might impact her moods, but a tiny pink tongue flickered out from beneath her headscarf, so he kept his damn mouth shut.

"It isn't all bad," he said instead, still warm from what happened with Josie. "They have donuts and bouncy houses. Legos. Debussy."

"Pfft." Maddy dismissed donuts and classical music with a flip of her hand. "For every bear claw there is a place like this, a pretension of order—a facsimile of choice narrowing the horizon until something as wild and uncultivated as a sunset is reduced to a two-dimensional image used to sell goods instead of recognized for the genius of the universe."

True, but Legos?

"Has anything else happened with the woman and her boy?" Maddy asked.

The abrupt change in subject made his head itch.

"What exactly do you mean by that?" he asked.

Maddy cocked her head like a predator watching its prey. "I *mean* has Number Five shown any more signs of recovery around them? Has the needle moved? What else could I mean?"

Pax looked over Maddy's head where Joey Z. and Denis were arguing at the entrance to the garden center. Joey wore rolls of different-colored duct tape on his arms like bracelets and Denis appeared to be objecting to them.

"Pax?" Maddy prodded. "What else could I mean?"

"Nothing," he answered. Aware he was as bad a liar as he was a humorist, Pax averted his face from Maddy's narrowed-eye gaze and grabbed a bucket filled with a purple stalked long grass.

"What do you think of this?" he asked, holding the plant in front of his face to hide his expression.

Maddy's black-leather-gloved hand reached through the grass and bent it to the side so she could examine him.

"Why do you look guilty?" she countered.

Pax shoved the bucket into Maddy's arms and grabbed another plant. This one was also a decorative grass, and the tasseled ends looked like a *dirkit*'s ass.

"I don't look guilty," he lied. "This one is nice, and it is on sale. Forty-seven cents less than the usual price."

Joey and Denis came up behind Pax, still quarreling.

". . . buy things because they look *cool*. This world is one where hard work is devalued and the elite want the masses to spend their currency on meaningless junk serving to keep them distracted from the atrocities happening around them." Denis punctuated each of his points by slapping one hand into the open palm of the other, applauding himself since Joey appeared disinclined to do so.

Each slap dislodged the tinfoil cap more from its precarious perch until you saw only the gnome's bulbous nose and frothy beard.

"You can't generalize about this whole world based on this one store," Joey argued, the acrid smell of decay accompanying him. "You're spending too much time on the YouTube. Miss Nekesa says—"

"Shut up. Both of you," Maddy snapped.

Denis huffed, pretending to be offended rather than terrified, and Joey's eyelids flew back, one of them getting stuck while his eyeball rolled wildly in its socket.

Maddy dropped the grass she was holding, grabbed the bucket Pax was hiding behind, and tossed it onto a nearby rack of potted ferns.

"The more I think about this plan, the less I like it," she said, arms crossed, toe still tapping. "Planting a garden suggests permanence. We don't want to put down roots, physically or metaphorically. We want to get out of this world and back to where we belong."

Denis pushed his hat up, revealing his beady eyes. "Agreed. The vampire is right. Use the young human as a blood sacrifice and get Number Five back into action."

Gasping, Joey held up his hands as though to deflect their words, the rolls of duct tape keeping him from bending his elbows. "What are you, monsters?"

"Um, yes," Maddy said, leaving no doubt how ridiculous she found his question. "Hello?" She pointed to the mass of "hair" hidden beneath her headscarf.

Spinning to face Pax, Joey waved his arms in distress. "What about you? You're supposed to be a champion of the Light. Isn't killing a little kid the work of the Dark?"

"Bah," Denis scoffed. "You're talking to The Butcher. Killing is as reflexive as breathing for Pax."

Not anymore.

"You're missing the point," Pax said. "Finding a sacrifice is the easy way out. What if we did use blood to feed Number Five and she started up again? Doesn't tell us what caused her to run out of fuel in the first place and certainly doesn't guarantee we won't get stuck again."

Rolling his eyes, Denis sighed and spoke slowly, as if to a

child. "If we can get Number Five healthy and moving, we can go someplace that's full of magic."

Maddy nodded. "We can't even send pigeons from this world. We're cut off from anyone that could help us. What is the life of one magicless child compared to the life of Number Five?"

Joey rocked back and forth, trying to hug himself and dropping duct tape rolls in the process. "But Pax is a paladin, he's sworn to uphold the Light. The kid and his mom are guests now. If you hurt them, you'd be breaking the Wayside's oath."

"Exactly," Pax said as he helped Joey pick up tape that rolled beneath a table full of spidery-looking plants with pink heart-shaped flowers.

"You're forgetting we paid a price to check into Number Five and were promised safe delivery in return," Denis snarled.

The price for a stay in a Wayside was supposed to be a secret, and Pax and Maddy weren't told what each guest sacrificed. Sometimes a wounded guest would volunteer the information ("I paid an arm and a leg for this trip") but usually the price wasn't something people liked to advertise.

Josie obviously paid in money.

One night when blood drunk, Raphe had insinuated he'd paid by losing some of his magic.

Denis would only say what he'd paid should guarantee him first-class service.

He might be the size of a human child but nothing about Denis was cute or sweet. Like most gnomes, he saved and polished his grievances like gemstones and saw his simmering anger as proof of his righteousness.

That righteousness, that's where the danger lay. Beings like Denis could do something heinous and have no guilt afterward if they believed they were in the right.

"*You* are forgetting you also swore an oath," Pax reminded him, slowly dropping his hand to his waist where his sword belt once hung, a crass reminder of a paladin's power. "Know this, gnome. Your and everyone else's safe delivery is now dependent on the lives of those two humans."

Denis was not cowed. "Know *this*, Paladin. I paid the price for a stay in a Wayside with the expectation I would get it all back and more when I arrived at my destination. I *will* be made whole."

"**My friend Mary Jean's** cousin's niece's friend is an expert in the satanic arts, and she assures me that statue there is a statue of Satan himself."

Once again, Gloria had figured out a way to put Josie on the defensive.

Tonight, when they dropped Amos off, Al had taken Amos upstairs and put him to bed so Josie and Gloria could have a "chat." Although she knew it was impossible, Josie's first thought was Gloria had somehow found out she'd kissed Pax.

Could it have left a mark on Josie? Was she walking around looking well kissed and delightfully groped?

Had her vow to make good choices crumbled beneath the onslaught of reawakened longings? Josie hadn't been held by anyone, other than Amos, since Dan died. She'd forgotten the joy in heated kisses.

"Needless to say, Al and I are deeply concerned," Gloria said.

No matter how ridiculous Gloria's claim the lobby gargoyles were proof of satanic rituals being performed on the premises, Josie now was in a position where she had to defend her choices.

How do you reason with someone who won't be convinced?

Josie never got more than her associate's degree—another black mark against her in Gloria's eyes—but if she'd had the luxury of attending a four-year college, she would have become a social worker. She wanted to help kids like herself who were pushed through a system like chickens through a packaging factory.

The highlight of her community college courses had been her psychology classes, and Josie leaned hard on what she'd learned when it came to dealing with Gloria.

The first step was to acknowledge Gloria's perspective.

"Well, Gloria," Josie said calmly, "while I have never heard of satanic cults occupying entire apartment buildings and advertising their presence with life-size statues of Satan, the idea of such a scenario would be upsetting."

Gloria's makeup palette skewed orange and her lips were the same shade as a can of orange Fanta. Beneath the dim lobby lights, the lipstick made her mouth look like the maw of a dragonfish, especially when she screwed it up tight in suspicion.

"Yes, yes, indeed. I am upset," Gloria agreed.

Josie took a deep breath in from the nose and blew out from her mouth. Now was the time to find common ground.

"It's important to both of us Amos lives in a safe place," Josie said.

"Exactly. Living in a city means exposing him to violence and drugs," Gloria said. "And Satanists. You're not going to find any Satanists in our neighborhood. The HOA frowns on that."

For Christ's sake. How would Gloria know what her neighbors believed? Did she think Satanists burned pentagrams on their front lawns instead of hanging flower baskets?

Never mind. Time to calmly present information.

"I have been to a few tenant meetings. In fact, Amos and I are on the Gardening Committee. None of the folks we've met have shown any interest in Satanism."

This made no difference to Gloria.

"They don't come out and announce their allegiance with the Devil," Gloria snapped. "They're trickier than that."

Josie's smile hurt but she kept calm.

"As for the statues," Josie continued, "I'm sure your cousin's niece's aunt . . ."

"Mary Jean's sister's niece's friend," Gloria corrected her.

". . . means well, but these statues are like the gargoyles on Cologne Cathedral in Germany. A church," Josie finished.

They weren't exact copies but came close. The resemblance was harder to spot when someone dressed the one on the right in NFL team jerseys. *Rival* NFL teams, at that.

Hmmmm.

Maybe there was something to Gloria's concerns.

"Have you noticed someone keeps dressing them in Kansas City jerseys?" she asked Gloria now, hoping for some common ground. "Does seem an evil thing to do in upstate New York."

"No one cares about basketball, Josie," Gloria huffed.

Okay. No more calm statements of facts or finding common ground. The woman was impossible.

"Al and I cannot sleep at night knowing Amos is living in a dangerous environment," Gloria continued.

A strange rattle shook the top rows of mailboxes. Someone on the first floor must have been cooking, because the lobby filled with the scent of cayenne pepper.

Gloria let loose a dainty sneeze, then scowled at Josie.

"Simply because you don't like the way they decorated the

lobby doesn't constitute an argument that this building is dangerous," Josie said. Her patience was fraying, and the rattle of the mailbox doors made her teeth hurt.

"... whining about me eating vegetables. Did you know Big Ag is part of the problem when it comes to ..." Denis's voice echoed from beneath the doors to the community room and Josie slapped a hand over her mouth to keep from cursing.

Shit.

If Gloria was freaked out by the gargoyles, what would happen when she met Denis?

Lucky for her, Al trundled down the stairs, humming the theme to *Magnum, P.I.*, and Gloria broke off her tirade to give Al grief about leaving on his coat inside and how it would give him a cold.

Al waved to Josie and walked out of the building without checking to see if Gloria was following.

The doors behind Josie opened a crack.

"... nonsense about gluten," Denis was saying to someone behind him. "Gluten isn't even real. Food scientists working for Big Ag made it up ... This door is stuck. Why won't this door move?"

Luckily, Gloria left off her torture and followed Al out of the building while asking him had he taken his vitamin C yet and reminding him her nephew's proctologist also said wearing a coat indoors was a surefire way to get sick.

Not until the outer doors closed on Gloria's backside did Denis manage to shove his body through the community room doors and out into the lobby.

"Oh, it's you," Denis said by way of greeting.

"Hello, Denis." Josie fought back her discomfort and raised her hand in greeting.

"Where is the boy?" Denis asked.

How long had Amos been alone in the apartment?

One minute? Five?

What if something happened?

No matter how ridiculous Gloria's complaints, they still stuck to Josie like burrs, pricking her with thorns of doubt, leaving behind a rash of shame.

"Have a good night," she said, unwilling—unable—to be so rude as to leave without a word. Wishing she had the self-confidence to run up the stairs to Amos without taking the extra minute to excuse herself politely.

The mailboxes rattled once more, and it sounded like the gnashing of teeth or a chorus of unseen observers voicing their condemnation.

It left Josie anxious, as though she'd been given a message but in a language she didn't speak. Amos was fast asleep when she looked in on him, multiple superhero stuffies surrounding his head like a halo. Al had neatly folded Amos's clothes and set them on the chair next to his bed, and a handful of books sat in a pile next to them.

She left the door open a crack and turned on the small light in the hallway but was too unsettled to go to bed yet.

Something was happening here. More than simply a wake-up call to her dormant libido from a tall, dark, and humorously challenged stranger. More than a prewar apartment building that seemed to exist in a world outside the reach of HGTV. More than a dysfunctional tenants' association and a pile of dirt that showed up right after Josie wished for a plot of earth.

Something was happening here, and it was Josie's job to figure out if she and Amos would be safe if they stayed.

Chapter Twelve

Josie stared at the blank wall.

Then she touched it. Next she smelled it.

Huh.

Sometime between Friday night and Saturday midmorning, this wall had changed color from white to yellow.

The roses had been unsettling.

This wall was downright freaky.

Not that Josie disliked the color. This yellow was the color of the walls she'd pictured in her daydreams about living somewhere beautiful and sipping coffee in a room drenched in sunlight. The perfect shade to catch the sun and reflect it back onto the warm wood floors and her beloved green velvet couch.

Josie and Dan had found the couch at the Salvation Army and had given it a good steam cleaning before they brought it home. Even so, Gloria had shit a brick when they'd told her where it came from.

"Who knows what is living in there?" she'd screeched, freshly manicured hands waving in the air as though hordes of cooties were going to come flying out of the cushions at her. Al had nodded in agreement, taken a seat on the couch, and turned on the TV to watch the Masters.

"Alan." The horror in Gloria's voice had melted into the scorn she reserved for lecturing her husband. "For Christ's sake don't sit on it. What if you catch something?"

Maybe a ghost had done it.

Maybe the ghost of an interior designer haunted her apartment and decided to paint last night. Having a haunted apartment would normally be a negative, but what was the alternative? Was she losing her mind? Having ministrokes?

The intercom buzzed and Josie tapped the wall with her forefinger twice before leaving the living room.

Josie pressed the speaker button. "Hello?"

"Hi. Ms. LaChiusa, this is Joey. Joey Z."

Shit. She'd promised to meet this morning with Joey and Pax to mark off the patio and garden design with stakes and tape so the committee could approve it and move on to the next stage.

"I'm coming right down," she said.

"Okay. Hey. *Hey*, we have the same name, sort of. Joey and Josie. We could both be Joes. That's cool, right? We could get our name on the back of T-shirts. Jo and Joe. People would . . . oh, there you are." Joey looked up from the intercom at her approach and waved. His left arm sported a ring of bracelets made from crocheted duct tape. The skin beneath was less patchy and red than it had been a few days ago at the garden center.

"Wow that was fast." His smile was so bright and genuine it took Josie a moment to process his next words. "Is Amos with his grandparents?"

A rush of fear scratched the length of her spine. "How do you know about Amos's grandparents?"

The words came out in a cold rush and froze Joey's smile into something twisted.

"I, uh, I saw them pick him up this morning?"

His widened eyes and drooping mouth could have been an expression of hurt or of guilt. Either way, the wounded-puppy look wouldn't work on Josie.

No siree.

"Are you ready?" she asked.

She'd softened her tone, but Joey's enthusiasm was visibly dampened, and he dragged his feet across the dingy carpet of the meeting room, silent until they exited the door to the courtyard.

Folks from the garden committee as well as a few onlookers stood in a semicircle around Maddy. She held up a sketch to pleased murmurs, and Joey went to stand at her side.

"I've marked the exact distance between each of the garden boxes so they are uniform in size," Maddy said. "Space is equally allotted between the concrete surface of the patio and the spaces set aside for plants."

Someone objected to the plan for shrubbery and another person complained about the square meters allotted to perennials. They sounded angry, and Josie turned her back on the group to investigate the pile of soil.

You could see it was good soil: black and rich with the faint hint of manure. To the side of the pile stood a wheelbarrow and shovel, yanking Josie back to her years on her grandparents' farm.

Mostly they grew feed grains like sorghum and milo, along with a few acres of corn and, best of all, sunflowers for sunflower seed oil. Josie had a small produce stand out by the main road, and when fall came, she'd pick bouquets of the sunflowers and sell them to the folks from San Antonio driving down toward the

Gulf. The color of the wall in her apartment was the same lemony gold of the sunflowers she used to bundle.

While the other tenants argued, Josie shoveled dirt into the wheelbarrow, memories of early adolescence woken by the scrape of the shovel's blade into the pile of earth and the smell of turned soil.

Kneeling at the side of the dirt pile, Josie took off her mitten and stuck her hand deep into the soil. Winter still had its grip on March and the promise of spring seemed like a cruel tease. The dirt was freezing cold and her fingertips tingled uncomfortably. Josie closed her eyes and inhaled the scent of stone, exhaling everything that had preoccupied her this morning. Couches, Gloria, kisses, and ghosts seeped out of her brain, and in their place, she planted hopeful seeds.

She visualized planting a garden like in Amos's favorite book, *Planting a Rainbow*. She planted a seed of hope that Barb went out to the movies with her husband instead of staying home and bingeing old episodes of *America's Most Wanted*. She planted a seed of hope that Gloria was being patient with Amos. She hoped . . .

"What are you doing?"

Josie didn't have to open her eyes to know it was Pax who crouched on the other side of the wheelbarrow. Even before The Kiss, she'd been hyperaware of his body, sensitive to how he took up space even when he stood across the lobby from her.

Pax, who touched her kitchen wall as though it was wounded. Pax, who tapped her kitchen counter to still the lights. Who appeared at the same time as roses and smelled like cinnamon when he hedged. Who looked at Josie as though she was a desirable woman and not simply a single mom.

She opened her eyes knowing it wouldn't make a difference.

His character and intentions couldn't be read on his expressionless face, but when he laid his palm on the top of the dirt heap, Josie sensed his presence. Solid and generous, like the soil beneath them.

His intentions?

If the heat from his hand was any indication, his intentions were genuine. Whether they were admirable was a whole other question.

"I'm planting the soil with hopes."

With anyone else, Josie would have never told the truth. She would have said something self-deprecating, then turned the question back on them.

He had the power to make her reckless, this man—something deeper than the lightheaded back-and-forth swing of attraction. A belief that flipping backward from the swing will be okay. That she will stick the landing.

"What kind of hopes?" Joey Z. stood next to Pax, wringing his duct tape–covered hands.

"It's something my grandpa used to do each spring," Josie explained. Her breath hitched when Denis came to stand behind Joey, but she continued.

Why the hell not?

"He would gather everyone around and say a prayer." Quoting Galatians, Grampa would hold his battered green John Deere cap in his supple fingers and remind Josie, Gramma, and the rest of the farm help that a man reaps what he sows. "Then he would put his hand in the earth and tell us what hope he'd planted that spring."

One of the tenants Josie hadn't met yet, a person with sallow skin and astonishingly wide blue eyes, plopped down and put their hand next to Pax's on the soil.

"Like what?" Blue-Eyes asked.

As folks gathered around them the warmth of bodies at Josie's back both comforted her and creeped her out.

"The kind of hopes you wouldn't think a farmer would plant. They were never practical," she said. "They were pie-in-the-sky kind of hopes. Like, everyone got to see a rainbow that year or everyone would get a gift in their favorite color."

Back when she was thirteen or fourteen, she'd cringed at Grampa's language, embarrassed in front of the men who worked her grandfather's fields. Not until years later had Josie appreciated the offhand poetry of his words.

"I would wish for pies from the skies, too," Joey Z. said earnestly.

"What kind of pies?" came the question from someone behind her.

One of the older folks who dressed in color-coordinated tracksuits knelt at Josie's side and stuck their hand on the dirt.

"Custard cream," they announced.

One by one, the tenants put their hands on the soil, planting hope after sugar-laden hope. The loamy smell of sun-warmed dirt and tree buds and pollen-dusted new shoots filled the air. Someone laughed and someone else hummed a tune Josie had never heard but remembered all the same. Even the breeze played along, whispering softly past Josie's cheek, riffling through Pax's hair.

Through all this, he kept his eyes on her, expression unmoving, intensity unwavering. Everyone around them could have been made of smoke for all the effect they had on the connection between Josie and Pax.

"*I* hope we finish yammering and get to planting something." Denis shoved his way in between Blue-Eyes and Joey. "Hope this wasted time won't leave us with nothing but boxes full of weeds."

Joey Z. sighed and Blue-Eyes shook their head as the faint scent of coconut cream disappeared. A reluctant agreement passed between a few of the tenants, and one by one they moved away from the soil and bickered softly among themselves about annuals versus perennials and the use of pesticides.

Maddy came over and pointedly cleared her throat. "Pax. Don't you have something to do over here? By me? You know, that thing?"

Pax held Josie's gaze for a moment longer until she blushed and looked away like a coward. He rose, brushed his hands together to rid himself of most of the dirt, nodded at her once, turned, and left.

She had wanted to ask Pax what hope he'd planted but kept her mouth shut for fear of his answer. Instead, Josie rubbed her hands down the front of her jeans, then tucked them under her armpits for warmth, deciding she'd done enough peopling for the day. Time for hot chocolate and the *New York Times* Games page.

The lobby was empty except for the gargoyles, both of whom sported New York Yankees ball caps. A faint scent of violet gum accompanied her up the stairs and Josie traced a finger along the wrought iron vines curling around the banister spindles, the occasional sparrow peeping out from the vines' leaves. The delicacy of this work never failed to amaze her. From the windows on each landing fell lemon-colored bars of light across the marble stairs and tiny motes of dust twinkled as they passed between them.

A long day stretched before her. Josie knew she should finish laundry, mop the floor, pay some bills, and myriad other weekend chores but that would kill a few hours at most. The rest of the afternoon and night she would spend alone, watching baking shows and looking at the clock more frequently as it approached Amos's bedtime.

The mix of silence and sunlight mesmerized her, and instead of stopping on the third floor, Josie kept her fingers on the banister and continued up the stairs. A vague notion of finding her way to the building's rooftop entered her mind, but the truth was she didn't want to go back to her empty apartment yet.

The fourth- and fifth-floor landings looked exactly like the others, but at the sixth floor, Josie stopped. Here, the iron banister turned so cold it burned her fingers, and Josie could see her breath.

Whoa. No wonder the rent was reasonable if the heat wasn't working on entire floors.

Josie tucked her hands back under her armpits. Opposite the sixth-floor landing was the elevator and a small alcove where a table stood in front of a rectangular window. On the table sat a gallon-size watering can and a calendar.

Josie ventured forward off the landing and walked into the corridor. Somewhere a tenant played Strauss on an out-of-tune piano, and the sound of hushed murmurs and occasional clink of glasses came and went.

There was no reason to stop on this floor, but the urge to explore itched at her brain. An uncanny stillness blanketed the hallway despite the piano and the muted voices. Each step felt weighted, and her shoes made no sound on the tiled floor.

Odd. None of the sixth-floor apartment doors had numbers on them. No welcome mats stood in their entrances, no seasonal wreaths or boot trays gave hints as to who lived here. Some strange optical illusion made the corridor seem longer than it should be, and although the piano continued at the same volume, Josie couldn't figure out from which direction the music came.

Despite the sounds, an oppressive silence swallowed her as she continued to walk. A ridiculous fear that if she shouted, no sound would emerge, formed in her brain. The composition ended and another piece began as the piano grew increasingly out of tune. Now the music reminded her of Chopin but played in four-four time instead of three-quarter and it scraped at her nerves.

Just turn around and go back, she told herself. *Something is wrong here. Something is very wrong.*

Even as she had these thoughts, Josie came to the point where the corridor branched into east and west. The door to the apartment at the end of the western corridor stood open, and from what she could see, the apartment was unoccupied.

Josie increased her pace toward the open door, relieved. It must be that there were no residents on this floor. That's why the temperature was so low and there were no hints of habitation. The piano player could be on another floor and the quirks of the old building created some weird echo so she could hear it up here.

Curious whether it had the same layout as hers, Josie walked into the empty apartment. The front door led into a small entryway like hers but wider. The molding was painted a dusty rose color that blended well with the cream-colored walls and deep brown wood planks of the floor. Past the entryway to the left was a large living area done in the same colors and a kitchen to the right.

Farther down was a crooked hallway with three doors. They must be two bedrooms and a bathroom, like hers. Josie opened the door straight ahead of her and let out a soft gasp.

Unlike the rooms in Josie's apartment, this room had only one window, circular like a porthole, high up on the outside wall. The window was small, but the room appeared well lit, the walls painted a faded peach color, the pale wooden floorboards pitted but clean. Against the wall to the left stood an empty crib.

Josie's belly fluttered at the sight. Gloria had foisted a suite of baby furniture on Josie when Amos was born. Between mourning Dan and trying to figure out how to keep a newborn alive, she'd had no energy left to hold her own against her mother-in-law's insistence. For the first two years of Amos's life he slept in a massive fake cherrywood sleigh bed bigger than a Lincoln.

This crib was perfect. Unadorned but sturdy, the crib rails were spindle shaped and the wood beneath her fingertips was satiny and warm. A moss green sheet covered the crib mattress and in the corner of the crib sat a handsewn teddy bear made from black-and-gold calico.

The bear was almost exactly like the one sitting on her bed back in Texas that day she left her gramma's house forever, except Josie's bear had lost most of its stuffing and had smelled like Jean Naté. She'd found it in the attic at the bottom of a plastic bin filled with leftovers from her mother's childhood alongside chipped spelling bee trophies, a pile of Wonder Woman comics, and an unused Hello Kitty diary.

Josie had left the bear behind as a gesture. When she caught the Greyhound to New York, she took only the clothes she'd bought with her flower money and nothing of her grandparents' except for Grampa's watch. As if to show her gramma that Josie needed nothing from her to survive and thrive.

Tears dripped onto the crib sheet when Josie reached over to pick up the teddy bear.

Fuck. She didn't want to cry, but this was the first time Josie realized Amos had been raised amid piles of furnishings and clothes and toys his father and grandparents bought for him but had nothing from her family.

"I wish I had taken you with me," she whispered to the bear. "I wish Amos had had something of Momma's."

Cradling the bear to her chest, head bent, the drizzle of tears continued while Josie's brain berated her stupid emotions and *stupid* reactions to an empty crib, for Christ sakes. The bear wasn't her bear. It was clean, the embroidered nose still bright pink, and it smelled like bayberry candles, not drugstore bath splash.

What did this mean, though? What was this place?

Despite the melancholy brought on by the sight of the empty crib there was no hint of danger. Nothing raised the hairs on the back of her neck. Once oppressive, the stillness now felt comfortable.

Cleansing.

Josie had two distinct memories of her momma. In one, they had gone to the pediatrician, whose offices overlooked a small canal-side park. It had been a warm, sunny day, so she and her momma sat on the bank of the canal and threw tiny bits of old bagels to the ducks.

In the second, her momma had come to her grandparents' house, desperate for a fix and begging for money. Gramma had shut the door in her face and locked it, but Momma went round to the sliding glass doors of the kitchen and stuck her head in.

Josie had been eating a grilled cheese sandwich and listening to a Rangers game on the radio.

"Hey, baby." Momma had stuck her head in the door and called to Josie. "Got any money on you?"

Josie couldn't remember if she'd taken change from the kitchen junk drawer or from her own pocket; she just remembered Momma blowing her a kiss as she ran out the backyard and into the alley.

"Ah, Ms. LaChiusa, I thought I—Josie?"

Pax stood in the doorway, eyes widened at the sight of Josie's tears when she looked over at him. "Are you hurt?"

Josie sniffed, then wiped her nose with the sleeve of her sweatshirt.

Slowly he approached her, his large body throwing off warmth in the chilly air. "Did something scare you? Is that why you were crying?"

Josie hugged the bear tighter, staring at Pax's chest instead of his eyes. She didn't want to see pity there. Or worse, disdain.

"It's hormones," she said. "No big deal."

Someone must be baking cookies, because Josie could smell the faintest hint of cinnamon.

Pax said nothing, just did that thing of his where he occupied space, comfortable in his own skin.

Josie sighed, then put the bear back in the crib.

"Whose apartment is this?" she asked.

Pax shifted away from her as if he could physically avoid the question, his eyes dropping to the teddy bear.

"No one's," he said, frowning at the bear. "This room hasn't been occupied in ages."

"Where did the crib and the bear come from?" Josie asked.

He answered with a small shake of his head and a shrug, indicating he'd no idea.

"My living room wall is yellow now."

Pax pursed his lips, brows raised as if in thought. "I see." He paused. "Do you like yellow?"

Josie didn't know how to react to the hopeful note in his voice.

"I don't know if I can stick to the lease," she said, apologetically. "I have to think of Amos."

Pax rubbed his hand over his mouth. The weighted stillness turned into something else. A prickling sensation awoke on the backs of her hands and knees as if someone was watching the two of them.

Waiting.

"What if we lowered the rent?" he blurted out.

Anxiety rippled through her belly. Josie shook her head, lifting her hand as though to ward off his words.

"Pax, that doesn't matter, I—"

"Is it because I kissed you without asking first?"

Josie froze, one hand still in the air, palm outward.

Reaching over, Pax grasped her wrist, gently, running his thumb along the faint blue streak of a vein. Like a magnet the pull of attraction drew Josie closer to him, unable to look away from his stare.

"No, it's not because we kissed." The words crackled as they spilled from her dry lips, Pax's thumb still sliding along her sensitive skin. His touch made her dizzy and glad there wasn't a bed in this apartment because—

A huge thump behind her made Josie jump, then squeeze her eyes shut.

No way.

No freaking way.

"Are you . . ." Pax drew out the last vowel, whether in amusement or horror, she couldn't tell because she wasn't going to open her eyes—or her mouth—until the universe finally did her a favor and opened a hole beneath her feet.

". . . tired?" he finished.

Goddammit.

Bowing to inevitability, Josie pulled her wrist from his grasp, turned, then opened her eyes. Sure enough, there sat a huge four-poster bed looking like one out of her favorite historical romances. A red velvet canopy covered the top and mounds of snow-white pillows sprawled against the headboard in stark contrast to a crimson silk coverlet.

"That . . ." Josie couldn't finish her sentence because Pax had stepped up behind her so close that if she leaned back, his chest would press against her, and what even were words when the rest of the world has disappeared, and you've gone from mourning your lost childhood to standing at the foot of a magical bed with a sexy ex-soldier.

She cleared her throat. "That's a little over the top."

The ornate bed disappeared, and in its place stood a black-metal-framed bed, tightly made up with cream-colored sheets and a plain blue comforter. Next to it was a small nightstand holding a pile of books and a glass vase filled with peach-colored cabbage roses.

Pax's gasp of surprise turned into a hum of desire vibrating up Josie's spine and woke a pulse at the center of her core.

"Okay," she whispered to herself, or to him, or to whoever was responsible for the parade of magical beds. "Okay. This is the last straw."

Josie swiveled, keeping both Pax and the bed in sight, and walked backward until her shoulder blades hit the light switch next to the door.

"Don't come any closer and don't touch me," she warned when Pax took a step toward her. "Neither of us is moving until you tell me what the hell is going on."

Pax had served in the Army of Light as a paladin for nearly one hundred of his world's years. He'd gone into service when still an adolescent and had—as had his fellow soldiers—remained celibate the entire time. Pretty sure one hundred years of celibacy was a valid reason to be distracted by the tidal wave of lust battering his body while he tried to figure out how to answer Josie's demand in a way that wouldn't cause the destruction of the known universe. He took his time picking out the right words.

"I . . ."

He rubbed his hand over his mouth as though he could pull the perfect explanation from his lips.

"You see . . ."

Pax glanced over at the bed—*his* bed—then at Josie.

"There's this . . ."

Shit.

"Tell you what," Josie said as she crossed her arms. "I'll start. The girls on the seventh floor are part of an all-woman Mafia drug cartel developing a designer hallucinogenic, and it got into the building's water supply by accident and all of us are tripping right now, and when it wears off, we'll wake up and the seventh floor will be abandoned except for a scattering of rhinestones."

He blinked. Then blinked again.

What?

"What?" he spluttered. "No. This is nothing to do with drugs."

"No?" Josie didn't appear to believe him. "Okay, how about this? You are all retired circus workers whose circus has shut down, leaving you without money, so you're planning a huge jewelry heist, calling upon everyone's special talents, and you're using Amos and me to throw the FBI off your tracks."

If he weren't so nervous, and horny, Pax would be impressed by the breadth of Josie's imagination.

"No," he said.

"Everyone here is under witness protection and—" Josie tried.

"No."

She rolled her bottom lip under her front teeth, her eyes darting from the crib to the bed.

"You're all dead," she posited, "and Amos and I can see ghosts."

"We're not *all* dead."

"An eccentric billionaire's last wish—"

"Josie," he interrupted her. "I'm going to tell you the truth. Just don't . . ." He looked up at the ceiling. "This would go easier if my bed weren't here."

The bed disappeared and Pax sighed in relief.

"That was *your* bed?" she asked.

"Look, before I make a mess out of this all, let's go downstairs to find Maddy and Raphe," Pax said quickly. "The three of us can explain everything."

Josie didn't move while she worried her bottom lip with her teeth. No doubt deciding whether to run screaming from the building never to return or to run screaming from the building and returning with the police in tow.

Pax waited.

Whatever this woman decided to do, he wasn't going to lift a finger to stop her.

Chapter Thirteen

Okay, but who stole the *e*'s from the Scrabble sets?"

A derisive snort broke the silence.

"The continued existence of life as we know it may depend on you," Raphe said, disdain dripping from his words, "and *that's* your question?"

Josie flushed. "It's—people kept bringing it up during the tenants' meeting, so I thought . . . never mind."

The vampire rolled his eyes. Josie crossed her arms over her chest and returned his scowl.

"How should I know if stolen *e*'s are of less cosmic importance than the exit light burning out or pigeons disappearing?" she demanded.

Maybe the problem was a gas leak.

What if they were oxygen depleted and having a group hallucination?

They—Raphe, Maddy, and Naliti—sat in a semicircle of mismatched chairs in the common room. Josie sat facing the three of them like a woman accused of witchcraft brought before the Inquisition.

Pax hovered between the two "sides," sometimes coming to

rest at Josie's shoulder, sometimes looming over his fellow . . . travelers? Tenants?

Co-delusioners?

"I bet Denis stole them because he's a poor loser," Naliti—*Princess* Naliti—offered.

"That is beside the point," Maddy interjected. She wore an amethyst-colored raw silk pantsuit, black patent leather high heels, black-rimmed glasses, and a black fedora to cover her *snakes.*

Actual live *snakes* living on Maddy's *head*. Snakes that if they weren't covered turned to stone anyone who looked in Maddy's eyes and lied. Because Maddy was a medusa. A monster!

One of the snakes poked out from beneath the brim of her hat right now, a tiny asp-like creature with yellow eyes and a flickering pink tongue.

Snakes!

"If it was Denis, I will cut off his balls," said Raphe.

Raphe the *vampire*!

That the hot, sexy guy with the accent was a vampire was the easiest of all this for Josie to believe. Too bad he was so uptight. She'd made one teeny-tiny joke about sparkles, and he acted like she'd spit on him.

"The point is"—Maddy spoke louder, giving Raphe and Naliti a dirty look—"the occupants of this building are in a precarious position now we've been unwillingly exposed."

Pax, who had been staring out the sliding glass doors at the back garden, swung around and put a hand to his hip as though expecting to grab something there.

A weapon?

"Number Five made the decision to tell her. How was I supposed to explain away appearing and disappearing furniture?" he asked.

"By 'furniture,' you mean 'bed.' Imagine *that,*" muttered Raphe. The vampire glared at Josie when he spoke and, yes, he was scary as hell, but it did nothing to diminish the hotness factor.

"Look," Josie said. "Let's forget the *e*'s."

Raphe mouthed the word *Never,* but allowed Josie to continue.

"The four of you are telling me this apartment building is a sentient being traveling to different planets—"

"Not planets," Maddy snapped.

The tenants' association—the assistant hotel manager's—anger at Pax when he told them about the apartment and the stuffed bear was what convinced Josie to take this seriously. Maddy's beauty and obvious intelligence had been intimidating enough but it was as if the truth had stripped away a mask she'd been wearing, and along with her amazing fashion sense, Maddy exuded an air of danger.

Menace.

Josie thought back to their conversation outside the clothing store the other week. Maddy never came out and said whether she and Pax were together or not.

Good God, what if a woman with snakes on her head thought Josie was moving in on her man? Did they bite? Were you turned to stone forever?

"Are you familiar with string theory and the quantum multiverse?" Maddy asked her.

"If we have to teach this human about superposition, we'll be here all day," Raphe complained.

"They're not different planets, per se," said Pax gently, once again serving as a buffer. "Think of them as different realities. In your reality there is only the slightest trace of magic. In other worlds, magic is as necessary as air."

Pax had tried to explain the nature of Number Five Wayside Hotel and World Travel Hub in the elevator down from the sixth floor to the lobby. As he'd spoken, he'd run his palm down the wall of the elevator car, gentling his voice as though soothing an anxious toddler.

Whether it was Number Five or Josie whose anxiety he addressed, Josie couldn't tell. No matter how hard she tried to keep her focus on this question of reality—realities?—that bed and what it meant kept intruding in her thoughts. Had the bed been a product of Josie's desires or Number Five's? When the bed changed shape, was that also Number Five's doing, or had it been Pax's idea?

Did this mean the building could read her mind?

Josie closed her eyes and wished for a dish of Abbot's chocolate almond frozen custard, but nothing appeared.

Why a bed and not frozen custard?

"So, each of you comes from a different reality, or world," Josie reiterated. "Princess Naliti, you are from a world where faery princesses are real."

Naliti cocked her head. "Yes, but not only on my world. Faery princesses are real on every other world as well."

Ungh. Josie's brain cramped.

"On my world, vampires are the apex predators. We rule all other species with a practical mix of stunning intelligence and piss-inducing terror." Raphe smiled with pride.

Naliti coughed into her fist something that sounded suspiciously like "bullshit."

"If I were to visit the faery home world," he said dryly, "I would still be the apex predator, but it would take some effort to convince them of my superiority."

Naliti scoffed. "Because you're a dick."

"Yes," Raphe agreed with false humility. "A large, *impressive* dick. A very carnivorous and ruthless one as well."

"Who needs his ass kicked," Naliti countered.

Overhead, a bank of fluorescent lights blinked in and out of existence. Pax looked at Josie with a concerned expression.

"No ass kicking," Pax said without a hint of a smile. "This is a Wayside."

The lights steadied themselves.

"All guests must take the Wayside Oath," he explained. "You cannot enter a Wayside without pledging not to kill. A broken pledge results in a considerable fee."

Josie wanted relief at this revelation, but her history taught her promises were lies waiting to happen.

"If we could get off the subject of dicks, please?" Maddy asked, then turned to Josie. "Every time a choice is made, two different possibilities come into existence. In one world, you live with Outcome A, and in a different world, all you know is Outcome B."

"So, there are an infinite number of worlds." Josie felt confident saying that much. In fact, she thought she'd heard something like it the few times she'd tried to watch *Doctor Who*.

Pax nodded.

"And these worlds are full of magic and magical beings," Josie continued.

"Like me," Naliti said cheerfully.

"Okay. Okay, but . . ." Josie groped for words to explain the uncomfortable realization forming in her brain. "I thought humans made up constructs like faeries and vampires to explain scientific phenomena. You're telling me they exist. Do all our constructs exist? Like the boogeyman? And do other worlds have constructs that exist in our world? Like, does Donald Trump eat little children if they wander into the forests by themselves on another world out there?"

Raphe shuddered while Pax stroked his chin in thought. "I . . . I've never heard of a Donald Trump before I came to this world."

Maddy twisted her lips into a Crimson Kiss–colored whirl as she thought. "I don't know for sure if the myths and legends from my world exist here or somewhere else. Simply because I've never encountered a *ksmor'ginşta* doesn't mean there isn't a world full of them."

A slight tremble moved through her hands as she spoke.

Yikes. "What is a *ksmor'ginşta*?" Josie whispered.

Maddy's shudder was more pronounced. "Imagine Barney the dinosaur but on meth, and he eats the children after he sings to them. And lives under your bed."

"Oh shit," said Raphe.

"Dude," Naliti said. "How am I supposed to get that out of my brain?"

Maddy tipped her hand as though to wave away the image she'd conjured. "The point is, the *ksmor'ginşta* serves the same purpose in my world the boogeyman serves in this world. That both exist somewhere else doesn't change their roles. The same for the fantasy books about elves and faeries Miss Nekesa from the library is always reading. They can continue to bring joy in an ugly world even if elves and faeries are right now fighting a pitched battle on another plane."

Whoa.

So much information. So much unwelcome information.

"Back up there. Elves and faeries are enemies?"

Naliti nodded. "Oh yeah. Those guys are pains in the ass and, for the record, none of them look like Orlando Bloom. Not a one."

An even worse thought occurred to Josie.

"Are you saying the boogeyman is real, too?" she asked. "He doesn't live here in Number Five, does he?"

"Even if he does," Pax tried to assure her, "the Wayside Oath will bind him. We vow not to harm another being within the walls of a Wayside."

He projected such certainty. Josie wanted to believe him but her brain deluged her with worst-case scenarios and her heart raced. What if the boogeyman lived beneath them and thought she and Amos made too much noise? Would he file a complaint or simply jump out at them?

"You said you were in the Army of Light," Josie said to Pax. "The boogeyman is bad, so you would have to fight him."

"Good and bad are absolutes for simpletons," Raphe interjected. "In your world he might be bad because he scares young children, but on his world, he might be the heroic leader of an uprising to liberate enslaved people."

Something wasn't making sense.

"Do you mean to say Light isn't the same as good?" she asked them.

The four of them looked to one another before any one person answered. No one spoke for so long it got uncomfortable, and a cold sweat sprang up on Josie's neck.

It fell, finally, to Pax. He dragged a folding chair over and set it next to Josie and leaned on the back of it.

"The Light is the force that protects the universe's magic," he said slowly.

Josie tried to pay attention to the meaning of the freaking

universe and not the distraction of whether a childhood nightmare roamed the halls.

Literally.

"Okay," she said. "What is the Dark, then?"

They did one of those stare-at-each-other things while Josie waited with an impressive amount of patience.

This time Maddy was the one to answer. "Dark is the force in opposition to Light. Dark is the end of magic."

"Is this theology or more physics?" Josie knew the answer, though. If it were theology, everything would have been simpler, and they could have stuck with good and bad.

"It is Universal Law." Pax's shoulders raised. "Physics is explicable. Universal Law just . . . is."

That was super helpful.

"Listen," said Naliti, "the Light is there to show us the truth about the universe. Truth hurts. It's messy, ugly, and hard, but without it, we can't thrive or grow straight or be healthy. If you are on the side of the Dark, you want to block out the Light. You want to twist and obscure the truth so you can manipulate circumstances to your own benefit. Snuffing out truth and getting rid of magic is the best way to control a population. Pump them full of fear, create imaginary enemies, and distract them from anything joyful or profound."

"Like fake news?" Josie asked.

Raphe nodded. "Or like gaslighting. Basically, like every lyric to every fourth pseudo-intellectual pop song written by an underfed pretentious blonde—ow. You keep your hands to yourself, Princess, or I'll rip them from your arms."

Josie would have run screaming from the room if Raphe had snarled that threat at her, but Naliti appeared unfazed.

"You better not be referring to Her," the faery said, arms

crossed and chin lowered. "If you are, *I've got a list of names and yours is in red, underlined.*"

"So, to sum up," Josie said quickly, "the universe consists of multiple dimensions or worlds with magic. To travel from one magical world to another, you book a room in a Wayside, and to get to a Wayside, you gotta travel certain roads, and you, Pax, were a soldier who protected those roads."

Pax's mouth straightened and he looked away, uncomfortable.

Raphe sneered. "Oh, he was brave, my dear. You should have Pax tell you stories about what he and his soldiers sacrificed during those campaigns."

Why were the best-looking guys always such asshats? Even on other worlds.

Josie continued her summary as though Raphe hadn't spoken. "Everything was normal until the elevator broke. Ever since, Number Five has degenerated to her present state and her fuel gauge shows empty, so you're stuck in my world, which has no magic, until you can figure out what's wrong with her, but you don't have a clue what that might be."

"Exactly," said Maddy.

"So . . ." Josie said, completely at a loss. "What the heck does this have to do with me?"

"You fucked up this time, Pax."

Every bit of patience Pax had stored was depleted after yesterday afternoon's revelations. Unable to sleep, he'd wandered the halls of Number Five, deliberately avoiding the sixth floor. At three in the morning, he'd begun stacking boxes in the lobby when the front door had opened and Raphe had staggered into the building, obviously having freshly fed.

Even Number Five, with her aversion to violence, wouldn't blame him if he reached over and grabbed the vampire by the throat. In fact . . .

"Erp perhchip muglecho." Raphe twisted in Pax's grip, feet two inches off the ground, unable to force anything more cogent than gibberish out given the hold Pax had on his windpipe.

"Oh dear. Um, Paladin?"

"Yes, Bert?"

The gargoyle sat across the lobby from the mailboxes in his usual alcove and dressed in a shocking orange-and-blue shirt with a large blue fish across the chest. Ernie's alcove remained empty, as he had declared himself on strike until his unique position of representing the welcoming spirit of Number Five was better respected.

"You are tasked with upholding peace and dignity in the eternal fight against the Dark," Bert reminded Pax in a melancholy voice. "Pinning the prince to the wall isn't dignified. Nor peaceful."

Pax did not let go.

"I am no longer a paladin," he pointed out. "I'm the hotel manager, and as such, it falls to me to discipline unruly guests."

"Hmmmm." Bert hummed a disappointed-sounding response.

Pax waited a second or two longer while Raphe's face turned a satisfying shade of purple, before he released his grip. He turned to the gargoyle and gave him a slight bow.

"I beg your pardon, Bertrand son of Betradette. You have the right of it. I should not—"

Pax lifted his hand, easily catching Raphe's retaliatory punch and squeezing hard enough to snap a finger, then continued. "I should not be lowering myself to anything below a paladin's standards, despite my retirement from service."

"Why don't you take your noble speeches and shove them up your—*ow*!" Raphe yanked his hand out of Pax's, whirled around, and confronted Bert. "Did you flick your tail at me? I am going to carry you to the rooftop and drop you to the ground, you pumice-brained knickknack."

Bert bared his rows of sharpened teeth.

"You are lucky my anger is too precious to waste on self-important decor," Raphe taunted, then turned back to face off with Pax. "You fucked up, O fearless defender of the Light. That woman cannot be trusted with our secret. Humans are one of the most ignorant, self-destructive, and violent races I've ever come across—and I'm a vampire. What will they do to us when our real selves are revealed?"

"Josephine is completely trustworthy," Pax said.

The vampire spoke over Pax's insistence. "Maddy—they'll stick her in a laboratory and cut off her snakes. Bert and Ernie? Supersoldiers. And myself? Well, no doubt I will rule over Russia and most of Eastern Europe," he preened, "but only after cataclysmic bloodshed."

"You cannot judge all humans by the media you consume," scolded Bert. "You've watched too many scary movies. I advise you to let Miss Nekesa curate your DVD selection like Ernie and I do. A little *Barbie: Life in the Dreamhouse* will lighten you up in no time."

"Ugh." Raphe held up his hands in a warding gesture. "None of that heavy-handed feminist malarkey, please."

Uninterested in the ensuing argument between Bert and

Raphe on Barbie and how she fit into postwar feminism, Pax returned to sorting boxes.

How *would* Maddy tell the rest of the tenants and what would be their reactions? Gut roiling, Pax acknowledged to himself many of them would agree with Raphe. Despite the faeries' wholehearted embrace of human culture, many looked upon humans with disdain and even outright hostility.

This world contained resources without end, but most humans went without them. The tiniest majority controlled its vast wealth. Anger drenched the airwaves, contaminating communication, and most governments equated peace with capitulation.

Even *Barbie: Life in the Dreamhouse* was not without its flaws; he had yet to see an episode featuring a neurodiverse or abjectly poor Barbie. Also, Ken did not get nearly enough credit.

The doors to the sixth-floor mailboxes sprung open with a low wheeze and black sand poured out.

What would the sixth-floor guests do in a world starved of magic?

What if they came to this world only to destroy it?

"There now," Pax said softly, and closed the mailboxes up with care. "We'll figure out how to mend you, don't you worry."

Bert and Raphe fell silent as Pax whispered soothing nonsense words, got a broom, and swept up the black sand, which promptly disappeared from the dustpan.

"The fact remains," Raphe said finally, "we're still missing something vital to Number Five's survival. We tried it your way with a new guest from a new world and it hasn't solved the problem."

"You are too impatient," Pax told him. "Give it time."

Bert set his elbows on his knees and made a cradle for his chin. "More time makes it worse. The guests grow restless as the weeks drag on, and the lack of magic puts them out of sorts. There are some who gave up everything they owned to travel the magical ways. Who knows how much time has passed since we came here? It could be years. Centuries."

Raphe nodded in agreement. "No matter how much we caution them, the guests are going to want to get out of here and explore this world. What's going to happen when Cierume stops yelling at the news, picks up her dancing stick, and takes matters into her own hands? Who's going to keep her from kicking ass from here to Washington, DC? Not me."

Pax had been worrying about this as well.

"Not to mention the sixth-floor guests," Raphe added. "If the human woman is scared by a big pussy like the boogeyman, wait till she meets her truly terrifying neighbors." Raphe talked a big game, but even he could not hide his apprehension when he brought up the sixth floor.

"Everything will be different now." Pax tried to appease the nervous vampire. "We explained to her she is to play a vital part in healing Number Five."

"Hmmph," Raphe grunted. "I noticed you never told the human her part could be played dead or alive."

"I'm not going to allow—"

Raphe cut Pax's protest short. "You seem to believe because you are the hotel manager you have control over your guests. You don't."

Pinpricks of rage heated the tips of Pax's fingers, and the stench of boiling tar stung the back of his throat.

"What are you saying, Prince?" he asked, hand to his hip. No sword hung there, but if it truly came down to it, he could have

Raphe's windpipe in his hands before the vampire had time to blink. "Is that a challenge?"

True to character, the vampire scoffed even as he stepped back. "Simply stating the obvious, Paladin. You can call as many meetings as you like, create as many gardens as Number Five can hold, sic Maddy on whatever poor fool comes by, but you cannot stop a guest from leaving out those doors and creating havoc if they set their mind to it."

Chapter Fourteen

"It's a wizard!"

Josie joined Amos at the living room window—the now completely yellow living room—and stared out into the snow.

"Yup. Our St. Patrick's Day blizzard, right on time," she responded.

One fun fact about that holiday in upstate New York. It either snowed or it was a hundred degrees out. No in between. Not up here.

"We hafta stay home?"

"Even more yup. Today is a snow day. Mommy doesn't have to go to work, and you don't go to pre-K."

Amos's eyes widened. "You don't hafta go at work? This is the best day ever, Mom!"

Josie picked him up and twirled him around fast in the hopes the air would dry the tears standing in her eyes.

Were there worlds where a woman didn't have to choose between earning a living and spending a few more hours a week parenting? Josie wished Number Five could drop her and Amos off there for a few years.

"Amos?" she asked as they settled themselves in the kitchen

for chocolate chip pancakes and hot cocoa. "If Momma could do magic, what kind of magic would you want me to do?"

She'd left the meeting with Maddy, Raphe, and Naliti after agreeing nothing would be said to Amos about the true nature of the building. She and Amos had walked over to the science museum on Sunday afternoon after church and treated themselves to pizza afterward. Josie hadn't seen any of the residents since the "big reveal."

Last night, Josie had tossed and turned in her bed, trying to figure out what she believed about Number Five and the people, or beings, in it. If Number Five was sentient, did that mean it—she—was aware of what Josie and Amos always did? Had Number Five been the one to decorate Amos's room? Was that creepy or cool, and why had the line between those two become so blurred since they moved in?

"If you were magic, you could make it always Christmas," Amos offered.

Josie considered this as she tossed a few marshmallows in their cocoa. "If it were always Christmas, it would never be summer and never be your birthday, and we couldn't go to the beach."

"Hmmmmm." Amos sat at the kitchen table and swung his feet back and forth furiously. "You could make tofu taste like pizza."

Now that was worth considering.

"That's all you can think of, buddy?" she asked. "Nothing else you wish you had that Momma can't give you?"

"Nope," he said, then licked the syrup from his plate. "I can watch *Dinosaur Train* because it's a wizard day?"

"Sure, bud."

Josie stayed at the kitchen table. She rolled her pancake into a tube and dipped the end of it in her cocoa, relieved. If she was utterly failing as a mom, Amos would have asked for her to do something about it with magic, right?

Saturday night, when Gloria had brought Amos home, she'd looked even more disgruntled than usual.

"Why is Amos not taking violin?" she'd asked before Josie could get out a greeting.

The buttons of Gloria's blue Talbots wool coat shone dully; her peach-pink lipstick greenish in the odd light. Josie had wanted to get Amos upstairs in bed as soon as possible, both because it was late and because the gargoyle in the left alcove was in a different position than it had been yesterday.

Was it alive?

Was it dangerous?

Pax would have warned her if the gargoyles ate people. Right?

"Well, we can certainly talk about that in the morning if you'd like," Josie lied, picking Amos up and giving him a squeeze.

"Josephine," Gloria had snapped. "Al and I have serious concerns about where Amos is developmentally. At his age, Dan played piano, tennis, and went to chess camp. Most of my friends have grandchildren in multiple activities."

Gloria waited a beat.

"And it shows," she said.

Did those same friends talk about their grandkids in front of them as if they didn't exist or couldn't understand when their abilities were questioned? The criticism pinched though and sat like a sharp stone in Josie's belly.

She'd kissed Amos's ears loudly so he wouldn't hear Gloria's words. "I don't know about violin," Josie had said, a forced smile squeezing her words too thin, "but I agree we need some music in our lives. How about after Christmas we sign this kid up for Orff?"

"Is that like yoga?" Gloria had asked.

Turning Amos upside down so he giggled some more, Josie had then righted him and set him on the ground, keeping her expression hidden, relying on her masterful powers of placation to make this end without conflict.

"It's a famous German music education technique," Josie assured her. "I was going to enroll him in the free class at the church—"

"I'll look to see if they are offered privately," Gloria snapped.

Right. God forbid Amos mingle with the masses.

"Great. Thanks again for spending time with Amos, I know he appreciates you two." Josie widened her fake smile and hustled Amos toward the staircase.

Gloria's insinuation had skittered through Josie's brain yesterday and in last night's crappy sleep.

Taking another pancake, Josie placed a line of whipped cream down the center, rolled it up, and dipped it into syrup while she brooded.

Despite being a pretty shitty human being, Gloria had managed to raise a good man. Dan had been smart and funny and genuinely warm with a big heart. If the secret to growing up into a decent person despite a parent's flaws was taking piano and tennis at age four, maybe Josie should look more into those sorts of classes.

What did she know about raising a kid?

What if, despite her attempt to escape her family, Josie was destined to repeat their mistakes?

The light over the kitchen sink dimmed and the whipped cream thickened and yellowed.

Holy hell.

Had Josie done that?

Was that Number Five reacting to Josie's anxiety, or was it a message telling Josie to relax, or was it a coincidence and the residents of Number Five had succeeded in their mad plan to drive her insane?

"Mom? I can watch *Arfer*?" Amos called from the living room.

"No more TV," Josie called back. Whatever had happened had unnerved her. Josie needed out of the building right now.

"It's a snow day, Amos," she called. "Let's get the last bit of use out of your snowsuit until it snows again at Easter."

"I can't look. It's too awful."

Pax, Bert, and Joey stared at Maddy, who had one hand over her eyes, dramatically twisting away from the lobby window. The four of them had been watching Amos and Josie making shapes in the snow on the front lawn.

Joey turned his attention back to the humans. "She isn't hurting him. It looks like they're making some sort of primitive art."

"They are making a mess of what was a perfect surface," Maddy complained. "It was a beautiful field of virgin snow this morning . . ."

Bert and Joey giggled when Maddy said "virgin."

". . . and is now a churning mass of soiled carnage," she finished.

Pax followed Joey's gaze to where Josie and Amos stood next to a rounded figure and pressed twigs into its sides, either to represent arms or as some sort of pretend torture.

Having no memories of playing in the snow from his time at the orphanage, Pax could only guess at what the little family was doing. Whatever it was, they laughed a great deal.

"I cannot let this go any further. They will put everything back the way it was, right now." With that Maddy put on her enormous sunglasses and stormed out of the lobby.

"Oh dear," said Joey. "I've been watching DVDs from Miss Nekesa's family-friendly section, and my research leads me to believe the LaChiusas are cavorting in a winter wonderland."

"What does that mean?" rasped Bert.

The boy turned away from the window, his nose stuck to the side of his face from pressing against the glass. "It is something humans do when it first snows. They cavort and afterward drink hot beverages and sometimes sing songs about kissing."

"Huh," said Bert, his sausage-size eyebrows drawn together in confusion, whether over the definition of "cavort" or puzzlement over why humans would choose to perform such an activity in the snow.

"Hmmm," said Pax, echoing Bert's puzzlement until a thought struck him. "So, if cavorting is what normal humans do in the snow, it would be abnormal for someone to insist they . . ."

Sure enough, Maddy stood out on the neatly shoveled walkway dressed in white with elegant white boots, long fur-trimmed white coat, and towering fur hat with a silken scarf tied beneath her chin. She gestured to the snow with her white fur-lined gloves, to the air, then back at the misshapen creature Josie and Amos had crafted.

He couldn't hear anything they were saying, but Josie's expression went from amusement to surprise to consternation quickly. Damn.

"I'll be right back," he said, although he doubted anyone was listening since Joey was trying to push his nose straight and grossing Bert out in the process.

". . . the whole effect is chaotic."

Maddy's voice slipped down the back of Pax's neck and left shivers in its wake.

Not good.

She'd been in a shitty mood ever since Josie found out about Number Five. No matter how many ways he asked her, however, Maddy refused to admit it. She kept telling him she was fine, even though her hair was so volatile she could barely keep her hat on.

"Oh. Hello, Ms. LaChiusa," he said loudly, waving like a fool. "Hello, Mr. Amos."

Amos waved back. "We is messing up Miss Maddy's snow," he announced.

"I'm sure that's not true," Pax said with false cheer. He came to stand next to Maddy while appreciating how the cold turned Josie's cheeks a pretty shade of pink. Her blue hat sat askew on her head, and a poorly knitted scarf was clumsily tied around her neck. Amos wore a yellow-and-green snowsuit, pink knitted hat, and a Spider-Man scarf to complement his Spider-Man boots.

"Oh, it's true," hissed Maddy.

"You see," Pax said over her words, "having watched Miss Nekesa's family-friendly holiday DVDs, I know it's perfectly *normal* for families to play with snow." He laid heavy emphasis on those last few words.

Josie lowered her chin and raised her eyebrows. "Is that what you've been doing? Researching what families do by watching Miss Nekesa's DVD collection?"

Maddy huffed. "It's not like we have families of our own."

"You no have a family, Miss Maddy?" Amos asked.

"Well, I do," Maddy said curtly after a surprised pause. She examined Amos as though he were an exotic-looking insect. "We aren't . . . close."

Amos's little forehead wrinkled: "We can share, Miss Maddy. Me and my mom will play on this part of the snow, and you can have the rest of the snow to look at."

When Maddy objected, Pax laid a warning hand on her shoulder. "That is kind of you to share the snow, Mr. Amos. That sounds like something a hero would do on those DVDs with those *normal* humans."

Josie ducked her mouth behind her scarf but the wrinkles beneath her eyes betrayed a smile. Did he sound ridiculous?

He certainly felt ridiculous. Would Amos understand what Pax was trying to communicate? When did human children develop a sense for subterfuge?

"Why play with the snow in the first place?" Maddy turned to Pax and set her hands on her hips. "What is the point if it makes a mess?"

"Play is how children learn." Josie crouched to Amos's eye level and retied his scarf.

Maddy and Pax exchanged glances. Neither of them had children, so on the one hand, what did they know? On the other hand, Pax couldn't recall a single moment of play during school at the orphanage.

"When kids use their imagination, they exercise their creativity." Josie looked over at them, eyes soft with what could have been either amusement or sympathy. "When they play with other people, they learn to problem solve and navigate social situations."

Pax scratched his head while he digested this.

"It's easier to learn a lesson if you're having fun while you learn it," Josie pointed out.

The door to the building burst open and Joey came running out. He wore an enormous blue puffy coat and giant snow boots that had the effect of making his legs look thin as pencils.

"Hi. Hi, guys. Hi, can I do what you're doing?" he asked, coming up on the other side of Pax and hopping from one foot to another.

"Do you have a snow day off from school, too?" Amos asked.

"Uhhhh, yes?" Joey said.

"We gonna build a snow fort," the child announced, then waddled back over to a heap of snow. "You wanna help?"

"Oh," said Josie, "ummm . . ." She sidled over to Pax and lowered her voice. "What if Joey gets hungry?"

Hungry?

Why would Josie worry about Joey being hungry, unless . . .

Ah. Another instance of a magical being having been smeared by this world's entertainment industry. She must think zombies' appetites were indiscriminate.

"It would be rude for Joey to bite a friend," Pax whispered back.

"Also, we're vegans," Joey announced. "I bet you didn't know that. My whole family are vegans now. We've never felt so good. Did you know veganism is proven to improve cardio health?"

"I have heard that," Josie acknowledged in a normal voice, cheeks flushing. "I'm sorry, Joey, I didn't mean to insult you."

"That's okay." Joey waved away her apology, bouncing on the tips of his toes. "Maddy told us you know everything now and it's new to you. New is scary. It's okay to make mistakes when you're scared."

"That's generous of you," she said.

Joey beamed. "Did you want to know more about veganism? I can tell you all sorts of important facts. For example—"

Pax and Maddy both turned on Joey with murder in their eyes and she held up a hand, palm outward, to forestall their irritation.

"I'll bet you have lots to say about it, but maybe you can help Amos first?" she asked.

"Yup, yup. I love to help." Joey bounced over to where Amos was sitting and eating a fistful of snow.

"I'm sorry about the snow, Maddy," Josie said.

With a sharp sigh, Maddy waved her hand to flip Josie's apology away. "If this is something normal humans do, there's nothing to apologize for, I suppose." She turned on her heel and headed back to the building only to come to an abrupt stop as the door opened one more time and all twelve faery princess ran, flipped, cartwheeled, and jumped out the front doors of the building.

"O-U-T-S-I-D-E! We're coming outside to slide and having snow much fun, uh-huh un-huh!" The faeries cheered en masse, dressed in blinding sparkly outfits of gold parkas with white earmuffs, gloves, scarfs, and boots—all covered in rhinestones.

Joey moved behind Amos as the group surged toward them, shouting and kicking up the snow. Princess Naliti waved to Maddy, then hurried over to where Josie and Pax stood.

"They wanted to come out here and practice stunts in the snow. I told them they couldn't use any magic while Amos was around, and they promised not to."

"I will—" Pax stopped abruptly when the front doors opened again and out came the Fate siblings, Past, Present, and Future. They wore their usual sweatsuits but had donned color-coordinated knitted headbands in deference to the snow. Behind them, holding on to a carved cane, was their cousin, Gbadu.

"What the hell is all this caterwauling?" Mx. Fate cried. "And is there liquor involved?"

"Who"—Josie tugged on the elbow of Pax's coat—"who are those three? I can't figure it out. Are they ghosts? Who is the older woman with them?"

"Let me introduce you to the Fates." Pax led her over and introduced her to Past Fate, his sister, Present, and their sibling, Future Fate. He then bowed slightly and introduced the fourth figure standing with them. Gbadu, the Goddess of Fate, was a tiny Black woman bundled into a pine green snowsuit with purple faux-fur trim.

"Aunt Gbadu," Pax used a traditional greeting from her world, where all people considered themselves related. "Welcome."

Gbadu wore a pair of wraparound sunglasses stretching around her head. Seeing as she had sixteen eyes, he appreciated her forethought in covering them all.

"I was expecting a parade in my honor." Gbadu sighed. "In the old days, there were parades whenever we left a Wayside. What do you call this? It's the goddamned sorriest excuse for a parade I've ever seen, if that's what it is. Why is everyone so cheerful?"

Present Fate shouted, "That's the shittiest snow fort I've ever seen. Did that child not learn physics?"

Aunt Gbadu and the Fates moved as one down the sidewalk and toward poor Joey and Amos, who were watching open-mouthed as three faery princesses did cartwheels around the foundation of their fort.

"I'm sorry your play was interrupted," Pax said to Josie. "I fear now the guests know you've been told of their true nature, they will take too many liberties."

"Well, you know what they say. The more, the merrier."

To anyone else, Josie's smile would be construed as wholesome. When she smiled at him, however, all Pax could see was an invitation to set his lips to hers.

It was a completely new form of torture, and he hated it almost as much as he enjoyed it.

"Paladins must not get a lot of time to play."

Play?

His expression must have answered her question, because those wide, gray eyes of hers grew soft and she frowned in an expression of sympathy.

"At the orphanage where I was raised, we had a regimented schedule. There was no time set aside for play."

He and his cohort were destined for the Army of Light. There was much they had to learn and many skills to master before they were old enough to serve. For the first time, however, watching Amos and Josie together, listening to the sounds of laughter and joy around them, Pax second-guessed that strict discipline.

Would he be a different man if he'd learned to play?

"What games did you play when you were a child?" he asked, curious now what the younger Pax might have thought about such activities.

Josie turned away from watching Cindy and a handful of her sisters building a slide in the snow.

"I remember one foster family had a toy oven with little dishes and wooden fruit," she said. "I would play for hours, pretending to be a regular mom."

Did that mean there were irregular moms?

A picture of a thin child in an ill-fitting dress standing at a blue plastic oven entered Pax's head. The certainty Josie's childhood had been difficult and lonely would explain part of the attraction he felt for her.

Often, those who had been wounded could find healing with someone who had been similarly hurt.

"I suppose your play stood you in good stead," Pax said, silently praying he would find the right words. "Now you are an admirable mother."

Her brows raised but her smile slipped, and his stomach contracted.

Was this the wrong thing to say?

"I don't know about that," Josie said, looking down. Thick, fluffy flakes of snow landed on her eyelashes, and the urge to sip them from her lids as they melted woke a tingle at the base of his spine.

Grateful they weren't inside the halls of Number Five—who knows what might appear—he hurried to assure her.

"I have spent decades discerning the Light from the Dark. You have raised a child who practically glows with courage and kindness. This makes you admirable."

"I . . . Thank you." Josie's head came up and stared at him as though he'd moved a mountain. "That is the nicest thing anyone has said to me in a long time."

"I should think Amos's grandparents say the same," Pax said. "They must be grateful instead of growing up knowing loss, Amos is growing up knowing only love and acceptance."

Josie shook her head quickly as if to dislodge something painful.

"I wish," she said. "Maybe it's because they are too close that they can't see how great Amos is doing or how hard I try. All they see is what he's missing out on and how little I can give him."

This struck Pax as unfair, but what did he know about the inner workings of a family?

"I see how great Amos is doing," he assured her. "I see how hard you try."

Would she believe him?

The tiniest of tingles scratched the back of his neck and Pax turned away from Josie too quickly to register her reaction to his words. He looked up and saw a figure standing in a sixth-floor window. Pax moved his body between Josie and the sight line of whoever stood there. Maddy would have told him if a sixth-floor resident had woken, so he could only hope Number Five was sending him a signal. He racked his brain for a reason Number Five wanted to bring the sixth floor to his attention, but the sound of Amos and Joey calling for help distracted him. Josie tugged at his elbow and Pax let himself be pulled away.

The unfettered joy of the moment before, however, was lost beneath a dull chill of foreboding.

Chapter Fifteen

Battles cannot be won if you see the enemy as anything other than targets. You cannot for a moment believe they love and hate and fear like you. Turn them into marks on a map or you will lose."

Pax whispered these words into Josie's ear while they lay on their stomachs next to each other behind a crumbling barrier of poorly packed snow.

"By the same token," he continued, his lips barely grazing the shell of her ear, sending jolts of arousal from her belly to her core, "you must remember your soldiers have lives and loves for which you are responsible. Protect them to the death."

Even during Josie's worst times, reality had never come into question. The revelations two nights ago, coupled with whatever this was sparking between her and Pax, had messed with her brain, though.

The world was spinning with her on it and the resulting dizziness could be mistaken for happiness.

Josie rolled onto her side on the bed of snow beneath them and studied Pax's face.

"That's intense. Were you in many battles?"

Raising himself on his elbows, Pax risked a quick glance over the icy barrier, then dropped and mirrored her position. Contrasting with the grayish light against the white snow, his skin looked ruddy, and his hair revealed strands of auburn amid the ebon black.

"I was a soldier in the Army of Light for nearly one hundred of my world's years," he said softly, eyes constantly tracking everything around them. "Before that, I was in the soldiers' training academy straight from the orphanage."

There were men like Pax on this world, too. Boys who lost families in brutal, long-running wars. Josie knew students in the local Sudanese community whose fathers wore the same expression as Pax when they spoke of the wars at home.

Not all of them were able to leave those wars behind.

Was Pax?

He seemed thoughtful and kind, but did his stoicism mask a deeper well of emotions? Did a man who fought others for an entire lifetime know how to set violence aside?

When Pax smiled, though, Josie pushed her worries aside; the smile reached his eyes. How could she doubt his character? Weren't the heroes in fairy tales always noble and righteous? The existence of faeries and vampires and other sorts of creatures meant there must also be handsome knights who would slay dragons for the love of a lady.

Still . . .

"Remember not to take this too seriously," she reminded him, keeping her voice light. "We're play—"

"Charge!" hollered Joey Z. as his spindly legs carried him over the barrier.

"C-H-A-R-G-E. We'll kick your ass we guarantee!" screeched a faery cheerleader as she and three of her sisters ran right past

Josie's head. Josie rose to all fours and peered over the snowbank at utter chaos.

As soon as he and Joey had completed their first fort, Amos had declared it was time for a snowball fight. Apparently, the idea of an all-out melee appealed to the other-worlders, because by the time teams were chosen, even more residents had spilled out of the building. There were at least thirty people—beings—now on the front lawn fully committed to the battle despite the snow falling and temperatures dropping in the face of a bitter wind.

"Left flank, retreat," Pax called, jumping to his feet with a shocking grace, considering his size. The sight distracted Josie so much she almost didn't react when the first snowball hit her right on her temple.

The second one smacked her in the chin—after that one she reacted.

Denis had thrown both.

Of course.

While the battle raged, Josie had the sensation of being watched. She couldn't make out any figures in any of the windows, and it might have been the building itself watching her. Now that she knew the part Pax hoped her to play in Number Five's recovery, the thought was less creepy than she'd supposed.

Mostly, she kept her attention on Amos, making sure no one slipped up in front of him and revealed their true selves. Any of their neighbors could be lethal when careless: Denis and his little troop of crony gnomes might be small, but some of them were downright feral with sharp teeth and short fuses. Bert, the gargoyle from the lobby, ran around on all fours dressed in an ugly Christmas sweater trying to pass as a dog. He weighed a good three hundred pounds if not more—and Josie worried he might accidentally step on Amos's foot.

Once Cindy and a few other faeries began hair-pulling, Josie decided it was time to take Amos home and make them both a snow-day dinner of grilled cheese and tomato soup when everyone around her went silent.

Josie blinked away the snowflakes from her lashes until she could make out the figure standing on the front steps of the building.

"Shit," muttered Future Fate. "Here comes the buzzkill."

Sure enough, Maddy's expression as she regarded the front lawn was of deep disgust. A few faeries halfheartedly cheered but trailed off as Maddy walked closer and closer. She looked like the White Witch from the Narnia books, her tall white fur-capped hat sitting regally atop her white headscarf, her white down-stuffed coat trailing off behind her.

Maddy hadn't offered any information about her home world other than the fact the boogeymen there were scarier than anything Josie could have imagined. Why was a woman as powerful as Maddy working as an assistant to Pax? He was amazing, yes, but there didn't seem to be anything magical about him. Maddy, on the other hand, could turn people to stone. Not to mention she exuded badass from her invisible pores.

Seriously. Maddy had the most perfect skin Josie had ever seen.

Was Maddy here to be near Pax?

"And what are you teaching your child with this play, Ms. LaChiusa?" Maddy asked now, her words icy and sharp. "How to be a soldier?"

"Well," said Josie, unsure whether Maddy genuinely wanted an honest answer, but since Amos had wandered over next to them, that's what she'd get. "This is a play fight. That means we are all friends when playtime is over, no matter which side we were on."

More than a few residents took issue with that.

"I wasn't friends with Denis before he threw a snowball at me," announced a stocky faery cheerleader with a bruise forming beneath her eye. "Do I have to be friends with him now?" she asked.

"If we can't be friends after a game, we can't play the game anymore," Amos answered in a serious tone. "'Cause if we lose our friends, no one is left to play."

More grumbling ensued.

"Or we can play a game wif no winners or losers. Then nobody is mad," Amos offered.

Maddy sucked her teeth and scoffed. "What's the point of playing a game if no one wins or loses?"

Her toes going numb, Josie took Amos's hand, ready to bring him inside to warm up.

Amos looked up at Maddy, his big eyes wide. "Games is fun. They make you happy. Happy is when you is your best self."

"Fun," Maddy muttered darkly. She leaned over and picked up a snowball. Some in the crowd gasped; others audibly caught their breath in anticipation of something terrible.

"Never tell Maddy something is fun," Denis whispered to another gnome. "She'll find a rule against it. No one kills a mood like—sphflunf de hoock!"

Amos clasped both of his mittened hands to his mouth in shock at the sight of Denis spitting out the snowball Maddy had thrown directly into his mouth. No one else made a move or said a word for a second or two after, while they tried to wrap their minds around the fact Maddy was out here for . . .

"Fun, eh?" Maddy tapped her chin with her gloved finger. "I'll have to try again to make sure I'm doing it right."

Sure enough, she leaned over and picked up another snowball, releasing whatever spell held them motionless. Joey Z. emitted a wailing battle cry, and the cheerleaders exploded into cartwheels and one-handed aerials.

"M-A-D-D-Y wants to play and won't be shy," they cheered as the Fate siblings and their cousin returned to their task of packing the snow into perfect spheres and tossing them lightly to whoever ran by.

Given the excitement, Josie let Amos stay out for another ten minutes. The battle devolved into neighbors throwing snowballs at their own teammates, tossing snowballs in the air and catching them in their mouths, and finally throwing armloads of snow into the air. Josie stood to the side and watched.

"This is a sight to remember." Pax had good-naturedly allowed a group of faeries to stand on one another's shoulders and dump snow over him, then dusted himself off and came to join her.

Josie laughed. "It's like if Disney characters came to life."

"Oh." Pax shook his head, the corner of his mouth pulling down. "Don't mention that particular multimedia conglomerate around the tenants, Denis especially."

"Why not?"

They ducked when a snow boulder came whizzing by accompanied by the faint scent of paprika.

"No *smells*, Cindy," someone shouted.

"Their specious infantilization of gnomes aside," Pax answered, "they would be considered allies of the Dark on many worlds."

"The Dark?" Josie saw the word as capitalized in her head. "How does Donald Duck contribute to the obfuscation of universal truths?"

"The concept is infinitely more nuanced."

Josie cringed when Bert knocked two gnomes off their feet and into a pyramid of snowballs Aunt Gbadu had carefully stacked. She didn't know who to be more concerned for—Bert or the gnomes who let loose a string of what she supposed were vile curses in a guttural language. Language that offended Aunt Gbadu, judging by the way she now wagged a finger at them.

Josie's stomach turned in foreboding.

"Pax?" Josie waited until Pax turned to face her. "I've been thinking about everything I learned Saturday night, and I have the sense you guys left something out."

When he reached over and clasped her hand, a tiny tremor shook Josie from her toes to her scalp despite the thick gloves separating their skin. If she had been bare-handed, her knees might have weakened.

"We have not lied to you," he said seriously. "You would know if we had."

Josie started to object when it hit her. "Cinnamon, right?"

"Mom, look!"

Naliti had picked up Amos and let him sit on her shoulders. She wasn't nearly as tall as Cindy and seemed more responsible, so Josie waved in acknowledgment, allowing it for the moment.

"Number Five is allergic to lies," he admitted.

"You may not have lied," she said. "But there's more to this story and to this place than a stranded hotel needing a new tenant."

The sun had never come out from behind the swollen storm clouds and the streetlights were still set to winter times. The orange cast of their bulbs turned the shadows between her and Pax into hollows of a sickly dark green and dirty blue.

"Mom, I'm cold," Amos called, dragging his Spider-Man boots in the snow while he trudged toward them. "We can have supper?"

"What about Saturday?" Pax said suddenly. "Can we have supper, too? It would give me time to tell more of the story and answer any questions you have."

"Supper?" she asked. "You want to come over for supper?"

His cheeks darkened and he rubbed his chin. "I thought I could make it for you. A meal. It doesn't have to be supper," he said quickly. "It can be lunch. It can be coffee." Pax nodded as though they were settling an argument. "We can go somewhere else and drink the coffee. Or water. We can . . . Do you drink water? We can do that."

Was he nervous?

Her own palms were sweaty, and her heart slapped against her chest.

"Supper is fine," she blurted before he could ask her if she liked to breathe air. "I mean, supper would be lovely. No one has cooked me a meal in years."

Josie's brain hissed in derision.

Way to sound desperate, Josie. Her gramma's scratchy voice itched behind her skull. *Practically begging for attention.*

Too late, the words were out. They stood there like fools, staring at each other. God. How embarrassing.

"Mom. We can have pudding for dessert because it's a snow day?"

Amos's arrival broke the tension. Pax recovered first.

"Pudding sounds most excellent, Mr. Amos. It is my second-favorite dessert."

"I likes the green kind," Amos offered.

Josie tugged at her scarf to cover her still-burning ears. "What is your favorite dessert?"

Pax cleared his throat. "You'll find out Saturday, I hope?"

"When pudding is green, it's called lickstacio." Amos kept

talking, oblivious to the heat and hesitation between the adults above him. "When ice cream is green, you call it mint."

"I . . ." Josie swallowed, trying to listen to her brain while her whole body screamed, *Yes!*

"That would be nice," she said finally. "I would like that. Dessert and water. Yum."

Pax smiled weakly, then bowed to Amos. "A most enjoyable battle, Mr. Amos. I look forward to more play with you."

Amos bowed in return, and Josie allowed him to tug her away from Pax and into the building.

"I like Mr. Pax. He's a funny nice guy," Amos confided as they made their way up the staircase, shedding clumps of snow as they moved.

"I like him, too," Josie said, nearly choking on the last word as the wrought iron vines sprouted pink heart-shaped flowers as they passed.

Holy shit.

"Tomorrow is going to be a wizard day, too, Mom?" Amos asked as Josie helped him off with his snow boots.

Would the flowers be there tomorrow? What did this mean?

"I have no idea, Amos," she answered, her head spinning with what-ifs and how-the-hecks? "But if I had to guess, I'd say we'll have plenty of wizard days ahead."

Chapter Sixteen

But, Mom, but, Mooooommmm."

Josie pushed opened the door to the lobby and Amos ran past her, his face red with frustration, tears in his eyes.

This morning it had been freezing, the snow from yesterday's blizzard measuring at least two feet. Josie had been held up at work, so Amos had to sit in the Oak Room at school, where the kids whose parents worked late were housed.

The teacher, Miss Monica, was wonderful, but Amos was the only "big" kid there. A handful of three-year-olds decided he was a monster and ran around screaming every time he moved, and it put him in a shitty mood.

It would put her in a shitty mood as well, so out of sympathy—and guilt that she'd been late—Josie had made an exception and gotten him dinner from McDonald's instead of heating up leftovers from last night.

The gesture was too little, too late to salvage a no good, very bad day, because before they made it home, Amos had discovered his Happy Meal had a blue Sonic the Hedgehog when he'd wanted the yellow one.

"We are not going back to McDonald's, Amos," Josie said for

the forty thousandth time. "The color of the hedgehog doesn't make a difference in how good your chicken nuggets taste."

She prodded Amos with her arms full of paperwork and rapidly cooling french fries but he collapsed on the bottom step of the staircase.

"My legs is broken!" he wailed. "I hafta go back and get a yellow Sonic."

Josie considered whether she should leave the child and go on upstairs. Eventually, hunger would force his legs to unbreak, but the determination of a four-year-old when it came to the specifics of a meal toy was akin to the hunger for a gold medal with Olympic athletes. Both groups were determined to break something—world records in the case of Olympians and their parent's will in the case of four-year-olds.

Worst-case scenario . . .

Even as Josie thought the words, the door to Pax's office opened and Maddy stuck her head out.

Today, Maddy was sublimely composed in a light beige skirt set, complete with a tiny gold pillbox cap settled onto the gold silk scarf covering her hair. Or whatever you called the snakes coming out of her head.

"This scene is loud and would appear unnerving to a being with less sangfroid than I," Maddy said.

The woman had a talent for stating the obvious.

"I wanted a yellow Sonic," Amos wailed.

Josie sucked in a huge bellyful of the violet gum–scented air and grasped for patience.

"You know, when I was a kid, we didn't have Happy Meal toys," Josie lied to her son, aware her words would mean nothing to this child, but pretty sure it was what parents were supposed to say. "We got chicken nuggets from the grocery store in no shapes, and if we complained, we didn't get fries."

This was the downside about living in an apartment building, magical or not: there would always be more witnesses to a child's temper tantrum and thus more witnesses on hand to judge Josie's handling of said tantrum.

She flinched when Maddy walked closer and tilted her head to examine Amos, who lay on his back, his legs out straight, feet flopping to the sides while he talked to himself about Sonic.

"It must not be easy as a single mother, trying to do your best for your little boy," Maddy said in a voice low enough that Amos wouldn't hear her. "He would do well with a man in the house."

He would . . . what?

How the hell would Maddy know what Josie needed to raise Amos?

Maddy wasn't a mother. At least, she'd never mentioned children.

"I don't think—"

"Hmm, no, I don't believe you have been. Thinking. Especially about the future," Maddy said. "If you were, you would know a permanent settlement here is impossible. We are leaving, Ms. LaChiusa, the sooner, the better."

Josie had been trying to get through the week with the promise of dinner with Pax sitting like a beacon at the end of a long, dark, absurdly busy tunnel. She hadn't even begun to process everything she'd learned about Number Five, but Maddy had a point.

This building wasn't just alive, it had a purpose: delivering these mythological creatures to the worlds where they belonged.

Amid all the explanations no one had given her a time line when they explained how the Waysides worked.

"Once you refuel, how long will it take you to leave?" Josie asked.

"What does it matter since you cannot come with us?" Maddy asked.

Well.

Well, that was blunt.

"Good evening, Mr. Amos, Ms. LaChiusa." Pax stood in the door to the office and Josie's humiliation was complete. He must have been fixing something, because his hair was covered with a red bandanna, a tight cream-colored thermal shirt stretched its seams at his chest, and he wore brown work pants with thick-soled black boots.

Maddy looked far too poised to have been up to anything with Pax in the office. There's no way any woman wouldn't look a little discombobulated if he'd been touching them in that outfit.

"What does it matter since you cannot come with us?" Maddy had said.

"Us" as in the residents or "us" as in her and Pax?

His boots made a soft pumping sound when Pax crossed the lobby and joined them at the foot of the staircase.

"I'm sorry for the noise, Mr. Pax," Josie said. "Amos has forgotten to use his inside voice."

Pax squatted and tilted his head, saying nothing while Amos described in detail why his heart had been broken and he wouldn't survive without going back to McDonald's for a yellow Sonic the Hedgehog instead of the blue one.

"My goodness, what a tragedy," Maddy said dryly. "I cannot wait to hear the ultimate outcome. Pax, we will speak more later."

Not only did she have incredible posture, Maddy's shoes today were pink patent leather heels with gladiator ribbon straps. How the hell did she walk in those things?

Josie had to fight the urge to flip her off.

By the time Amos finished his soliloquy with a wet, mucousy inhale, Maddy had disappeared, and it was only the three of them in the lobby.

The gargoyles must have been out doing whatever gargoyles do on a Wednesday night.

Pax, of course, being a magical sexy knight with great hair, did not tell Amos about what sort of indignities he'd suffered in his childhood. Josie could only imagine the kinds of stories a guy raised in some sort of military orphanage might have.

Instead, Pax twisted to sit next to Amos on the bottom most step and asked the obvious question.

"What is the difference between the yellow Sonic the Hedgehog and the blue Sonic the Hedgehog?"

At first, Josie thought she might cry in relief when Amos sat up, tears forgotten, and launched into a long, detailed explanation of Sonic Hedgehogs. Could have been true, could have been completely made up—to her knowledge Amos had never seen a Sonic the Hedgehog movie—whatever Amos was saying, however, animated him enough so his legs became unbroken.

Then Josie thought she might cry for another reason when Amos reached out and put his hand in Pax's, still talking, and walked up the stairs with the giant knight in tow.

Josie fell into step behind them, trying to label her feelings.

Overwhelmed? Yes.

Exhausted? Always.

Other emotions lay alongside these, emotions she couldn't tease apart. What exactly did she feel at the sight of Amos's hand being held by a man who wasn't his father?

Hope? Hesitancy?

Was allowing Pax to help a wise choice or was she letting him get too close too soon?

What *would* happen if and when Number Five got better?

As always, Josie's brain treated her to worst-case scenarios ranging from the fatal to the merely humiliating, but each stair the pair touched turned to a dark forest green marble beneath their feet.

Wrought iron birds followed them, hopping between spindles on the staircase, tilting their heads back and forth and stopping occasionally to peck at the sculptured ivy leaves, some of which had turned the same dark green as the stairs.

As Amos and Pax passed the small table on the third-floor landing, the vase atop it holding dried flowers suddenly overflowed with pink and white peonies.

What was Number Five reacting to? Was it to the energy produced between the unlikely pair in front of her? Or was Number Five coming back alive in response to Josie's fervent wish that whatever was happening between Amos and Pax would turn out well?

Magic.

If asked, Josie would have predicted magic would manifest itself in tremendous and terrifying ways. This magic—real magic?—seemed quiet but also marvelous and more to Josie's liking. Why use magic to conquer the world when you can just as easily gift your neighbors with fresh flowers when they come home from work?

The pair came to a halt in front of Josie's door, still discussing various Sonics. Apparently, the blue Sonic turned into the yellow Sonic when he needed special powers.

Fascinating.

"I can show you in my book," Amos was saying. "You wanna come inside?"

Pax, who'd been staring at where his and Amos's hands were joined, now looked over at Josie. His eyes, so often unreadable, were a little bit wild—Amos's creative liberties with classifications of superheroes could make things confusing—and definitely hopeful.

More magic?

What if this was Number Five's doing? What if Pax was only interested in them because of some weird spell?

"It is your mother's decision," Pax said.

If it was a spell that brought Pax to them, did that necessarily mean he needed a spell to remain with them?

"If you don't mind leftover lasagna, you are welcome to join us for supper," she told him.

At her invitation, the door to the apartment opened.

Amos, chattering once again, walked into the apartment without missing a beat.

"Number Five is not subtle," Pax said to Josie, ducking his head as two iron birds flew by.

"You don't have—" Josie's words faltered when Pax tapped his pointer finger gently against her lips.

"She's not subtle, but I'm not unhappy about it," he said quietly. He lifted his finger and lightly traced the arc of her cheek.

How could the lightest of touches throb like a pulse between Josie's legs?

"What happens if this doesn't work?" she asked, unsure whether she meant what was happening between herself and Pax, or reviving Number Five. "No matter how hard I try, I can't imagine a scenario where this turns out well," Josie said. "What happens when Number Five's tank fills back up? What if . . . ?"

Pax smiled, an occurrence so rare it called up butterflies in her stomach and made her dizzy.

"What if you told yourself a story?" he said gently. "By the end of the story, you are guaranteed to have a happy ending. Can you imagine that? Being happy in the end?"

"I don't know." Josie was too tired not to be honest. "I've never tried."

Pax lifted the palm of his hand and cradled her face.

"You don't believe you deserve happiness."

Josie blinked hard against her tears, but she didn't move away from him.

"You do," he told her. "You do deserve to be happy."

To hear the secret words of her heart, the desire for a happy ending, scared her. To hear them in a man's voice made her even more frightened. What if Josie once again believed in another person's promises? How many times could her heart break before there was nothing left of it?

"How can I believe in a story so filled with magic when magic doesn't exist in this world?" she asked. "A brave knight, a troupe of faeries, a changing staircase—all of this is something out of a lonely girl's fever dream."

Pax's smile widened to the point where it bordered on goofy. Josie's insides turned from mushy to actual liquid at the sight.

"I'm your fever dream?" he asked happily, the goofiness spreading to his wide, surprised eyes.

Josie couldn't help but smile back even though she knew her smile was probably as goofy.

"Mom, I can has some lasagna with my nuggets?" Amos called from inside the apartment.

At the sound of her son's voice, Josie stepped away and shook her head. The critic who lived in her brain wouldn't let her hold on to maudlin wishes like happy endings and trustworthy hearts for long.

The goofy smile on his face melted into disappointment. For the first time since she met him, Pax was easy to read.

Dammit.

Damn her for a sucker.

"Lasagna and nuggets are a terrific taste combination, Mr. Pax," she said, forcing lightness into her words. "C'mon in and let us open your culinary horizons."

In the orphanage where he grew up, the children had been taught to read, but there had been no storybooks for children. They learned to read for practical purposes. Pax's old commander used to say an army runs on stomachs and shitters, and even the most lowly of soldiers should know how to build a waste pit and make a hot meal.

As such, Pax read books on engineering, botany, geology, and accounting. Accounting had been the most important class, because if you were going to fill those stomachs (and those shitters), you had to pay for the food.

He'd wager Josie hadn't grown up with a lot of storybooks, either. If she had, she'd be more comfortable with happy endings.

"You can read 'nother book, Mr. Pax?"

Pax sat on the floor of Amos's bedroom on a blue carpet decorated with red webbing. Next to him sat Amos, and surrounding them both were heaps of children's books. Amos had eventually calmed down and eaten his chicken nuggets, then had a second dinner when Josie warmed up the lasagna.

After, both Pax and Amos were disappointed there was no screen time because of Amos's behavior earlier, but high spirits had been restored when Amos was allowed to have four books before bedtime.

"I gonna pick the longest books, Mr. Pax," Amos had confided. "We'll stay up for a long time."

First, they'd read a book about Busytown. Pax found this world fascinating and resolved to find out more about why animals dressed as humans made such compelling characters. They read a book about trucks, complete with smells and textures. Amazing. Next came *The Cat in the Hat*, which had Pax on the edge of his seat. Having visited a world full of beings remarkably like the cat, Pax was thrilled when everything ended up with neither bloodshed nor loss of limbs.

Amos had tried to get Pax to read a Sonic chapter book, but Josie had caught on to Amos's plan, and they finished with *Don't Let the Pigeon Drive the Bus!*

Pax would have continued to read through Amos's entire collection, but Josie was as disciplined as his old commander although, happily, softer and better smelling.

"I am afraid we have reached our limit, Mr. Amos," Pax said.

He'd hovered in the doorway as the little family completed their ritual. Kissing Amos on the forehead was standard human tradition as he'd seen it before on Miss Nekesa's Barbie DVDs. The rest—a song, a hug in a certain position, a recitation of blessings and discussion of which donut is the superior donut (neither of them were correct in pointing out the obvious superiority of chocolate peanut-covered) appeared organic to the two of them.

At the thought of them partaking in this exchange every night, Pax had to smother an intense jealousy that growled in his gut like hunger.

"Have you read every book in Amos's library?" he asked Josie later as they drank tea in the living room.

Josie raised her brows as though the answer should be obvious. "Many, many times over," she said.

"And, afterward, the two of you sing a song and do the other things you did tonight?" he asked.

"Mmmm." Josie nodded in the affirmative as she sipped her tea. She caught her bottom lip with her teeth. "Did you think it was weird, or too much, or . . . ?"

Pax shook his head no. "How is it you can have such a beautiful child and still have such great doubt about your abilities?"

Setting a hand to her chest, Josie winced. "Ow. Okay, straight to the heavy stuff, huh?"

He shrugged. "I apologize. I was genuinely curious. I did not see it as 'heavy stuff.'"

Josie set her tea on the low table in front of the sofa, and her hair fell from behind her shoulder into a wave of brown and gold. Her hair smelled like a candy back on his world, one made from extraordinarily tiny flowers called Harpsingers.

Normally, a man like Pax, even though he was a paladin, would never have been able to taste a Harpsingers candy. One ounce of the sweet was worth more than an ounce of gold or diamonds. He'd attended a crowning ceremony as a guard, however, and each guest had received a fingernail-size piece of candy wrapped in a bag made of silk shot through with gold. The bags had been placed on the center of each plate when the guests sat at the coronation dinner.

Lady Vanigna, aunt to the new king, had picked hers up and sniffed in dismay. "How exceedingly banal," she'd announced, and thrown the bag over her shoulder. It had hit Pax in the chest and he'd caught it, but when he made to return it to her, she told him to keep it.

For a long time, he'd treasured the candy, taking it out now and again during the worst of campaigns just to smell it. The scent alone could make him forget the carnage feet away from his tent flap and instead remember hot summer afternoons and the relief of a quick plunge into an icy river.

Josie's hair smelled like that candy.

This was the perfectly sound excuse for why, when she sat up, he didn't move away quickly enough, and she caught him sniffing her head.

Pax's face heated at her amused grin. How was it a man as universally feared as himself turned into a foolish child in the company of one tiny human woman?

"It's pretty easy to second-guess yourself as a parent these days," Josie said, graciously ignoring his embarrassment. "Especially as a single mother from a 'broken home.'"

Unfamiliar with the motions she made with her fingers when she said, "broken home," Pax frowned and shifted his body to face Josie's and better see her expressions.

"It's what some people call families where there aren't traditional parents, like a mom and dad, or conventional supports." Josie sighed. "Usually, it describes the household of a poor single mother."

"In the Princess Barbie movies, she often comes from a broken home," he informed her. "Shocking, how often parents die or are taken away by enchantment in these worlds."

"Yeah," she said lightly. "Well, my mother was taken away by an enchantment to drugs, and I don't know who my father is, so not as exciting as Princess Barbie. I've been alone since I was sixteen. I'm flying blind with a lot of this parenting stuff."

"Flying blind means . . . ?"

"Making it up as I go along," she answered. "Gloria knows this. It's why she's waiting for me to fuck it up, and oh my God, here I go complaining to you again."

Not for the first time, Pax wished for his sword and Butthead and an enemy he could cleave in two.

"Gloria wants you to fail?" he asked.

"She wants to take Amos away from me."

Anger at the thought nearly choked him.

"She cannot," he said firmly, shaking his head while Josie explained about custody and laws and whatever other stupid human rules governing parents and children there were that made no sense to Pax. Genuine anguish underlay Josie's words but the source of it wasn't anything he could touch . . . or kill.

"It helps to talk to someone about it. Now that I say it out loud, it doesn't sound as bleak as it did when it was running around in my brain."

"I wish I could do more than simply listen," Pax said. "I want to . . ." The words dried up when Josie shifted her position to sit facing him, one arm on the back of the couch and that hand holding her head, fingers entwined with her candy hair.

She was not the most beautiful woman he'd encountered in all the worlds. Nor was she the most clever or the most amusing. Instead, she embodied a mix of these traits that seemed to be tailored specifically for him.

"Yes?" Josie asked softly, waiting for him to finish his thought.

The time for thinking had passed, however.

"I want to kiss you again, Josie," he told her, eyes on her mouth with lips the color of spring flowers. "I want to listen to your fears as well, but after that, so we don't forget, I want very much to kiss you."

Josie's lips parted and his body tensed at the sight.

"I want to kiss you, too, Pax."

Her eyes sparkled in the dim light and a thread of desire ran up his spine when he leaned forward to kiss her, gently at first, the briefest brush of his lips against hers like a shower of sparks until the flame took hold and he kissed her deeply, taking her breath and returning it with his.

Her mouth tasted sweet like vanilla tea, and he stroked the satin skin of her cheeks with the tips of his fingers, relishing the friction when she shivered at his touch. Unlike the last time, they moved slowly, building heat. He kept the kisses long and slow until she pushed against him and lapped at his tongue like a cat.

The sensation went straight to his cock, and he leaned forward, caging her in his arms. She arched into his chest, but when he stroked her waist, letting his fingers casually pull up the sides of her shirt, she pulled back.

Although unaccustomed to wooing women, Pax was accustomed to watching and learning. He was hyperaware of every move she made, the speed of her pulse, and the tiny ways she adjusted her body to his.

Reluctantly, Pax broke the kiss and rested his hands on her shoulders. "I do not wish to overstay my welcome. Thank you, for dinner. For letting me read with Amos. For . . . this."

Josie panted as though they'd run a race, her eyes unfocused. "It felt good," she assured him. "I'm overwhelmed. It's been a long time since I—" She stopped and looked away as though suddenly pained. "Since I've been kissed," Josie finished.

Foolish man, why had he wanted her to say something else, something more?

One last kiss, a sweet note of finality, and he said good night.

Pax kept his composure until the elevator doors closed on him, and he slumped, banging his forehead against the wall.

"What is wrong with me?" he said aloud, secretly hoping Number Five was listening and could send him a sign of what he might do next, but all that happened was a shower of thick, soft cabbage rose petals fell on his head.

Chapter Seventeen

All I'm saying is the pigeon should know bus drivers are unionized. How is it appropriate to have a children's book glorifying a scab?"

The attendants of Miss Nekesa's Thursday-night Story Time stared at the speaker blankly.

"I likes to eat my scabs," Amos offered.

Miss Nekesa, head librarian of the East Avenue branch of the public library, glared over her copy of *Don't Let the Pigeon Drive the Bus!* at Denis, who had interrupted her for the third time. Denis, who sat cross-legged on the carpet in the middle of a group of wet-headed children as if he hadn't a care in the world.

Story time was the endcap of the traditional Thursday-night routine for a gaggle of neighborhood four- and five-year-olds and was preceded by tofu hot dogs at Dogtown, then swim classes at the Y, after which most kids changed into their pj's instead of back into their school clothes.

Josie and Amos were regulars at Story Time. From the exchange of scowls between Miss Nekesa and Denis, tonight was the first time he'd been to Story Time but not the first time he'd been in the library. Josie glanced at the glass vestibule in the front of the library but no Pax or Maddy were in sight.

Was this even legal, letting Denis out unsupervised among the general population? Dammit. He was going to blow Number Five's cover.

"Mr. Denis, we wait until the book is finished before we ask questions," Miss Nekesa said. With doe-like brown eyes, a snub nose, and a smile that lit her face, Miss Nekesa held a goddess-like place in the eyes of the children—and most of the adults—who frequented this branch.

The fact Denis had interrupted her during story time earned him the awe and enmity of the crowd of kindergarteners surrounding him.

Denis huffed, but even he must have had some sort of survival instincts, because he held his tongue until Miss Nekesa finished the story.

When he tried to restart a discussion about the connection between union busting and the Freemasons, he was quickly shut down by the little girl to his left, who explained he hadn't held up a hand first, so he didn't get to talk.

"Oh, I have to signal my subservience to the institutional leadership if I want my opinion to be heard?" he retorted.

"You stayed past your turn on the computer and Miss Nekesa had to give you a red checkmark," the little girl said matter-of-factly. "You're lucky she lets you sit on the alphabet carpet for story time and not on the fruit carpet for kids who can't listen to directions."

Josie was saved from intervening by the little girl's mother, who'd caught sight of her daughter chastising an unfamiliar adult and come to scoop the child up and hustle her out the doors. The rest of the kids slowly drifted away after picking their allotted three picture books.

Having nabbed the coveted beanbag chair, Amos would stay put until the library closed if Josie let him. He sat contentedly with a pile of Busytown books, searching the illustrations for Lowly Worm and making up a story to go along with them while squirming around and enjoying the satisfying crunching sound beneath his butt.

"As a woman of color, I would think you of all people would promote children's literature upholding the importance of unions," Denis whined.

Josie cast one last glance outside in case help was coming, then turned her attention back to Denis. He'd left the carpet and now stood in front of Miss Nekesa in a confrontational pose, arms crossed, tinfoil-hatted head tipped back so he could glower.

Miss Nekesa, for her part, appeared nonplussed by Denis's scolding, looking every inch a cool librarian from the blue-and-silver-rhinestone pin at her throat to her glow-in-the-dark star-print skirt falling in neat folds from her hips to mid-calf.

"Tell me more about what I should do as a woman of color," she said dryly. "I find it fascinating coming from a White man."

If by "White," she meant gray?

If Josie hadn't known about Denis's gnomic origins, would she have seen clearly what he was? Did Miss Nekesa not wonder about his skin and his hats and his general . . . gnomeishness?

"We'll see what you say when I show up to the main library's Community Input Forum next week," Denis countered. "I am organizing a large group of constituents who share my concerns about the messages these Story Time readings promote."

A mental image of members from the tenants' association piling into the downtown library's meeting room and quarrelling over the propriety of Mo Willems books sent a shiver of fear down Josie's spine.

"Uh," Josie blurted, completely at a loss about how to defuse the situation. It couldn't be a good idea for Denis to make himself the center of attention. "Uh, Miss Nekesa. Thank you for story time tonight. I wish there had been amazing books like the Pigeon books when I was growing up."

Miss Nekesa appeared relieved at Josie's interruption. "Yes, Mo Willems is a national treasure, isn't he?"

Josie nodded vigorously and Denis turned his scowl on her.

"Huh," he said. "What kind of literature was your generation force-fed that you see union-busting pigeons as literary heroes?"

A flush heated Josie's face and she clenched her fist at his dismissive tone.

"The message of *Pigeon* is when you make a promise, you have a responsibility to follow through no matter what arguments people might make," Josie explained. "It's fun for kids to be the ones who say no for a change."

Denis issued a derisory snort in response but signaled his disinterest in further argument with a one-shouldered shrug.

"Amos and I were heading home," Josie said, taking advantage of her momentum. "Did you want to walk back with us, Denis?"

Josie did not want Denis anywhere near her and Amos, but it wasn't a good idea to leave him here with Miss Nekesa, either. He was bound to say something that couldn't be explained away.

Her resolution nearly deserted her when Denis's gaze fixed on Amos, now singing to himself while hanging upside down on the beanbag. Surely, if the guy was dangerous, Pax would have told her.

"I'm not leaving," Denis declared.

"Everyone is welcome to stay until closing," Miss Nekesa said in a tight voice, no doubt thinking how *lucky* she was to have chosen a public-facing job at the library. "If you'll excuse me, I'm off to help Mr. Raj check out some books."

Denis stared at Miss Nekesa's back with a frown, then turned his attention back to Josie.

"It's not working, you know," he said.

"No," she said honestly. "I don't know. What's not working?"

Denis crossed his arms and tapped his foot, the picture of impatience. "You. You're not helping. The golden needle hasn't moved an inch."

This was one of those times Josie wished she could channel her coworker Barb's energy. What would Denis do if Josie told him to fuck off?

The thought was equal parts terrifying and thrilling.

"It might have worked if someone could tell me what exactly I'm supposed to be doing," she snapped, the closest Josie could come to a "fuck off."

As soon as she said it, Josie wished she could take it back.

Ridiculous as it was to feel responsible for something she hadn't known about or offered to do, Josie nevertheless struggled to breathe through a surge of guilt. When Pax had explained about the—well, there was no way for her to pronounce what they called the gauge measuring Number Five's fuel—he'd assured Josie she didn't have to find any magical grails or solve ancient riddles.

She just needed to trust Number Five.

Hard to figure out how to trust an apartment building but Josie had promised to try.

Now Denis was over here insinuating Josie was supposed to be doing something and not only that, was doing it wrong?

"How am I supposed to know what you should do?" Denis asked. "Those big shots like Maddy and Raphe, they'd never let someone like me near the precious Wayside Handbook. They think I'm no danger to anyone, just a cute little gnome."

"No one thinks you're a cute little anything, Denis," Josie said dryly.

Luckily, Denis was the right amount of self-absorbed not to take offense, assuming Josie agreed with his complaints.

"I have places to go, little missy," he snarled. "Important places. I am an important person where I'm from."

This is where Josie would usually tell Denis of course *he* was important and she would do whatever it took to get him to that important place.

Except.

The way he said it, he implied Josie was *not* important.

Dammit, she was important. To her son. To herself. Maybe to a few other folks.

Screw Denis for poking at her sore spots.

"I have lives depending on me as well, Denis," Josie shot back. "I do the best I can do with what I'm given. No. I do *better* than most with what I'm given. Back off and trust Number Five."

"Whatever," was his stimulating retort.

Whatever? Where were the high fives and trumpets? Josie had clapped back for the first time in forever and hadn't been slapped down by an immediate wave of guilt when she did it.

That felt awesome.

Maybe Denis would have a little more respect the next time he spoke to her. Maybe he could treat her like a fellow tenant and not like an interloper.

Maybe they could someday be friends.

"I'm going out and getting drunk." Denis readjusted his cap and stalked toward the exit.

Okay.

Maybe not.

Either way, the thought of Denis getting drunk and going off on a rant did not sound like a good idea. Damn Pax for not having a cell phone.

Josie hustled Amos into his coat and jiggled with anxiety as Mr. Raj checked out Amos's books. Denis had already left. She spotted him through the window, trudging down the slushy sidewalk.

"Mom, I can have a snack?" Amos asked as they made their way up the walkway to the entrance of Number Five. "I can have some carrots, or celery, or ice cream?"

"Sure, buddy," Josie said, distracted. As soon as they entered the lobby, the lights flickered, and a row of mailboxes rattled. "I'm going to talk to Mr. Pax real quick."

Josie knocked on Pax's office door and tried the handle, but the door was locked.

"Mr. Pax," she called, and knocked again. "I have to tell you something."

The doorknob twisted beneath her hand and Josie stepped back, but the door didn't open. A muted curse came from behind the door and the knob twisted back and forth again.

"Umm." Josie looked around, but Amos was counting birds on the staircase and not paying attention. "Umm, Number Five?" Josie whispered. "Can you open this door? I need some help."

Josie didn't know if she was relieved or creeped out when she heard a quiet *click* and the door finally opened.

It wasn't Pax, though. Maddy stood in the doorway, clearly annoyed.

"What?" Maddy asked.

Josie tried to peer around her to see if Pax was there, but Maddy stood so none of the office was visible behind her.

Whether Pax was with her or not behind a locked door wasn't important.

"Denis is on his way to a bar to get drunk and he's in a mood."

That was important.

"I'll kill him." Maddy stepped out of the doorway and closed the door behind her so quickly Josie had no time to see if she'd been alone.

Not that this mattered. Because Maddy sounded as though she really was going to kill Denis. Josie didn't like the guy—gnome, whatever—but she didn't want him to die.

What better reminder she shouldn't be crushing on Pax than the fact he was a knight from another dimension who managed a hotel full of mythical creatures who could wreak serious havoc on her world if they got it into their heads to do so.

This entire situation gave Josie a headache. And a stomachache. Any high she'd experienced from her bravery in the library was now extinguished.

"Don't kill him," Josie said as Maddy stalked toward the front door. "That would attract attention."

Maddy turned and shot her a disbelieving look. "I watch your television. People kill each other all the time here."

"Mom says there's a lot of bad stuff on grown-up TV." Amos had left off counting birds and wandered over to Josie's side. He took hold of her hand and pulled. "Can we haves a snack now?"

Josie nodded at Amos although she aimed her words at Maddy. "That's right, buddy. There is a lot more violence on grown-up TV than there is in the real world. Those shows make us feel unsafe so we stay home and buy more stuff. In the real world we don't go around killing each other in bars because the *police* would come."

A movement in the corner of her eye caught Josie's attention and she glanced over to see Bert, this time in a Lions jersey, shaking his head and mouthing something unintelligible to her.

Maddy must have understood, because she sighed theatrically. "Fine. I'm going to go get Denis and have a long talk with him about his actions and their consequences." She coated that last word with such sweetness it hurt Josie's teeth.

"Before I go, do you know what set him off?" Maddy asked.

Josie cut a glance to Bert, then at Amos, who was now holding her hand and leaning toward the stairs, essentially using her as a pole for his I-want-a-snack dance.

"He said"—Josie lowered her voice and leaned in toward Maddy—"he said I wasn't working."

Sympathy from Maddy was the last thing Josie expected, but the derisive snort the other woman let out still stung.

"I suppose I can't blame him for being frustrated," Maddy said. "This whole experiment has been deeply disappointing."

With those warm words, Maddy left the building.

Bert shrugged sympathetically, but Josie's headache intensified and lasted even after her and Amos's nighttime snack of carrots and celery and ice cream.

Experiments had a beginning and an end.

How long would this one last, and would she and Amos be allowed to stay once the experiment was finished?

Pax knocked softly on the door and counted to five. If Josie didn't answer, he would leave. It was after ten, and she went to bed early, and this was a dumb idea, and he should . . .

"Hi."

Pax blinked.

Josie's hair was again in the shape of a cinnamon roll atop her head, but pieces of the roll had fallen apart and framed her face. She looked as though she were staring out at him from behind a heart. She wore an enormous blue-and-red shirt with a white buffalo on the front, and baggy blue-and-white flannel pants.

Something about the combination of big clothes and messy hair caught him off guard. Before he could pinpoint what made her enticing in this state, she frowned.

Damn. How long had he been staring?

"Maddy didn't kill Denis."

That's all he wanted to tell her. There was no other reason he should be standing here, disturbing her rest and gawking at her.

"I wanted to let you know," he said.

Josie nodded. "Thanks."

That was it.

The kisses they shared last night must not have been very memorable or enjoyable.

Pax was going to turn around and leave.

Right now.

"In case you were worried," he said.

In case she hadn't understood the first time and wanted to ask him a question.

"Okay," Josie said.

So, that was that. Message delivered. Time to go.

He remained standing.

Josie blinked, then took a step back. "Do you want to come in for a—"

"I don't want to bother you," Pax said, even as he crossed the threshold. "Maddy told me about earlier tonight and I wanted to set your mind at ease."

Did she believe him?

Pax couldn't tell. He didn't know Josie well enough to be familiar with the shape of the frown now bowing her lips and drawing her eyebrows down to bump into each other at a deep furrow above her nose.

"Denis said I wasn't working," she said.

Ah. That was the frown Josie wore when worried. He would remember and try to erase it when he saw it.

"Denis has a way of twisting everything into a complaint," Pax replied. "He cannot know if you and Amos are helping or not. Simply because events aren't happening fast enough to his liking doesn't mean they aren't happening."

The frown hadn't completely disappeared, but now Josie pushed her lower lip out farther than her top lip, and she appeared less anxious and more thoughtful.

She had a compelling lower lip.

A buzzing sensation came to life at the base of his spine.

"What happens if this doesn't work. Do Amos and I leave?" she asked.

His stomach dropped and Pax put his hand on the wall to steady himself. This meant he was half caging Josie against the wall. Another step closer and his chin would be brushing the crown of her head.

"No," he said firmly. "No. If this isn't working, we will find another way, but Number Five wants you here."

He paused, then lifted her chin gently with his other hand. Her eyes widened and the buzzing grew stronger.

How could a woman's skin be so soft?

"We both want you here," he confessed.

He should back away. It wasn't right for him to crowd her like this. He'd been through the mandatory HR training and seen the videos. But the sconces to the left and right of them had dimmed and she set her palm on his chest, not to push him away but to settle over his heart.

Still. Consent was key.

"Pax," she whispered. "I don't know . . ."

"Say the word and I will leave," he told her, his eyes locked on her lips when she wet them with her tiny pink tongue and his cock hardened. "I will not take anything further than what you want."

The floorboard directly beneath Josie's toes lifted up and she grabbed Pax around the neck, gasping in surprise.

"Number Five, behave," he scolded, but Josie was giggling and the sound made him lightheaded, so he had to hold on to her in return. The closer they held each other, the less the world around them—the walls and bricks enclosing them, the responsibilities awaiting them, the looming questions of what if and when—the less *any* of it mattered.

Kisses were magic. Not in the strict sense, but in the sense that the simple brush of lips against lips could conjure a lust so sudden and strong at the exact same time it also filled you with a sense of satisfaction as comforting as finding a warm spot directly in the center of a sunbeam.

Pax could say with certainty that Josie could perform some magic; her kisses were soft and damp, starting out hesitant and sweet. So sweet he was back to his boyhood when tag was foreplay and holding hands made his heart explode. They changed after the first few seconds to adult kisses, long and hard, tongues and teeth.

Even though he canted his hips to rest his hard-on in the

valley of Josie's thighs, Pax remained focused on kissing her. She tasted like nothing else he'd ever had on his tongue, better than whiskey, better than pie. Because of the difference in their heights, he had to pick her up to hold her close. He didn't want her to break off from kissing because her neck hurt.

Pax didn't want anything of Josie's to hurt.

Josie pulled her lips from his, bending her head until their foreheads touched.

"We can't be out here. What if Amos wakes up?"

"Number Five will tell us if he wakes up," he said to Josie. "Won't you?" he asked Number Five.

In response, the sconces winked off and on.

"Whoa," Josie whispered. "Does Number Five like frozen custard?"

Panic squeezed his stomach. "Is that a joke?"

Josie's head tilted back when she let out a laugh that sounded like a satisfied sigh and the noise gave him a charge, like the slick sting of electricity, and he pulled her even closer, relishing the way her thighs pressed around his hips.

"We should get out of the hallway," she whispered.

Out of the hallway to the bedroom?

Thankfully, Pax didn't ask this out loud.

Too much, too soon. For them both.

Instead, keeping Josie held tight against him, Pax walked into the living room and settled them both on a soft green couch.

They resumed their kisses, finding a pace in between furious and languid; she trailed the tip of her tongue along the side of his neck until he made a noise, then returned her lips to his. He licked the skin above her pulse and relished the tiny lift of her hips in response. Sweet soft touches, tentative exploration, the sound of night falling gently outside, and the plush slide of cotton against velvet combined to leave him lightheaded and vulnerable.

Not once since he'd joined the army had Pax felt this vulnerable.

Vulnerable and weightless.

A thousand warriors of the Dark could challenge him right now and he'd surrender. Happy to leave this plane on the heels of such a carnal yet pure experience.

Who knows how long they kissed, slowly tumbling to the side and rearranging themselves so Josie lay on top of him, free to let her hands roam where they wanted and discover whatever she wished to find?

In return, she allowed Pax to slip his hands beneath her shirt to find a clingy short chemise, and beneath this, the sweet, heavy fullness of her breasts.

Another time or place, he would have pulled the sweater off over her head to better see her body. From the cushioned thighs and the plumpness of her breasts, he could tell she would be stunning, but Number Five would only do so much to give them privacy.

Rather than wishing for something he hadn't yet earned, Pax let Josie tell him how far he could go and what gave her pleasure. By midnight, the two of them lay facing each other, her hand down his sweatpants and his palm between her legs, adrift in a cloud of sated lust, self-conscious laughter, and the potent scent of what could be.

"Please," Pax whispered, relishing the invisible sparks tickling his lips when they brushed up against Josie's earlobe, "don't let Denis scare you off. If I could get rid of him, I would, but he paid for his room, and I can't kick him out unless he violates the Wayside Oath."

Josie shivered at his words.

He pulled her tight against him. "I'll keep him away from you and Amos, I promise."

"Don't," she said quickly. The return of the frown from before, the one that unsettled him so, gave him a low, dull ache in his belly where before there had been contentment. "Don't promise me anything, Pax. I'm not ready to believe it."

Later, after they'd detangled themselves, after he'd kissed her a long good-night, after he'd walked through every corner of the building making sure all was quiet, Pax thought back on Josie's words.

What kind of world was this where a woman would believe in magic before she would believe in kindness?

Chapter Eighteen

Stop looking at me."

Silence met Josie's demand.

"I mean it, you two. You're weirding me out."

Barb's and Jenna's desks faced each other's in the rectangular-shaped Financial Aid Office. Unlike the outer office, which looked out into the lobby of the Admin Building and Ben's office and the meeting room along the outside wall, the space where Josie and her coworkers sat had no windows.

There was a massive corkboard on one end stuffed with flyers about every conceivable on-campus or university-affiliated event as well as rideshare ads and help wanted notices. The rest of the walls held a smattering of framed Monet prints hung crookedly over the institutional butter yellow paint, and one lone copy of the university's official calendar. Not much there to capture a person's attention.

Not that Barb and Jenna cared enough about what Josie thought to pretend to be looking at anything other than her.

They'd been at it since eight this morning.

Josie had even looked up harassment guidelines in the university employee handbook.

"I'm admiring the fact that a lovely color has returned to your cheeks," Barbara said with a straight face.

"Uh-huh," Josie scoffed. She turned to Jenna. "What about you, Jenna? Want me to blink my eyes at something? Looking for my cyber ransom note?"

"I've never seen you wear that shirt before," Jenna said. "It brings out the blue in your eyes."

The shirt was five years old. Josie had worn it at least three times a month for the past two years.

Josie narrowed her eyes.

Enough.

"Fine," she spat. "I have a lovely color and my eyes are sparkling. Was there a question you had for me? A guess as to *why* my eyes are sparkling?"

Jenna and Barb traded glances.

Barb shrugged and batted her eyelashes, the picture of innocence. "I don't know, Josephine. Why are your eyes sparkling?"

"And does it have anything to do with that bouquet of flowers on your desk?" Jenna asked in a high, questioning tone.

The flowers.

They were on Josie's desk when she arrived at work this morning.

A huge arrangement of sunflowers.

There was a card, but it was a get-well card with no name or message on the other side.

"Have you been sick?" Jenna asked the instant Josie set foot inside the door.

"I bet it was the only free card left," Barbara whispered to Jenna five minutes later when they stood at the copier pretending to copy but staring at Josie's flowers instead.

"You know," Josie said now, "it's possible I have a social life.

Maybe I went out last night and met a nice man and he's sending me flowers because he likes me."

"Out," repeated Jenna, enunciating the word. "Out, like someone with a social life."

Was that so hard to believe?

"We all deserve flowers, dear. You can tell us you bought them for yourself, you know," Barbara said.

My God, was Josie truly so pathetic that neither woman entertained the idea an admirer would send Josie flowers? They acted as though the bouquet was one more symptom of whatever they thought was wrong with Josie lately.

Despite her constant protestations that no, she wasn't being threatened, and no, she hadn't tweaked her meds, and *no,* she wasn't going to the new church two blocks away that smelled like burnt popcorn, the women persisted in coming up with the most outrageous theories for her recent "personality change."

"I'm going to go in there and tell Ben we need a weekly meeting to discuss the premeeting meetings needed for the number of meetings we've scheduled for the week," Josie threatened.

Barbara gasped in horror and Jenna held up her first two fingers in a crooked V and shook them in Josie's direction.

"You wouldn't," Barbara insisted.

"I will give you each one direct answer to one direct question, then you will stop speculating about my emotional state," Josie said. "After that, no more staring at me and muttering to yourselves unless you're trying to figure out how to tell me I've won the lottery."

"The lottery is rigged," Barbara said.

Jenna swung around in her desk chair and gazed intently at Josie. Her thin nose quivered as though readying itself to sniff out the truth.

"Have you joined a cult?" she asked.

Oh, for fuck's sake.

"No," Josie said. "No cults. I'm Catholic. We frown on organizations that ask you outright for donations instead of guilting you into it by standing next to you with a basket."

Cracking her knuckles, Barbara took over. She stood, wobbling in her pink-yellow-and-purple Fluevogs on the uneven carpet. Like a shark circling its prey, she stalked around Josie's desk, eyeing the flowers, eyeing Josie, eyeing Josie's desk until Josie almost called the whole thing off.

"Does he make you happy?" Barb asked.

Oh.

There was something to contemplate.

"I thought I was responsible for my own happiness," Josie countered.

Did Pax make her happy?

Was he truly the reason Josie had felt more confident of late?

Yes and no.

Pax's attentions made her feel good—better than good. Attractive. Interesting. All the things a woman should feel when a man kisses her with enough passion to wobble her knees.

However.

This confidence, it wasn't born solely from those kisses. Life had been tough lately, but Josie hadn't fallen apart. She hadn't turned into her momma, either.

She was living in a magical apartment building that was a living organism, and her neighbors were faeries and vampires, and instead of losing her mind, she was making a garden with them.

Choices had been made, and although they terrified her every time, Josie had made some solid and healthy ones.

The world was bigger than she'd ever imagined, but Josie hadn't lost her place in it.

Unsettling, really, Josie was growing up simultaneously with her own child, but she held a suspicion even the most adult-like of adults struggled with indecision and insecurity, just like their kids.

Barb shrugged. "You can't make yourself happy if the person you love doesn't want the same."

He did, though. Deep in Josie's soul, she knew Pax wanted happiness for her. Even if it came at his expense.

Except. She didn't love him.

Right?

These emotions, they weren't love. A responsible parent wouldn't fall in love with a magical knight whose kisses were disorienting and who made them feel cherished. A responsible parent would know things, like what political party they belonged to and the relative toxicity of their childhood, and what they've done lately to stop climate change.

This wasn't love.

It couldn't be.

"**The tokoloshe on** the second floor set a fire in the waste bin of the community room," Maddy said.

Pax nodded.

"That's the third fire they've set this month."

Did Josie like her flowers?

On Pax's world, a knight brought his lady favors when they were courting. Flowers. Books. Ribbons.

Wait, did Josie know they were courting?

How was courting defined on this world?

"They got into a fight with Harry, the sulik in 3F, and dented the window shade," Maddy continued.

Pax nodded again.

On Pax's world, a male relative needed to give permission to the knight to court a lady.

"The residents of the sixth floor have woken and eaten everyone in a three-mile radius."

Pax made a sound of encouragement.

Would Pax have to ask Amos if he could court his mother? How would he phrase it to the boy?

"Shit!" Pax jumped at the sharp pain in his hand where Maddy stabbed him with her pin. "Why did you do that?" he asked.

Clad in a suit made from a blue shiny sort of material, Maddy sat cross-legged on the corner of his desk, while he was trapped in his rickety chair with a broken backrest. Reams of paper sat in untidy piles behind her and the carcasses of two laptop computers lay in front of him.

She repinned a large sparkling brooch to the lapel of her jacket and sniffed slightly in that way she had of insinuating you were stupid or small. Or both.

"You're not listening to me," Maddy said calmly.

"I am," he argued. "The sulik is being a dick, and the sixth floor . . ." Pax stopped. "Okay, you're correct. I wasn't listening."

"You need to do your job, Pax."

"How—"

She held up her palm near his face and he swallowed his question. Obviously, Maddy was in the mood for a lecture. Having been on the receiving end of lances, flaming arrows, sword points, and acid attacks, Pax could easily stomach a lecture, so he pushed himself away from the desk and leaned back, ready to listen.

He'd forgotten about the broken chair, though, and fell backward off it onto the green linoleum-tiled floor.

Perfect.

"I did not want you for the job of hotel manager," Maddy said, ignoring Pax's prone position and occasional painful groans as he pulled himself up to stand.

"I know," Pax groused. "You told me within the first five minutes I started."

Maddy had preferred working with the last hotel manager, Manny Quintas. Quintas had let Maddy take control of most everything from check-in procedures to schedules.

By the time Pax arrived, she'd expanded the Wayside's Rules and Regulations from 38 rules to 843.

"You are too lenient with the guests and far too lenient with the staff," Maddy began.

"You and I are the only staff," Pax pointed out. He rubbed his tailbone and gazed at the heap of metal and wood that once was his desk chair.

"Because you let them go," she countered. "We shouldn't be cleaning up after tokoloshes and dealing with Denis's plumbing issues. We have more important things to do."

Had this office shrunk? Pax spun on his heel and examined the walls. It might have shrunk; it might be his own suffocation projecting onto the walls. He didn't want to be inside listening to Maddy lecture him, worrying about an empty tank and missing Scrabble letters.

He wanted to be with Josie.

"I can't keep them asleep forever, Pax."

Pax pushed his palm into his forehead as though he could contain this obsession with Josie and place it somewhere out of reach. She was one woman, and the fate of hundreds of beings depended on the health of Number Five. *That* is what should be filling his brain.

Sighing, Pax walked around the desk and faced Maddy. Not too close, though, because he was admittedly scared of her snake hair. It was unnerving when those little tongues flicked out at him.

"I cannot imagine the strain of having to keep a floor full of gods and goddesses asleep until they reach their destinations. We are alive and well because of you and your power."

Maddy sniffed. "I'm not looking for compliments." She examined her nails, as though what she should say next was written in minuscule letters on the red acrylic.

Perhaps it was. Nail art was a mystery to Pax.

"I'm looking for a way off this lump of coal," she said. "Has the needle moved at all?"

Pax sighed and Maddy's lips thinned to a sneer.

"You are besotted with that woman and her child," she accused.

What was Pax to say? Was "besotted" the same as "obsessed"?

Both words meant a loss of control, meant placing the importance of the LaChiusas over the importance of the people he'd sworn to protect.

Maddy slipped off the desk and pointed her forefinger into Pax's chest.

"Ow," he objected.

"The reason I didn't want you as hotel manager was I knew the responsibilities. To most people, this appears to be an easy job. It's not."

Was she worried Pax couldn't handle the stress?

Of course, Maddy knew what he was thinking. "I know you can handle the job, Pax. My concern was you shouldn't have to.

You should have been given a respite after your years at war, and instead you were given even more responsibility."

"I don't mind," he objected. "It's not more than I can handle."

She scoffed. "Right. You can handle anything, because you're a brave war hero who can stick people with a sword, yada yada."

What did "yada yada" mean?

"Even if you can work past the point of exhaustion, you shouldn't have to. If what's happening with Number Five is to teach us anything, it's we all need to refill our tanks now and again. Have you ever considered what you need to fill yours?"

If Maddy had even a hint of sympathy in her eyes while delivering this speech, Pax might have fainted in shock. Her expression, though, was of supreme annoyance.

Maddy went to the office door, put her hand on the doorknob, then paused. She didn't look back at him when she spoke, but Pax felt the heat of her stare anyway.

"This infatuation with the woman and her son. Ask yourself, will this help you fill your tank or will it drain the last of your energy instead?"

Chapter Nineteen

"I don't know, Josephine."

Gloria stood outside the running car holding Amos's overnight bag with two fingers, mouth twisted into a spiral of disdain. "Given the vomit incident a few weeks ago, I am having second thoughts about this whole endeavor."

When Gloria and Al came this morning to pick Amos up for his regular day with them, Gloria had—without any advanced notice—asked that Amos spend the night with them.

The woman couldn't possibly know Josie had plans for dinner. Expecting Josie would say no, Gloria immediately backpedaled when Josie had surprised her with a yes.

Not because Josie thought anything would happen with Pax, just because Gloria's reaction had been funny.

Nothing to do with Pax at all.

"Well," Josie pulled the word out like a bite of taffy. "If taking care of Amos for an overnight is too much for you two at your age, I unders—"

"Get in the car, Amos," Gloria interrupted.

The only thing Gloria disliked more than telling people her age was acting it.

Josie waved goodbye to Al and Amos until the car drove out of sight, then walked back into the building. Bert sat in his alcove reading while Ernie's niche sat empty. He looked up at Josie when she walked in and gave her a terrifying smile.

Not on purpose. Gargoyles in general looked pretty scary.

"What an unhappy woman," Bert said, pulling the reading glasses from his nose. "If you'd like, I can make her disappear."

The offer stopped Josie dead in her tracks. For a long, shameful second, she envisioned life without Gloria breathing down her neck.

"No, thank you," she said. "Gloria is Amos's grandmother. I genuinely believe she wants the best for him. It's not okay to disappear someone because they're not nice. Not on this world, at least."

"If you say so." Bert sounded unconvinced.

Josie had become better acquainted with Bert yesterday when she ran home during lunch to pick up a book for Jenna. He struck her as kind and somewhat of an overthinker.

"What are you reading?" Josie asked now, squinting but unable to make out the title along the paperback's spine.

Ironically, Bert's frown was far less intimidating than his smile.

"I'm reading *The Little Prince* by Antoine de Saint-Exupéry," he said, holding up the books so she could see the cover. "It's for Miss Nekesa's Tuesday-night book club."

Josie had heard of the book but never read it. "How do you manage to attend a book club without blowing your cover?"

Despite Bert's well-intentioned attempt at pretending to be a dog during the snowball fight earlier this week, the disguise would never fly if he wasn't twenty feet away in a blizzard.

"It's on Zoom," he said. "You usually can't get reliable Wi-Fi in Number Five, but Tuesday nights she grants an exception. There is a big group of us who do it together in the games room in the basement, where the discussions don't disturb anyone." Bert paused and looked over at Ernie's spot. "Some people have strong opinions about the difference between an allegory and a fable."

Trying but failing to visualize a group of zombies, faery cheerleaders, and gargoyles getting heated over semantics, Josie decided not to probe further.

"Last month we read *Charlotte's Web,*" Bert said. "That was a disaster. The Kokopelli in 5D still isn't speaking to the chupacabra in 2C because they disagreed violently about whether Wilbur was the hero, and Nuwa, the dragon in 4E, was so devastated by Charlotte's death her tears flooded the apartment below her."

Every time Josie thought she'd wrapped her mind around this place, that mind was reblown. "There is a dragon in 4E?" she asked. "Like, a real fire-breathing dragon?"

Bert cast a curious glance her way before putting the reading glasses back on. "Never heard of a dragon breathing fire." He settled back and opened the book while shaking his head. "Your Mr. Disney has a lot to answer for."

By the time six o'clock rolled around, Josie had left aside the question of where the fire-breathing rumor started and picked up the all-important question of what she was going to wear for dessert and water.

Hopefully, Pax was not a man of his word and had cooked an actual dinner. Josie planned to eat heavily and drink nothing, thereby ensuring she'd be home in fleece pants and in front of the TV by eight.

Why wait until your thirties to live the good life?

Standing in front of a closet that was miraculously full of clothes and at the same time contained nothing to wear gave Josie's brain a shot of lightning-like energy.

That dress?

Slutty.

Those jeans?

Pooch-projecting.

That top?

Forever way past twenty-one, why did Josie think she could pull off anything white anymore?

The longer she stood there, the stronger the stench of Pall Malls.

Once she was dressed, it was time to open the bathroom cabinet.

What a treat.

Josie's brain began to spiral in a familiar loop. Foundation made her look as though she were the sixty-year-old Handy Andy cashier from back home, which made Josie sad, because no one had ever explained to Brenda, the cashier, the importance of blending, which made Josie think of Barbara, because both women still read the *Enquirer* in its hard copy at lunchtime, which made her think about the fact she hadn't had any lunch and thus was hungry and would embarrass herself by eating like a heathen (that last word pronounced with three syllables, like her gramma), which brought her brain back to the subject of Pax.

Josie's brain pointed out she was attracted to a *man from another world*, for Pete's sake, and if that wasn't enough, he was searching for a way to leave this world as soon as possible.

How many ways can you spell "emotionally unavailable"? Josie's brain asked.

Her libido vehemently disagreed, but Josie's libido had gotten her into terrible circumstances in the past, so its vote counted for less.

Way less.

In the end, Josie opted for plain black panties instead of her pretty lace ones and a pair of loose jersey pants instead of a skirt.

Nothing special happening tonight.

Nope. No siree.

No reason for her skin to tighten or her heart to pound way too hard. By the time the elevator doors opened on the basement level, Josie had halfway convinced herself she was experiencing a stroke and not the jittery anticipation of a date with a handsome man.

She would just let him know she was stroking out and take a rain check.

Relief at this decision lightened her step as she walked away from the laundry room and games room and toward a part of the basement she hadn't yet seen. Unlike the games room, which looked like a rec room from the 1950s, or the laundry room, which could have jumped out of a Martha Stewart article from the 1980s, this part of the basement seemed to be furnished in the style of an Old West bordello. The walls were papered in a crimson paisley print, and beneath her feet were warped wooden floorboards covered with a narrow Persian carpet runner. Brass candlesticks affixed to the wall lit the way, each holding fake candles topped with pink fabric shades adorned with red-and-pink tassels.

"Who decorated the basement?" she asked Pax when he

opened the door to his apartment before he could greet her. "Was that you or Number Five?"

"Neither," he said. "Welcome."

Since she was still standing upright and her heart had calmed, Josie supposed she couldn't wimp out with the stroke excuse, so she girded her loins—as in told her loins to shut the fuck up and stay quiet tonight—and walked past Pax into his home.

"Thank you for having me." Josie fell back on her manners, holding out her host gift.

Pax took the bottle of wine and examined the bow. "This isn't water."

Josie's laugh died on her lips at his shocked expression.

"You don't have to drink it if you don't want." Had she insulted him somehow? "It's a human tradition to bring wine when you are invited to someone else's house for dinner."

He looked relieved. "Oh. It's a tradition on my world that you bring a bottle of wine to a person after you've assassinated a relative."

Pax showed her where to leave her shoes and brought her through a narrow corridor. Unlike Josie's apartment, there were only four rooms off the hallway. One might have been a bedroom and another one a bathroom or a closet—she couldn't tell from the closed doors and Pax didn't elucidate. At the end of the corridor stood an entire freaking suit of metal that looked like beaten gold. To the left was a small sparsely furnished living area and to the right of the freaking suit of gold was a slightly larger kitchen.

"Whoa," Josie said. "This is . . . Is everyone's apartment like this? I mean, like the resident's home world?"

Unlike her kitchen, which came complete with a refrigerator, oven, sink, and counter, Pax cooked in what looked like the kitchen you'd find in a castle. The floors were made of a reddish stone set amid earthen-colored grout. Against the back wall stood an open fireplace with a sculpted wrought iron grate decorated with tiny iron salamanders, which held four burning logs. Above the grate, an iron arm held a cast-iron pot, the contents of which released rosemary-scented steam. Instead of a granite or Corian countertop, Pax had a waist-high wooden chopping board table next to a deep ceramic sink. Cast-iron and copper pots and pans hung from a thick beam overhead and the plaster walls were painted a deep burnt sienna hue. A wooden shelf held a set of pottery dishes, cups, and bowls, and in the center of the room next to the fire was a round table—about the same size as hers—holding two place settings and a squat clay vase filled with cabbage roses.

Pax pulled a chair out for her and Josie took a seat while he went to a small door set in the side of the fireplace and used a wooden peel to remove two beautifully browned loaves of bread.

"To answer your question, yes. Number Five listens to what every guest needs to feel safe," he said, tipping the peel and sliding the loaves into a bread basket. "Many of our guests need specific accommodations."

Josie leaned over and inhaled the gorgeous scent of the bread. Next to the basket lay a knife and a small dish with a square of creamy yellow butter.

No need to worry about the state of her panties. There was no way her libido would be able to fight any postmeal drowsiness, not with stew and bread on the menu.

A thin wicked-looking blade arced through the air in front of her and Josie jumped as Pax speared the wine cork right through the foil, twisted his wrist, then yanked the cork right out.

For some reason, the action turned her on.

And . . . just like that, Josie's libido was back in the game.

Pax poured her wine first, then poured a glass for himself.

"I keep forgetting this is a hotel, not an apartment building. And you manage the hotel?" she asked as he took her bowl to the fire and ladled in a helping of stew.

"I do," he said, then served himself a bowl.

"What exactly does that entail?" she asked.

Josie waited for him to explain but he said nothing more until he sat.

Pax must have showered—or dumped rainwater from a wooden bucket over his head like an old-timey knight—right before she arrived, because his hair was damp, and the ends curled slightly.

Josie found it easier to read Pax's face and gestures when they were alone. Pushing his spoon to align with his bowl and placing his napkin on his lap, he might appear to have not heard her question. His eyes were unfocused, and his jaw moved slightly as though he were talking to himself.

He wasn't ignoring her. He was considering his answer.

Despite Josie's talent of second-guessing herself, her newfound ability to read Pax felt genuine.

"My job is to be an interpreter between the guests and Number Five," he said finally, lifting his gaze from his food to her face. "She has her own language, as you might have observed."

Josie took a bite of the meat and a sip of her wine. She let the delicious flavors of rosemary and baking spices meld while she considered Pax's words.

"What about Maddy?" she asked. "Is she an assistant interpreter?"

Pax frowned but Josie could tell it was because he was considering her question and not because he was annoyed.

"Maddy . . . has a separate set of tasks than I," he said slowly.

By the way he paused between words, Josie knew he was holding something back.

"The two of you seem to be together a lot," she said breezily. *Hopefully* breezily. "Is that because of your job, or are you good friends?"

"Friends?" he echoed with genuine surprise, then shrugged. "I suppose."

Josie's gaze fell to Pax's spoon. Heavy and unwieldy in her palm, it sat tiny and delicate in his hand. The softness with which he spoke and the fluidity of his movement made her forget how much larger he was and the strength he must possess with his muscular frame.

Friends.

What if, as the night went by, he wanted more and she didn't? Josie would have to trust Pax wouldn't cross any lines she drew. The fire dimmed and thick shadows wreathed the room. Josie glanced behind her and the only door to the kitchen was farther away than she remembered.

Pax set down his spoon and lifted his hands in the air as if she'd trained a gun on him. A log on the grate popped like a cap and Josie straightened at the noise.

"Even if I were not the hotel manager," he said, his voice a velvet rumble from deep in his chest. "Even if I were not bound by the Wayside Oath. Even if I had not spent my life as a warrior for the Light, I would always respect your wishes, Josephine."

"Can . . ." Josie took a quick sip of wine. "Can Number Five read my mind? Is she telling you what's in my head?"

The idea of it felt like a violation.

"No. Number Five is sensitive. If you become frightened, she becomes anxious." He tucked the streak of white hair behind his ear and looked at the table, hiding his expression as he spoke.

"You have no reason to feel safe. Nothing you've seen or heard since last week comes close to what you know as reality. We are strangers in many ways and you've no proof we mean you no harm."

This is true and would explain the nameless foreboding she'd felt all week.

Her hunger deserted her.

"It's almost like a conversion," she blurted. "If I accept this"—Josie made a twirling gesture with her finger to encompass him, the kitchen, the whole building even—"the world will never be the same again. I won't ever be the same person."

With all her heart, Josie wanted to believe Pax was the kind of man who kept his promises, and his instinct to believe the best about people, his patience, and his kindness were genuine.

But good and bad were too simple—he'd said it himself. What if one tenant's heroics meant something terrible would happen to her and Amos?

"If I believe in you and in Number Five, that means having faith in both fairy tales and nightmares." Josie's thoughts spun out into a web, and she spoke slowly as she tried to keep from losing track. "If fairy tales and nightmares are real, where do I go to hide? The stories we tell about people in your worlds are supposed to stay stories."

"If magic is real, it becomes mundane," Pax said. "Is that your worry?"

"'Mundane' isn't the word I'm looking for," Josie said.

Josie stood, her napkin falling from her lap, as her vague worries coalesced into words.

"If monsters are real and my worst nightmares live down the hall from me, nowhere is safe."

What if those scary men who lived on the fringes of her

dreams, the ghosts of near misses and stupid choices, what if they walked the corridors of Number Five?

"That's not how it works," Pax objected. He came around the table and took her hands in his warm palms and held tight. His freshly showered skin smelled like bergamot, and Josie could not look into his eyes in case they were a trap.

"Look, Pax. Even if the boogeyman in 5M is a hero on his world . . ."

"The djinn twins live in 5M," he corrected her.

". . . the boogeyman is a terrifying monster on my world."

Pax nodded and she kept going.

"I don't want to live next door to a monster," she said.

The fire went out.

"Oh shit, what did I do?" Josie looked around the kitchen. "I'm sorry. I'm sorry, Number Five."

The coals flared, casting a carpet of orange light barely reaching her knees.

Pax smoothed his thumb over the back of her hand and Josie watched the movement, mesmerized. "You know, on some worlds, I am a monster."

She jerked her head up and examined his face.

He meant it.

"One of my names is The Butcher."

"Why?"

Why would Pax tell her this now? Was he having second thoughts about whatever this was between the two of them and wanted to scare her away?

Her breath came in short, shallow pants as Pax slowly lifted his hands and set them on either side of her face, the same way he'd touched her the last time they kissed.

"Soldiers are killers," he said, tilting her head slightly. "I was a good soldier."

Josie licked her bottom lip, and his eyes fastened on her mouth. "You aren't at war anymore. You're supposed to keep anyone from getting hurt. The boogeyman or any of the other . . . tenants . . . it's only their oath that keeps them from hurting someone, and that only works when they're inside Number Five."

Although the coals still glowed, Josie shivered and moved closer to Pax, relishing his heat.

"What happens when they walk out the front door?" she asked. "How can you keep us, everyone, safe? What about the Zombino family? All vegans cheat at some point, no matter how good they claim vegan ice cream has gotten."

"I won't let anything bad happen to you."

What if he did? What if something happened to Amos?

"The stakes are high," she said.

As if it hurt to remove his touch, Pax let go of Josie's face and took a step backward.

"You are thinking of Amos," he said.

"Always."

"Never yourself?" he asked.

"It isn't a zero-sum equation."

When you loved someone with your whole self, their well-being was your well-being. At least, that's the way Josie believed parenting should work.

"I can only offer my word Number Five is a safe haven for you and for Amos, and I truly believe it is the will of the universe that you stay."

Josie shook her head as though she could dislodge the webs made of what-ifs and worst cases.

"Do you mean in the apartment or . . ."

Tentatively, Pax reached out his hand. "Let's take it slow. Perhaps we will begin with you remaining to finish your meal with me?"

Over the piny scent of rosemary came the faintest odor of roses. If Josie had any doubt about Number Five's intentions, the return of that smell laid those doubts to rest.

She could walk away right now and there would be no repercussions. Pax, for all his professed flaws, was obviously a man who took trust seriously. If he said he would respect Josie's wishes, he meant it.

In the end, what made her comfortable enough to stay was the certainty that she was free to leave.

Pax would have said nothing if Josie decided to leave. Still, his relief jellied his knees, and he was grateful to sit before she could notice.

"Do you have a favorite world of all the ones Number Five has visited?" Josie asked.

Pax would have been content to simply stare at Josie for the rest of the meal. He'd mistaken her hair for brown when he first saw her. The gentle light of his kitchen fire revealed individual strands of gold and red in between the brown, allowing him glimpses of the treasures he would have otherwise overlooked.

When Josie cleared her throat, Pax blushed.

Look at him staring at her like a stupid boy staring at a fine lady passing by—of course she would be worried.

"A while ago we had a siren as a guest," he said, hoping his story would distract Josie from his embarrassing behavior.

"What is a siren?" she asked.

Pax explained about the creatures born from the marriage of the sea-foam and the shoreline, whose language was wordless song that told of tides and storms to come. Their voices were so startlingly beautiful that sailors had to traverse the seas with their ears stuffed full of cotton, lest they jump to their deaths in the freezing water in pursuit of them.

He cleared away their dinner plates and brought out a covered dish that had been sitting to the side of the hearth, keeping warm.

"Will you have coffee?" he asked.

When Josie said yes, Pax busied himself making the coffee and told the rest of the story.

"They are unpopular on many worlds because males often mistake their warnings for invitations," he said.

Josie huffed softly. "This sounds familiar."

He continued. "Their home world, however, is different. There are no landmasses on that world, only an ocean."

Lifting the lid from the covered dish, Pax smiled at Josie's delighted reaction, clapping her hands and rolling her eyes in anticipation.

"Cherry cobbler. Pax, you are amazing."

The compliment fizzed through him like champagne and the sight of Josie licking her lips, chasing crumbs with the tip of her tongue after the first bite, heated the fizz into lust. Once again Pax was grateful he could take a seat, this time to hide his reaction to her pleasure.

"The sirens live on coral reefs jutting out from the surface of the water. Because of the different colors of sands and rocks, different parts of the ocean appear violet, blue, and green. One large swath of water rests above a coral mountain range and appears bright pink when their suns are on opposite sides of the sky."

"Oh," Josie said. "That sounds beautiful."

"When Number Five stopped to take on the sirens, this was the first time I had ever seen an ocean."

Pax paused.

Josie didn't push. She took a last sip of her coffee, rose, and began clearing the dishes from the table.

"You don't—"

Josie waved off Pax's words and continued to clear.

"Words are hard," he said. To her.

To himself.

Josie turned from the sink and wiped her hands on a dishcloth.

"They are," she agreed.

The sirens hadn't used words, not in the way other beings used them. Their songs would wrap around you at the solar plexus and pull you until you felt the ocean floor beneath your feet and the currents pushing your skin this way or that.

"The only words to describe that ocean are meaningless. 'Awesome.' 'Overwhelming.' 'Majestic.' 'Terrifying.'"

None of these descriptors did justice to the intense beauty of the sirens' world.

Josie walked back over to the table, picked up her half-full glass of wine from dinner, and took a sip.

"Number Five doesn't use words," she noted. "That's a good thing. They can be slippery, meaning one thing if said in one tone of voice and the opposite if spoken in a different tone."

He stood as well. Josie's lips were slightly damp from the wine and her solemn gray eyes looked up at him from beneath her dark brown lashes.

"Would you like to see it?" he asked.

A wave of crimson bled across her face. "See it?" she asked, her voice breaking on the last word.

What did she think he meant?

He'd no idea, but Pax blushed, too.

"The sirens' world," he said quickly, his tongue heavy and thoughts skittering around his brain like pebbles shaking before an avalanche. Why is it he could fight off a dozen rabid werewolves and barely raise his heart rate, but when it came to carrying on a conversation with this woman, he lost complete control over his bodily reactions?

"Oh." Josie's blush turned an even deeper red, bordering on purple. The two of them were going to pass out from the blood rushing to their faces, and other parts, and it was purely out of self-preservation that Pax took her wineglass, set it on the table, and led Josie out of the kitchen and into his study.

"When they check in, we keep a record of each guest's departure point," he explained. On one wall of his study hung a rectangular slab of *hežžĐuriŒ•ñlett,* and opposite stood a well-worn couch. Pax turned on the reading light at the end of the couch, pulled back a thick woolen blanket, and gestured for Josie to sit.

Once she did, he grabbed the remote and sat next to her—close enough to be almost touching—and messed with the buttons until he found the hotel guest ledger.

"Oh my *goodness.*"

Pax smiled at the awe in Josie's voice as the scenes from the sirens' world appeared on the *hežžĐuriŒ•ñlett* screen. Having rewatched many times the breathtaking waves of pink, blue, and green smashing together to create iridescent foam, he could now turn his attention to watching her reactions.

As beautiful as the rainbow ocean might be, it was plain in comparison to the beauty of Josie's face when full of wonder.

Maddy's warnings had been in the back of his head all night but the sight in front of Pax drowned them out.

Number Five wanted Josie here, of that he was certain. He was doing his job by making the case for her and Amos to remain with them.

If Pax's job meant he and Josie grew closer, who was he to fight it?

Chapter Twenty

Only once had Pax been held captive in his many long years as a paladin. A band of trolls had caught him unawares and, as it was winter and they were far from home, decided they would rather eat him for dinner than hold him for ransom.

Reasonable.

They bound his hands together, then his ankles, and hung him by both from a sturdy oak branch. While they built up the fire over which they would hang and roast him, Pax underwent an excruciating exercise in patience as he twisted his wrists back and forth, ever so slowly, so the trolls wouldn't know what he was up to.

The threat of imminent death combined with the need for stealth was reminiscent of the torture Pax now underwent sitting next to Josie. Her attention was rapt on the unfolding scenes of the sirens' home world, the majestic waves of indigo and burgundy smashing midair to create a lilac-colored sea-foam.

Meanwhile, all Pax could focus on was the half inch of space between them on the couch, how the heat from Josie's body crept like vines to caress his own, how, if he moved achingly slow, he could curve his arm along the back of the couch in such a way that her neck would rest against his elbow.

The buzzing sensation in his bones from sitting close but unable to touch her skin caused his heart to race and his fingertips itch to brush against her. He knew from before that Josie was soft and smelled like cherries and sugar, her kisses were warm and her touch was sure, but now, now Pax wanted to see her.

She wore a black cotton shirt with a neckline barely reaching the top of her cleavage and loose pants that went to her ankles. He stared at her shoulders as if the heat from his gaze could melt the cloth away and reveal the line of her clavicle, that magical place in a woman's body where grace and gravity come together.

Like the time he was powerless to use his strength against the trolls, Pax was unable to dominate Josie in any way physically. That wouldn't be fair. He wanted her to turn to him, to touch him first, to be in control.

While he waited, watching her expression as she soaked in the beauty of another world, his breath stuttered, and his heart raced as though he were waiting to be roasted over a troll fire.

Should he say something?

What could he say?

Enough of the ocean, can I see you naked?

Even with such limited experience with romance as Pax had, he knew this was not an appropriate conversation starter.

So he simmered and hardened and ached in the most horribly delicious state of banked desire until the screen dimmed and Josie turned to meet his gaze.

"That was amazing," she said quietly. "Thank you for showing this to me. I've never seen anything so beautiful."

"No," he said, slightly stupid from the buzzing and the banking and everything in between. "Never."

When she smiled, he lost his mind a little. How could one not after such torture?

"Can I kiss you again, Josie?" Pax asked.

When she tilted her head to consider his offer, her cheek brushed the inside of his forearm, and it had the same effect as a blow to his head. He stopped breathing and every single inch of him from his toes to his eyebrows thickened in need.

Not simply a sexual need, although there was enough lust in the air to choke them both. Need for the sort of touch that came accidentally when you sat next to a person who trusted you, who let their bare skin graze yours without jumping back, who sidled into your lap and oh . . .

Oh.

Yes.

Josie slid one thigh over both his and straddled him. The V between her legs pressed against his half-hardened cock and Pax had the fleeting worry if she touched him there, he might explode.

Simply because he'd never heard of anyone exploding from lust didn't mean it couldn't happen. He'd never heard of a world without magic and yet here they were.

"Can I touch you first?" she asked.

"Yes," he squeaked. Sheer horror at the sound he'd made was forgotten in the wake of an even more powerful shudder of pleasure when Josie followed through on her request. Her fingertips traced the features of his face from his brow to his lips, then skimmed along the tops of his shoulders.

With a tilt of her head, Josie's hands stopped moving at the hem of Pax's shirt and he nodded permission to the unspoken question. Frustratingly slowly, Josie unbuttoned the black collared shirt he'd worn in hopes of impressing her. Josie's hands were small, fingers thin and capable as they freed each pearl-colored button.

When she'd finished, Josie pulled the shirt from his torso and paused again with her hands curled under the hem of his tight gray undershirt.

"You wear a lot of clothes," she teased—at least, he hoped she was teasing and not complaining.

"Say the word and I will never wear another stitch again," Pax vowed solemnly.

When she tilted her head back and let loose a quiet laugh, he could not help but to rise and sweep her into his arms.

"I made a joke," he informed her as he walked them from the living room and into the small bedroom at the other end of the hallway.

"You did," Josie said. "It was a most excellent joke. Top tier."

Pausing on the threshold, he asked permission to enter, and Josie consented with a nod.

Pax couldn't rid himself of his proud smile even after he settled Josie atop his bed and pulled the T-shirt off, toed off his boots, and unbuckled his belt. The smile widened at the rapt expression on Josie's face, the way she scrambled up on her knees and reached out to help him with the belt, and the quiet hum of appreciation she made when his pants fell to the floor.

The smile remained when Pax joined her on the bed and, with her permission, slid her black shirt off to reveal the body beneath.

Under the smell of whatever lavender soap she used to clean her skin was Josie's true scent. Salt and earth, something sharp, like lemon or antiseptic—nothing unfamiliar but enigmatic all the same. Pax breathed it in and held it in his lungs, letting it suffuse his blood while she lifted her hips so he could take off her pants, leaving on her undergarments. On the exhale his lips traveled the length of her, spreading kisses to every soft, rounded part of her that called to him.

"May I?" he asked when he reached the bottom of her brassiere.

Josie's laughter was soft and easy when Pax struggled to figure out how to untangle her from the contraption, the laces to which he'd been accustomed had been traded in for hooks and eyes. Not very romantic, if you asked him.

His disappointment was forgotten in the rush of appreciation that took his words away when Josie set her brassiere aside.

"How are you . . . ?"

He was going to ask how she could be real, this woman resting next to him, biting him with tiny kisses, lips pulled over teeth, stroking her delicate fingers along the dips and hollows of his musculature. Redolent of summer, she was formed of curves and lines and everything beautiful the universe had to offer, and more besides.

Leaving off that question, leaving off any speech requiring higher-brain functioning, Pax turned instead to exploration. His lips and tongue and fingers traversed a continent of woman, discovering secret territories of salty and sweet. There was the soft slope of her belly, the berried peaks of her breasts, and the plunging line of her neck.

All these places opened to him with a "please" and a "yes, there" and an "oh my God."

The entire time, his own body hummed with need, but Pax did not, could not, rush his exploration. It was slow work to learn a woman in this way. Slow, exacting torture that fogged his brain and hardened his cock, and turned his nervous system inside out. His skin was so sensitive when Josie moved beneath him, a thousand fires licked his limbs, burned him up, and sent him flying into the ether.

Pax rested on his elbows, holding himself above her while he laid searching kisses on every inch of her skin.

"This part of you here," he whispered into her neck. "I don't know why, but I want to taste you here."

True to his word, Pax traced the curve between her neck and her shoulder with the tip of his tongue, pulling a response from the center of her. Josie arched her back, wanting more contact, wanting some sort of friction, and opened her legs so his hips rested between hers.

"Closer," she said.

He obliged, but only enough to tease her. The pressure of his erection against her folds was hampered by the cotton of his boxers and the cloth of her panties. Josie wrapped her arm around his shoulders and gently pulled him to her, letting her palm explore the expanse of his muscled back while she ran the fingers of her other hand through his hair.

It was thick and soft, and when she made a fist and tugged it gently, Pax growled and left off the small bites on her shoulder and turned his attention to her breasts.

"So pretty," he said before laving the pink outline of her areola. "Tastes perfect."

He covered her nipple with his hot wet mouth, and his eyes held Josie's captive. Clenching his teeth slightly, he bit at the same time he sucked her deep into his mouth and lightning shot down her spine.

"Closer," she demanded, but it was more like begging and Pax gave her what she asked for. His other hand grasped her hip, and they rocked together in time with the lapping of his tongue on her breast.

Josie threw one leg over his hips and moaned at the friction. Her panties were soaked, and she wanted to feel more of his skin, grip the muscles of his ass, ride this out into bliss, but she couldn't speak because they were kissing again. Grinding against each other, unable to stop and pull off the rest of their clothes, indulging in kissing that grew more intense as though they could devour each other, press so close nothing could peel them apart.

Breaking the kiss, Josie threw her head back and took a breath, pulling all the air she could into her lungs while the tension between her legs grew tighter until Pax reached between them and asked, "Can I touch you here?"

Words were beyond her, or maybe she answered something like "yes" or "now" but probably just moaned. Josie took his hand and pulled it to the hem of her panties, welcoming his touch.

All it took was one, two, three circles with his thumb and a thrust of his finger for Josie to come on his hand, letting loose a low half sigh, half moan pulled deep from her belly.

God, it felt good, but it wasn't enough.

"More, still," she said, then suckled his tongue and urged him on with her hips. Pax didn't pause, he shifted his weight and worked her with the palm of his hand, slowly pushing one finger then two deep inside her, twisting them slowly.

It was her turn to ask, and she took the low grunt as the answer yes. Quickly, she slipped her hand below the waistband of his boxers and wrapped her hand around his erection. He was hot and thick, and the need to taste him nearly overcame her desire for completion but Pax was determined. His fingers moved faster and as his palm made circles, faster and faster until she came again with a strangled cry and saw stars behind her eyelids.

Her skin expanded, a wave of satisfaction moving her from beneath his body to on top of him. Josie pulled down his boxers, her hair covering her face and sweeping over his cock as she unhooked the boxers from his ankles, then settled herself back on her knees, bowing low and capturing the engorged head of him between her lips.

Whatever word it was he yelled when she licked him from root to head and back again, it wasn't a name, so Josie paid it no mind. Instead, she focused on the sweet tremors still coursing between her thighs and the salty taste of Pax's skin, and reveled in the way his hands flopped out to his sides and grabbed at the sheets, as though he was holding himself back from touching her too hard or too fast.

"Your mouth," he groaned. "Never felt anything as good."

The praise excited her even more than his shouts and Josie rewarded him by taking as much as she could of him into her mouth until he hit the back of her throat.

"Never," he promised her. "Never so *good*."

The hitch in his voice was her only warning before his hips thrust up against her and he came into her mouth and down her throat, his hand lightly stroking her hair in contrast to the strength of his thrusts against her lips.

"So good," he said one last time in a voice filled with reverence, in such a way Josie knew it for the truth.

"Very good," she agreed, when she crawled back up his body to come lay herself atop his limbs and traded soft quiet kisses of wonder and delight.

Words too small for what happened, but neither of them was

inclined to search for another because some words were better left unsaid unless they were meant to be spoken outside of the bed.

Instead, they lay tangled in a knot of limbs, listening to the other person breathe, and tucked words away for later, content to speak with fingers, lips, and tongues in a language both were learning together.

Chapter Twenty-One

Mom, Mr. Tim says if it stays warm this week, we can have outside time again."

"That's super news, buddy."

Was it a postorgasmic hallucination, or did the sun shine brighter today?

Walking to Wegmans for a treat after church, Amos and Josie turned a corner and were hit with a wall of wind hard enough they had to grab their hats and pull them over their ears to keep them from flying away.

"Mom, Miss Alysha says there are only three more days until spring."

"That's cool, buddy."

Everything Josie touched, smelled, and tasted today reminded her of what happened last night with Pax. What had yet to happen.

What she could imagine happening.

"Mom, one time Jalyn put his boogers on a piece of paper, and they turned another color after they dried."

"No way, buddy."

Stupid.

Sex made Josie stupid.

She should have remembered that.

She'd been naked with only two people before Pax. The first time she'd had sex, it had made her stupid enough to believe in a boy who had promised to save her and ended up ghosting her. After that, Josie had guarded her heart and her body until she met Dan. Even then, a long time passed before sex made her stupid again.

If Dan had lived, Josie was sure she'd have let herself fall in love with him.

"Mom, if we had a dog, I could name him Jingle Bells."

"You sure could, buddy."

Given her track record, why was Josie tempting fate again? If she . . .

Wait.

What?

Before Amos could open his mouth again, she warned him, "Too bad we can't get a dog."

Shit. What else had she agreed to when she should have been listening to her child but was instead reliving what happened last night with Pax?

Pax from another world. Who managed a dimension-traveling hotel. A hotel filled with monsters and ghosts and mythological creatures.

Pax who touched her with reverence.

Pax who made her come so hard she'd seen stars.

Whoa.

Whoa, these were not the thoughts she should have while hanging out with her four-year-old son. She should be thinking about pedagogical enrichment and positive reinforcement, not orgasms.

"Grandma Gloria says when I come live with her, I can have a dog."

"Grandma Gloria said *what*?"

Josie stopped in her tracks and stared at Amos, who, oblivious to the bomb he'd dropped, was blowing bubbles with his spit.

"Amos, did your grandmother say you were going to live with her anytime soon?"

Palms up, he shrugged. One of his red knitted mittens had a hole above his pointer finger, and the sight of his pale pink fingernail sent a crushing wave of protective love through Josie's body. She wanted to pick him up and hold him, breathe in the perfect mix of boy sweat and crayons and Nilla Wafers that made up Amos's unique scent.

"I don't know when. She said I can have a dog. Maybe college I'll live with her? In like thirty-six years?"

"Right." Josie took his hand in hers and they continued their walk, but now the delicious memories of last night were replaced with frantic calculations.

The last time Gloria spoke about Amos coming to live with her and Al had been after Amos had a series of fainting spells last year. The pediatric cardiologist assured Josie the arrhythmia that caused them was often seen in children post cardiac repair. Gloria had demanded Josie seek a second opinion with another cardiologist—a guy who called her "Mommy" and was way too scalpel happy for Josie's comfort.

Luckily, the second cardiologist agreed with the first that there were no obvious leakages, but in the lead-up to the consult, harsh words had been spoken and doubt cast on Josie's ability to care for Amos.

All the energy Josie had, she put toward being a good mother, a stellar coworker, and a model fucking citizen, and it exhausted her. Gloria, however, never got tired of calling out the very same flaws that kept Josie from living a louder, larger life.

If Gloria was going to put up another fight, Josie didn't know how long she could hold out.

She and Amos rapped on melons and ate samples of salami while he tried out a series of knock-knock jokes. From the outside, they presented a picture of normalcy. Didn't they? Could anyone passing by see an outward sign of her deficiencies?

Knowing she wouldn't get a signal once they got to Number Five, Josie called Gloria on the walk home. The wind and Amos's questions made it hard to hear sometimes, but the message was clear.

". . . say he could have a dog. I said we could get him a dog and have the dog live at our house," Gloria explained, as though she didn't know what that would do to Amos. As though she hadn't mapped the consequences out in her head before making that promise. "Since you insist on living in the city in an apartment too small for a dog and are gone all day . . ."

Gone all day working to support herself and Amos.

Living in the city so they didn't have the expense of a car and could access the discounted childcare at work.

Too small for a dog because rents were up to 50 percent of folk's after-tax income.

". . . stay with us for the whole weekend. He will learn responsibility caring for the animal and . . ." Gloria droned on about intellectual and emotional development, companionship, and the twist of the knife ". . . spending time with other people, and not dependent on you."

Josie had seen this coming but hadn't wanted to admit it.

This was the first volley in Gloria's battle to take Amos away.

Brilliant move.

"This is something we should have discussed together, Gloria, before you told Amos," Josie said, hoping the intermittent connection would make her sound unruffled and determined.

"Yes, well. There's a lot we need to discuss, I agree."

The censure in Gloria's voice came through clear as a bell and Josie closed her eyes against the memories of Gramma it conjured.

What the hell was Josie supposed to do now? Get a puppy?

Out of the question.

Sacrifice even more of her free time with Amos? The drive from Gloria's suburban neighborhood was twenty minutes by car, forty minutes by bus. Commuting to see a pet would be nuts—one more arrow in Gloria's quiverful of arguments against Josie and Amos living in the city.

If she and Amos were to move out to the suburbs, would Pax be able to get away to come and see them?

What if Number Five woke when he was inside and he had no time to warn her?

Worry had gnawed holes in her belly by the time she and Amos got home. Sunset lit the lobby with orange-and-reddish-gold light, and unwilling to let the rare cloudless day disappear yet, they went out into the courtyard to inspect the garden.

The garden boxes had been built according to Maddy's dimensions. The entire space was divided into perfect rectangles and squares, the soil measured evenly between the sections. Each of the tenants had received a notice in their mailboxes earlier in the week that this month's tenants' association meeting would be about the common garden—specifically garden rules, regulations, and privileges.

They wandered past box after box. The basketball hoop was

gone and hadn't been replaced, and despite Josie's request, the open space looked to be made of paving stones instead of grass.

"How I'm gonna run back here?" Amos asked.

"I guess there aren't any other kids in the building, buddy," Josie said. "They must not know kids like green space to play."

She stumbled when they rounded a box and nearly stepped on a gargoyle. The gargoyle was bigger than Bert and lay unmoving on his back with an arm tucked under his head staring up at the sunset.

"Hi, guy," Amos said cheerfully. He squatted next to the gargoyle and patted him on the forehead.

Josie held her breath, but the gargoyle remained frozen.

"Have a nice day," Amos told the gargoyle. He wandered over to where the benches and tables had been mapped out on the ground by duct tape.

When nothing happened, Josie nodded to the gargoyle and followed her son but stopped when she saw a tiny sign posted in one of the beds.

NATIVE SPECIES ONLY

This made sense. They wouldn't want to introduce plants from other worlds into the ecosystem. Who knows what damage they would wreak? They could let loose the next kudzu on the country.

But.

How much joy would flowers bring to the tenants if they didn't evoke any memories? What if there was only one world on which the most beautiful flower grew? What if there was someone in the building who missed gardening as much as she did?

Like everything else about Number Five, the sign presented difficult questions without yes-or-no answers.

Josie knelt and put her hand on top of the soil. What flowers would the Fates plant if given the choice? How fantastical might the flowers be where the faeries came from?

The soil beneath her skin vibrated with the sensation of anticipation, and tiny spikes of blue and pink poked out of the dirt.

Holy crap.

"Josie?"

Pax's voice was soft as velvet and curled round her neck like a shawl. Closing her eyes, she breathed in the scent of cold fresh air and dried orange peels that made her knees weak.

"Hi, Mr. Pax. I has some good jokes for you," cried Amos.

Too soon, she thought. She needed time to organize the parts of her that had spilled out when he touched her. Time to steel herself against rejection or temptation, depending on what she could see in his eyes.

Too soon to lose her composure when Amos was nearby. What if her son could sense her attraction to a man he barely knew?

The anxiety about Gloria's comments coupled with her fear and choked her breath.

"What happened here?" he asked.

Josie opened her eyes.

The pink-and-blue spikes had shriveled into tiny black curls.

Pax walked around to the other side of the box and squatted opposite her. His black hair was pulled back today, and he wore a blue cotton henley beneath his Carhartt jacket. A pair of work gloves hung from his side pocket, and his feet were hidden under a pair of work boots.

The stray regret she hadn't paid attention to his naked feet streaked through her brain.

She was pretty sure he had sexy feet.

"I have a joke for you, too, Mr. Amos," Pax called, his eyes never leaving Josie's face. "I googled them," he told her quietly. "I think I understand now."

Longing, fierce and bittersweet, squeezed her chest.

Even if she weren't a single parent struggling to overcome a lifetime's worth of head-fuckery, she couldn't be with this man. Whatever rebooting she and Amos were supposed to provide meant Number Five would eventually be on its way to other worlds, taking Pax with her.

It gave extreme *Men Are From Mars, Women Are from Venus* vibes.

"I must tell you. I've been to visit Number Five's heart and—" Pax broke off at Amos's arrival.

"Knock knock." Amos came and sat next to Pax.

What was it Pax wanted to tell her?

"Who is there?" Pax asked, looking at her boy with a smile.

"Worm," said Amos.

Pax considered him, eyes narrowed in thought. "Hmmmm. Perhaps I do not understand after all. Worm who?"

"It's worms outside!"

Amos threw his head back and laughed. As the first silver note left his lips, the wizened black curls in the garden box popped back up into blue-and-pink spiked plants again. The laugh felt like it lasted forever while little red vines joined pink-and-blue spikes, and next to them grew yellow stalks with iridescent buds. In the next box over, black mushroomlike plants sprung up, their undersides spotted with eggplant-colored heart shapes. Behind that box, a row of bushes appeared, dark copper leaves dotted with opal berries.

Pax was still looking at Amos. "Worms outside?" he repeated, then slapped one thigh in excitement. "Worm outside—'worm' sounds like 'warm.' See?" He glanced over at Josie. "I got it and . . . ah . . ."

"Mom, where did these plants come from?"

The three of them stared at the strange flowers, then one another. Josie's mouth opened and closed rapidly like a flounder.

Pax appeared more dignified, but he'd nothing to offer, either.

The impossibility of what happened in front of her and the unreality of the past week came crashing down, and Josie, true to form, decided it was time to get the hell out of there.

"I don't know, Amos. Let's go on upstairs and have some ice cream, why don't we?"

Just like that, her son forgot about the plants and raced to the building entrance.

Pax mirrored Josie's slow rise to her feet.

"Words are hard." Pax echoed his complaint from last night. "I tried to send you some in a note, but they curled up and turned to nonsense as soon as I wrote them down."

Josie swallowed and nodded. Words were hard.

"I wanted to tell you I have never touched anything as soft as your skin, the memory of that touch is wrapped around my fingers, and all I want to do is bury my head in my hands and remember touching you."

Oh. Oh, goodness.

"Those are beautiful words, Pax," Josie said.

He shook his head, objecting. "They aren't enough. You are a siren's song and impossible to translate, but I want . . ."

Josie wanted as well. She wanted to go back to Pax's bed, to be held, to be comforted, and to be supported when her energy was depleted.

"I wanted to tell you this before I told you my other news," he said, "so you wouldn't think what I felt . . . how I feel . . ." Pax rubbed his chest. "I want you to know that I want you here even if it has no effect on Number Five."

Nothing Josie had experienced had ever taught her good things happened to good people. Instead, she'd seen time and again that opening yourself to happiness meant inviting weakness. Succumbing to pleasure was selfish.

Even if it wasn't, there were garden boxes full of flowers from alternate dimensions right here on boring Earth. This wasn't sustainable, was it?

This couldn't last.

Nothing beautiful ever lasted.

"I have to tell you—" Pax said, but stilled again when Amos interrupted.

"Mom, we going upstairs?" Amos called.

Josie consoled herself with the thought that she would have left Pax even if Amos hadn't called her. She wasn't using her son as an excuse to leave.

"I have to go. We can talk later," she told Pax, hurrying off to join Amos before he could object.

Whatever news Pax had could wait.

Josie had some decisions to make.

"How could you let this happen?"

Raphe, Denis, and Maddy stood in a line in front of Pax, identical expressions on their faces.

"Right," said Pax. "I should have known Number Five would react to the sound of a human child's laughter because we have *so* many of them running around."

Raphe's head jerked back and Maddy set a hand to her chest.

"Was that . . . was that sarcasm?" Denis asked. "I didn't think you had the emotional range."

Truth be told, Pax hadn't known he had the emotional range, either. Sitting at his desk while the three harbingers of doom hovered over him, Pax dropped his head into his hands. This must be why paladins were sworn to celibacy. One night of sex, breathtaking, beautiful sex, and his emotional range was the height and length of a mountain range. One second, he was mindless with desire for Josie, the next he was outraged by Denis's selfishness, and the next he was practically floating with pride for understanding a joke.

Who was he and where the hell did The Butcher go and disappear to?

Pax couldn't be sure, but perhaps the men and women of his world had more in common with the humans than he'd originally thought? Humans had names for conditions like this. "Besotted." "Head over heels." "Lovesick."

There were names for it on his world as well. "Heartcharmed" and "off the ground." "Loveblind."

Words he and his soldiers would use as curses when someone acted the fool.

"I don't know what 'emotional range' means," said Raphe. "I *do* know when you're thinking with your cock that cock-ups are inevitable. This goes beyond exposing ourselves to a little boy. Those plants are out there for any would-be burglar or even curious neighbor to walk around back and see."

True.

"They aren't even in the correct boxes," Maddy added. "I specifically set aside three boxes for annuals, and of the flowers I recognize, all of them are either perennial or carnivorous. Why did I invest in a new label maker if no one takes the time to read the labels?"

"You are overlooking the importance of what happened." Besotted or no, Pax knew when to listen and when to lead. He'd been commanding troops for decades, and although he listened attentively when his soldiers made their points, final decisions always came down to him.

"Number Five grew those flowers. Whether the boy had laughed or not, Number Five reacted to an expression of joy."

Amos's laugh had the shining tones of Pax's favorite throat singers. It had been a gift, that sound, and Number Five had answered in kind by offering up a gift of her own.

"This is exactly what needs to happen," Pax said. He placed both palms on the desk and pushed to standing. "For months Number Five has been shutting down. Since Jo . . . er, Ms. LaChiusa—"

"You can say her name, Pax," said Maddy, huffing with annoyance as she sat in a chair opposite his desk and pulled off her spikey-looking shoes, rubbing the arch of each foot. "We know you're sleeping with her."

"What?" Pax reared back. "How do you . . . ? What are you . . . ?"

Denis grimaced. "The stairs to the basement vanished Saturday night and the elevator would only go up."

"The entire building reeked of roses," said Raphe. "Meanwhile I was stuck on the first floor all night. The couches in the common room are lumpy. I want the ballroom back."

"Not to mention you have this goofy heart-eye-emoji look on your face all the time now," Maddy complained.

Pax glared at her.

"I don't even know what that means," he said. "Goofy emoji

look," he muttered. He'd show them a goofy look after he rearranged their features with his fist.

Sparks flew from the small brass lamp on Pax's desk and a tin candlestick appeared in its place.

"Unh-uh." Raphe waggled his finger at Pax. "You're going to have to rein in that temper if you want Number Five to keep getting better. Remember, hands are for helping, not for hurting."

Denis pushed his tinfoil hat back and peered up at Raphe. "Where did you hear that nonsense?"

Raphe raised one brow in a supercilious expression. "You are not the only being who can navigate the interwebs." He leaned down and smiled, revealing his razor-sharp bloodteeth. "I *know* things, gnome."

"*Can* we stick to the point?" Maddy demanded. She slipped her shoe back on and grimaced. "The point being Number Five cannot let her enthusiasm cause our unintended exposure. More importantly"—she looked at Pax—"has the needle moved?"

"Yes."

The three beings gasped.

Pax nodded. "I went to check after the flowers appeared, and the needle is up to the three percent mark. This is working."

What he hadn't told them is the needle had moved after his night with Josie, not because of the flowers.

"What did she do?" Maddy asked.

Pax didn't know. It couldn't have simply been what they'd done in his bed. There were other couples, whole families in the building. If it was sex fueling Number Five, they shouldn't have run dry.

If it wasn't simply the physical intimacy, that left certain possibilities. Possibilities that were none of these folks' business. Private possibilities too fragile to take into the light and examine.

"It could be whatever the humans are made of or excrete is working to help cure Number Five," Raphe said thoughtfully. "Like a vaccine. We inject Number Five with magicless beings and Number Five reacts in defense by making more magic."

"They are a people, not a disease," Pax objected.

"If this is the case, it doesn't matter who comes to live here," said Denis excitedly. "We can get any old human, preferably one with bad hearing and poor eyesight, to live here and it would have the same effect."

"Yes," Raphe agreed. "We should get rid of the woman, seeing as she's become such a nuisance, and replace her with a less attractive human."

Rage, dark and heavy, filled Pax's veins.

Denis asked, "What if the woman goes public with what she knows?"

"Is the altar back up to code, Maddy?" Raphe asked. "I still think a blood sacrifice would be helpful."

In some men, a red haze descended on their vision, a precursor of blood. With Pax, the decision to kill had never been taken lightly, and when he drew his blade, he'd always been certain his vision was clear, his mind in order, and his heart beating slow and steady.

Scratching beneath his beard, Denis nodded, then belched. "There's more than a few guests who will pitch in to pay the penalty fee, if it comes to that."

Right.

The little dirt-sucking conspiracy fanatic was going to die.

Before Pax could reach for Denis's throat, the lights dimmed, and a freezing wind blasted through the office. Papers flew off the desk, Manny's beer hat toppled over, and Raphe's cape smacked Maddy in the face.

Who wears a cape inside at three o'clock in the afternoon?

As abruptly as it began, the wind died, leaving a chill and the smell of burnt sesame seeds behind.

"Number Five has spoken. The LaChiusa family remains where they are." Pax's fists clenched so hard the entirety of his knuckles showed beneath his skin. "Anyone touches a hair on their heads, and I will kill them on the spot."

Leashing the violence coiled in his gut, Pax left before anyone could point out his hypocrisy.

Chapter Twenty-Two

Which direction do you think she went?"

Cindy, Ashley, and Shelly, the three oldest faery princesses after Naliti, rolled their eyes simultaneously—whether at Maddy's tone or the fact she was repeating the same question she'd asked two seconds earlier, Pax couldn't tell.

Faery princesses were champion eye rollers.

"I don't know. Naliti is in charge of us, not the other way around." Cindy was the second-born princess, and when Naliti was gone, it fell to her to manage her sisters.

Maddy and Pax looked at each other in dismay.

This was the one who ate silicon packs on a dare.

"Does your father know?" Pax asked.

The sisters gasped but Maddy shook her head. "No. I'd have warned you."

Oberon, king of the faeries, was asleep on the sixth floor.

None of those guests would enjoy being awakened on a world with no magic. Oberon would be even less amused to be awoken and told his eldest daughter was missing. If peeling Denis out of a bar two seconds before picking a fight with a motorcycle gang was enough to put Maddy in a pissy mood for days, Pax couldn't imagine how she would handle cleaning up after Oberon in a rampage. Entire cities had fallen the last time that guy was in a mood.

The snow had melted into formations resembling black coral sticking to the curbs and undersides of cars. Everything was cold and wet, and the sky threatened bad weather to the west.

The five of them stood in the parking lot of Donuts Delite, the last place Naliti had been seen.

"Can you use your phone oracles to get me a list of the clothing and jewelry markets nearby?" Pax asked.

Shelly, the youngest of the three faeries, snorted in derision. "That's what you think? Naliti hasn't returned because she was shopping?"

What else would she be doing? There weren't any woodland fields nearby in which to cavort, nor were there male faery brothels to be found.

Shelly shook her head. "Shopping wouldn't keep her out all night. Now, a museum might. She's kind of obsessed with the Corning Museum of Glass."

"I'll bet you a tube of Clé de Peau concealer she got stuck in a book or a lab somewhere while wearing an invisibility spell and was locked in overnight," Cindy said. "It's happened before."

"Happened before?" Maddy exclaimed. "Why didn't anyone tell us?"

Cindy rolled her eyes. "Right. Like we'd be all, hey, Maddy, a bunch of us were out—"

"A bunch of you were out?" Pax yelled. A man getting into his car carrying two boxes of pastries looked over at them with concern.

"Sorry," Pax apologized. "Sorry, that was too loud."

"You never said we couldn't leave the building," Cindy objected.

"What part of the memo entitled 'No One Is to Leave the Building' gave you the impression you could leave the building?" Maddy asked.

The princesses looked at one another.

"Ummm, which memo was that?" Ashley asked. "We get about ten a day from you, Maddy."

"Honestly, it's like you're single-handedly bent on taking down the entire rain forest with the number of notices we get from you," Cindy said. She held up a finger, "Monday we got a memo about not slamming the lobby door, Tuesday"—she held up two more fingers—"we get two memos, one about weather strips on the windows and one about the *e*'s from the Scrabble games, six memos on Wednesday—"

Shelly crossed her arms. "Besides, Denis and Joey Z. are always going places. So are you and Pax."

"Because we can fit in and act like humans," Maddy scolded. "No one would know we were from another world."

"We fit in," Shelly objected.

Cindy was a six-foot-tall Black woman with dark skin, blue hair, several nose rings, and today she was wearing a black lace top covered in rhinestones and a pink fluffy sort of skirt barely covering her tail. Shelly was four foot eight inches with light bronze skin, had recently shaved her head, sported a pierced tongue, pierced cheeks, and was dressed in a tube of material. Ashley was five foot eight, had yellow horns, and her skin was the color of a birch tree.

"Well, Naliti fits in and that's the point," Cindy reminded them. "She looks like a small woman with brown skin, which is low status on this world. Except for people like Miss Nekesa and the lady behind the register at Dogtown, these humans aren't nice to those with low status."

Pax did not inquire as to what was a Dogtown and why the faeries were familiar with the employees there—mostly because he knew the answer would make him yell again. Instead, he had to agree with the princess.

"You are correct," he said, not without sympathy. "A small woman with dark skin is at a disadvantage on this world. Even more reason, once we find Naliti, you and your sisters stay home from now on. All of you will be at risk."

"We should split up." Maddy spoke directly to Pax, tired of dealing with the princesses. "The Hag in 6G can make up a searching spell bound to work for at least a little while before it loses its potency out here."

Pax nodded. He set a hand on Cindy's shoulder, aware of their fear. None of them had spelled a word or shouted a "Yeah" since he'd arrived. Even their rhinestones appeared dull in the wan sunlight.

"Don't worry, we'll find her. Naliti has more common sense than most of the guests. I'm sure she's keeping a low profile and will be back soon."

Cindy nodded, but Ashley and Shelly glanced at each other and frowned.

"Ashley, you come back with me and get the money to pay the Hag," Maddy said. "Cindy, you and Shelly buy three boxes of donuts to keep up our energy. Do not forget to order some of those cannoli donuts while you are there. Pax . . ."

Whatever Maddy was going to say was left forever unheard in the wake of an explosion that shook the ground beneath their feet.

"OMG, never mind," Shelly squealed. "I know where Naliti is now."

The days were getting longer now and much of the snow had disappeared. Although Pax had left the rubber mats out in the lobby on which to wipe the slush, the walk up to Number Five had been clear for a few days and three enormous snow boots sat at the end of a mat so dry its edges curled.

The boots struck a melancholy chord as Josie and Amos walked through the lobby on their way to the science museum parking lot. Al and Gloria were taking Amos to a special showing of The Night Sky with Disney Princesses at the museum's planetarium.

"Mom, what are you going to do tonight when I'm with Grampa Al and Grandma Gloria?" Amos asked as they exited the building and began the trek three blocks north.

"Probably go to the library," Josie said. It was only a little bit after four and Amos was going out to dinner after the show, so she had her evening free. "Maybe do some grocery shopping and laundry."

"That sounds fun," Amos said, jumping over puddles and getting dirty water on the back of his corduroys. "You wanna come to dinner wif us?"

"No, but you be sure to tell me everything you and Grandma Gloria talk about, okay?"

Josie had looked up family lawyers in the area, wanting to be prepared if the worst case happened. Eventually, she would have to confront Gloria head-on, but that fight would require resources.

It was fine standing up to gnomes and demanding orgasms

from magical knights, but facing off against her mother-in-law took a whole other level of courage.

"What if we goes to McDonald's?" Amos asked. "You don't want to come?"

Josie opened her mouth to say something nice, and not the truth, when the ground shook beneath their feet and an enormous pink-and-lime-green cloud blew out the glass atrium of the science museum.

Oh shit. Josie would know those colors anywhere. She took Amos's hand and ran toward the explosion, rather than away from it.

"What was that, Mom?" Amos cried as they made their way to the back of the museum where the parking lot was located.

A crowd had gathered on the street in front of the museum and folks who had come for the planetarium show were out of their cars and pointing toward the sky.

That was a pastel mushroom cloud slowly dissipating into the pewter-gray sky, leaving behind the scent of Bath & Bodyworks Cherry Blossom Shower Gel. The shattered glass strewn across the museum roof glittered like rhinestones, although who knew? They could be actual rhinestones.

"Oh, man," Josie whispered to herself. "Oh, man, oh, man, oh, man."

From the east side of the lot, a gaggle of faery princesses appeared, Cindy front and center.

"Mom, look, it's Cindy. She has blue hair today," Amos cried.

Yup. Yup, she did.

"Amos?"

Oh, look. The cherry on top of the shit sundae. A few cars over, Gloria and Al were frantically waving, Gloria's horrified glance hopping between Cindy's blue hair, the pink-and-green tendrils of smoke wafting from the roof of the museum, and Amos.

As soon as Gloria called Amos's name, Cindy and her sisters' heads turned in unison and they changed their course, now heading directly for Josie and Amos.

Having spotted them, Gloria began pulling Al away from the car and toward what was shaping up to be a giant clusterfuck right at Josie's feet.

Yay.

"Hi, Ms. LaChiusa. Hi, Amos." Cindy waved.

"Hi, Cindy. Hi, Shelly. Hi, Ashley. Did you see an esploshun?" Amos cried.

"What is happening?" Josie asked Cindy, her attention split between Gloria and Al and the people who were finally emerging from the damaged museum. Thankfully, none of them were screaming in terror or shouting anything about faery cheerleaders.

"Naliti is missing—was missing," Cindy said, turning her attention to the museum as well. "She's been gone all night. We were out looking for her when we heard the explosion."

As Josie suspected from the color of the cloud, Princess Naliti was behind this. But why? She was the most sensible of the faery cheerleaders. If Naliti couldn't be counted on to keep a low profile, there's no way they would be able to keep the tenants of Number Five under wraps.

"We need to evacuate!" Gloria cried. While Josie was talking to Cindy, the older woman had snuck up on them. "It's completely irresponsible to be standing out here at the site of a terrorist attack!"

While her words expressed distress, Josie knew this explosion would entertain Gloria for weeks if not months afterward.

Not as exciting as a plane crash, but fodder for all sorts of *National Enquirer*–fueled speculation.

My God, what were Barb and Jenna going to make of this?

"This is my Grandma Gloria," Amos said, happily. "This is my friends Cindy and Ashley and Shelly. They have superpowers."

Oh shit.

"Friends?" Gloria asked, taking in the sight of the three princesses and their wardrobe choices while Al came huffing up to the group. Her eyes narrowed and stuck on Cindy's blue hair. "How do you know them, Amos?"

Josie cleared her throat. "These are our neighbors, the Smiths."

Neighbors, Al mouthed with delight.

Neighbors, Gloria mouthed with disdain.

Before Amos could elucidate and maybe let slip the existence of eight more Smith sisters, a young woman behind them squealed.

"OMG. Are you Cindy Smith? From TikTok?"

Cindy turned around and flashed a blinding smile as the young woman proceeded to take pictures.

"What is TikTok?" Gloria asked. "Is that a gang?"

Josie might have known the faeries were on TikTok. Within minutes, they were surrounded by teenagers taking selfies with Cindy and her sisters, gushing about their social media accounts, and exclaiming over their boots, clothes, and hair.

"Influencers." Al had to raise his voice to explain to Gloria over the sound of the faeries' fans. "Famous for being famous. Lots of money in it. *Tons* of money."

"Were you here for the experiment?" a girl asked Shelly. "It was cool. Dr. Naliti is one badass scientist."

"Mom," Amos whispered, "she said a bad word."

Distracted—*Dr. Naliti?*—Josie nodded. What in the world?

"I follow her YouTube channel, like, religiously," the same girl told them while taking selfies with the cloud in the background. "She is so inspiring. I'm going to change my major from art history to chemistry."

Sure enough, the crowd exiting the museum was mostly young women, many of them in pink and green.

This was bad.

Or was it good? Josie didn't know the answer.

Amid a flurry of fans swirling around the faeries, the dark, solemn forms of Pax and Maddy stood out. The two of them approached the gaggle of selfie takers with apprehension.

Seeing Pax outside of Number Five did something to knock Josie's center of gravity askew. How was it a man who came from another world, dimension—whatever—could appear so solid and real? As if the people milling about them were poor copies and he alone was genuine.

"She lives upstairs from me," Amos volunteered to the starstruck crowd. "They all live upstairs."

Al's eyebrows rose in muted delight, but Gloria grabbed hold of this information with both hands.

"What kind of doctor blows up a museum?" Gloria asked the girl, lips tight with disapproval.

Pax surveyed the crowd as he approached. The pull to go stand at his side, soak up some of that calm, was strong enough to make Josie hesitate. She wanted him, but what did she want from him?

"These are your neighbors? People who blow up museums?" Gloria asked, her intonation making it clear the questions were rhetorical. "Flicktok people?"

"You are Amos's grandparents?" Pax asked as he reached them.

Oh shit.

"Ummm, ah, let me introduce you," Josie stammered, stumbling over the introductions. Was Pax her building super or her friend? Was it obvious to everyone they were more than friends? Were Maddy's snakes going to stay put?

Josie could barely breathe, terrified by the possible consequences of the collision between two literally different worlds in the most bizarre of scenarios.

"Pax is the building superintendent, and he works closely with Maddy, who is the president of our very active and involved tenants' association," Josie said brightly.

"Oh, *you* are responsible for the upkeep of that building." Gloria gave Pax a once-over, her upper lip pulled back in a sneer. "Do you have a process for investigating prospective tenants, or can *anyone* move in?" Gloria asked.

While Josie doubted she and Maddy would ever be friends, she had no doubts about how committed Maddy was to Number Five. The instant she sensed Gloria's disapproval the medusa raised her chin and narrowed her eyes.

Terrifying.

"The Wayside is an *exclusive* private residence," Maddy announced, coating her words in a frozen shell of condescension.

"I am afraid there are no apartments to let in the building," Pax added. "If you are interested, however, there is a three-year waiting list, a one-hundred-dollar fee for an FBI background check, and a minimum salary threshold."

Maddy sent Pax a look of approval, and Josie hid her smile with her hand.

This line of defense flummoxed Gloria, but she rallied quickly. "Well, if you have so many famous tenants and it's exclusive, you must have problems with strangers getting into the building. I can't recall seeing any security cameras or even a doorman. In our neighborhood we have a watch who checks on our properties."

"Hmmm." How Maddy could make a hum of agreement sound like a derisory snort was one of many questions Josie still had about this woman. Person. Being. Badass.

Pax crossed his arms. "You wouldn't be able to spot our security. Not for what we pay. I can assure you no one enters my building without permission."

Gloria appeared displeased and about to argue the point, but Maddy interrupted. "Considering the statuary in our lobby is insured through Markel, it would be the height of foolishness not to have top-tier security."

That shut Gloria up.

Shut Josie up, too, because what statuary was Maddy even . . .

"The gargoyles?" Josie asked.

"Exactly," Maddy said.

"Our security is impressive, but even more impressive is the care Ms. LaChiusa takes of her son. You do not have to worry for Amos," Pax said with an edge of finality.

No doubt the former knight thought he'd put an end to the argument. How kind. Whatever sort of monsters he'd faced in his past, Josie was willing to bet they had nowhere near the tenacity of her mother-in-law.

Gloria's face, as readable as a child's, was twisting into various permutations; a frown signified her inability to use building security as a weapon against Josie when she remembered she could hold the dog over Josie's head and she straightened her mouth.

"An apartment building requiring security, explosions right

next door, a mother who works all day and no backyard, no pets, no neighborhood friends. This isn't how a boy should grow up. Of course I worry."

The words sounded practiced—and practical—but beneath the plaintive tone, Josie heard genuine confusion. Gloria truly didn't believe families could thrive on love rather than things.

Posing with Cindy for selfies, Amos laughed, unaware of his fate being discussed at this very moment.

"I have to ask myself if Amos is better off being closer to us," Gloria said, her eyes never leaving Josie's face. "Many people would agree with me."

Many people. Many people like social workers or judges or whomever else Gloria called upon to get her way.

Maddy scoffed. "I would certainly disagree. A boy needs to be with his mother."

The medusa's words were almost as shocking as the explosion. Josie gaped at the woman who, only days before, had told her Number Five was set to leave her behind and Josie needed a man in the house.

"I would disagree as well." Pax looked to Josie as if asking permission and she nodded once, speechless at this defense. "I grew up given plenty of food, outdoor activity, rigorous academics, and went on to become a high-ranking officer in the military. Looking back on my childhood, the one resource I lacked and will always regret not having was the affection of a parent."

Pax's voice never wavered, his expression remained enigmatic, but no one who heard his words doubted for a moment his regret was real. Josie would be damned if Amos was going to experience that same regret.

Stepping up close to Gloria, Josie held her gaze and drew the line.

"I know you love Amos. I know you want what is best for him. Believe me when I say every choice I make, I make with him in mind," she said firmly. Yes, she was angry at Gloria's constant diminishment of her parenting, but Josie couldn't let anger be the deciding emotion here.

They had common ground, she and Gloria.

Even though Dan was lost to them, they still had Amos.

"He loves you, too," Josie said. "You and Al are the most important people in his world besides me."

Gloria's eyebrows rose in surprise.

"Spending time with you and Al gives Amos confidence that he is loved. I want that for him as much as you do," Josie said. Her throat closed a little, but she kept going, pushing out the words she needed to say.

"I need you to support me so I can focus on being the best mom possible and raise Amos to be the same sort of wonderful man you raised Dan to be. You cannot undermine me by questioning where or how we live, or by pitting your lifestyle against mine. If you continue to do this, it will hurt your relationship with Amos, because I am never, ever, letting my son go until he is grown and ready."

Gloria schooled her features to unimpressed, but the avid gleam in her eyes had dimmed and she tilted her head quickly to one side as though trying to shake Josie's declaration from her brain.

"I see," she said. "Well, I—"

"We do support you, Josie," Al said, speaking over Gloria. "Amos is a lucky little boy and reminds me of Dan at that age. Doesn't he, Gloria? Remind you of Dan?"

Gloria whipped her head around and frowned at her husband. Al smiled at her, sympathy radiating from his expression.

"We all miss Dan," he said gently, holding her gaze. "Grieving for Dan isn't the same as loving Amos, though. Those are two different things."

The moment felt heavy in a good way: solid and pure despite the pain at the root of it. While around them the crowd laughed and chattered with excitement, the five of them—Pax, Maddy, Al, Gloria, and Josie—shared the weighted silence in unexpected solidarity.

Her shoulders slumped and Gloria nodded once in agreement. "Yes. I suppose they are."

Deciding the excitement would most likely result in the planetarium canceling or at least delaying the show, Al proposed they take Amos out to Don's by the lake instead. He generously extended the invitation to all of them and Gloria didn't even object, but Pax and Maddy declined politely, and Josie told Al she would come with them the next time. Amos's departure was punctuated by the clicking of cell phone cameras and Josie's last-minute reminders to wash his hands before he ate and use his best manners.

A cheer rose up outside the museum when Naliti finally emerged, flanked by a bevy of older men and women in various states of distress. Josie would not want to have been Naliti at that moment, but the faery appeared nonchalant, and from where Josie stood, the ensuing discussions appeared calm enough.

Once Gloria was out of earshot, Josie turned to Maddy and Pax. "Thank you—"

Maddy held up a gloved hand, palm forward, blocking Josie's thanks.

"This"—she continued to hold her palm in the air but dropped all fingers except her pointer—"this was a debacle."

True. "Debacle" was an excellent SAT word for what was happening around them.

"Hurry up and *get to work*," Maddy spat from between clenched teeth.

Before Josie could ask her exactly what "work" she needed to get to, the crowd parted and Naliti stood before them.

While the princess huddled with Pax and Maddy, Josie was pressed into service as a photographer. Almost twenty minutes later, all the pictures had been taken and all the water bottles signed. As the group made its way back to Number Five, Josie found herself walking next to Pax.

"Is everything all right?" she asked him. "What did Naliti say?"

His eyes met Josie's and he reached out his hand. Before she could think better of it, they linked fingers and even that small a touch sent her heart rate soaring, and a bittersweet contentment settled in her bones.

She wanted to stop in the middle of the sidewalk and climb him like a tree, wrap her limbs around him, and lose herself in his touch. She wanted to run in the opposite direction and never feel this kind of need again.

"Unbeknownst to us, the princesses have become social media phenomena. Naliti has been conducting scientific experiments online and today was her first in-person event."

He sighed. "Maddy is livid, and I cannot say I am happy, either."

Famous faeries didn't exactly help the rest of Number Five's residents keep a low profile.

"I'm pretty surprised," Josie said. "She seems sensible, I can't imagine why she would blow up a museum."

Pax squeezed her hand lightly. "She claims it wasn't on purpose. She was conducting a simple experiment when something went wrong." His gaze shifted between their clasped hands and the group of faeries in front of them.

"The experiment was a demonstration of bases and acids—elemental science on this world. No magic whatsoever until she used her powers to heat a flask of liquid. Her hypothesis is the unused, latent magic on this world exists in a volatile state, and our presence is exciting it."

"Not exciting in a good way, I take it," Josie said.

Pax agreed. "Not good at all."

He held the door to Number Five open for Josie and she let go of his hand to brush by him, sparks prickling at her wherever their bodies touched.

"Pax," Maddy called. She was in the office doorway ushering Naliti inside, looking unaffected in that way you knew she was furious.

"You better go," Josie said.

"I must go," Pax said at the same time.

Before she could turn and make her way to the stairs, Pax caught her by the elbow.

"You were generous back there with Gloria," he said. "I have . . ." Pax paused and looked upward as though the words he needed were hovering up by the decorative plaster arches crossing the lobby's ceiling. When she'd moved in, they had been a dirty white with missing chunks. Now, though still dusty, they were almost whole again.

While conscious of the crowd of folks milling around them, they spoke quietly within a bubble of their own making.

"Whatever happens, you have changed something within this place. Changed something within me. Please, don't leave until we speak again," Pax said. "Please."

He knew.

He knew Josie had one foot out the door.

Gloria might back down for now, but blowing up the science

museum wasn't going to go unnoticed, and the magical plants and gargoyles aside, Number Five wasn't a place you could put down roots.

Josie and Amos were only two people, but they made up a family, and a family needed a place to grow and thrive, like plants in a garden.

"I'm not going anywhere tonight," she said. "We can talk in the morning."

The elevator opened and Raphe stalked out, bedecked in a puffy white shirt and tight black jeans.

"Paladin," he called to Pax. "What happened now?"

Pax ignored the question, keeping his eyes on Josie's face, but he frowned, and she knew it was time to let him go do his job.

"We can talk in the morning," she repeated.

He nodded, reluctantly. Before Raphe could say anything more, Josie turned her back on them and walked up the stairs toward the third floor. Amos would be home in a few hours and she had some thinking to do.

Chapter Twenty-Three

Glistening scales appeared a dull silver and black in the wan moonlight.

Josie stood unmoving in a darkened bedroom, the draft from a warped window casing bumping up against her chest. The window stood about three feet from a thick mat made of cotton or linen—difficult to see in the dark—upon which a serpent sat.

The sensation of cold and the sweet scent of rot almost tricked Josie's brain into thinking this was real, but when she cataloged the size of the creature and the fact that the walls of the room were carved of sandstone, she understood it was a dream and she faced something much grander than a snake.

Josie wore a long pink flannel nightgown with tiny bluebonnets embroidered at the neckline. It had been her momma's, and in real life, Josie had never worn it. Instead, she'd kept it in a plastic bag in the back of her closet to preserve her momma's smell.

Josie had forgotten it when packing her duffel bag the day she left Texas and for years fantasized about going back to get it.

Beneath her toes, the bare floor was icy cold, and she wasn't wearing socks.

"You have disturbed my rest," the serpent said.

Not that the flickering red tongue darting in and out of the serpent's mouth had shaped those words. The words simply hung in the air between them.

"I'm sorry," Josie said.

The following pause made her slightly nauseous. Still trying to parse sleep from wake, Josie couldn't discern what kind of serpent she faced. In her religion, serpents were the symbol for forbidden knowledge. Then again, some of her neighbors in Texas had believed handling snakes proved you were pure in the eyes of the Lord.

Would that make a serpent part of the Light or the Dark?

"Can I do anything to make it up to you?" Josie asked, the polite response coming automatically despite the obvious ridiculousness of the offer. What the heck was she supposed to do? Sing the giant serpent a lullaby? Make it a cup of hot milk?

The serpent's coils shifted and more of its massive body came into view.

Josie had the urge to kneel.

"You have a child," the serpent said.

Cold raced up the back of Josie's knees and she trembled.

"Don't touch him." The warning slipped from her lips and sounded more like a plea in the torpid air. Josie licked her lips to repeat her warning, but words deserted her as the serpent rose above her.

There was no ceiling above them, just a sky so black it was purple, and the only illumination came through the window. Josie couldn't see the whole of the creature, but the occasional shine of its scales hinted at something larger than would fit in an apartment.

Too many strange things had happened for her to question

how a dream could feel this real. Instead, Josie focused on the basic question of whether she was going to die right here in her momma's nightgown without having made arrangements for Amos or saying goodbye to her friends.

"You are brave for such a tiny being," the serpent said.

Josie wasn't brave. She was scared and cold and beyond confused.

A dry flapping sound accompanied the serpent's moving tongue, and without warning, it came closer as the great beast lowered its head. Josie shook hard enough her teeth rattled.

"The universe is out of balance and sickening the Waysides," the serpent said, its words dry and unemotional. "The cure for the Waysides is the cure for everything."

Okay. Great. That was helpful.

"How do I find the cure?" Josie asked.

Like the roar of a waterfall, the serpent's hiss pounded the walls and shook the floorboards.

"Are you truly so stupid as to ask *me*?" the serpent demanded. "Little speck, if it were in my power to cure the Waysides, I would have done so at the beginning."

Josie stumbled back, her feet now numb from cold.

"Okay, you don't have to be mean," she admonished. "I figured you brought me here to give me a clue or something."

The dim light finally allowed Josie a glimpse of the serpent's head.

Holy. Shit. Holy *shit* this thing was huge.

Golden eyes at least two feet wide stared at her, unblinking.

"I brought you here because I need a warm snack before I can fall back asleep," the serpent said.

If Josie could have moved her legs, she would have run straight through the window, broken bones be damned, but her body wouldn't respond to her brain's order to flee. The vertical black crevasse in the serpent's eye widened, and as it did, all sensation left Josie's body. She slumped to the floor and landed on her back, one leg bent outward.

I hope you choke, you overgrown worm! Josie shouted. In her head, of course, since her mouth couldn't move, not even to draw breath.

The moving coils made a sandpapery sound as the serpent lowered itself closer, and as terrifying as the sight was, Josie wouldn't look away.

All she could think was she'd failed Amos, sentencing him to the same hollow ache that had sat inside Josie for years. Why wasn't she enough for anyone to stick around? What was she lacking that sent her momma and her daddy away?

Tears of rage blinded her. How dare this creature do that to Amos?

"Hello, Mother. What are you playing with?"

The serpent raised its head away from Josie and faced someone, or something, on the other side of the room.

"Daughter," the serpent said in greeting. "Are you hungry, too?"

"For one of them?" The daughter made a gagging sound.

Oh jeez, thanks, lady.

"You wouldn't eat it anyway," the woman said. "They're full of bile and contradictions, both of which you can have only in moderation. Stop teasing the poor thing."

"Who is the mother and who is the child here?" the serpent demanded. "I've been eating mortal souls for longer than you've been sentient."

Sensation came back into Josie's limbs. She clenched and unclenched her toes and fingers while the pair bickered about cholesterol levels and diets. Once the conversation veered into how the serpent spoke to her daughter about weight gain during adolescence, Josie knew it was time to run. Nothing good ever came out of those conversations.

". . . never said you were fat. I said the outfit you were wearing—"

Josie didn't bother to look behind her to catch a glimpse of the daughter. Instead, she heaved herself off the floor and ran for the window, the serpent's surprised hiss ruffling the hair on her neck.

Just as she covered her face with her arm and launched herself toward the glass, Josie was wrenched backward. The daughter had one arm wrapped around Josie's waist, the other over her eyes.

"Ballsy move," the daughter whispered in Josie's ear. "Now go limp and let me get you out of this."

Recognizing the woman's voice, Josie did as she was told.

"I am going to take great pleasure in squeezing the life from that thing," the serpent declared.

"You can't eat it. Even if it didn't make you sick, it still has a young in the nest who can't care for itself."

Amos.

An image of him and his sweet blinding smile flashed through her brain and Josie whimpered.

"I could eat the young," said the serpent.

The daughter made a sound of disbelief. "Let this one go and I'll order us takeout."

"Hmmph," the serpent snorted. "Not Thai again. I'm sick of Thais."

The woman lifted Josie off the floor and carried her to a door carved from the rock wall that hadn't been there two minutes ago.

"As for you, little human . . ." the serpent said.

The daughter paused but Josie kept her glance straight ahead, willing herself not to react.

"I am sparing you on account of your young," the serpent informed her. "If you wish to stay out of my lair and my belly, however, I suggest you find that cure."

Before Josie could make any promises, the world went black.

Pax hadn't been able to get away from the triage following Princess Naliti's experiment gone wrong last night until it was too late to go visit Josie. He'd waited till an hour past the sunrise to walk up to Josie's door but his courage deserted him. He'd raised his hand to knock, then dropped his arm and walked away, toward the elevator.

He would have pressed the button to go down, but it melted into the wall as he approached.

"Very subtle," he whispered.

The elevator disappeared and several iron birds swooped over his head.

Pax sighed and rolled his eyes, turned on his heel, and walked back to the door. Considered leaving Number Five to purchase a cell phone to call Josie but he didn't have her number. Stared at his shoes for a little bit and thought about kisses. Kisses and the destruction of the universe.

"Hello, Mr. Pax. Why is you walking around out here?" Amos stood at the open door and stared up at Pax's fist, once again raised as if to knock.

"Hello, Mr. Amos," Pax replied.

Amos wore yellow sweatpants, a blue sweatshirt with a pony wearing goggles on it, and a white cap with a blue buffalo across the top.

Were human children color-blind until a certain age?

"You are not wearing any superheroes today," Pax said, stalling.

What was he going to tell the child?

Oh, I'm walking around until I find the right words to convince your mother she is perfectly safe but at the same time under my protection and to sniff her hair and figure out if she'll let me have sex with her again.

Nope. Can't say that.

"I got Hulk on my underwear," Amos informed him. "And I got Batman on my socks."

Sure enough, the caped defender stared up at him from the little boy's feet.

"Excellent." Pax craned his head and peered into the apartment. "Where is your mother, Mr. Amos? She wouldn't want you to answer the door without her."

Amos shrugged. "I'm not allowed, except the door opened by itself."

No going back now.

"Can you tell her I am here? I will wait out in the hallway if you . . ."

"Hi." Josie came out of her bedroom dressed the same as her son, except her sweatpants were black and her blue sweatshirt had **Kamala** across the front of it.

"Hi," he said.

She didn't smile as they stared at each other. Pax felt the space between them widen.

"You wanna watch a cartoon, Mr. Pax?" Amos asked.

"Come in," Josie said. "I was going to make coffee."

Pax followed Amos into the living room and sat on a large green velvet couch. Amos clambered up next to him.

"You wanna watch 'Pidey and Fwends?"

Boy, did he ever.

Pax had now read eighty comic books and watched twenty hours of programming concerning Spider-Man. He had several questions regarding this show, which purported to follow Spider-Man's childhood. Specifically, what was behind the introduction of Dino-Web powers in season three? How did dinosaurs fit in with superhero mythology?

Amos expertly clicked through the symbols and categories on his television remote until he found his favorite episode. Though it happened to be one from season two, Pax was content to watch and leave his dino questions for later.

"What do you take in your coffee?" Josie stood in the archway to the living room. Her hair was pulled back tightly, and she wore no makeup.

She looked young and fragile.

Like she was ready to run.

Damn.

"I shall return, Mr. Amos," Pax said. "Would you like a drink as well?"

"No thanks." Amos barely reacted, transfixed by the television screen.

Josie cleared her throat and sent Pax a speaking look. He sighed and left the television behind.

In the kitchen, a blue glass bowl filled with lilacs sat on the table and the curtains were now red-and-white-checked gingham.

"Have a seat." Josie gestured to a wooden chair and Pax obeyed. A creamer in the shape of a cow was already on the table next to a sugar bowl in the shape of a strawberry. She set down a mug emblazoned with the words Male Tears in front of him and Pax took his time inhaling the marvelous scent of fire and earth.

"Thank you. This is delightful. We do not have coffee on my world," he said, spooning in enough sugar to make it palatable—about six spoonfuls—then taking a sip and nodding his thanks.

"Don't leave—" he said.

"We have to talk—" Josie started.

They broke off at the same moment, staring at each other through the silence. Josie took a sip of her coffee.

Wait.

Wait, what the . . .

"Did you drink your coffee without sugar and milk?" he asked.

"Mmmm." Josie blinked at his shock, as if what she'd done were completely normal. "I take mine black."

Pax gaped. Perhaps he'd misjudged her this whole time? Perhaps Josie was a masochist or born without taste buds.

"Why?" he asked. "Why would you drink something that disgusting?"

Obviously, she thought he was joking, because she took another sip, pushed the mug away, and leaned back on the chair, assessing him. The purple shadows under her eyes hinted the coffee had been a necessity and not a whim.

"Last night I had a dream."

Pax waited while Josie gathered her thoughts. He, too, had had a dream last night. He could tell from the exhaustion written on her face that Josie's dream hadn't been nearly as pleasurable as his dream.

"Is there . . ." Josie lowered her voice on the off chance Amos was listening to them instead of Spider-Man.

Doubtful. Spider-Man already occupied a huge space in Pax's brain. How could it not hold Amos's entire attention?

"Is there a huge serpent on the sixth floor?"

Pax choked on his coffee.

Mortified, he took the Buzz Lightyear towel Josie handed him and wiped up the liquid that had come out of his nose while examining her face.

"You . . . I don't . . ." He coughed again. "A *huge* serpent, you say?"

Josie nodded, appearing calm. Calmer than Pax might have expected given how little time she'd had to accept the reality of Number Five and the mostly benign nature of the guests she'd met so far.

"I don't know."

She frowned. "What do you mean, you don't know?"

"The sixth-floor guests are accorded a great deal of privacy." Pax leaned back, then forward, trying to find the words to explain the nature of the sixth floor. "The only person who knows for certain is Maddy. It's her magic keeping them docile while they reside within a Wayside."

Beneath the heavy odor of the lilacs was the faint scent of dried lavender and eucalyptus hand cream. Josie had folded her hands and set them on her thigh. Pax gave in to an urge and reached over to take one of her soft hands in his.

Aside from a small gasp at the contact of skin to skin, Josie said nothing, but she let him keep hold of her and squeezed his fingers in consent. For a moment, Pax allowed himself a heady peace. He felt for her pulse beneath his fingertip and marveled at how incredibly soft yet at the same time how marvelously strong this woman was in a way only women could be—a strength forged through trials of the heart rather than physical exertion. Trials Pax did not know if he was equipped to pass through.

"So," Josie said. "The serpent I talked to . . ."

Pax's hand spasmed in fear and he pulled her hand to his chest. "You spoke with him?"

"Her," she said, eyes wide.

Damn. He'd scared her.

"She said she was sparing me because of Amos and I needed to find a cure to what's making Number Five sick."

The list of entities who might appear to a human as a large serpent was vast.

"How did she entice you into her chamber?" he asked. "Did you hear a noise or the notes to a familiar song?"

Josie shook her head. "It was a dream. I went to bed and woke up in front of her."

Likely a summoning. Not as bad as having a sixth-floor guest awake and roaming the hallways, but not a good sign, either.

Pax rubbed the bridge of his nose and closed his eyes. "Even the gods are impatient. Why will no one give Number Five the time to fill at her own pace?"

When Josie slipped her hand from his, he opened his eyes to see an expression of confusion on her face.

"Didn't you say these guests had places they needed to be?" she asked. "If they paid a steep price to get to whatever their destination, it makes sense they are impatient. With Number Five's tank still empty—"

"But it isn't!" Pax exclaimed.

Josie blinked and Pax smacked himself in the forehead.

"I haven't told you?" he asked, then continued before she could answer. "I haven't told you. The golden needle has moved. This is, we are . . . you are working."

This didn't elicit the response Pax had been expecting.

Well, he might have been expecting Josie to jump up and

wrap her arms around him and cry, *You've saved us!* or something equally laudatory, and kiss him.

Who could blame him?

That was a reasonable expectation for a knight to have when in the company of a lady.

"It moved?" she said. Instead of joyful, her voice sounded accusatory. "When were you going to tell me this? When did it move? I could have told the serpent, and she might not have wanted to eat me."

Pax opened his mouth, but his brain was stuck on that last part.

"It doesn't matter," Josie said sharply, as though she knew where his brain might catch. "Did this just slip your mind?"

She made the gesture with her fingers he hadn't figured out but was certain did not mean anything good.

"Yes," he admitted. "Yes, I've been distracted by Naliti blowing up the science museum and Raphe going on about blood sacrifices and everyone wanting Number Five to be fixed yesterday and the endless debates over mini clover versus grass."

"Blood sacrifice?"

Shit.

Pax bit his top lip. This was going cockeyed. Why wasn't Number Five stepping in to help him like she'd done before? Where were the roses? Where were the dimmed lights and tipping floorboards?

"Ummmm." Pax pulled at the collar of his shirt. "You see—"

"Shhhh." Josie held up a finger and cocked her head, listening for Amos. Pax waited, expecting to soon hear the boy ask for another episode or the tinny, high voices of Spidey's friends coming from the television.

Instead, there was silence.

Something was wrong.

Amos was quiet.

Too quiet.

Of course, it could be the boy had turned off the television and was reading a book instead.

Only, if the sixth-floor guests were reaching out in their sleep . . . what if one of them . . . ?

Whatever Josie saw in Pax's face caused her to blanch, and she ran to the living room, one hand out toward the wall as if to prop herself up if her legs gave out.

Pax maneuvered his body out from behind the table without knocking anything over and followed Josie into the living room.

The room sat empty.

"Amos?" she called, but there was no strength in her voice.

Pax rushed to Amos's bedroom and threw open the door.

This room sat empty as well.

Down the hallway Josie called her son's name as she searched the bathroom and her bedroom, but Pax felt in his bones she wouldn't find him.

A terrible, terrible thought occurred to him.

What if Amos hadn't wandered off?

What if he'd been taken?

Chapter Twenty-Four

You promised me Amos would be safe," Josie whispered around the claw squeezing her lungs. "You said nothing would happen to him."

A low throb rippled along the walls of Number Five, and Josie fought the urge to vomit.

The front door to the apartment was wide open. Outside in the corridor, dozens of wrought iron birds flew in intricate loops and circles.

"Amos?" Pax called, his skin a sickly gray color beneath the flickering lights. He stepped out into the corridor and the birds scattered.

"Amos!" His voice shook the walls and set the glass teardrop crystals in the overhead light to shaking so hard that two or three of them fell to the floor.

She followed him out of the apartment and looked both ways down the hallway, but Amos wasn't in sight. He wasn't gone completely but Josie knew he wasn't on this floor.

She should be crying or screaming. She should be running up and down the corridors and calling her boy's name, but Josie was too numb to move. Pax turned and set a hand on her shoulder but remained silent, shaking his head with an aura of helplessness that scared her even more.

An iron bird swooped close enough for its wing to brush the top of Pax's head.

"Those birds," Josie said, "They must be what drew Amos out of the apartment. But why?" She enunciated her words carefully in case the numbness that froze her legs reached her lips and soon she would be unable to speak. "Why would Number Five let him leave?"

"Pax." Josie put her hand to her throat, fighting the invisible ligature threatening to send her to the floor. "Tell me now. Why do you look scared? What the hell is happening here?"

He squeezed her shoulder lightly, then let his hand drop to his side.

"There's something I have to tell you."

Pax had fought battles that went on for days. Hour after hour beneath a dying sun, he'd stood knee-deep in mud and shit, swinging his sword until he was so exhausted he would swear he'd fallen asleep while hacking.

He would one hundred times rather be back on those killing fields than tell Josie the truth right now.

He was a coward.

He deserved her hatred. Because she would. Hate him.

"Number Five would never hurt Amos," he said. "But there are some guests who disagreed with the plan to invite humans into the building as tenants."

He paused to gather courage, wanting more than anything to look away from Josie's terrified gaze, remaining where he was because he owed this courageous woman his complete attention.

"And?" Josie prompted, looking up at him expectantly. "What does this have to do with Amos?"

Every so often the Light makes you choose. Those choices can cut you off at the knees faster and far more painfully than the stroke of a sword.

Pax could tell Josie everything he'd been keeping back from her. The consequence of course was she'd never trust him again. She'd take Amos and leave, and he'd never see them again.

Or he could lie.

Make up another story.

Pretend her terror was unreasonable. Speak to her as though she were a child and cut down her growing self-confidence with a blade made of shame or distaste.

"Denis, Raphe, and a few others believed the key to saving Number Five was not to embrace new life within its walls. They suggested instead we sacrifice the new life. Sacrifice you." His mouth dried and he had to force himself to tell the entire truth. "Sacrifice Amos."

Josie crumpled like a scrap of paper beneath a fist but Pax caught her before she could hit the floor. He wanted nothing more than to cradle her, meld his body to hers, stay in a cocoon for as long as they could. Her low moan of horror nearly drowned his words, but Pax knew she heard him.

"No," she whispered.

"No," he echoed.

No. No, no, no.

A lifetime lived in service of others. A lifetime of duty he'd never asked for. A lifetime without a single word of thanks, without a single night of comfort, without a single legacy other than a reputation for bloodshed.

"No," he said again, pulling Josie up and pulling her along with him toward the stairs only to find a wall where they once stood.

No.

"They won't touch him," Pax said. "I swore to you I would keep him safe. I swore on my life, and I will die before anyone touches a hair on his head."

"Where could he be?" she asked.

The sacrificial altar.

Raphe's lair. The incinerator.

Nightmares.

He turned and raced for the elevator, but when the doors opened, the only button on the panel was for the first floor. Josie hesitated outside the elevator, but Pax slammed the panel with his fist, something in the back of his brain telling him this was the wrong thing to do, but a buzzing noise made of pain and rage deafened him to his conscience.

"Where is he?" Pax yelled.

Number Five remained silent. No guests popped their heads to investigate the noise, not a single sound could be heard over the rasp of his and Josie's ragged breaths.

"Send him out to me right now," he commanded, staring down as if he could see to the basement. "Give him back or I will slit your throats and burn your corpses to ash."

Josie gasped but Pax's fear had taken hold of his tongue at the thought of Amos in danger. An innocent. The purest thing he'd encountered in a long—perhaps too long—lifetime.

"I need my sword," he told Josie. "I will slay them where they stand and burn the whole world down." Rage and terror and the empty sensation of loss writhed beneath his skin.

Josie said nothing but she came to stand next to him into the elevator car.

When the elevator didn't move, red stars burst before Pax's eyes.

"I will—"

"Stop," Josie whispered. "You're scaring her."

Pax's hands fisted and opened as he tried to catch his breath. He hoped he was scaring Number Five. He wanted to scare her, to show his strength, to be a hero.

"You're scaring me, too," she said softly. Although she turned her head toward him slightly, Josie's eyes remained fastened on the place where he'd slammed the button.

The words were spoken so quietly he almost didn't hear them.

Why wasn't Josie screaming? Where was her anger?

The life of a child hung in the balance.

Josie's child.

Amos.

The delicate little being who was terrible at jokes with a voice that sounded like bells.

Of its own accord, Pax's rage abated when he thought about the tone of Amos's laughter. Like silver. Something rare.

His pounding heart eased.

The most powerful faiths on all the worlds Pax had encountered venerated the attributes that came easiest to children.

Forgiveness.

Love that was unconditional even if undeserved.

Awe for the everyday. Appreciation of stories.

Applause for the mundane.

Acceptance of flaws.

The more Pax listed the qualities that make children special, the more he recognized how many of those qualities he did not himself possess and it humbled him. His breathing slowed, his fist unclenched, and the dignified, intractable hope that kept Josie standing filtered into him.

On those worlds where divinities used brute strength to ensure loyalty, violence to convert their followers, or venerated war and rage, Pax had encountered hellscapes. Fear could twist even the most noble aspirations into something dangerous and shameful.

Those worlds best described as paradise, the worlds with the happiest residents, the most beautiful vistas, the least conflict—those worlds were ones where children were cared for, where curiosity was praised, and kindness valued more than anything else.

Reason returned to him along with breath.

Being a hero had nothing to do with the promise of strength. Cutting down the enemy in front of him wasn't going to protect Amos and Josie forever. Being a hero meant finding the fortitude to give the LaChiusa family a place to live—to thrive—surrounded by tolerance, kindness, and community. A formidable challenge compared to what he'd faced as a soldier. Formidable, but not impossible.

"I am sorry I frightened you," Pax said to Number Five.

He turned to face Josie and waited until she looked at him.

"I am sorry I frightened you as well," he told Josie. "I let my fear overwhelm my better self. I lost control and I never want to do that again."

Terror had bleached her skin a terrible shade of gray, but when she took hold of his hands, her grip was warm and steady.

"I forgive you," she said softly. "When a child you love is in danger, we often mistake the fear for anger."

Pax bowed his head in relief that Josie had forgiven him. When a low chime vibrated up from the floor and the elevator doors closed, he knew he'd been forgiven by Number Five as well.

Chapter Twenty-Five

The elevator doors opened onto the lobby, but Josie didn't move.

Her brain had latched on to the stupid idea that if she remained in place, the world would pause, and nothing could move forward.

If she left the elevator, it would be to find Amos, because Amos was missing. If she stayed here, whatever happened to Amos would be suspended.

"Stay," Pax said. "Stay and I will find him."

A stalwart paladin had replaced the terrified man looking to smash someone with his sword. No vestigial anger or fear remained on his face. Pax stepped out of the elevator, and as his foot touched the marble tiles, his clothing changed. His legs were encased in rough woolen pants tucked into black boots, one with a knife peeping from the cuff, his broad shoulders covered by what looked like a linen tunic with a thick leather vest over the whole. Across his back lay a leather belt with two scabbards attached, one of which held a broadsword.

He looked at his hand, which now held a mace, then over his shoulder at Josie.

"Did I do that?" she asked.

Shrugging, Pax crossed the lobby and peered through the windows of the common area's double doors. Josie followed, staying a few feet away from the huge blade strapped across Pax's back.

"I just want him to be okay," Josie whispered. The wrought iron vines wrapped around the balustrade had turned green and began flowering as she passed them, pink flowers with gold thorns, dark green leaves with veins in the shape of complicated designs. The birds flew in and out of the vines and the scent of violet overwhelmed her.

"I hear voices," Pax said. Josie tore her attention from the vines and joined him at the doors to the common area. "Stay behind me. Whatever happens, my aim is to get you to Amos. Once you have him, run."

"Run from Number Five, you mean?" she asked.

Pax nodded.

"And afterward?" she asked.

He canted his head to the left as though she'd said something unintelligible and frowned.

"If we leave, will Number Five stay sick? Will she die? If she does, what happens to you?"

Pax frowned. "It must be difficult enough to be the only humans in a building full of other beings. Knowing some of your neighbors saw your lives as less valuable because of that difference, how could you stay?"

"Because . . ."

Number Five had given them roses and a Spider-Man quilt. There had been kisses and snowball fights.

"Because this is our home," she said. "Because you made us welcome."

Along the baseboards, purple and white violets sprouted while the mailboxes for the sixth floor burst open and iridescent pink sand poured out onto the floor.

Pax shook his head quickly as though her answer stung, then pushed open the doors to the common area.

The fluorescent lights remained but beneath them lay a black-and-white-tiled floor. Small side tables flanked the windows, atop which sat brass vases full of cabbage roses. Like the moment before the cymbals crash in a symphony, a low, promising vibration hummed through the air.

Right when Josie thought she might fall over with dizziness, a high-pitched scream split the air.

Josie and Pax ran across the room toward the glass doors that led out into the courtyard but stopped short before they reached for the handles, shocked into stillness at the sight greeting them.

The courtyard had been transformed.

The garden boxes and warning signs were gone. In the center of a mossy lawn stood an enormous magnolia tree with yellow blossoms. In the back corner where the broken bench had been, water tripped down a stack of shale stones and fell into a small pond full of water lilies and large rocks upon which sat albino turtles.

The Fate siblings gathered on a blanket next to the pond, laughing at something Joey Z. was telling them. Close by, the owl shifter was doing Tai Chi with Bert and Ernie, the djinn twins were engaged in a fierce game of hearts at a small table, and a nymph sat beneath the basketball hoop playing a fife.

"Amos." Josie was out the door as soon as she spotted him doing summersaults with the faery cheerleaders.

"Mom, Mom!" he cried when Josie grabbed him and squeezed his tiny body, then set him down to check and make sure nothing was broken or bruised. "Did you know we have a backyard now? And did you know I can hears the birds from the staircase sing a song? Did you know if we wish together, we can has more gardens?"

Pax watched Josie fly unfettered to her son—the collision of two pieces of light.

The sight left him . . . affected.

Sharper than hunger, more than lust, Pax longed for what connected Josie and Amos. Whatever that was called, he wanted it so badly it left him hollow and shaken.

"Love," said a voice.

While he'd been staring at Josie and Amos, someone had come up behind him from the ballroom. Pax cursed himself for the inattention and swung round to examine the person.

A woman, a human woman.

She wore a green T-shirt and ripped jeans. Her plain brown hair was twisted into two braids, and beneath her thick eyebrows she'd a pair of unremarkable pale blue eyes.

"It's called love, what you see there," she explained, gesturing to Josie and Amos.

Ah.

No wonder Pax hadn't known what to call it.

Love.

"Who are you?" he asked.

"Momma?"

Josie stood, holding Amos in her arms. She took a step toward the woman, her mouth opening and closing.

"Momma?" The words came out high and tight, pushed out from a place of pain. Or joy.

"Hey, baby," the woman said in greeting.

"Is it really you?" Josie asked.

Pax turned his gaze to the woman, searching her worn face for a hint of truth.

"Sort of, if that's what you want."

The answer wasn't what Josie had expected. Her shoulders sank. Pax frowned.

"It's kinda complicated," the woman continued. For an instant her image sputtered, in and out like a candlewick at the end of its use. "Aren't you a treat? Lookit you and your boy, there. You done good, little Jo."

"Mom, Mom, I'm gonna go feed the turtles." Amos was halfway to the pond before he finished the sentence, his feet barely touching the ground.

Josie watched her son, then turned back toward her mother. Pax thought maybe she would run to embrace her, but Josie took a step then stopped.

Certainly, there was compassion on Josie's face, but also something that looked a lot like regret. A palpable misery came off Josie in waves even from a distance.

"What do you want?" Josie asked, her voice thin and hollow.

"Wanted to ask you to stay," the mother said.

Josie winced as though her mother's words had sharp edges. "You didn't stay."

Although her tone was level, Pax heard a note of censure. A *broken* home is what Josie's mother had left her daughter. He doubted he would be half so calm as Josie were he in her place.

"No, we both know it was for the best. If I'd stayed, you'd have learned to take care of someone at the expense of yourself. This way, you learned to take care of someone who can love you back the right way."

Josie's mother looked as though she would smell like laundry detergent and cigarette smoke, but instead she smelled like nothing at all. Again, she winked in and out of existence.

"Number Five?" he asked.

The image canted her head and lifted her palms as though weighing the truth.

"Sort of," said Number Five.

"Why?" Josie asked. She came closer now that she knew it wasn't her mother, turning her head every so often to check on Amos's whereabouts.

Number Five smiled. "I don't know, little Jo. You're the one who decides how to see me."

Josie frowned and Pax rubbed his chin.

"I've never seen you," he said, trying to keep it from sounding as though he was jealous.

He wasn't.

Not really.

"You have," said Number Five. "You didn't know it."

"For Pete's sake, Cindy!" a faery cheerleader hollered. "How should I know you'd be dumb enough to stick your finger in there? Someone, go get Naliti."

A scrum of residents formed over where the faeries had been practicing their moves. No one seemed to notice Number Five or even to glance over to where the three of them were standing.

"Anyhow, I'd be real grateful if you 'n' your boy could stay for a while," said Number Five. "I'm in some trouble and I need your help."

"How?" Pax asked. A strange reluctance to hear her answer pressed on his breastbone. What if it was a simple fix. Where would Josie and Amos go?

How could he leave them?

"How do we fill you back up?" he asked.

"You know already, Pax Nomen, Paladin of the Ways, Protector of the Light," Number Five said, thrusting one angular hip to the side and setting her hand on it, nodding toward Josie. "It's what you saw when those two found each other."

Oh.

So.

Simple, but not easy.

Number Five cocked her head. "What do you say, little Jo?"

Josie looked over at the other residents, who had somehow conjured up a ball and were kicking it around while Cindy argued about something with Denis.

"I have to think of Amos," Josie said.

Number Five nodded. "Wouldn't it be nice for him to have a community like this?"

Josie's mouth opened and closed. Pax watched her for clues, slowing his breathing so he could hear her words.

"What about the magic part? Amos couldn't keep a secret if you tied it to him," Josie said.

"Eh. We'll come up with something. I'll watch out for him, make sure no one does anything too dangerous around him," Number Five assured her.

Rather than answering, Josie caught Pax's gaze.

"A lot could go wrong," she said to him.

What he should do was agree with her, then show her the size of his sword. Threaten to behead anyone who looked twice at her or Amos. Nod without saying a word, implicitly promising his eternal vigilance.

He opened his mouth to say something to that effect, but these words came out instead.

"Sometimes, I dream about us. I dream of waking beside you, having spent the night before making love with you. I dream your hair is messy and you are wearing my shirt, and my heart pounds with such longing I fear it might pound out of my chest."

Number Five disappeared and the raucous cries of the tenants' kickball game faded.

"Sometimes I dream about us. The three of us, eating tofu scrambles and discussing the evolution of Sonic the Hedgehog—I have a few thoughts on that."

Josie's beautiful gray eyes shone extra bright, but Pax was sure he knew why those tears had appeared.

He kept going.

"I dream about love. I dream you and Amos teach me the different ways of it, that you have patience when I cannot speak of it or grow frustrated and want to beat it into a shape I recognize."

"Love?" she whispered.

"That's what sits here, isn't it?" Pax rubbed his chest. "That's what aches when I see you and when I don't. What pushes against the walls of my skin when you wear your blue hat, or talk to Joey Z. without acting disgusted, or lie to the faeries about how you like their outfits."

He took a step toward her, but his knees shook too much, so he stood like a fool as she approached him.

"I didn't lie," she said. She closed the distance between them and reached up to set her hands on his cheeks. They held each other like an Ouroboros, with no end and no beginning. "I like the green-and-pink color scheme."

"Please," he begged, "don't tell me something horrifying when I am making a declaration of love. It unsettles me."

"I beg your pardon," she said, laughter creeping into her voice. "Continue, please."

She smelled like candy and sweat and the triumph of spring, so Pax kissed her because he had to, then finished his thought.

"Please, stay so I can learn how to love you."

Josie swallowed, tears threatening to spill from the corners of her eyes.

"What happens when Number Five is able to leave?" she asked, the words coming out thin and reedy, as though her throat were tight around them.

"You will decide," he said. "If you and Amos want to stay in Number Five, we will visit the sirens' home world together."

Josie gasped and her hand flew to her chest.

"That would be wondrous indeed," he said. "The universe is a vast and marvelous place. I would be happy to travel through it with you."

A bank of clouds pulled apart over their heads and a warm spring sun poked out.

"And if I don't want to take Amos away from this world?" Josie asked, the two lines between her eyebrows deepening.

Pax faltered. He'd already told her he loved her. Why was it hard to say the next part?

"I would stay with you no matter what you chose, if . . . if you want me?"

With a laugh reminiscent of her son's, clear and pure like the sound of a stream or the dawn chorus, Josie wrapped her arms around his chest. Pax took a deep inhale of her hair, relishing her soft body clasped to his.

"Oh, I want you," Josie declared, pulling back and looking up at him. "I've never wanted anything more. I love you."

Pax lifted her up and the crowd around them began clapping in appreciation for the enthusiasm of their kiss.

It wasn't only Number Five who had been empty.

This woman, this child, this love—this was the magic that would save them all.

Epilogue

Are you certain you don’t want me to eat your mother-in-law?”

Josie smiled and thanked Bert for the umpteenth time for offering to get rid of Gloria, and for the umpteenth time, she declined.

“If you ate her, who would babysit Amos for Pax and me?” she said instead.

“I would look after him if I were two hundred years younger,” Bert assured her. “He has a staggering amount of energy, that boy.”

“I suppose he does,” Josie agreed. She said good night and climbed the stairs to apartment 3C. There was a wreath on the door made of red, green, and silver crystals and a welcome mat with a picture of a snowman below it.

She came inside and walked past a closet full of winter coats, past her photographs beautifully framed in copper and gold, and went into the living room. A baby grand piano stood in the corner of the room with a plastic red-and-blue bench in front of it. Both she and Pax had tried to open the cover, but it wouldn’t budge. Pax theorized it waited for Amos to be interested before it would let them play it. Josie had doubts they would ever see those keys.

"I take it Gloria did not want to come upstairs again this week?" Pax came out of the kitchen, a Wolverine apron slung around his narrow hips, drying the last of the dishes with a Buzz Lightyear dish towel.

"On the one hand, telling her this building was rent controlled for retired circus performers was a stroke of genius," Josie said.

Amos could tell his grandparents the most fantastical stories and they wouldn't bat an eye now.

"On the other hand, Gloria gets to use rude observations about carneys and trained seals as her excuse not to interact with you. It galls her that you and Al get along."

Upon learning they were dating, Al had taken Josie aside and confided that Dan would have approved of Pax. The unexpected admission had touched her deeply.

"The lobby looked presentable?" Pax asked.

"The sixth-floor mailboxes still rattle when you walk by, but nothing else has changed," she assured him.

He sighed and flipped the dish towel over his shoulder, joining her in the living room on the green couch. Like he often did, Pax let his fingers comb through her hair, touched her cheeks, her arms, her cheeks again as though assuring himself she was truly there in front of him. That she was going to stay.

"I checked the needle this morning," he said. "It's still stuck at ten percent and none of us have any idea how much fuel the ±Þ˜š¬¥‡ needs before Number Five can start up again."

Josie rested her head on his shoulder knowing she would never get enough of the comfort and security flooding her veins during the in-between times, in between the fervent kisses and existential crises, in between the boundary drawing and the Sunday morning bliss.

Pax, focused on twisting a lock of her hair around his finger, suddenly stopped.

"What if you and Amos aren't enough?"

Before Josie could answer that awkward question, Pax spoke again.

"That was such an awkward question." He let go of her hair, leaned over, and kissed her an apology. "What I meant is, what if it takes more than our love to fill Number Five's tank?"

"I'd say love grows, and the longer we are together, the more we can fill her tank," Josie answered. "But that kind of growth happens over years. Can Number Five wait that long?"

"Denis had an idea . . . I know, he's a soulless jerk, but he's motivated to help in this matter."

Josie bit her lip and sighed. She would never forgive Denis for advocating for her and Amos's sacrifice, and Pax didn't blame her.

The Wayside Oath still held, however, and killing the little asshole was off the table.

"I can't imagine what Denis could come up with to try and fill Number Five's tank with love," Josie said.

Pax took her fingers in his, and as he kissed her knuckles, the candles on the sideboard lit and cabbage rose petals fell from above.

"What do you know about speed dating?" he asked.

CITY MAGAZINE

Events Page

DECEMBER 22

BINGO NIGHT at Holy Cross Church. Coffee and cookies begin at 5:30 p.m. in the church basement with Bingo to follow. $1 a card, winner takes half the pot.

FRIDAY MOVIE NIGHT Join Miss Nekesa at the Frederick Douglass Public Library for Friday Movie Night's feature, HOW TO TRAIN YOUR DRAGON, starting at 6:30 p.m.

SPEED DATING AT THE 5555 Join other singles in the community room of 5555 East Avenue for a free mixer. Music provided by THE FATES AND FURIES, cash bar, from 7 to 9 p.m.

Acknowledgments

Thank you to my husband, my real-life romantic hero, and to my children, who constantly amaze me with their creativity and compassion. Thank you especially to my mom, who went and kicked cancer's ass to the curb and back, for sticking around and being an inspiration. Thank you to my editor, Sarah Blumenstock, for making me a better writer; to my agent, Ann Leslie Tuttle, for her patience and professionalism; to Liz Sellers for being a champ; and to everyone at Berkley and Ace who has worked to make this book a reality. Thank you to Kim-Salina I in marketing and Jessica Mangicaro for calming me TF down when I need it. Special thanks to Peggy Dean for the beautiful cover design and illustration! Thank you to Alison Cnockaert, the interior designer; Lynsey Griswold, the production editor; and Will Tyler, the proofreader. Thank you to Anita Mumm, whose kind words and terrific guidance convinced me I really could write something other than historical (although I'd rather not). Many thanks to the Campers (Serena, Meg, Libby, Mazey, and Ali), to Neely Tubati-Alexander and Liana De la Rosa, to my beloved OG Berkletes, and, as always, to the Park Ave moms and the Highland Hotties. Thanks go to the bookstagrammers for being awesome human beings as well as voracious readers, to the booksellers and librarians who champion the romance genre, and to all my readers who made the leap from the world of secret scientists to the world of Waysides.

Turn the page for a look at Raphe's story

The Wayside Guide to Baking and Bloodlust

from Elizabeth Everett!

"You need to leave."

Sophie didn't bother to look up at the woman issuing the demand—her friend and coworker Destinee Hodges. After all, she'd told Sophie the same thing every night for the past year only to get the same response.

"I *am* leaving," Sophie replied, not bothering to move. The words she'd just typed careened crazily into one another on the screen so that it looked to her like she'd strung random letters together for shits and giggles. She'd need to use the read aloud function to be certain her brief made sense, but that could wait until tomorrow.

"You said that two hours ago," Destinee countered.

Sophie sighed and saved the document, finally acknowledging Destinee with a level gaze.

"Don't tell me what to do. You're not my mother," Sophie deadpanned.

Destinee wasn't Sophie's mother, but she sure acted like it with no shame whatsoever, and vice versa.

Sophie and Destinee had started at Vulpis, Anguis, & Partners on the same day a little over ten years ago. A decade working together in mostly white, mostly male trenches creates family like nothing else.

Both became criminal defense attorneys because they believed that everyone deserves representation regardless of their income and status. However, instead of eventually moving on to Legal Aid or other nonprofits once they paid off their law school debts, they'd decided to remain at VA&P. The firm was wealthy enough that they could take up to a quarter of their cases pro bono and never have to eat ramen again once the loans were finished.

Destinee had just become the first Black senior partner and only the second woman senior partner since the first Reynard Vulpis founded the firm almost two hundred years ago. Sophie hoped this meant VA&P was ready to make her the *third* woman senior partner.

In their ten years together, Sophie had watched as Destinee bought a house, found a partner, had two kids, and gained a live-in mother-in-law and an incontinent dog.

In the same amount of time, Destinee had watched Sophie find a house, a husband, and an incontinent cat.

Then offered her a shoulder to cry on when Sophie lost them all.

Her divorce had been, in a word, devastating.

For the first time in her life, Sophie had failed.

Spectacularly.

The consequence of this failure had cracked her foundation, and ever since handing over her house keys to her ex-husband, she'd struggled to find solid ground. Every morning, Sophie woke ready to command the day, only to remember her sole responsibility now was an apartment empty of all life except a succulent she'd won in an office raffle.

She'd named it George and given it a fifty-fifty chance of survival.

Sophie shut down her computer and left with Destinee, who caught her up on the latest with her kids, Devon and Charlotte. Sophie was their godmother and took great pride in their commitment to driving their parents up the wall. Once upon a time, Sophie would hoard the stories, saving them like acorns for when she and Adam had their own kids. She had been determined to be the ideal mom.

Ideal mom, perfect wife, loving daughter, successful lawyer—exceling in all the things and never breaking a sweat.

Unrealistic?

That last part, yes. No matter how much time Sophie spent at the fitness studio, she had the endurance of wet cardboard. Everything made her sweat.

"Wait," she told Destinee. "Before you go, I made the kids salted-caramel-and-chocolate-chip cookies for their lunch this week."

"The *kids*?" Destinee huffed as Sophie pulled out a Ziploc full of cookies from her padded lunch bag. "Salted caramel is wasted on their immature palates. How do I get the cookies in *my* lunch? The kids will never know what they're missing."

"I made you a dozen, so no one has to go without."

Destinee did a happy dance, then hugged her goodbye and drove off in her sticker-ridden minivan. Sophie walked home via a route that took her down city streets bustling with university students and young professionals enjoying the heady comfort of late spring in upstate New York. By next week, it would be either a hundred degrees or forty degrees, but whatever weather summer brought, you could be sure the humidity would be in the seventies.

Stopping at the corner store, she picked up a carton of strawberries, then made her way home to the Wayside apartment building.

Home.

Before the divorce, "home" meant a suburban three-bedroom, two-bathroom, architecturally ambiguous house with a big backyard. A house that reaffirmed her status without being ostentatious and radiated stability from its tasteful Nordic decor to its Ernesta welcome mat.

Never in a million years would she have imagined living in the city. Or that turning down a walkway toward a redbrick apartment building with flashing purple lights in the windows of the seventh floor would make her shoulders drop.

Or that, when entering a lobby with a tiled floor that had seen much better days, a bank of mailboxes would randomly rattle, as though in welcome, and the faint smell of crème caramel would make her smile. She raised her hand in greeting to the two enormous stone gargoyles she'd named Frick and Frack, which sat in hollowed recesses on either side of the elevator. Someone had put a Washington Commanders scarf around Frack's neck.

Sophie frowned. None of that nonsense, now. This was Bills country.

At her mailbox, she withdrew a handful of envelopes. Most of them were confirmation of bills she'd gotten via email, but the lawyer in her liked to have paper backups. The bills came less often now that the divorce was finalized and the prenup had been honored.

Sophie stared at the rectangles of white paper: documentation that her marriage had existed, redundant memorials to the limits of love. The acoustics of the lobby were such that her quiet sigh returned as an echo of wings. She lingered in the lobby, soaking in the peace of a place without computer screens that gave her headaches when she tried to read them and without people who also gave her headaches when she tried to read them.

"Oh, a rare sighting of the elusive Sophie Cooper in the wild." A low voice made of velvet stopped Sophie in her tracks.

Chills went up her spine as the summoner of the velvet voice walked out from the building's common room and into the lobby.

Raphael Darksson.

Raphe.

When Sophie had moved in, Pax, the building's super, had assured her most of the tenants kept to themselves.

"It's an . . . older population," Pax had said. "Very quiet."

Indeed, the whole place gave off an air of faded grandeur that appealed to her after having lived in a bland development for so long. She'd imagined her neighbors were a bunch of genteel residents who smelled of lavender and put Christmas wreathes on their doors.

There were plenty of elderly residents, but nothing about them said "genteel." Three older niblings walked around the games room in pastel running suits, barking orders at everyone, including one another, to make sure they put back every single card and game piece. A man named Denis would complain about the insurance industry and its biases if he cornered you in the elevator. An ancient-looking Black woman with wraparound sunglasses would smack you in the ankles with a scary-looking cane if you didn't move out of her way fast enough.

As for Raphe? He was one tenant who did *not* keep to himself. At six a.m. on the first morning after Sophie had moved in, Raphe had knocked on her door.

"Raphael Darksson," he'd said without preamble. "Welcome to the building. Are you seeing anyone?"

The abrupt introduction wasn't what left Sophie speechless. Nor was it that it was six a.m., she hadn't brushed her teeth, and she wasn't wearing a bra, so it looked like she had three stomachs.

No, it took her far, far too long to find her voice because the strange neighbor with questionable social skills standing in front of her was *ridiculously* gorgeous.

Silky, shiny black hair fell straight across his forehead like he was an anime hero. Once, she caught the scent of whatever shampoo he used, and it had made her mouth water. He had piercing blue eyes, cheekbones so sharp they would slice you if you got too close, and beneath his tight black T-shirt and jeans, a body that must be a full-time job to maintain.

He was, in a word, hawt. So hot that, after three years without even the slightest sexual interest in anyone—masculine, feminine, or nonbinary, and including her husband—Sophie's attention had been caught and piqued by the man's sculpted body and disconcertingly beautiful face. Add to it he spoke with a faint European accent? Yum.

"You missed another event," he told Sophie now as he joined her by the mailboxes. "The tenants' association sponsored a speed dating night. It was free for residents, and this time they had snacks."

Snacks?

"A Wegman's sub platter," he continued, despite her silence.

And so it went. Every time Sophie ran into Raphe—and it was uncanny how often she ran into him—he would speak to her in non sequiturs about the fantastic happenings (in his words) associated with the tenants' association.

Which might have appealed to her, except he used the same tone of voice and facial expressions to describe said happenings that one might use when describing scenes of torture and abuse.

Raphe made game night sound like the apocalypse.

"Plenty of attractive and well-adjusted men and women and people free of definition by a binary gender system were there," he informed her, making "attractive" and "well-adjusted" sound like "disease-ridden" and "categorically insane."

"There's been an uptick in attendees who have employment, as opposed to graduate students looking for free food," he told her. "In case you're looking for a partner with similar tastes." He lifted his chin in the direction of her strawberries.

"What do you mean?" she asked, looking down at the berries. Similar tastes as in a propensity for fresh fruit or similar taste as in dinners that can be eaten over a sink?

"Seven dollars for a carton of berries," he said, shaking his head. "What the youth today won't pay for phytonutrients."

"They pair really well with salted caramel chips," she said sheepishly. "I was going to add them to cookies and ice cream."

"That sounds"—his voice lowered to a growl—"sublime."

Sophie's knees went a little weak. Holy cannoli, this guy was something.

"Would you like a cookie?" she asked. Embarrassed by the slight waver in her voice, she turned away from him and shoved her mail into her shoulder bag, then kept her eyes down while she rooted around inside for a second bag of cookies. She'd meant to give them to her paralegal but could always whip up another batch.

When she gave him the cookie, he held it up to the light as if examining it for flaws.

What if he found some? What if he thought her cookies sucked?

The thought depressed her, even though she knew it shouldn't. Suddenly, Sophie was ready for soft pants and bed.

"Mr. Darksson," she said, putting the bag of cookies away and clutching her strawberries to her chest. "Thank you so much for keeping me informed about the tenants' association activities. Hopefully, when my work schedule slows, I will have the pleasure of finally attending one of them."

"The next meeting is this Saturday," he said without glancing at her. "You are a lawyer, are you not? A professional of the white-collar variety? There should be no obstacle to you attending a Saturday-morning event."

Part of the oddness of their encounters was that Raphe, though he looked no older than thirty-five, had the speech and mannerisms of an octogenarian aristocrat straight out of a PBS miniseries.

"Saturday morning?" Sophie said. "I have work I have to—" She broke off her sentence when he finally took a bite of her cookie.

"Mmmmm." Raphe closed his eyes and made a sound of pleasure so sexy it felt like fingers against her skin.

Whoa. She looked down, and there were goose pimples on her arms. Could this be a sign that Sophie was finally getting past the pain of the divorce?

"Delicious," he said. He opened his eyes and, holding her stare, flashed her a smile that hinted at a shared secret. Sophie nearly fell over in surprise when her nipples tightened at the sight.

As though he knew what effect he was having on her libido, her neighbor's smile grew larger, wolfish almost, giving her a glimpse of straight, white teeth.

"Excellent," he said. "It is settled. I look forward to seeing you Saturday morning at ten."

He winked and headed for the elevator.

What? No way was she spending her Saturday morning doing anything but eating Corn Pops and watching Season Six of *GBBO*.

God, she missed Mel and Sue.

Before she could object, the elevator doors closed on him.

Shit.

The elevator operated as though it had a mind of its own. Who knew when it would return and, once returned, how many people would be in it? She'd once witnessed twelve cheerleaders pile out of that thing.

Instead of risking an elevator ride with a squad of bedazzled adolescents, Sophie took the staircase.

The stairs were made of deep green marble flecked with gold, and the balustrades of the railings were beautifully fashioned from wrought iron. Some of what might be the original paint was still clinging to the sculpted ivy, and tiny wrought iron sparrows peeped out from the faded green leaves.

Her labored breath and aching calves were forgotten once Sophie had climbed the five flights to Apartment 5B and entered her black-and-white-tiled vestibule. The little room contained her coat closet and a low bench, beneath which she stored her winter boots and over which hung a thrift-store mirror, the paint peeling from the faux–gold leaf–covered frame.

This would never have hung on the wall in the house she'd shared with Adam. It would have looked like the five-dollar find that it was against the Brunschwig & Fils wallpapered background. Here, though, the mirror looked like a well-loved antique, and Sophie always felt a little boost of self-confidence when she glanced in it on her way to work in the morning.

From the vestibule, she walked into a short hallway flanked on either side by two archways, one leading to the living room, the other to the dining room. A few feet farther in to the left was the bathroom, and to the right, her kitchen. At the end of the hallway stood the door to her bedroom.

Her habit had once been to go straight to the kitchen after work and eat dinner standing in front of the refrigerator. Adam was often asleep by the time Sophie got home, and she never wanted to bother with heating anything up or washing dishes. The unspoken rule in their house was that food was to be consumed as fuel only.

Much of their life together had been centered around such unspoken rules. More specifically, around Sophie trying not to break rules she didn't know existed until she broke them. Rules like no crying when she was exhausted, no expectations of Adam in excess of what he was willing to provide on any given day. Rules like not taking up more space than was necessary and not asking for more than she'd earned.

The kinds of rules that spread like moss and suffocated whatever spark the two of them had in the beginning.

Tonight, Sophie skipped the kitchen and went straight to her bedroom. She'd picked out a neutral cream paint for the room when she moved in, but whatever paint the previous tenant had used before her had the oddest chemical reaction with the paint she'd bought. No matter how many layers of cream paint she put down, the walls turned a beautiful mother-of-pearl pink that glowed in the low light of the setting sun.

The room faced west and had a small decorative balcony. On warm nights like tonight, Sophie pulled the two tall windows back and stepped outside to admire the silhouettes of the buildings on the next block over set against the backdrop of violet skies. Her shoulders dropped, and she leaned against the brick wall of her building, which held residual heat from the day.

Home.

More than all the self-help books and podcasts and advice Sophie had turned to after the divorce, it was this space that brought her the most peace during her pain. While the remains of the day bled into night, she relaxed in a place that seemed made just for her.

* * *

"Did you do this?"

Shit.

Maddy, assistant hotel manager of Number Five Wayside Hotel and World Travel Hub, strode down the hallway toward Raphael Darksson with a crumpled sheet of paper in her hand. As a medusa, Maddy had the power to turn people who lied into stone. Raphe wasn't exactly scared of her, but neither did he want to be the one who pissed her off.

Medusas were known for creative punishments.

Maddy had taken to wearing the fashions of this world like a *repƷƷuut* to fire, and today's outfit consisted of a cream silk suit dress matched with ivory high-heeled pumps and a silk head-wrap meant to hide her snake hair from any humans that happened by.

"How can I assist—" Raphe began in a conciliatory tone.

Maddy came to a stop in front of him and thrust the paper in his face. "Is this your questionnaire from speed dating on Tuesday?"

Raphe raised one eyebrow and smirked, cognizant of the effect his looks had on all the genders of most species. "Did you see something on there that piqued your interest? Rushing to find me and ask me more about my *hobbies*?"

Maddy reached over and grabbed Raphe by the chin. Hard. She smushed his mouth when she drew him toward her.

"Did you put 'raw dogging' and 'blood sport' under the likes section and 'woke anything' under dislikes?" she demanded.

Raphe rolled his eyes. "You can't blame me for trying to find some amusement during these events," he said. Or at least tried to say, what with his lips mashed together.

Maddy's chartreuse headwrap shuddered, and a tiny, pink, forked tongue flicked out near her temple.

"The reason these events aren't working is that no one takes them seriously." Maddy let go of his chin and set her hands on her hips.

"Oh, for fuck's sake," he complained, rubbing the skin where she'd pinched it with her razor-sharp nails. "It doesn't matter if I play nice or not; the fact is we need a human to fall in love with one of us. Instead of putting on social events, we should be going about this like any right-minded vampire."

Maddy scoffed. "We are not kidnapping a reasonably attractive human and dosing them with a love potion, then keeping them prisoner until—"

"At this point, they don't even have to be attractive," Raphe interrupted. So long as no one looked at him to get involved, he didn't care what the human looked like.

Six months ago, Number Five Wayside Hotel and World Travel Hub was going about its business, traveling the rivers of magic that cross the universe and stopping at whatever magical world necessary to drop off or pick up a guest—the key word here being "magical"—when something unprecedented happened.

Number Five ran out of fuel.

The magical hotel and every one of its guests were stranded. Not only were they stranded, but they'd also been stranded in a world seemingly without magic.

A wasteland, as it were.

The hotel manager, Pax, tried to "reboot" Number Five by renting a room to a human. Pax and the woman, Josie, had fallen in love, and Number Five's fuel tank had gone from zero to 30 percent filled.

A Wayside couldn't start until it had a completely full tank, so it was up to someone else in the building to take one for the team. One human, that is. Take them and love them.

Love.

For fuck's sake.

Merely thinking the word summoned a gag reflex.

"Hairball?" Maddy asked.

"Existential dread," Raphe answered and pounded his chest with his fist. "Gives me reflux."

Dread because they had to keep their existence a secret from the humans of this world or they'd all be carted off to be dissected—or, in Raphe's case, worshipped adoringly. Dread because they lived with an entire floor full of gods, goddesses, and miscellaneous magical beings who were so dangerous to other creatures that they had to be put into a deep sleep to journey in a Wayside. Dread because not only was Number Five Wayside a magical Hotel and World Travel Hub, but she was also a sentient being with the penchant for the *romantic*. Dread because the longer Number Five remained stranded on this world, the longer his late father's throne remained empty, and the more chaos would ensue on Raphe's home world.

He'd been on a diplomatic trip to the Gnomic Empire when he received word of his father's death and had been subjected to assassination attempts ever since. A low-grade hum of worry droned in the back of his head every time he thought about how long it was taking to return to his world.

He owed it to the glory of his family to go home and bang some skulls.

Raphe shivered with pleasure. How amazing it would feel to end an argument with the satisfying squelch of smashed skulls. In this world, smashed skulls were a last resort. Humans preferred to "talk it out" and "compromise."

This world sucked.

To make matters worse, right after installing a new tenant, Pax had left his post to go do something called a vacation with his human partner and her offspring, abandoning the residents to Maddy's dictates.

Vacation.

Betrayal, more like.

"You might be the presumptive king on your world, but here, you are just another stranded guest," Maddy reminded him. "Stop dicking around."

"I'm not dicking around," Raphe replied. "Unfortunately."

It had been a long time since his dick had been seen "around." Too long.

"Sophie Cooper," Maddy said. "What about her?"

Ah, the new tenant.

[illegible]nother few days and she'll be putty in my hands," he as-[illegible]r.

[illegible] air around them reeked suddenly of cinnamon.

[illegible]ophie Cooper was frustratingly elusive. For Raphe, who was [illegible]d to the adoration of the faery princesses on the seventh floor [illegible]nd the not-so-subtle thirsting of the owl shifter and his poker buddies, it had smarted a bit when the human appeared to avoid prolonged interaction with him.

Raphe found her pleasing enough in appearance. Toothsome, even, with her curved belly and supple thighs. He admired how her corkscrew hair evaded attempts to tame it and sprung from every headband and hairpin with a defiant attitude. Pity she dressed like a *ri℘Kieeeee* with a case of *ΣvIOΥpis,* because she'd a lovely decolletage. Even more compelling, she accessorized herself with delicious baked goods.

The slump in her shoulders when she crossed the lobby to the stairs after returning late at night, however, gave off an air of defeat at odds with the amount of time and energy she seemed to devote to her work. Every time Raphe had tried to lure her into his company, she'd used her profession as an excuse to turn him down.

"Pax rented her an apartment over a month ago. Since then, she hasn't been to a single TA meeting or event," Maddy complained. "She's never in the courtyard playing kimchi ball—"

"Pickle ball," Raphe corrected her.

"Whatever," she growled. "How are we supposed to make her fall in love with one of us if she won't come out of her apartment?"

"You're asking me? Vampires are not a sociable species, you know."

Raphe's father had been an exception. King Claudius had reveled in his position and held court more often than necessary simply to be among others of his kind. Raphe would be a different sort of king. The kind who issued declarations from behind a desk instead of in front of crowds. Another disappointment in the long list the vampire court had about Raphe.

A chill wind brushed up against the back of his neck, and he glanced around in case Number Five was trying to give him a message, but the only things he could see were the faux wood paneling and ugly fluorescent light fixtures.

This was a symptom of Number Five's illness.

This building had been a showplace of tasteful décor before it got sick, but now it resembled a run-down dump. Oh, some things had gotten better since Pax and his human had fallen in love—the ballroom was no longer carpeted in a smelly brown Berber carpet, and the courtyard had been transformed into a delightful garden.

The rest of the place was the stuff of nightmares. Literally.

Maddy's impatience wasn't caused by her dislike for the dingy surroundings so much as her nervousness about what would happen with the sixth-floor residents if Number Five didn't recover soon. The sixth floor housed some of the most powerful beings in all the known universes, and the hotel's magic alone kept them asleep. No one at Number Five wanted to witness the havoc wreaked on a nonmagical world by a cranky god being woken too early from a nap.

"There will be a preplanning meeting for the planning meeting of the TA on Saturday morning," Maddy said. "I want Sophie Cooper there."

Preplanning meeting for the planning meeting for fuck's sake. Raphe used his considerable willpower to keep from rolling his eyes in disgust. He'd seen the young zombie, Joey, get his eyeballs stuck doing that, and the sight had . . . made an impression.

"I've already asked her—" Raphe began.

"Your attempts have been halfhearted at best," Maddy snapped. "I know you can be charming. I've seen you make faerie princesses tremble with longing and gnomes bend over backward—and forward—to catch your eye."

Any number of things could make a faery princess tremble, but Raphe wasn't about to argue.

"So go coax Sophie Cooper out of her apartment and into someone's bed before we are stuck here, forever."

Photo by Asa Shutts

USA Today bestselling author **Elizabeth Everett** lives in upstate New York with her family. She likes going for long walks or (very) short runs to nearby sites that figure prominently in the history of civil rights and women's suffrage. Her writing is inspired by her admiration for rule breakers and her belief in the power of love to change the world.

VISIT ELIZABETH EVERETT ONLINE

ElizabethEverettAuthor.com

ElizabethEverettAuthorBooks

ElizabethEverettAuthor